"SPELLBINDING STORYTELLING . . . A superbly crafted love story."
—*Pasadena Weekly*

"A SMASHING JOB of recreating the intensity and intrigue of the auction business."
—*Palm Beach News*

"A TOTALLY ABSORBING, INTRIGUING, INSIDE LOOK into the seamy luxury of the art world, where sex, money, power, love, and greed are dangerously intertwined."
—Bill Tice, Coty Award-winning designer and author of *Enticements*

"A DELICIOUS PORTRAIT OF DOUBLE-DEALING . . . In this artful romp, family skeletons come to life, unveiling dark secrets of black market intrigue and hidden passion."
—Cara Saylor Polk, author of *Images*

"FASCINATING AND SOPHISTICATED."
—Charles Strouse, composer of *Annie, Applause, Bye Bye Birdie,* and *Golden Boy*

The Golden Circle

Ferne Kadish
and
Kathleen Kirtland

ST. MARTIN'S PRESS/NEW YORK

St. Martin's Press titles are available at quantity discounts for sales promotions, premiums or fund raising. Special books or book excerpts can also be created to fit specific needs. For information write to special sales manager, St. Martin's Press, 175 Fifth Avenue, New York, N. Y. 10010.

This novel is a work of fiction. All of the events, characters and names depicted in this novel are entirely fictitious with the exception of a few people, primarily from the art world, whose real names are used but who are depicted in an entirely fictional context. No representation that any statement made in this novel is true or that any incident depicted in this novel actually occurred is intended or should be inferred by the reader.

THE GOLDEN CIRCLE

Copyright © 1986 by Ferne Kadish and Kathleen Kirtland
All rights reserved. No part of this book may be used or reproduced in any manner whatsoever without written permission except in the case of brief quotations embodied in critical articles or reviews. For information address St. Martin's Press, 175 Fifth Avenue, New York, N.Y. 10010.

Library of Congress Catalog Card Number: 86-13153

ISBN: 0-312-90871-7   Can. ISBN: 0-312-90872-5

Printed in the United States of America

First St. Martin's Press mass market edition/December 1987

10 9 8 7 6 5 4 3 2 1

For Ilene and Michael for being what you are—the strongest link in my golden circle.

—F.K.

To Ron: May the circle remain unbroken.

—K.K.

Acknowledgments

We would like to express our deepfelt gratitude for the invaluable help given to us by Robert Crowningshield, Gemological Institute of America, Gem Trade Laboratory; Barbara Feldman, Grolier Club; Nancy Little, M. Knoedler and Co.; Elaine Markson; Peter Schaeffer, A La Vielle Russie; Ron Winokur; Richard Winston, Harry Winston Salon; Richard York, Richard York Gallery.

CHAPTER 1

It was one of those beautiful Los Angeles afternoons. A drizzle early in the day had cleansed the city of pollution. Clear sunshine made streamers of light from the high windows of the Rasten Gallery to the polished concrete floors below. Dale Kenton rushed to the back of the gallery, then turned and stood pensively, regarding the painting being mounted on the clean white wall opposite her. It was fashioned of odd-shaped panels of raw wood, fastened together then painted in random swirls and slashes of strong black, neon pink, and white.

"I don't know," she fretted. "Maybe the four-panel piece was better there." Her lean, tanned fingers wandered up to her dark hair and began unconsciously twisting it into thick loops. She squinted to get the room into perspective. Two movers put down the massive piece and gave her looks of frustration.

"What do you think, Mark?" she asked, looking to the doorway where he stood watching her.

Mark Rasten stroked the chain of his antique gold pocket watch as he considered his reply.

"I think you should calm down. It's not our first showing. He's the artist. Try to remember I've been in this business for thirty years."

Dale shrugged her shoulders, then rested her five-foot-nine-inch frame against the wall in an effort to relax.

"Tony Lamm's special," she explained. "I know it. I feel it. This opening's important for him. I want him to get good reviews, and some sales. He's worked hard."

Mark took one step backward and positioned himself to examine the mass of jutting wooden forms on the opposite wall. The clash of pink and black had a near-blinding effect in the strong afternoon sun.

"Are you sure he'll turn out to be someone?" he asked. The inquiry was nothing new. Mark was always tortured by doubt when his money or his ego was at stake.

He walked into his office and slipped behind his desk. It was a simple slab of granite set on round glass cylinders. Gray industrial carpet covered the office floor. Shelving on the back wall held confetti-colored ceramics, while an enameled steel and copper sculpture took up one corner. Dale had redecorated it the year before. She followed him in and settled herself on the tailored muslin couch in the corner.

"How's the press for this show?" he asked her.

"*Art World* was here today. *Art in America* and the *Los Angeles Times*, too," she said, ticking them off on her fingers. "With this much press, Tony Lamm would be a success even if he couldn't paint. And he can."

"Are they going to interview me?" Mark inquired with sudden interest.

"They already have," Dale assured him. "I told them to use your name on all the quotes I gave them."

Mark nodded, then reached into his jacket pocket and withdrew a pair of gold-framed glasses. Putting them on, he began searching through the clutter of his desktop. "There it is," he said, withdrawing some typewritten pages on the gallery's distinctive letterhead. "I want you to have your friend Pat Shore arrange a lunch with Maurice Goldman at the museum. You two are still friendly, aren't you?" Dale nodded. She couldn't imagine anything that would break up her friendship with the woman who had been her department head when she was hired at the Los Angeles County Museum of Fine Arts. It had been her first job, and she had counted herself lucky to be able to work even as a gofer in the contemporary art department. It was Pat who had recognized her promise, who had made sure she got beyond that spot, showing her the ropes and spending incalculable hours teaching her. She had given her all the responsibility she could handle, and because of it Dale had learned as much in two years as she would have in four years of graduate school.

In the end she'd gotten a new title, Second Assistant, but not a raise. Money was tight for public institutions, and the voters were making it tighter. When Mark offered her the gallery job at double her museum salary she'd had no choice but to leave. Pat had made it easy for her. There was never a hint of resentment, and they had managed to keep up an easy friendship over quick lunches and Saturday shopping expeditions.

"Have him sign these," Mark told her, holding out the papers he wanted her to present to Goldman.

She looked down at the papers. They were typed estimates of the value of a group of paintings that one of the gallery's clients was proposing to buy and donate to the museum. Mark's signature was at the bottom attesting to their worth. A blank space waited for Goldman's signature as head of the museum's contemporary art department.

Dale paused, measuring the consequences. "They're overvalued, Mark."

"People rarely want to undervalue things when they're getting a tax deduction," he pointed out with a hint of sarcasm. "Besides, once Goldman gives us a letter of acceptance from the museum, that *will* be their value."

"But Goldman isn't going to accept the paintings at these values," Dale protested.

"If he doesn't we're going to be out one sale," Mark said in a clipped tone. "Which would be a disaster since I've decided to take a trip to the south of France later this month. And you know," he said, leaning forward and speaking in a tone of confidential intimacy, "how much I like traveling first class. Which is why," he finished, straightening in his chair and handing the papers back to Dale with an air of finality, "you're going to talk him into it, my dear."

Dale sat silently. Her long, expressive fingers began to drum an anxious tattoo on the arm of the couch. Somehow she managed to mask her resentment as she listened to him.

Mark looked up, realized she was distressed, and came across the room to sit next to her. "Don't get that way again," he said, putting an arm around her shoulders. "You've come such a long way. You learned a lot while you were at the museum. You've learned even more here. You're bright, and you're a quick study. You're a natural in this business. But that's just what this is—a business. This is the real world. Don't blow it," he cautioned her. "You've got to make sales to survive. Sometimes that's just not as clean as you'd like it to be. God knows it bothers me, too. But it's a fact of life, Dale," he insisted. "You do understand that, don't you?"

For a moment Dale didn't move, then she shrugged and stood to leave. "On your way," Mark told her, patting her on the shoulder. "Opening's at seven-thirty. The show must go on."

Dale walked back to the main gallery to finish hanging the paintings. She had rarely felt so tired, as if all of the spiritual energy and the drive had been sucked from her. She knew as well as Rasten that if she did the persuading, it was her reputation on the line. She was barely twenty-eight and already it seemed as if life was one long compromise. She had already given Mark every ounce of her energy and talent. Now he expected her to hand him her ethics as well. She reached for her purse and headed for the door.

By seven-thirty the gallery was filling up. Dale mingled with the crowd, scrutinizing the converted warehouse with satisfaction. Heavy, whitewashed supporting beams still crisscrossed its cavernous ceilings. Weeks of work stripping stains and patches of oil had resulted in the high-gloss gray floors where hundreds of art lovers were now standing. Movable white walls divided the building into smaller gallery spaces. To its rear a storage area held canvases of every size supported by wooden racks that reached from floor to ceiling. Despite her mood she felt a sense of satisfaction; she had planned every last inch, then put in as much effort as any of the construction workers to finish it.

Tonight it looked its best. Exotic bird of paradise and long ropes of ginger blossoms were arranged in the entrance to the print area. Wineglasses were placed on the portable bar in the rear. The city's leading social reporter was milling with pencil in hand making notes on the crowd.

She saw Pat in one corner of the room. She considered going over to her immediately, considered arranging the lunch before she'd had enough time to think about it and develop more qualms about its possible consequences. But when Pat spotted her,

her smile growing wide and her fingers flashing a victory sign and motioning to the bustling gallery, Dale felt her anger at Mark rise again. It was too good a night for moral compromises. She didn't want to spoil it. She returned Pat's wave, then gave her attention to the rest of the room.

Goldman was talking animatedly to collector Frederick Weisman by the wine bar. On the other side of the room, artist DeWain Valentine posed for a picture with a group of collectors. That will look good in the papers, Dale thought with satisfaction.

She spotted Tony Lamm in the middle of the room, engrossed in conversation with a girl whose thin, almost childlike body was caught within clothes that seemed one size too large and a generation too old. Hardly Tony's type, she thought to herself, and probably not someone he should be wasting time on during the opening.

Dale crossed the room to break them up. The girl followed Tony's gestures with round childlike eyes. She had high cheekbones, and a porcelain white face that flushed easily and often as Tony gave her the benefits of his usual unorthodox and unpublishable comments. From a distance there was something vaguely familiar about the slump of the shoulders under the khaki beige that hung from her slight frame. Dale waited for him to finish, then stepped more obtrusively forward.

"Hi. I'm Dale Kenton," she began politely, extending her hand only to look into the suddenly smiling face of Katherine Bruner. Dale felt her face break into the same warm smile as she gathered Katherine into a warm hug of reunion.

"What's this?" demanded Mark, who with his usual ability to scavenge bits of gossip had materialized at Tony's elbow.

Tony ran nails that were underlined with traces of paint through the inky black spikes of his hair.

"Might have something to do with the fact that she offered to buy two of my paintings," he suggested. "Though I could have sworn that she'd have been happier getting that sort of thank you from me." He straightened his varsity baseball jacket, and centered the weathered Chicago Cubs cap that he regularly sported on an untroubled head as he waited for an explanation.

Dale didn't even notice. Her thoughts flashed back to Paris on a quiet afternoon a good six years before.

CHAPTER 2

There is a certain kind of hush that settles over the Louvre late in the day. The air is heavy with the thousands of conversations that have been held there. An almost cathedral silence flows through its rooms in the wake of groups of departing French schoolchildren and tourists. It's the perfect hour for serious students to prowl the maze of its corridors, taking uninterrupted looks at its treasures.

Dale circled the Winged Victory. She'd been battling the tops of heads and hands and faces all day. Everywhere she'd stood they'd popped up in her way like so many jack-in-the-boxes bent on spoiling her view. Being able to take a leisurely look without interference was a blessing.

Cautiously she approached it. Looking to her right and her left she confirmed that she was alone. She dropped her knapsack on the marble floor. Reaching up, she ran a tentative hand over the statue's carved draperies. They felt cool, almost moist to the touch. She closed her eyes and traced the lines of the figure as if she were reading in Braille, imagining as she went the hands of the sculptor moving, fashioning valleys and peaks and roundness out of a solid shape.

"Pardon, mademoiselle." The voice at her shoulder startled her. The guard seemed firm but sympathetic, as only a fellow art lover can be. She quickly removed her hand and retrieved her pack. He smiled to himself as he strode down the corridor.

Dale turned away from the sculpture and found that she had had an audience. Across the room a small blonde girl watched, doing her best to contain a smile. Dale hurried toward the door feeling like a fool.

"I do that too, you know." The voice from behind her was tentative. "I imagine I've carved them myself." The girl caught up with her, touching her lightly on the elbow to slow her down. "I can't tell you how many times they've threatened to throw me out of New York's finest museums." She glanced down to the floor shyly.

Dale looked sympathetic, then skeptical.

"Really," the girl assured her. She looked delicate and fine-boned. She had nervous hands. Her bitten nails, shredded at the cuticle, argued against her totally sheltered look.

Dale shook her hand. It was small enough to have been a child's. "Glad to meet you," she said. "You're American?"

"New York," the girl told her, "Katherine Bruner."

"Dale Kenton," she said, extending her hand and smiling. "From Los Angeles. Art student?"

"I'm hoping to be accepted at the Art Students League next year," she replied seriously. "You, too?"

"I just graduated from Art Center. I'll be starting to work at LAMFA next year."

Katherine recognized the nickname for the Los Angeles museum and looked impressed. "What a break," she said. "You must be really excited."

"I am about the job," Dale agreed. "But the salary's nothing to be excited about. This is the last time I'll be in France for a while. I plan to see as much as I can before I have to go home," she told Katherine, indicating with a sweeping gesture the paintings that lined the corridor.

"Want some company?" Katherine suggested shyly.

"I might consider it. If you promise not to embarrass me by touching anything," Dale teased.

"It's a deal," smiled Katherine.

Dale followed her new friend into the Grande Galerie. Immediately they sensed the classical form and stately beauty that it had been designed to convey. On either side of the long, straight hall great oils were hung, some as old as the Louis Sixteenth room that housed them. Dale felt the eerie prickle of goose bumps start on the back of her neck and run over her entire scalp. "Have you ever seen anything like it?" Katherine asked her, a note of reverence in her voice.

For nearly an hour they circled the room finding something that they had missed before, some delicate brushstroke or detail, on each trip. At last they were before the Mona Lisa, newly intrigued by the smile that had fascinated so many generations. If the guard hadn't gently asked them to leave they might have stood there for hours.

They were subdued as they left the museum, each occupied with her own thoughts about the challenge that lay ahead. There was no denying the years of work and sacrifice that were bound up with the masterpieces they had just seen, as much an ingredient as the paint and marble of which they were composed.

They spent a thoughtful hour strolling through the Tuileries. They didn't have to share its raked gravel paths with much of Paris. A few children played among its trees, nannies waiting on shady benches. But parents were at home planning and packing for their August sabbaticals by the sea.

Katherine stopped by the wrought iron fence that separated the park from the sidewalks of Paris. Golden fleurs-de-lis topped its even black bars. "It's a lot to think about," she said solemnly. "How about coming back to the hotel with me for some tea?"

Bulky black cabs and honking Mercedes rushed by as people ended their day and headed home. Dale had been in Paris for almost a week, but this was her first look at the Place Vendôme. They entered from the busy Rue de la Paix, and immediately she felt the sense of security in its quiet sidewalks. Dignified sixteenth-century buildings circled its perimeter. She studied the brass plaques that noted with precision the businesses that were housed behind each imposing door. Among them were the finest jewelers in the world. The smell of money was everywhere. The people who walked the street seemed filled with the sense of power that comes with being able to afford to patronize those shops, more institutions than stores.

The uniformed doorman at the entrance to the Ritz helped couturier-clad clients into a succession of limousines and cabs. He nodded to Katherine as the girls climbed the steps to the front door, then he diplomatically removed Dale's rumpled knapsack from her hands, indicating he would check it for her.

Katherine walked into the small, elegant lobby with the assurance of someone who belongs. Marble columns swooped from the floor to the high ceiling above, with fine Oriental rugs coloring the space between them. Massive arrangements of hothouse flowers bloomed on antique tables scattered throughout the room. Shy though Katherine might be, Dale realized ruefully, in some ways she shared the self-confidence of the rich.

Katherine led Dale to the galleria, which stretched the length of one side of the hotel. They sat in two satin upholstered chairs as tea was served from heavy silver pots. Dale chose from an array of finger sandwiches and pastries that dwarfed any she had seen in her life. Looking at her jeans and tennis shoes, she felt embarrassingly shabby.

"This is where you're staying?" she asked.

"You're whispering," Katherine pointed out. "It's a hotel, not a church."

Not like mine, thought Dale, picturing the room she shared with three other girls in her hostel on the outskirts of the city. "Do you always stay in places like this?"

"When I'm here with my father," Katherine told her. "We're traveling through Europe for two months visiting artists. He's a dealer."

Dale was excited. "I'd love to meet him," she told Katherine.

Katherine paused, as if she feared the addition of her father would spoil the special communion that had been established between herself and Dale. "Maybe you could come with us tomorrow," she said finally. "We'll be visiting some studios."

"Not if it's a bother," said Dale, seeing her new friend hesitate. "You better check with him before we make plans."

Katherine seemed reassured. "It's no problem," she told Dale.

"What time do you start in the morning?" Dale ventured, wondering how she could possibly have been lucky enough to stumble into someone who would ease her entrance into the inner sanctum of Paris artists and dealers. They made plans as Dale picked up her knapsack from the front desk.

She couldn't help but compare her world with her new friend's. Fate had a habit of placing her in circumstances where she had her nose pressed against the window of the candy store, able to appreciate but never partake. But tomorrow was going to be different, tomorrow she was going to be part of that private world, if only for a while.

The weather the next morning was beautiful. Katherine pulled her chair close to the iron railing of the tiny balcony. The tall French windows of the suite's living room had been flung open to let in the morning sounds and smells of the city below.

She peered over the iron railing to the Place Vendôme. Their tiny slip of a balcony was obviously more an architectural detail than a functional space. Still, by working her way to its very edge she could get the front half of her chair into the open and have a partial view of the square.

She tightened her grip on the sketch pad that rested in her lap, then carefully studied the cobblestones of the street below. They were irregular, and yet they had a sense of repetition. The bulky inequality of their edges was accented by bright summer light that seemed to give the stones a sense of life all their own. Grasping her charcoal she methodically began, taking care to observe each edge. Finished, she looked at the street below, then to her sketch. Satisfied that she had captured the lumpy solidity of its cobblestone texture, she leaned her body to one side, letting her head rest against the frame of the tall French doors. Summer sun warmed her face. She felt a fine sense of satisfaction with her work.

The moment was interrupted by a knock on the

door. *"Entrez,"* she called to the room service waiter, who used his passkey to open the entrance hall door. He emerged into their spacious living room bearing a large tray fragrant with the smell of fresh, strong coffee and croissants. Katherine rose from the balcony and walked back into the living room. As she poured hot chocolate into her cup she could hear the sound of her father's door opening, and the slight rustling of his starched cuffs as he came across the room working cufflinks into his shirt.

Her first sense of him was the great long draught of aftershave she breathed in before she looked up. There wasn't another man in the world who smelled like her father. He had his scent blended to his own formula. It was as if they had bottled a day on the sea, full of salt spray and the bursting sweet odor of warm summer air.

"Bonjour," he said, bending to kiss her lightly on the cheek. *"Bonjour."* She looked up to him smiling hello, then watched as he added steaming milk to his coffee, reached for the basket of pastries and took out a large brown brioche.

"Tell me about this girl who's coming with us today," he said. "There were so many people at the opening last night I didn't have much of a chance to ask you about her. Is she someone you know from home?"

"I told you. I met her in the Louvre. You just never listen to me."

"That's not true, angel," he said, reaching over to give her a pat on the cheek and then quickly looking back to his breakfast. "I just don't always remember what you've said," he added.

"I think you'll like her. She's about my age. Maybe a few years older. She comes from California."

"What part?" interrupted Ronald with interest. "I have a lot of friends out there."

"I'm not sure," said Katherine. "We spent most of our time talking about art."

"Did you get a chance to meet her parents?"

"They're not here, Daddy. She's traveling by herself," Katherine answered, a note of impatience creeping into her voice. "Don't worry, she's quite respectable, if that's what you're concerned about."

"Darling, if you invited her to join us for the day, I haven't any doubt. What's that?" he asked, indicating the sketch pad that Katherine had put down on the table beside her.

Katherine picked it up and handed it to him.

Ronald looked at the sketch thoughtfully. "You're improving every day. Your strokes used to be abrupt, as though you wanted to get the drawing over with. Now there's a smoothness to your work. When it's time for you to run our gallery you'll be good, very good. All you need is a few more years of study and a little more knowledge.

"Perfect timing," he said, finishing the last bite of brioche as the phone started ringing.

Katherine thought back to Dale as she listened to her father on the phone. She could hear him in the background rattling on in rapid French. It was important to her that he like Dale. She'd found more in common with Dale in a few short hours than she had in all her life with most of the girls she'd grown up with.

"Good news," said her father, striding back toward the couch. "Villeurs reorganized his plans. He'll be meeting us in Italy after all."

"That's great," said Katherine, though really her reaction was divided. She'd already begun hoping that her father would agree to invite Dale along on the Italian leg of their trip. The addition of Villeurs was almost surely a death knell for that. He was an important collector and curator who was developing a modern museum in Provence. Her father had been trying to get closer to him for years. He wouldn't want Dale traveling with them now that he had his chance.

"Finish your coffee," she said, leaping out of the couch at the brash ring of the phone. "It's probably Dale. I'll ask her up."

Ronald looked at his watch. "We have a lot of ground to cover. Tell her we'll be right down."

Dale shifted nervously on a large chair in the lobby. She was wearing one of the two dresses that she had brought with her. Normally she dressed in pants or shorts; but her instincts told her that Ronald Bruner would appreciate more formality. Her trim, unpolished fingernails were an unpretentious finish to the long hands that rested peacefully in her lap. Her composed facade showed no trace of the nervousness she was feeling. She waited with an air of sophistication that made every action, whether large or small, appear to have originated in a natural wellspring of knowledge about what is appropriate.

She stood to greet them. "Good morning, Mr. Bruner," she said, giving him her best smile. A sense of promise was strong in her clear eyes. "I hope I'm not intruding on your day. But I've been looking forward to it since Katherine invited me."

"Nonsense," he replied. "It's a pleasure."

A driver was waiting for them when they reached the sidewalk. He swung open the shiny black door of the Daimler to let them enter the back seat.

"First stop is St. Simon's studio. Have you heard of him, Dale?"

"I'm afraid not. I've found a lot of artists here now who don't get much press in the States."

"True," agreed Ronald. "Katherine, why don't you fill Dale in?"

"He emigrated to Paris from Belgium in sixty-six," she complied. "The French government helped him out. They gave him a grant and moved him into La Cité des Artistes."

"Have you been there?" interrupted Ronald.

"No," Dale said, "but I've heard of it."

"We'll take you before we leave for Italy," he told her. "As long as you're in my care I'll take full responsibility for your artistic education. Not the museums," he said with a deprecating wave of his hand. "Anyone can take you there. I'll take you to where they live and breathe. Right into the bedrooms and the brothels."

"What's St. Simon's work like?" Dale asked.

"You'll soon see," said Ronald, "but you must promise to tell me exactly what you think."

"There's no problem about that. If there's one thing I have a reputation for it's getting in trouble over telling people exactly what I think."

Ronald looked at her appraisingly as the car pulled up in front of a six-story building.

St. Simon's apartment was on the top floor. Dale's anticipation grew with each flight of stairs. Their knock was answered with an energetic shout and within seconds the door was flung open by an elfin man who couldn't have been more than five and a half feet tall. His forehead was on a plane with her chin.

"Come in," he said suddenly, ushering them into his entrance like a small flock of children.

Ronald and the girls followed his tiny figure up the stairs to the mezzanine level of the apartment. At the top of the stairs Dale paused, surprised by the size and airy lightness of the studio that filled the entire floor.

"Ivan," shouted St. Simon to a young man who stood at the other side of the room examining a large, freshly painted canvas. "Come, let me introduce you."

The guest who came across the room presented an

interesting picture. His high Slavic cheekbones combined with slightly slanted eyes of a strange shade of gold-flecked tan made Dale think of a leopard. His hair was a fine, true brown. It was rare to find such a color, with no blond or red highlights. Just the warm, even brown of the top of a loaf of newly baked bread. It was fine as a baby's, and fell over his forehead, molding itself with the unresisting malleability of a child's locks. There was something gentle about him, an ease of manner that seemed to come from deep within. But she sensed something disturbed as well. She guessed that there was less than ten years' difference in their ages, but he seemed a world older than she.

"Ivan Wolnovitz. This is Ronald and Katherine Bruner. And . . ." St. Simon paused, waiting for her name.

"Dale Kenton," she told him, extending her hand.

Ronald greeted Ivan warmly. "We've met," he reminded him. "At Kenneth Fraizer's several years ago." Recognition dawned on Ivan's face.

"Of course," he said, smiling. When he spoke it was in an interesting mixture of cultivated English with the slightest coloring of a French accent. "Excuse me," he said, turning from Ronald, "but that's a most interesting new painting you have over there, Jean."

Dale looked toward the large oil at the other side of the room. Soft sunshine filtered through the large windows overhead, washing it in a luminous halo. From afar she saw slashes of vivid, unexpected color. She had trouble stifling a gasp when she got close enough to make them out.

The gaping wound of a woman's vagina spread out before her, nearly enveloping her in its huge maw. Legs, heaving and taut, spread out at right angles to either side of it. They were strung up by heavy, painted ropes that seemed knotted at the top of the canvas. The throes of labor had been depicted with savage energy that shocked Dale and Katherine as they stood in front of the massive painting. Emerging from the woman's straining vagina were the rear legs and tail of a large white rat. Out of the corner of her eye Dale could see Ivan watching her. He seemed to be struggling to contain a mischievous grin. One hand was held up in front of his mouth.

"Remember," Ronald reminded her. "You promised to tell me the truth."

Dale looked back to the painting. She was repulsed, and at the same time fascinated. She turned away and walked over to St. Simon, who was pulling some sketches and watercolors from the racks of work that lined one side of the room.

"Last year," he said, holding up a sketch of three rats trussed for dissection. Scissors lay next to them, and small piles of intestine. They were drawn with a moving, slashing energy that took them out of the realm of anatomical drawing and into the racing mind of the man who had drawn them. Dale looked at St. Simon's clear, pleasant face. It must be good therapy, she thought.

"What do you think?" asked Ronald.

"I think Jean's a very different man than he appears to be on the surface," said Dale.

"Oh," Ivan laughed, "any of his friends could have told you that."

"I find them disturbing," she told him. "And yet I keep finding myself looking back to them. There's an ugliness to them. A meanness. But I like them."

"Which ones do you like best?" asked Ronald.

Dale paused to think, then pointed to two canvases. The first was a huge depiction of birth and vivisection that was dominated by the running figures of a man and a greyhound.

"And the small one over there," she said, walking Ronald back to a pen-and-ink sketch of a bird, which was hanging on the west wall of the studio.

"And this one?" he asked, indicating a sketch of a folding box that hung next to it. "It's rather nice."

Dale examined it carefully. "I like the others better," she told him. It would have been easy for her to agree with him. But where art was concerned she had her own convictions and wasn't shy about giving them.

"Jean, my friend," Ronald said, wheeling on one well-polished heel. "We will honor Miss Kenton's choices, don't you agree?"

"I rarely disagree with a beautiful woman," St. Simon said, shrugging helplessly. "And as for you, your taste in art is improving with age. I'll have them packed and shipped to you this week. This deserves a toast," he insisted. "Ivan brought some Beaujolais. Sit down." He led them over to a corner of the studio where a small table with a wine bottle and glasses stood among an assortment of chairs that casually spread out around it.

"They say the Beaujolais is good this year," Ivan told them. He casually lowered himself into the chair next to Dale as he spoke, brushing against her and treating her to the touch of a tweedy male jacket. His clothes seemed an integral part of him, as if he'd been born in them and they'd merely grown with him, changing size from year to year to suit his developing physique. He seemed so unconcerned about them that he managed to make other men's suits look contrived.

"You must be working in your father's gallery by now," Ronald said as he sat down across from them.

"My father died last year," Ivan said quickly. A shadow of depression seemed to darken his expression.

"I'm so sorry," Ronald told him. "You've had the whole weight of running the gallery fall on you?"

"I'm not working at the gallery," Ivan said. "I'm

not working at all right now." He shifted in his chair, uncomfortable under Ronald's curious gaze.

Ronald quickly changed the subject. "We'll be going to see Maurice Concorde from here," he said to Dale. "Have you ever seen his things?"

"Just in photographs," Dale told him. "There was a big spread on him when he wrapped the columns of the Musée d'Art Moderne in plastic. What a job. Those columns must have been a hundred feet high."

"He's doing something even more interesting now," Ivan told them. "Turning the countryside outside Paris into an environmental work. I was planning on going out there at the end of the day. Would you all like to come with me?"

"Katherine and I have promised to go to a new show at the museum tonight," Ronald told him.

Ivan looked toward Dale, waiting for her answer.

"I'm afraid we won't be finished in time today. We're going to several studios."

"Then dinner?" he suggested. "You shouldn't have to be alone in Paris."

Dale looked hesitant. Katherine took her hand affectionately. "Go with Ivan," she told her. "It will be fun."

"I could meet you around eight," Dale told him.

"Eight it is," he agreed. "At Chez Allard." As they walked to the door he told her how to get there.

Chez Allard proved to be a small place jammed with dinner customers. As she stepped through the front door Dale felt a giving softness underfoot and looked down to see an old-fashioned cork floor lightly covered with sawdust. It was probably as close as you could come to a country kitchen in the city of Paris, with cheerful paisley-patterned walls and the quaint etched-glass windows.

They were ushered to a well-worn leather banquette where Ivan made himself at home, eagerly drinking in the aroma of good Burgundy cooking.

Monsieur Allard rushed from table to table as his father had before him, describing the specials of the day and recommending the bottles of rich Burgundy that were obviously among his favorite vices. His face had the flushed rosy glow that comes with a small but steady intake of fine French wine. He nodded approvingly as they gave him their selections. They didn't need much urging to add a carafe of the house Burgundy to their order, and Monsieur Allard produced it with the alacrity of a man who's eager to share his pleasures with others.

"You just can't find a stew like this anywhere else in the world," said Ivan as the deep china bowl of *boeuf à la mode et navarin* was placed in front of him. Chunks of beef and tender lamb swam in a thick broth of meat stock and red wine. Tender young carrots and peas rose to the top, offering inviting flashes of orange and green. "If you don't lift your fork soon," he said, looking to Dale, "I'm going to faint from hunger and longing right before your eyes."

She quickly lifted her heavy pewter fork and dug into the small crockery casserole of white beans, ham hock, and country sausage that was steaming in front of her. They ate in silence for several minutes, each one savoring the flavorful mixture that had been served to them.

"Where did you meet Ronald and Katherine?" Ivan asked, ripping a crisp heel of bread from one of the baguettes that had been placed in the center of the table.

"I met Katherine in the Louvre," Dale replied. "She invited me to join them for the day."

"That explains it," Ivan said sagely. "I couldn't place you as one of her friends from New York." His tone was blunt and disapproving. There was something unpleasant about it, and yet Dale found herself intrigued by him.

"What's that supposed to mean?" she asked him.

"It means that you're not socially prominent enough. Katherine's mother is dedicated to finding her daughter the right kind of husband, and she's decided that won't happen unless she keeps the right kind of company."

Dale looked embarrassed. "I gather you've known them a long time."

"My father and Kenneth Fraizer were partners in an art business in Russia when they were young. I used to go to New York with my father to visit Kenneth. He's a good friend of Ronald's. We always spent a lot of time around the Bruners while we were there."

"Ronald seems to know a lot of people."

"Politicians. Artists. Plus every interesting eccentric who ever passed through New York. It's no wonder Katherine grew up on the quiet side. But she listened and absorbed. I wouldn't shortchange her. I would bet that Katherine Bruner can be very determined once she gets it into her head to do something."

As he talked Dale watched him closely. He had nice eyes, but there was a certain restlessness to them. They danced past her face to the table as he spoke.

"It sounds as if you and your father were there a lot."

A hint of sadness crossed his face. She tried to decipher it. There was some mystery to him. It was his manner more than his features that disturbed, and yet fascinated, her.

"You're sensitive about your father," she said. "His death must still hurt a lot." She could sense his surprise at her direct question, but something about the way she asked it made him answer.

"You're right," he admitted, and, to his surprise, he found himself pouring the whole story out to her. "I watched my father's spirit break," he explained. "I watched him give up and die.

"He'd been working on the biggest transaction of his career. A portfolio of da Vinci drawings was about to come on the market. It was much too big a buy for him alone, and so he was putting together a consortium of dealers to make the purchase. He had the money together within the week. He never told a soul. He was too afraid that someone else would come in and get it before he had the partnership put together. Except for one of his best friends. He did tell him. When he called the portfolio's owner, he was told that they had decided to put it up for auction instead. It was going to be the crowning achievement of his career. He was truly devastated."

"It just didn't work out," Dale said.

"Oh, it worked out," Ivan answered bitterly. "For my father's friend. A man named Whytson. They were auctioned off at his auction house. Whytson called Dad the same day. He said they'd approached him independently. That he'd tried to turn them down, but that they insisted they would just be taking them to another auction house if he did."

"Your father didn't believe him?"

"He said he did," replied Ivan. "They stayed friends. But I think that underneath it just kept eating away at him. By the time he died the gallery had dropped off quite a bit. Not that that matters. The whole thing left me with such a distaste for the gallery business that I don't want to deal with it any more."

There was a moment of silence, when neither of them could find the right words. As she realized how soon her trip would be over, Dale felt a sense of regret. He might be having a difficult period, but her gut told her there was more to discover about Ivan.

23

"Thanks for being such a good listener," he said quietly. He reached over to fill her wineglass, and then his hand went to her face, stroking it gently.

She pulled back, the warmth of his touch still lingering on her face. She was startled by the quickness with which it had happened. She felt the familiar fears welling up in her. He didn't seem to notice her quick retreat.

"Tell me about yourself."

"I'm from Beverly Hills," Dale answered, halting the progress of a spoonful of plump white beans to her mouth. She quickly popped them in once she had.

"Your parents have lived there for some time?"

"Since I was five," she answered, then hesitatingly added, "That is, my mother still lives there. My father has been traveling a lot."

Her words came out slowly. Ivan couldn't miss the sudden pallor that blanketed her face. It was obvious to him that she would prefer not to pursue the subject, so he tried a different tack. He didn't understand, but he was willing to explore until he found a subject that caused her less discomfort.

"Tell me," he inquired, "did you get your interest in art from your family?"

"Well," she said, answering slowly, "my mother was a costume designer before she got married. But she hasn't done that for years. And my father . . ." Dale felt the words stick in her throat. She didn't want to be rude, but his questions about her family were making her not only upset, but uncomfortable as well. She might as well spit the whole thing out and be done with it. "He was in the film business for many years. He and my mother aren't married any more. He married Cynthia Pauling last year. You might have seen it in the papers." Her statement ended harshly. She'd tried so hard to black it all out of her mind, and his questions were stirring up all the old hurts.

He didn't say anything for a moment. In fact, he'd seen the coverage. The headlines had been blatant. "Aging Actress Takes Seventh to Altar." "This Time It's Mr. Right." Real *National Enquirer* items. It was no wonder that she was touchy about it. If he followed the pattern of the husbands who'd preceded him, her father was nothing more than a kept man. "I don't think I remember anything about it," he lied quickly as he directed their waiter to bring the pastry tray.

Dale felt the energy drain from her with a suddenness that surprised her. It had been such a crude reminder of the difference between her world and Katherine's. It was history, she reminded herself. Her father didn't believe he could make it on his own and he'd chosen the easy way out. He'd married a woman who would support him, her mother and herself be damned. She'd gotten over her anger at him. Or so she'd thought until she saw the closeness that Katherine had with her father. Dale couldn't ignore it. She might have had that relationship too. She had shared it once with her own father. But when the going got rough he'd turned into a little boy. No man would have done what he had, Dale was sure of that. If he preferred a fantasy life to his family, that was his business. She couldn't stomach it. It was just easier to put him out of her life and out of her thoughts. How lucky Katherine was, she thought. She really had it all. Is that a twinge of envy? she asked herself as she pulled her thoughts up short.

"You're beautiful when you're engrossed. You do know that, don't you?" Ivan wasn't in any way hesitant about it. She found him interesting, forward, and frightening all at once. Her cheeks flushed with color as she raised her eyes to his, not knowing how to respond.

"I think you should concentrate more on your dinner and less on me." As her lips mouthed the words he leaned over the table and kissed them lightly.

She found herself choking on the words. He was making her not only upset, but uncomfortable as well. She should have been able to handle it, another woman could, but her memories were too strong. They didn't leave room for any man to get close to her.

"I'm not interested, Ivan. Not right now. Is that clear enough?"

He half closed his eyes, as though her words amused him.

"I think I'm going to enjoy getting to know you," he started to tell her.

She felt the anguish start all over again. She stood up from the table quickly and then, dizzy, braced herself against it with her hands.

"Where are you going?" he asked, alarmed. He placed one of his hands over hers to hold it in place.

She jerked it back and turned to the door, in time to conceal the tears. When she hit the sidewalk she began to run, knowing even as she did what a fool she must seem to a man who had no way of understanding what was wrong.

CHAPTER 3

"Your change, mademoiselle." The clerk smiled as she pushed twenty francs across the counter to Dale, who had been about to leave without picking them up.

"Thank you," she said, hiding her embarrassment by quickly pocketing the change and immersing herself in the guidebook she had just paid for.

The Jeu de Paume. It was one of Paris's smallest museums, a tiny jewel box of impressionist works, a rich dessert that had been saved until after all the others had been savored. She had been upset earlier in the morning when she had phoned the Ritz and learned that Katherine was too sick to join her. Now, having thought about it, she realized it might be for the best. By this time Katherine and her father both had probably heard what an ass she'd been the night before.

She found herself flushing at the memory of the way she'd rushed out and left Ivan, who had tried nothing more than a light kiss. The warmth of his fingers on her face. She could still feel them there. Why couldn't she have accepted it and gone on to have a nice evening? She'd overreacted—she always did. She felt like sitting down and crying, but she forced herself to go in to the museum instead. She'd saved for this trip. She'd paid for it. By God, she was going to learn from it.

And she did. Her eyes raked the works of Manet, Degas, and Matisse that hung on the first floor with the thoroughness of a comb searching for secret tangles. They were so numerous and so beautiful that despite her mood she was mesmerized for an hour before she felt ready to go to the floor above.

At the top of the stairs she was greeted by Toulouse-Lautrec's poster-sized paintings—colorful glimpses of life as it had been lived in neighborhood bistros and traveling circuses. She followed them along four walls, carefully examining the entire room, then moved on to the door that led to the Van Goghs.

He stared out at her from a self-portrait as she walked through the door. His painted eyes riveted hers with their expression of sheer madness. Clashing canvases of gold ochre and reds and violent greens were lined up on the wall one upon another. She might have felt up to them another day, but not this morning. She turned and looked at the next wall, trying to find relief.

Instead, her heart dropped in an instinctive reaction of fear. For a moment she didn't understand why, then she recognized it. It was the tweed, the tan and golden tweed that had done it. The tweed of Ivan's jacket. She looked at the figure standing in front of the painted landscape just long enough to recognize the jacket, then she wheeled and hurried out of the room before he had a chance to see her.

She clung to her bag as she ran down the stairs, trying to make her feet light, trying not to clatter too much, trying not to draw attention to herself as she fled.

Halfway down she heard the steps behind her. They were coming quickly, catching her. She felt a sense of panic begin to overcome her, and as quickly tried to control it, to tell herself that the way she had behaved wasn't so terrible, wasn't so different from the way that any other girl would act. Even as she tried to convince herself she knew that she was wrong.

She gasped as the hand grabbed her shoulder, a sharp intake of breath she couldn't control. She stopped unwillingly, then slowly began to turn, framing an apology, any apology, for the way she had acted the night before.

At first she kept her eyes down, level with his tweed chest. Then she looked up into a pair of deep brown eyes. Confused eyes, staring at her from under a thick thatch of dark hair. Eyes which, to her relief, she had never seen before.

"*Votre livre,*" the young man said, handing her the guidebook she had purchased on the way in. He looked at her as if she were a madwoman. Dale stared at it, didn't recognize it, then in a sudden flood of understanding realized she had dropped it as she'd run from the room. He gave her a short, clipped bow, then hurried away, glad to be rid of her. She considered going after him to explain her mistake. But instead of following him back up the stairs she found the nearest bench, sat down, and, putting her head in her hands, began to cry quietly.

She wondered if it would ever change. Once she had been so trusting of everyone, so sure that they were exactly as they appeared to be. Running her hands through her hair she vaguely remembered the girl who had been so open, so loving, so giving of herself. No barriers or walls had surrounded her then. She had been able to control her feelings, to participate in life, to let the days take her from one to the next. Bobby Adler had once told her she was too idealistic. That she should question a little bit more. But there had never been any reason to until she had found out the truth about her father. Now all she could think about was how it had changed her life. It had been the most difficult time of her life, yet it had all started out on a day that seemed to hold out so much hope.

It had been a sunny, summer day.

Fred Kenton closed the door behind his daughter as she settled herself in the front seat of the car. She was still tying the laces of her Adidas as he pulled out of the driveway. He looked over at her with satisfaction.

Dale started to give her tight-lipped smile, then remembered the braces were gone and let her mouth open to reveal the row of perfectly regular white teeth they had produced. Like everything else in the Kentons' life Dale's braces had come late, delayed and saved for and finally given in to as one of those

29

expenses that had to be faced on the day of her sixteenth birthday.

She was wearing a freshly washed Lacoste shirt, its bright red knit looking richly vivid against the tan of her slim neck. Where her white shorts stopped, the sun-bleached gold of her downy upper legs continued. Fred had hesitated when she begged to go along with him to his meeting with Brad Simon, but had finally given in. Looking at her he knew he had made the right choice.

"Are you nervous?" she asked, trying to gauge the thought processes that were at work under the curly, wispish cluster of her father's hair. He still had a youngish face. Over the years Dale had watched it distort into an incredible series of grimaces in his attempts to make her laugh.

"Nothing to worry about," he reassured her. "If this doesn't work out I've still got my television job. It may not be the most prestigious show in the world. But it's kept us eating so far."

Dale didn't comment. She knew her father was hiding the excitement he felt about this interview. The best movie projects always eluded him. The stink of failure was beginning to penetrate his self-esteem. He desperately needed to do something of importance for a change, and Brad Simon's pictures always were. Dale allowed herself to hope. Her father wasn't one of those figures around whom Hollywood legends grow. He was simply a man who discovered early in life that he liked to earn his living by making people laugh. Things were always a little tentative for the Kentons, but budgets were stretched so that Dale could stay in Beverly Hills schools, and, like the palms that lined Wilshire Boulevard, she had grown tall, lean, and brown while learning to bend to accommodate the winds of chance that constantly made Hollywood more interesting.

"You'll get it," she said with confidence, as they pulled up to the entrance.

The Beverly Hills Tennis Club was familiar to her. From the time she had been tall enough to see over a net her father had gotten her tennis lessons. As she grew older, she met friends there daily. The Club had been a little subdued lately. The economy was down, which meant the picture business was quiet. There was paranoia in the air. Men who hadn't conceived of living without six-figure salaries were frightened for their futures.

None of this had caused Brad Simon to turn a hair. He ran an independent production company that was rumored to be running an entire studio from behind the scenes. He could afford to keep smiling, and he did. He showed Dale a row of polished white caps as he took her hand and guided her to the seat next to his. His wife of fifteen years, Cynthia Pauling, sat to his left.

As Fred could well remember, Cynthia Pauling had been gorgeous. When she had arrived from Eastern Europe to do her first American movie, she was slim, pale, and romantically withdrawn. As the years passed, the legend lingered on. In reality she had become an increasingly plump Polish sausage of a woman.

Lunch went well. Cynthia seemed to like Fred, and Brad seemed to want anything that made Cynthia happy.

"It's not easy to keep her content," he complained. "Especially on a picture. She's demanding. She makes you shoot slowly. Then you have to put in extra work to keep from going over budget. I'll leave it to a younger guy like you," he added.

Cynthia flashed a beguiling smile, as if the whole conversation was just in fun. Fred knew it wasn't. He realized now why Simon had called in a television producer to work on this project—someone who could work with smaller figures and cut corners when necessary. He also realized as he looked across the table that Simon was resting one pudgy paw on his daughter's knee.

Dale looked her father straight in the eye. She looked like someone had rammed a hot poker up her back. She didn't say a thing. She waited for him to do something about it.

"How does two thousand a week plus expenses sound?"

Fred realized that Simon was talking to him. It was more than he had ever made in his life. Simon's hand moved several inches up Dale's thigh, enjoying the trip.

"Twenty-five hundred," he answered, "would be more like it."

If Simon knew how far that was above Fred's normal salary, he made no mention of it. His hand was slipping under Dale's shorts. "When could you start?" he asked.

"I could replace myself on the show in two weeks. How would that fit into the preproduction schedule?" Fred was beginning to sweat. Dale looked stricken, though she sat without a word.

"Fine," agreed Simon, reaching out to shake on it with the same hand he had just withdrawn from between Dale's legs.

They were silent during the ride home. Fred seemed at a loss as to what he could say to her, how to explain how humiliated he was by what he had been willing to ignore to get the job. As he pulled to a stop in the driveway he reached over to her. "Dale . . ." he started.

She interrupted him. "Sometimes . . ." she said, kissing him on the cheek then putting her head wearily on his shoulder. "Sometimes, you just do what you have to do."

Dale soon learned to endure her father's constant

absence. The better things got, the less they saw of him at home. Dale's mother looked discontented. Her face took on the look of dead white plaster. Her eyes were increasingly blank and defeated. Their dinners were lonely affairs during which Dale often had to defend her father against her mother's tirades.

When Fred did come home for dinner he was interrupted by a series of phone calls from Cynthia. Dale dreaded hearing that voice on the phone. Cynthia threw herself shamelessly at every man who came within arm's length, Fred included. Still, he seemed to be surviving with her, though she was infamous in the business for her ability to halt shooting and shred producers in the process.

Not that all the consequences of her father's new job were unpleasant. For the first time in her life Dale found herself as a social equal of friends who had previously valued her on the basis of looks, humor, and total honesty alone. To her delight she found a white Rabbit convertible sitting in the driveway on the morning of her seventeenth birthday, a gift from the father who had wanted for so long to let her keep up with her contemporaries. The next thing she found there was Bobby Adler's Alfa Romeo.

Bobby was the son of Sheldon Adler, the head of production for one of the majors. Landing Bobby was a coup. Not only did it entitle a girl to order anything she felt like at dinner without having to worry about the price, it was a lifelong pass to all the good screenings in the city. Dale saw every movie Hollywood made before it hit the theaters.

It was late in the shooting schedule when Dale, leaving a screening one night with Bobby, saw Cynthia and Fred together. They stood by Cynthia's Jaguar, closer than Dale would have thought necessary. Bobby stopped her as she started to walk over to them.

"Give your father a break," he suggested. Looking at Cynthia's plump posterior she made a statement she would live to regret. "No job's important enough for my father to do that," she sneered.

"Dale, you're not a kid anymore," laughed Bobby. "Cynthia snaps her fingers and your dad's right there. It has nothing to do with you."

She was determined that she should have a talk with her father. If Bobby was thinking the worst, other people might be too. And the last thing Fred needed at this point was to have a rumor like that reach her mother's ears. She left a note that would be waiting in the kitchen for him the next morning, and by ten his secretary had called to confirm a luncheon reservation.

The Bistro Garden was the same on any summer day. Umbrellas shaded white iron tables on an open patio bordered by tumbles of azalea and white-washed brick wall. Some of the patrons' time was spent picking at poached salmon in dill sauce. The rest was devoted to speculating about the cost of the clothes and the number of possible facelifts of fellow diners.

Dale entered as tentatively as a gazelle among water buffalo. She wore a simple white linen skirt, slit just far enough up the side to reveal tanned legs with the provocative molding of healthy young muscle playing beneath the skin's surface. Above the jut of her hip bones was a sweet young waist which had yet to spread wider than the circle of a man's two hands. Around the patio, men placed bets among themselves as to whether she had reached the magic age of eighteen.

Dale waited nervously for her father's arrival. She knew it would embarrass him to hear of the rumors that were circulating.

He was late. Dale toyed with the kiwi in her fruit salad as she waited. She bit slowly down on one fragrantly juicy piece trying to decide if she liked it and reached no conclusion. Her concentration was centered on the upcoming conversation with her father.

When he came, she was too lost in thought to see him. He was at her shoulder before she even realized he had arrived. Eight male diners changed their bets, now wagering on whether he was her father or her lover. He kissed her on the cheek. They sighed. Too early to tell, they agreed.

"How's work?" she said, responding to his kiss with a smile.

"Have you ever heard about Napoleon's problems at Waterloo?" he replied, wrinkling his forehead in mock pain and looking for all the world like the beleaguered victim of circumstance.

"I have two actors who've just finished shredding their scripts into bite-sized pieces. A screenwriter who refuses to cancel his flight to New York. And the threat of a directors' strike in two days. Business as usual."

Dale grinned. Fred had never lost the ability to make her laugh.

"But I knew," he said somberly, "that if my princess asked for a private meeting it must be important. I respond to your call." He bowed cavalierly and waited for her to begin.

Never one to be indirect, Dale moved to the point. "Bobby says you're making it with Cynthia. I know it's silly, but I thought you should know about it so you can talk to Mother."

Fred didn't answer. He just looked at her. Suddenly Dale felt as if she were in a capsule. Around her people moved in slow motion. Waiters took hours to go from one table to the next. People rose slower than flowers grew, while within her own little bubble everything raced with the sudden frantic heartbeat of fear. Why didn't he say anything?

"Princess, it's just not working for us, your mother and me. We've grown in different directions. It's not her fault. My life's just expanded so."

Dale looked at her father, not quite believing what he was saying.

"Dad, that can't be. If you and Mom talk, you could work it out."

"Princess, please don't make it worse on me."

"Worse on you," flashed Dale, real anger in her voice. "What about Mom and me? Our lives? You have an affair and we just walk into the sunset. Happy ending for you. What are you going to say to her? 'Darling, today I fell in love with Cynthia'?"

Her father's face was a shambles. "I don't have the guts to tell her. Maybe you could lay the groundwork for me," he said hopefully. "It might be easier for her to hear it from you."

Dale felt faint. She stood up slowly, staring at her father like a stranger. Then she turned and raced out of the garden, a flash of white and tan leaving questioning faces behind her.

Dale knifed her car into the heart of Beverly Hills traffic. With the top down, her long black hair blew behind her like a starry streak. The afternoon sky had become a sticky crimson, the glow from a fire in the Santa Monica mountains spreading like a fatal wound.

She realized that a film of ashes had begun to settle on everything. A fine gray dust dulled the polished white of her hood, and was working its way into the custom white glove-leather seats. Dale looked down to see her hands taking on the grimy look of a coal miner's face. It was the final blow. She pulled over to the curb, choking on hard-fought tears mixed with the grit of other people's dreams quickly going up in smoke.

She shook her head, trying to leave the memories behind. It was impossible. For her own special reasons Dale was determined to be a success. She was determined not to let any man ever again get close enough to her to hurt her. It was only those you cared about and loved who could do that. All I can do, she thought, is to make a little progress with this every day. First I'll be a good friend to Katherine. I'll commit myself to her without reservation. That will be the start. She got up and went to the nearest pay phone to call the Ritz and check up on her friend.

"It's hepatitis," Ronald told her when he picked up the receiver.

Dale felt a chill of panic as she heard the words.

"The doctor thinks she picked it up while we were in Spain," he went on.

"Oh dear." Dale's voice sounded frightened.

"He says she'll be fine if she spends a few months in bed," he reassured her.

"Are you sure?"

"You two have really gotten to be close, haven't you?" he asked rhetorically. Not waiting for an answer he continued. "I'm sorry about all the plans we had for the rest of the week. I know you must have been looking forward to them."

"That's not important," Dale told him. She realized she was holding the receiver so tightly her fingers had lost their color. She eased up on it, and relaxed a bit when she did.

"Can you excuse me now?" Ronald asked. "I have to make some arrangements for Katherine. I don't really see how I can get out of going to Italy, and I don't feel right about sending Katherine home alone. She's too sick to travel by herself. The hotel doctor has given me the name of a private nurse he recommends. I'd like to call her now and get that worry off my mind."

Dale stopped him. "I'd like to travel home with Katherine. I can fly directly back to Los Angeles from New York. I'd really like to," she added, hearing him hesitate.

"Dale," he told her, "that's a generous offer. But you don't have to do it. It's not as if you owe us some debt of gratitude for taking you under our wing here in Paris. I don't want you thinking that."

37

"There's no way she's going home with some strange nurse," she interrupted him. "I won't let her." Her concern for Katherine was obvious in her voice.

"All right," he agreed. "I've already booked flights back to New York for Katherine and the nurse. I'll just extend one ticket to get you back to Los Angeles. You turn your own in at the airport for a refund. I insist," he said firmly, as she began to protest. "I'll make out a list of emergency numbers in New York for you, though I'm sure you won't need them. Katherine's mother will be at the airport when you arrive, and she'll probably have Kenneth Fraizer with her. Betty doesn't handle crises too well on her own," he confided.

"So it's set?" Dale asked.

"Katherine's lucky to have found a friend like you," he answered sincerely.

Remembering what Ivan had told her the night before, Dale wondered if Katherine's mother would see it that way, too.

CHAPTER 4

Dale looked toward the ocean, shading her eyes with one hand. On the other side of the rise where the sand dropped off, scooped low by that morning's high tide, a boy was throwing a Frisbee for an eager retriever. The dog, springing up for his catches, appeared in the air over the hillock, then disappeared once again behind it. Dale envied him the twisting freedom of his exhilarated leaps. Gauging the position of the sun she flung a blanket out facing it, covering the sand with the bright geometry of a Navaho weave of brilliant turquoise, yellow, and green. She dropped to it, motioning with a hand for Katherine to join her.

A light breeze stirred the palm trees overhead, and whipped the corners of their blanket into the air. A spider web of dark hair tangled itself over Dale's face. She threw her head forward, her hair falling away from her neck and over her head like an inky sheet, then tossed it back again revealing eyes that looked the color of Dutch Iris in the summer sun. She looked relaxed as she turned to study Katherine with an expression of affection. She was amazed to find that her feelings toward her friend hadn't faded during the years since they had last seen each other. "You're looking better," she told her.

Katherine examined herself doubtfully. The baggy, almost matronly suit of the night before had been replaced by a pair of shorts and a T-shirt in cotton knit. She kicked a pair of flat black ballet slippers from her feet and reached up to adjust the heart-shaped red sunglasses that rested on her nose. "Long Island will fall off into the ocean before my mother approves of this outfit."

"You're a little old for your mother to be taking you shopping," advised Dale. "I'm sure she's a wonderful woman, but between the clothes and that hairdo, she has you looking like you're fifty. Life's too short!"

Katherine patted her hair self-consciously. "She had to do everything for me when I was sick," she said. "I was in bed for almost a year. It was like I was her baby again. We've never quite gotten back to normal. She doesn't want things to change, and it doesn't really bother me so long as she's so happy."

"They are going to have to change sometime. You'll be leaving home, won't you?"

"There's no need to rush it."

"Sounds like a girl who isn't involved with anyone," Dale said wryly. "Find a man you want and you won't be so patient."

Katherine began to smile. She rolled over on one elbow. Her face turned up toward the sun and toward Dale. "There already is one," she said, breaking the quiet moment.

Dale's face lighted up with pleasure. "Good for you. Want to tell me about him?"

Katherine's face glowed. "It's amazing, Dale," she said, reaching over to squeeze her friend's hand. "All these years and we can still pick up right where we left off."

"I know what you mean," Dale answered. "Not having to explain who you are. Skipping all the phases that new relationships have to pass through. So who is he?" she asked, suddenly curious.

"Steven Fraizer," Katherine replied. "You remember me talking about Kenneth Fraizer?" Dale nodded. "Steven's his son," Katherine explained.

"Well, at least you know what you're getting into. That's more than I can say for most couples."

"True," Katherine agreed. "We've practically grown up together. In the beginning we were just friends. It's more than that now. Sometimes I wonder whether I was always in love with him."

"He feels the same way?" Dale asked.

"I'm sure he does," Katherine told her.

"Well, has he said so?" she probed.

"Not exactly," Katherine admitted. "But he acts as though he does. He knows how I feel. He wouldn't continue our relationship if he didn't love me."

"You certainly haven't changed in the last six years," Dale told her. "You're naive. Lots of men play along with anything as long as it suits their needs. The minute they're inconvenienced, it's a whole new ball game."

"Steven isn't like that, Dale," Katherine stated with certainty. "We've been too close. I'm sure we'll get married."

"I'm surprised you haven't been to Tiffany's to order your new stationery," Dale said, laughing to show she wasn't being mean. She thought for a moment, and then went on. "If you're all that close, why hasn't he asked you to marry him?"

Katherine paused to organize her thoughts. "I think he's too proud. I think he wants to feel established before he makes that move. To feel as if he can really offer me something. It's so complicated," she added in frustration. "He's been working with his father for years, and he still doesn't really know what his position is at Fraizer's. Kenneth doesn't seem to delegate any authority to him.

"Not that Kenneth isn't a wonderful man," she corrected herself quickly. "Fraizer's has grown from nothing under him. He knows everything about the art world. He has the patience of a saint when he's helping someone to grasp his business. All his employees love him. He just can't seem to let go," she wound down.

"Sounds like it's time for Steven to get out on his own," Dale commented. "It might teach Kenneth not to take him for granted."

"He tried that," Katherine told her. "Six months ago. He went over and interviewed for a job at Sotheby's. Kenneth had a fit. Went on and on to Steven about its being a family business. About loyalty to his own blood. The truth of the matter is that when it comes to the auction business he's right. He is the best teacher. Steven's learned more from him than he could have from a dozen department heads somewhere else."

"My instincts tell me you may not be seeing this

realistically. I want you to be happy," Dale said with concern in her voice.

Katherine reached up and hugged Dale. "I will be. You'll see. You'll dance at my wedding yet. What about you?" she asked, turning her face to follow the sun. "Anyone in your life?"

"My work is my life," she answered, only half in jest. "What did you think of the showing last night?" she asked. She pulled a bunch of grapes out of her bag and tossed half over to Katherine.

"I've never been to a better first showing," Katherine told her. "I listened to what the people were saying. They loved it. And you sold five paintings," she added. "That seldom happens on the opening night of a first showing."

"Two to you. Does that only count as one sale?"

"When you get paid for two, you count it as two," said Katherine practically. "Rasten is lucky to have you."

"I wish someone would tell him that," she sighed. "He was surviving more on his past reputation than on taste before I got there."

"I can imagine," Katherine laughed. "My father knew him years ago in New York."

"Your father was friendly with him?"

"Hardly," chuckled Katherine. "Daddy used to call him the used-car salesman of the art world. He'd do anything to make a sale. The other dealers hated him."

Dale nodded sagely. "That sounds like Mark. No thirty-thousand-mile warranty, but other than that the business approach is about the same."

"You don't like him much, do you?" observed Katherine.

"I guess I'm feeling a little victimized right now," admitted Dale. "I've spent five years trudging from one artist's loft to the next while he's stayed in his office giving interviews to the press on his hot new finds. I was grateful for a chance to break into the business. But he's done more than take my recommendations, he's taken all the credit."

"That's rough," Katherine sympathized.

"Even that wasn't so bad until he got greedy," Dale complained. She picked up a handful of sand and threw it down in frustration. "He's started doing things that aren't quite ethical."

"I think he started that quite some time ago," Katherine told her. "Judging by what my father used to say about him."

"But he didn't start by asking me to compromise myself quite some time ago," Dale said quietly. "That only happened a few months ago."

"Compromise yourself? What are you talking about?"

Dale's words came slowly now. It was obvious that she was in a great deal of emotional turmoil. "Little things at first," she said. "Fudging on the timing of his payment to artists. Selling paintings they'd given him on consignment, then waiting a month or two to let them know they could collect their money. But now it's gone beyond that. He's asking me to do something that's really wrong. It's just not honest, and it's my reputation he's putting on the line.

"He's asked me to pull some strings to get the museum to sign off on an overblown valuation on a group of paintings he's just sold. He's not only overvalued them to get his client a bigger deduction, he's backdated the sale so it will fall into this tax year. He thinks my friend Pat can get it accepted by the museum if I'm just persuasive enough. And maybe she can," she said, her voice rising under strain. "But it's wrong, Katherine. It's dishonest. I don't want to do it and I think he'll fire me if I don't." The tears came silently down her face. Katherine simply looked at her, completely at a loss for words.

"Damn that man anyway," Dale said when she had

recovered her composure. "Men do this type of thing so easily. They just call it business and get on with it. So why do I have to feel this way? How is a woman supposed to get ahead if she doesn't have the nerve to do things the way men do?" She slammed her fist into the sand as she finished.

"Not all businessmen are that way, Dale," Katherine said. "Not really. You ran into one that's a rat. There's only one thing for you to do. Leave."

"I can't afford my principles. Jobs aren't all that easy to come by in the art business."

"The art world's small," Katherine cautioned her. "Do the wrong thing today and it will follow you forever. When you sell a client you're selling your reputation as much as your paintings."

Dale started to nod her head negatively.

"Listen to me before you say no," Katherine stopped her. "You're independent. You don't have anyone in your life. Or children to worry about. You know the center of the art world is New York. You've already got a network of intangible assets to bring with you—your experience, the museum and the gallery, and your connections. Rasten or not, it's where you should be."

Dale was silent, suddenly frightened by the thought of leaving her security and the city she'd known from childhood behind.

"And you've got a friend there," Katherine added quietly.

The sun caught her cheekbones as Dale looked down. She looked suddenly fragile. "What would I do for an apartment, a job? I've got some money saved up. That could carry me for a while. But it's not a hell of a lot, Katherine."

"I'm going home tomorrow," Katherine pointed out. She reached over and took Dale's hand. "Give me a week or so and I'll find you a furnished sublet. The rest . . . Well, honestly I don't know. Let me talk to my father. Between the galleries and the museums and the auction houses there's bound to be something. He'll know. You've got a decent résumé. And your time at the museum will help."

Dale studied her friend with new appreciation.

"Just call and I'll be at Kennedy to meet you," Katherine finished.

Dale felt as if a weight were being lifted from her. "Lend me some change for good luck," she insisted. "I'll be using it soon."

CHAPTER 5

Dale stood by the conveyor belt. It was still rolling by empty. She looked to the top of the luggage chute where the strips of black rubber flapped undisturbed. She checked the sign one more time. TWA Flight 840, Los Angeles.

Hurry up and then wait, she reminded herself as the growing crowd of disembarking passengers started to shove and jockey for position around her. She opened her purse to look for an aspirin and got bumped by a heavyset woman dragging a cardboard box tied with twine and labeled on every side with a name and address in Brooklyn. She started to snap at her, then realized it wasn't her fault that they were jammed in like sardines. It's really getting to me, she thought, amazed by the case of the jitters her move had brought on. She thought back to the good-bye lunch that Pat had given for her, and for a moment she felt misty-eyed and sentimental again.

"Welcome to New York," said Katherine, looking less frail as she cleared herself a path through the crowd with techniques she must have learned from a football coach. "I see you're getting the feel of it already."

"Is it too late to change my mind and go home?" Dale asked plaintively.

"Follow me," said Katherine, ignoring her. "The driver will get your bags."

She proceeded to elbow her way through the throng with the efficiency of a native New Yorker. "Got your claim checks?" she asked Dale, then handed the four tickets to a uniformed driver. "We'll wait in the car."

Dale sank into the seat of the Mercedes limousine. Its gray plush cushions molded to her body as comfortably as a shoe that had already been broken in.

"Are they evacuating the city?" she asked. "I've never seen such a crowd—"

"New York is like this all the time," laughed Katherine. "That's part of the fun."

Dale shook her head in disbelief. "I'm exhausted. And I've only been here fifteen minutes."

"Don't worry. Tonight you're coming home with me. Hot tub, bed rest, and dinner with Mother and Daddy. I'll show you the apartment in the morning. By then you'll be ready to tackle anything."

"Tell me about it," Dale prodded.

"It's a sublet, fully furnished. I'm sure you'll love it—well, maybe not love it. But it's a good location, Twenty-first and Third Avenue. It's near Gramercy Park, and the rent's only eight hundred dollars a month."

"Eight hundred dollars? Jesus, that's sure going to cut into my savings."

"Well, there is only one New York City," Katherine said trying to make light of it. "Space is at a premium."

The driver appeared at the window. "Just the four bags, miss? Then we're all set."

"How'd Rasten take it when you told him you were leaving?" Katherine inquired as they pulled out into the stream of traffic that had been jostling and honking its way past them. "I bet he had a fit."

"He did bluster on about me leaving him high and dry after all he'd done for me."

"Bet that made you think twice about your decision," Katherine said sarcastically.

"Sure," Dale replied.

"Didn't he want to know why you were leaving?"

"I tried to make that easy on him. I told him I'd gotten a good offer in New York."

"Did that work?"

"No," Dale admitted. "He kept at me until I finally had to admit I didn't have another job. I ended up telling him I couldn't live with his ethics any longer."

"How'd he take that?" Katherine asked.

Dale looked nervous as she answered. "Not very well, Katherine," she admitted. "I thought for a minute that he was going to come right across his desk and smack me. I was honestly afraid of him for a while there. I didn't know what he was going to do."

"He didn't have the nerve to touch you, did he?"

"No. But I have to tell you I didn't like the look on his face as I left. Mark is used to having the last word. He doesn't like surprises."

"Admit it. You felt good, didn't you?"

Dale began to smile and slowly nodded her head to Katherine's question. "I'd waited for that moment for years. I've never felt more independent in my life. And I'll tell you one thing, Kath," she went on, "I'm going to make sure that I'm never in the position of having to rely on someone like that again."

Katherine gave Dale's arm a reassuring squeeze as they took the Locust Valley turnoff. The car slowed, then made a careful left turn. A large electric gate opened before them, and they entered the driveway of Katherine's home. Five acres of well-manicured grass rolled as flawlessly as green carpet from the road to the house that had been settled at the crown of the hill. It was a modern structure, all steel I-beams and glass walls that staggered themselves over a number of different levels and gardens. In the middle of the circling front drive a single Henry Moore sculpture rested, a humanoid family that sat solidly before the house, its mellow bronze sheen giving a softening touch to the sharp angles and reflections of its architecture.

"Here we are," said Katherine, oblivious to Dale's awestruck silence.

Ronald greeted Dale with fondness, making her feel immediately welcome. Betty Bruner's greeting was more reserved. She announced that dinner would be at eight, and instructed her to rest until then. Dale gratefully accepted. The strain of the trip had stripped her of energy.

She was quickly settled in the guest room. More than comfortable, it was an enchanting cocoon of warm beige and blue. The inviting chaise longue that had been placed by the window begged you to curl up with a good book. She saw that morning's edition of the *Times* by her bed, a carafe of ice water to its side. On the other bedside table a vase of fresh roses breathed their garden scent into the surrounding air. Setting the alarm for seven-fifteen, she slipped between soft percale sheets. The feel of them against her skin was like a sedative. Within moments she had dozed off.

Dinner with the Bruners started out unlike any family gathering Dale had ever witnessed. The spirited conversation at the table centered around the Manet show that had recently closed and a Bob Graham bronze door that Ronald had commissioned for the back garden. A feeling of warmth and mutual respect was apparent.

As they were about to start dessert Ronald clinked his knife against the crystal of his water glass to catch their attention. "I think Katherine may have an announcement to make," he stated, then having whetted their appetites he turned to his daughter. She shifted uncomfortably in her chair. "I'm sorry, sweetheart," he said once he realized he'd made her uncomfortable. "But I just couldn't wait any longer. I saw the envelope from Paris in the mail this afternoon when I came home. I'm dying to find out what it said. Tell us, can't you?"

Katherine looked reluctant, but she did. "They're offering me the grant," she announced.

"I knew it," Ronald said enthusiastically. "That's cause for celebration." He pressed the buzzer on the floor near his chair and a maid appeared at the dining room door. "You can bring in the champagne now," he told her, then he turned back to Katherine. "I took the liberty of putting it on ice when I saw the letter," he smiled.

"I'm a little behind," Dale said. "What grant?"

"From the Sorbonne," Ronald told her. "They give three a year. It's a special course of study in art history and curatorship. Half the time is spent in the art school; the other half is spent in an apprenticeship at the Louvre. I just wish I'd had an opportunity like this when I was starting out. You'll come back with a whole new dimension to your experience, won't you, sweetheart? She won't want to come into the gallery with me," he joked, turning to Dale. "She'll want to take it over instead."

Dale looked across the table at Katherine. She felt torn between happiness at her friend's good fortune and the queasy feeling that had started in her stomach when she'd heard her only contact in New York was planning to move to Paris the very day that she had arrived. To her surprise Katherine looked more confused than glad.

"It's probably something you'll want to think over," Betty Bruner said softly. "You can't just pick up, hop over to Paris for a year, and then come back to start all over again. Do you think Steven will just sit here and wait for you? Nice young men from good families are not that easy to come by," she cautioned. "He might not be here when you get back."

Katherine looked over to her mother. Her eyes pleaded with her to take the words back, to change the verdict. Dale could tell as she looked at Katherine that Betty had confirmed her daughter's worst fears.

Ronald looked across the table sternly. His eyes quieted Betty temporarily. "Steven's starting out himself," he pointed out. "He's no more sure of himself than you are. He can use the year's seasoning as much as you can. You'll both be more ready to make a decision at that point."

"Are you just going to leave Dale and move to Paris?" Betty broke in. "She's just moved to New York, at your suggestion I might add. Do you think this is quite fair to her?" She looked at Dale, expecting to be backed up.

Dale couldn't keep silent at the cost of letting Betty use her as an excuse. "Don't let the decision hang on that," she told Katherine. "I have my museum experience. I must admit I didn't make the greatest career choice to follow it up, but at least I have that gallery experience, too. I'll get a job somewhere. If they'd offered me that grant I'd take it in a minute. Besides," she added, "who knows? You might meet someone in Paris and fall in love. Then she'd have it all, wouldn't she, Mrs. Bruner?"

Katherine looked doubtful. Her eyes traveled from her father's face to her mother's, then back again. Ronald walked over to his daughter's side.

"Think about it, sweetheart. Get a good night's sleep. You have a few days to decide. And don't worry about Dale. I have a few ideas of my own for her. I'll let you in on them in the morning."

His eyes caught Dale's and held them steadily. She thought back to the day in Paris when she had met him, the day when she had told him in no uncertain terms that she wasn't afraid to speak her mind. He had seen proof of that in Paris, and he'd seen it here again tonight. His approval was obvious.

As Dale undressed, she thought of the next day and her first glimpse of the tiny flat that Katherine had found for her. She went to the bathroom imagining what it might be like. It was strange, she thought as she bent over the painted porcelain basin to soap her face, the difference a few hours can make. Running warm water onto her washcloth, she looked up to the mirror and realized to her surprise that she was about to cry. It wasn't that she was angry with Katherine for thinking of leaving, or jealous of her for her house, or even of the chauffeur or the paintings or her clothes. But a sadness came over her when she compared this life to her own family dinners. Even with their disagreements the Bruners had seemed so civilized, not given to loud arguments and hostilities bursting forth in angry tones and harsh words that could never be taken back. Get into bed, she warned herself, before you start thinking about the rest of it.

As she lay there she put her hands over her face to try and push back the memories. Then she lay very still, willing herself to sleep. Her mind sneaked back to Katherine. It disturbed Dale that her friend seemed so confused. It was no wonder from what she had said about Steven. Every time she tried to get close to him and find out where their relationship stood he put her off. Maybe he loved her, but it seemed more as if he were running away than delaying things until the right time. She wished that she knew him so that she could give Katherine some input. Her body, pushed to its limits, finally gave in.

Dale awoke the next morning to find her room awash with sunshine. Shaking the sleep from her head she walked to the window. From her second-floor vantage point the entire expanse of the Bruner garden spread out. A small stand of birch trees was directly below her, their leaves half shed in preparation for the winter, peeling strips of their ivory bark highlighted in the autumn morning. Behind them groups of maple and oak bounded the property, their foliage in various stages of the transition from green to the rich reds, yellows, and oranges they would wear for fall. Caught up in the scene, Dale had the exciting impression that nothing could go wrong with the world.

"Fresh orange juice, croissants, strawberry jam, butter and hot coffee," Katherine called through the closed door. "It's eight-thirty already. Just put it on the table," she said to the maid who followed her in with a breakfast tray.

Without pause for breath she began to pour Dale's coffee. "You'll have to hurry. Daddy's leaving for the city in half an hour. If we catch a ride in with him we can go over to the apartment before I have to be at the gallery. Oh," she added, "I won't be able to be with you tonight. My parents are having a dinner for Red Grooms. I feel so bad about leaving you alone your first night at the apartment," she told her, and in fact she did look sad.

"Don't worry about it," Dale told her. She broke one of the warm croissants and watched the pat of butter that she spread on it soften, then melt. "You've really gotten to see a lot, haven't you? Everyone who's creative ends up at your house at one time or another," she commented as she reached for the juice.

"It's nothing to do with me," Katherine told her self-deprecatingly. "Daddy never stops wanting to see and to listen. It's been quite an education."

"So while the rest of us were playing with paper dolls and coloring books, you were listening to Rothko and Nevelson," Dale noted with envy.

"And listening to my mother reminding me how lucky I was to be surrounded by the greatest artists of our day, to be a part of their golden circle," Katherine added. "At the time I thought it was boring," she admitted. "Obviously it must have penetrated."

Dale nodded with total understanding. "Don't worry about tonight. It will give me time to unpack and adjust. Not to mention reading the want ads." She looked down for a moment. She'd stopped seeing Katherine; she was seeing her own father's face, filled with longing and the desire to be part of Hollywood's own golden circle. Well, he'd entered it all right. Even though it had meant leaving his wife and his daughter behind. The pain was too great. She forced his image from her mind and turned her eyes and thoughts back to her friend.

"My God," exclaimed Katherine, clapping a hand to her forehead. "I almost forgot the most important thing of all. Kenneth Fraizer's agreed to talk to you. Eleven o'clock tomorrow. Daddy told him you needed a mentor, and he's agreed to see you tomorrow."

"He got me an interview with him?" said Dale with delight.

"Daddy says he didn't promise anything definite," cautioned Katherine. "Not a job. But he did say he'd give you whatever help he could."

It was more than enough for Dale. You have until tomorrow morning at exactly eleven, she told herself, to figure out why Kenneth Fraizer's auction house can't survive without you.

The city looked agreeable in the daylight. The ac-

53

tivity seemed more lively than frantic. Dale felt reassured. Her apartment building was that anonymous gray that's found in any city. The sole source of its personality was the flashy turquoise awning that it sported like a jaunty scarf. A floor of black-and-white tiles could be glimpsed through its open doors. Two nicely potted bushes marked the spot where the canopy met the street.

Dale followed Katherine up the stairs. On the fourth floor they started down a hallway that had the distinctively musty smell of a New York apartment building. "They're all like this," apologized Katherine as they stopped at a shiny black door marked 4E. "Until you get inside." She fumbled with three locks, then swung it open. Dale experienced a wave of trepidation as she started in.

The room was a surprise. After California, small was too big a word for it. There was just enough space at the end of its L-shaped interior for a sofa, a table, and a couple of chairs. There was a tiny bathroom to one side and a Pullman kitchen—two burners, a small oven, a tiny refrigerator, and a smaller sink.

Dale scanned the room, hoping that with a little money and a lot of style she could turn it into something she could call her own. She forced a smile onto her lips. "It'll be fine, just fine." God in Heaven, she thought, what had she done? It looked like a cell, not an apartment. Suddenly the fear that she had kept under control seemed ready to break out.

"I even did the shopping," bragged Katherine. "Juice, Perrier, and ice cream." She realized that Dale was waiting for her to finish the list. "That's all there is. I'm rotten when it comes to marketing. You can find anything else you need on Second or Third Avenue. And Fraizer's is at the corner of Park and Eighty-sixth. The phone number and address are on the table by your bed and your phone is connected.

I'm off to the gallery," she concluded. "I'll call you tonight to check up on you."

Dale closed the door behind Katherine. Dead bolts, chains, and locks were mounted on its side like an armor against the city outside. She looked at them in disgust, started to walk away, then thought better of it and turned back to fasten each one. Shaking her head in dismay she went into the bedroom area where her bags were waiting to be unpacked. The closet space wasn't lavish, but then neither was her wardrobe. An hour later she was finished. She quickly stripped down and walked to the closet. After considering her choices she took out a pair of gray flannel slacks, a red turtleneck, and the present she had treated herself to before she left home, a gray cashmere cape. She put on a long strand of large fake pearls, added matching earrings, ran a brush through her hair, and let herself out the front door. She repeated her fumbling performance from the outside, finally succeeding in getting every lock and bolt secured. Now I know what Houdini went through, she thought ruefully as she turned to go.

She considered stopping for a light lunch, but decided to go straight to Fraizer's instead. She was eager to take a look at it before her interview the next day. By the time she reached Park and Eighty-sixth her hair was windblown and her cheeks had a healthy pink glow. To her delight she discovered that an auction had been scheduled for that afternoon.

Dale paused for a moment before entering, trying to get the feel of the place from outside. She didn't know the building's history, but she was sure from the look of it that it was interesting.

In fact, the House of Fraizer was an architectural monument built by one of the city's notorious robber barons during a time when Fords were nonexistent and "summer cottage" meant a fifty-room castle like the Vanderbilts' Breakers in Newport.

Its solid door was flanked by two Doric columns, supporting the triangular entranceway roof above. The entire first story consisted of solid blocks of granite and windows that had been covered with ornate but heavy iron grillwork in defense against the city's onslaught.

The most imposing feature of the next floor was the windows, bound at their foot by carved granite balustrades, vaulted at the top with high arches that revealed the fact that the rooms were two stories high. Above the ornate carvings was another smaller story whose simple square windows looked out over the busy avenue below. It was there that the offices could be found.

Dale finished her inspection and felt pleased. Taking a deep breath, she took her first steps through the gleaming front door.

The entrance to the building had originally been the great house's foyer. It was three stories high, and culminated in a vaulted dome whose painted ceiling hung dramatically over stairways that led to the upper floors. It now housed Fraizer's information desk and the sales counter for catalogues of past and upcoming auctions.

"May I see a catalogue for today's sale?" she asked the neat young woman who stood behind the desk. She was handed a glossy booklet on whose cover a magnificent diamond necklace and ring had been photographed against a deep black velvet background. Auction of Fine Jewelry was printed in classic lettering across the top of the page. She quickly flipped through its pages, surveying the various lots that had been photographed and captioned within.

"How much is the catalogue?" She reached for her purse and paid, then tucked it under her arm and looked around in confusion.

"Can I help you?" She turned, following the smooth voice that had addressed her.

He must have been standing right behind her, watching her hesitate. His build was tall, but slight. It gave him an appealing vulnerability that bigger, raw-boned men don't have. He was young, late twenties or early thirties she guessed. His thick dark hair looked casual until she realized how perfectly each strand fell into place. He had obviously devoted a great deal of care to his appearance. Everything about him—clothes, manicure, and handsome head—spelled money. It was an impression that usually put her off a man, warned her from the outset that he could prove to be too self-involved. But this one's dark and wide-set eyes looked at her with such candor she quickly forgot her prejudices.

"It's my first time here. Do you know which way the sales room is?" He led her down a short corridor toward some large double doors. They had fallen into step with a crowd hurrying to the same destination. "Are you bidding on anything special?" he asked.

"No. Just watching. And you?"

"I never bid," he replied. "I work here," he added, seeing her surprised expression. They jostled their way into the sales room before she could ask him anything more.

Rows of chairs had been set up within the room. A uniformed guard was checking passes and admitting selected members of the crowd to the front seating area, where a few chairs still appeared to be empty. In the rear two-thirds of the room, chairs had filled and people were beginning to line up in the standing room against the walls.

"I guess we can forget about getting a seat," said Dale in disappointment. "Is it always this crowded?"

"Wait here a second," he commanded her. "I'll be right back."

Dale watched him as he walked away, confirming her original impression. He might be good-looking and smartly dressed, but there was more to him than that. As he crossed the room his eyes took it in with an intelligence she found appealing. Within a few moments he returned.

"It's all taken care of. I managed some seats." Taking her arm he escorted her toward the front of the room where they found two empty seats near the center aisle. As Dale settled herself, the auctioneer walked from behind the movable partition at the rear of the stage and approached the podium.

"Is that Kenneth Fraizer?" she asked.

"No," her new acquaintance answered. "He'll come out later to auction the important lots."

Within minutes Dale found herself caught up in the excitement of the bidding. It went so quickly, the auctioneer's chant of "Do I hear two thousand. I have two thousand. Do I hear two thousand two hundred," she could hardly keep track of his bids and replies. She barely restrained herself from raising a hand at times when he convinced her and the rest of the crowd that a piece was about to go well under its true value. She wrote the price near each lot as it was sold. Each page she turned brought them closer to the sale of the important lots of the day. There was a buzzing murmur as Kenneth Fraizer finally strode onto the stage.

"Look at him," her friend said, motioning to Kenneth Fraizer. "He's in his element."

Dale looked toward the stage. He did look as if he could feel excitement stalking the room. Dale felt it, too. As she scanned the crowd she could see it flushing the faces of the waiting bidders like the warm breath of a would-be lover.

"He looks calm," she commented.

"Oh, there may not be any change in his expression," her friend said. "But inside he's burning. He's got a volatile group in front of him today. One that can go hot or cold. They may catch fire and set a bidding record, or they could get scared off and retreat. It's up to him to hold the reins."

"And if he rides them past their limit?" Dale asked.

"He never does," he told her. "He's got an uncanny ability to stop just at the point when they're about to refuse. When they reach the risk they won't take. I don't know how he does it."

Kenneth Fraizer's eyes were filled with anticipation. They were set in a head that was large, almost overly large. It added an imposing note to an appearance that might otherwise have been too small, too dapper. For while he was well-built and self-assured, his height was only average. His salt-and-pepper hair was slicked back from his forehead, giving full play to a profile that was chiseled to the point of being severe. He rested his ivory auctioneer's hammer on the podium and gave smiles of recognition to some of the spectators in the front rows, and Dale got the feeling she was looking at a man who could make the transition from charm to demanding toughness without missing a beat. The anxiety about her interview with him that she had suppressed began to mount within her.

Kenneth stood at center stage. The lights were strong, but not harsh—just right for showing detail without revealing flaws. He brushed the podium every now and again, never leaning on it like so many did. There was no need. When Kenneth auctioned, every nerve was alert. Every muscle taut. The need for external support was unnecessary to him. From time to time his fingers lightly touched the lectern, reminding the viewers of why he was there.

"You're lucky to see him. He doesn't auction much

any more. Most of his time is spent running the house."

"Why is he doing it today?" Dale asked.

"Today's different. Any auctioneer would give a year of his life for the chance to sell the Mayapur Diamonds. He's no exception."

Dale looked at her catalogue. The Mayapur Diamonds were Lot 170. There were nineteen more pieces before they reached them. Among them were diamond-studded Tiffany brooches in the playful shape of mayflies. Weighty, flawless rings. Each one a miniature masterpiece that Kenneth could use to move his bidders into a frenzy before Lot 170 arrived. He had used his wiles to gain the privilege of auctioning those diamonds, and now he would stretch them even further to set a world-record price.

Smaller pieces were auctioned. Waves of enthusiasm ebbed and flowed. An occasional lot brought real excitement, its sale a spurting half-climax presaging the main event.

Trinkets were being bought and sold for thousands—gemstones not even visible to the eye of the audience when brought onstage. To give the bidders some idea of what they fought for, a picture of each item was projected on a four-foot screen that turned even the most finely faceted diamonds into nebulous, blurry yet recognizable lots.

"Check your catalogues," intoned Kenneth before starting the bidding. When paid for in the hundreds of thousands, mistaken identity is hard to live down. Dale didn't take her eyes from Kenneth's face. He seemed to be waiting with barely contained excitement for the sale of Lot 169 to be properly recorded. No emotion betrayed itself on his face, and yet his hands had undeniably begun to have a slight quiver that revealed itself in the flutter of the price list he had held so casually until that moment.

The faces of the crowd before him grew suddenly stilled, awed by the sheer size of the thing as the picture of the Mayapur Diamonds was projected in front of them. Those in the first few rows were slightly altered by the glow that the screen now threw off.

The necklace had been fashioned decades before in the workrooms of Smythson from a grouping of rare blue-white diamonds that the Maharajah of Mayapur had entrusted to the hands of their master craftsmen. The stones had been set in an invisible platinum mount—circlets of glistening diamonds surrounding three massive round stones the size of a boxer's thumb. The hanging baguettes were linked with a neck-circling rush of diamonds that weighed in at ninety-five carats. Enlarged on the screen the smaller diamonds looked for all the world like a bed of crushed ice at a seafood buffet.

Kenneth waited for the exclamations to hush, then he singled out the serious bidders, giving each a direct and meaningful look before he set the terms.

"What is he waiting for?" Dale asked.

"He knows who the serious bidders are. He's just making sure they're ready." Her friend pointed discreetly to a middle-aged couple at the front of the gallery. "Joseph and Sophie Ableman," he told her. "The New York department-store magnate. She wants these jewels so badly she had Richard Smythson come here the day of the preview to look at them."

"Who else should I watch?"

"Olivier Jarre," he said, indicating a man several rows in front of them.

Dale studied his face. "He looks bored," she said.

"I don't think so. He flew in from Geneva to battle for this one."

"Who else?" she asked.

He scanned the crowd again. "No one else that I

can see. But it's unpredictable. You never know where the bid's going to come from." He hushed her next questions as Kenneth started the bidding.

"Lot 170. The bidding will commence at $500,000."

Joseph Ableman's paddle shot up. Kenneth acknowledged it. "I have $500,000," he said, then immediately raised it. "I have $520,000." As the audience tried to follow the bidding, heads clicked from side to side in an effort to search out the bidders.

Olivier Jarre sat quietly, arms folded over his chest. Both he and Kenneth understood that so long as his arms were unmoved he remained in the bidding. Kenneth checked him each time he called for a bid, next scanning the sides of the stage from the corner of his eye. From time to time he caught a signal from one of his assistants on the phones to his left, one taking bids from a hotel owner in Chicago, the other bidding for a developer from San Francisco. In between he checked the order bid sheet that rested on the podium before him. Listed were the written bids that had been mailed in by customers who could not attend the auction. They were placed at the house's discretion, with the stipulation that Fraizer's would go no higher than necessary in filling the order.

Up to $750,000 Kenneth caught bids from assorted members of the audience.

"Tourists," her friend told Dale. "Always ready to jump in to the bidding on a famous piece just for the high of telling their friends about it at the next cocktail party."

"Why do you call them tourists?" she asked.

"They visit the bidding for a while, then they drop out before they get too close to actually purchasing something they can't afford."

He may have been right. Perhaps most tourists

faded fast. But this time one hung on, riding the bidding with each new wave. As Ableman raised it to $3 million. As Jarre sat immovable, taking it to $4 million. Phone bids moved it to $4,300,000, and the tourist stayed with the trip.

His most distinguishing mark was his lack of the extraordinary. Clothes nicely cut but not stylish, in a medium gray. His manner was tentative and his bids hesitating. Washed-out blue eyes flickering with nervous excitement peered out from behind thick glasses.

"He's playing chicken a little past the comfort point," her friend said. "If he's not getting nervous, I am."

With a prearranged scratch of his head Kenneth signaled Bob Bentley, who was standing at the back of the room, and sent him to the front office to check their mysterious bidder's credit.

Bentley disappeared as Ableman took it to four million five hundred. Sitting beside her husband, Sophie Ableman was beginning to look slightly manic.

"Look at her. You wouldn't believe the changes auctions can bring out in people. The Jekyll and Hyde personalities that betray themselves in the heat of the bidding never fail to amaze me. She heads half the charity boards in New York," he went on. "Today she looks as if she's been flown in to a crap table on a Las Vegas junket. We get a lot of them like that. Addicted to possessions and excitement at the same time."

"And without them the business would die," Dale pointed out.

Kenneth took another bid from Jarre, then one from the Chicago phone. As the mysterious tourist moved his paddle up, Kenneth reached for the glass of water that always stayed at his side, trying to stall long enough for Bob Bentley to get back to the room with his answer, but he did not appear. He took another bid from the phones. He tried to avoid looking at the Maharajah of Mayapur's secretary, who sat prominently in the front of the room. The man skewered him with hard, dark, questioning eyes.

Bentley appeared as the tourist's next bid had been accepted. He slowly nodded no.

"Damn," said the man sitting at Dale's side. "We've been stuck."

Kenneth looked to Ableman, who was conferring with his wife. He had reached his limit. Sophie was trying unsuccessfully to persuade him to go up one more time.

He glanced at Jarre. Those folded arms had moved, and were now stretching out to the Swiss dealer's knees. Smiling ruefully he gave Kenneth a negative nod.

The order-bid list yielded nothing. The top mail bid had been $3,800,000. They had passed that, and then some. The phone bids had died, too.

Reaching down, Kenneth started coaxing. "Do I hear $5 million?" He scanned the audience, but he let his eyes come to rest on Sophie Ableman.

"Pull him out," Dale heard her companion mutter under his breath. "Save him from knocking it down to someone who can't pay for it."

Sophie Ableman turned to her husband one last time. She whispered something to him. Ableman's paddle slowly raised with five million dollars.

"I don't know what she said," her friend chuckled. "We'll never know. But it sure worked. I'll bet that Kenneth sends her flowers. Dozens of them," he smiled as he turned to Dale.

As the tourist raised his paddle one more time, Kenneth pretended not to see him. He looked in the opposite direction and knocked down Ableman's bid.

64

Dale sat glued to her center aisle seat. She made no movement. She said nothing. The frenzy of the bidding washing over her had brought her thoughts to a wild pace. She had come to Fraizer's to observe, to watch, and to think. She had taken this job interview very seriously. But instead of hard facts, she had gotten auction fever. She was determined to get a job at Fraizer's. No matter how low the salary, or how dull the apprenticeship, she would make her future in the auction business.

"Come on," he said. He took her arm lightly and led her through the excited clamor that followed the sale of the diamonds. Before the sound died in her head Dale had begun to make her plans.

"Congratulations," he told her when they had reached the lobby again. "You didn't give in and bid." He favored her with a mischievous grin that was particularly appealing on his youthful face.

"It wasn't easy, but I managed to restrain myself," she told him.

"Would you exercise as much self-control if I asked you to dinner? Or would you give in to temptation?"

Dale felt a pang of doubt. He was a strange man in a strange city. Still, he was attractive and pleasant. "I don't think so," she declined slowly. "I don't even know your name."

"You're right on that count." He stopped for a moment as Dale waited expectantly. "It's Steven Fraizer. And yours?"

She was too surprised to answer. But then she realized she should have known. He was so familiar with the way the house worked, and with Kenneth Fraizer as well. The age was right, even his appearance, so close to the man that Katherine had described to her that afternoon on the beach. "Dale Kenton," she answered, finding her tongue again.

She waited for him to recognize her name. He didn't.

"Miss Kenton," he asked, assuming a formal pose. "May I have the pleasure of buying you an early supper? No strings attached." He looked at her with such interest she was sure he hadn't made the connection between herself and Katherine.

She sifted through the possibilities quickly. She didn't like the idea of having dinner alone with Steven Fraizer. He was involved with Katherine, and he was an attractive man. But it would give her an opportunity to answer some of the questions she had about him. She remembered their dinner the night before, and Katherine's confusion about whether she should stay or go. It couldn't be just an accident that fate had produced him here for her to talk to. The synchronicity was too perfect. "Miss Kenton accepts," she agreed.

He guided her down Fraizer's front steps, then hailed a cab. "Where would you like to go?" he asked. The driver sat waiting impatiently for directions.

"I don't know," she said with a helpless shrug. "This is my first day in New York." There it was. To be fair she had given him one more chance to realize who she was. But he didn't.

He looked happily surprised. "Your first day? We've got to welcome you properly. No tourist spots for you. I'm going to show you where the native New Yorkers hide out."

He was a tour guide as they drove across town. He took her through the theater district, which looked strangely deserted and a little grubby in the hours before the marquee lights went on and limousines would begin disgorging theatergoers at their doors. The Village was livelier. Street musicians played. Flea market stalls, where everything from vintage dresses to closeouts on sheets could be found, were being folded up for the evening. Near Washington Square a troupe of teenagers thundered from one end of a schoolyard basketball court to the other.

They turned on Houston Street and entered a neighborhood where red, white, and green tins of olive oil were stacked up in grocery store windows under hanging curtains of dry salamis and clusters of garlic that had been knotted with heavy twine into oversized necklaces. The smell of spices and freshly cooked sausages drifted through the cab window. Dale's mouth began to water. The cab slowed, and then stopped. She heard shouted words of Italian as mothers called children home for dinner, and men bid each other good evening.

"We'll stop at Regerrio's," he said, steering her firmly through the front door of the restaurant to a center table. "And if you're good and finish your dinner I'll introduce you to the bakery across the street. The best Italian cookies in the world," he confided.

Dale slipped the slim tube of waxed paper from a bread stick and broke it in half. She took one crunchy bite, savoring its wholesome brown crispness, then looked across the table to Steven Fraizer. He was slim and dark, and had the face of a fine-boned aristocrat. A look Dale called sleekly strong. He observed her intently with the expression of a man who is fascinated by what he sees, watching her every move. She finally became nervous. She started to ask him about the menu, when he suddenly interrupted her.

"Tell me about yourself. What do you like to do?" The question was asked so distinctly, so seriously, and with such honest interest that it caught her off guard.

"Well," she replied. "I love art. I wanted to be an artist when I was younger. I ended up as an assistant to the director of an art gallery in Los Angeles instead. You might say it was an apprenticeship." It was difficult for her not to go on, to tell him about the next day and her interview with his father. She wondered how much she could tell him without jeopardizing her purpose for being there. It was hard not to be totally honest, but her need to help Katherine was greater.

His eyes never moved from her face. She shifted nervously. She was beginning to feel an attraction to him. The energy that was traveling between them was so real it was almost tangible. His silence left a gap that she filled by rattling on. "I love to play tennis. But then everyone from Beverly Hills plays tennis, most better than I do." She ran out of words and reached out for the wine bottle that stood in the center of the table. He moved to help her and they collided, his hand touching hers with a soft, personal pressure. "Excuse me," she apologized, quickly withdrawing. He smiled as he filled her glass. Then he looked directly into her eyes.

"Anyone special in your life?" he asked. "Pardon me for asking so abruptly, but it's important to me. It isn't very often that I find someone who makes me feel the way you do."

Dale started to laugh nervously. "I've been in New York for twenty-four hours. Almost," she corrected herself, looking at her watch. "No. I can't say I've found anyone special yet." Her heart was racing with staccato speed. His touch had been like a shock. Get ahold of yourself, she thought. He's Katherine's boyfriend. She looked back up to find him observing her. "How about you?" she asked, quickly shifting the subject. "Is there anyone in your life?"

"Well," he hesitated. "Yes and no. There is someone. I guess you might say that we've been going together. I'm not sure where it will end up. She's ready to settle down and become a Manhattan matron. Be a good wife, serve on charity boards, execute perfect dinner parties with the right mix of people—the arts, politics, theater. Actually she's been brought up to do just that sort of thing. I'm not ready for it. I'm still young. I'd like to get settled in business. So since I'm not ready to make any commitments and she's ripe for the picking, I guess it will dissolve in a natural way," he said, shrugging it off. "She'll find someone else and I'll become an old bachelor waiting for the right girl to show up at the right moment."

Despite the casual way he delivered his comments, Dale sensed that this was something he had been struggling with for some time. The right moment. When does anything happen at the right moment? At least he'd been open with her about it. She wondered why he couldn't be as direct and honest with Katherine.

"It would be wrong to make a commitment if you're feeling that way," she answered tentatively. She suddenly realized she was in a position to affect the direction Katherine's life would take. The thought frightened her. "Commitments should be honored. They shouldn't be taken lightly."

She looked back at him, then dropped her eyes. She was frightened. She had found out more than she wanted to know. She was out of her familiar environment and felt thrown off her pace. Normally she was able to control relationships, their depth and progression. But she felt this one pulling at her.

Steven looked at his watch. "I think we'd better get a cab," he said reluctantly. "As much as I hate to say it, I have a busy day tomorrow. How about you? Anything planned?"

She couldn't meet his eyes as she answered. "An interview," she told him. "A job interview." She was relieved that he didn't pursue it.

She was sad as they rode back toward her apartment. Under different circumstances they might have been strolling through the streets spinning tales of the things they would be doing together, and getting to know each other better. She had felt wanted. And she realized that she wanted him, too.

As they pulled up in front of the distinctive blue awning of her new building he suddenly turned and lifted her face in his hands and kissed her. It was soft and sweet and tender. It lingered on her lips as she turned away. There was nothing rough about Steven Fraizer. She could understand only too easily why Katherine felt about him as she did. Dale felt a warmth spreading from her belly and turning into lightheadedness as it went higher. She longed to know how his hands would feel, how his muscles would flow if they were together. She knew he wasn't in love with Katherine, not truly in love. But the thought that Katherine loved him intruded as her own passion grew. Why was it that men seemed to be able to play these games so carelessly with the women who care about them, she wondered.

"May I come up for a minute?" he asked softly as they sat in the back seat of the cab. "I hate to let you go so quickly."

She sat for a long minute while the battle raged inside. Then she answered just as softly. "No. I have an early interview in the morning."

"Do you have a phone yet? A number?"

"Not yet," she lied as she reached for the door handle.

She tried not to turn as she went through the front door of the building, not to turn back and look at him one more time, but she couldn't help it. He was watching her closely as she went in. She wondered if he could read the hint of fear in her eyes from that far away.

CHAPTER 6

Dale awakened with a start, forgetting for an instant where she was. The room was unfamiliar and a sense of uneasiness was there waiting for her when she opened her eyes. Then she remembered the night before and pulled the covers more tightly around her long frame, pushing her head back into the pillow in a vain attempt to shut out the night's memories and the day that was already beginning.

Her stomach began another flop as she thought of her interview at Fraizer's that morning. She tried to eat breakfast, then gave it up as her nervousness at the possibility of seeing Steven again built.

How she wished she'd told him who she was before he'd pulled away. It seemed too hard at the time, but now she realized that the consequences of letting him go were worse. If she didn't get the job, she might be able to slip out of Fraizer's without seeing him. If she did get it, there was no way he could be avoided. She wouldn't blame him for thinking her a liar, at least by omission, once he found out who she was. She agreed. It wasn't a way she liked to think of herself, even if it had been for the best of motivations. She wouldn't even blame him if he tried to kill her chances for getting the job.

Then there was Katherine to face. They had planned to meet later in the day. Her friend would be waiting for her when she got home. She dreaded seeing her and not telling her the whole truth, but she knew that if she reported what Steven had said it would be even more cruel.

Dale stepped out into a cool autumn morning. She looked crisp in a black-and-white houndstooth suit, nipped in at the waist and softened by an ascot, carefully knotted at her throat. Her inner worries didn't keep her dark hair from shining as it swung free in the clear morning light, and the effect was attested to by the men who stopped, turned, then looked back over their shoulders as she passed. She was oblivious, her energies centered on the upcoming interview. She had planned it out as she dressed; now she had to find a way to lead Kenneth Fraizer down the proper path.

She stopped for a moment in front of the auction house. Then, adjusting her jacket and squaring her shoulders, she strode through the imposing front doors.

She passed through the halls of the House of Fraizer. To one side was the auction gallery, to the other viewing rooms. She knew from her careful questioning of Steven the day before that the basement was devoted to storage, and the upper two floors to appraisal and executive offices. As she took the elevator up to Kenneth Fraizer's third-floor office she began to pray. Then the door opened and she found herself standing in his anteroom.

It had once been the library of the mansion. Before its fireplace the richest men in America had held discussions of how to wipe prairie off the map and replace it with railroad track. Much of the room's original spirit still lingered.

The room was immense, easily forty feet by twenty, its floor enlivened by a stretch of Persian rug adequate to carpet the tents of two sultans.

Dale answered the inquiring glance of the woman who sat in the reception area. Her desk, a long Italian writing table, was anchored in a sea of books, busts, and velvet reception chairs in such a way that she could run interference between the world and Kenneth. "I'm Dale Kenton. I have an eleven A.M. meeting with Mr. Fraizer."

"Yes, Miss Kenton. He's expecting you. If you'll

have a seat for a moment, I'll tell him you're here." Within moments Dale was shown into Kenneth's office. It was small, but it had all the quiet trappings of the successful, dignified connoisseur of the arts. An antique European gilt and crystal chandelier draped like an expensive fantasy from the high ceiling. The parquet floor was covered by a priceless Aubusson carpet. Eighteenth-century French and Italian drawings, powdery red chalks being carefully preserved under glass, were grouped in intricate displays upon the silk-covered walls. He stood behind his desk to welcome her, and extending his hand with a smile said, "Ronald's told me a lot about you. Please sit down." He waved her to a large velvet couch in front of the room.

He was even more intense in person than he had seemed to be on the stage the day before. He had one of those experienced faces, early fifties she guessed, that had grown more defined, rather than slackening, with age. Under silvering hair, cheekbones were growing stronger and eyes more insightful. As he stood to join her on the sofa she saw that his body seemed taut. He obviously paid attention to it, and it showed to good advantage under the close-fitting Italian tailoring he seemed to favor.

"Yes, I do remember you," he started. "You were on the plane with Katherine the summer she got sick. You met in Europe, didn't you?"

"In the Louvre," said Dale.

"She talked about you a lot when she got home. I spent a lot of hours with her while she was sick." He shook his head at the memory.

"She told me you were especially kind to her during those months," said Dale.

"Her father and I are close," explained Kenneth. "I could see how difficult it was for Betty to handle everything while he was gone. And quite frankly," he added, "I think of Katherine as my own daughter."

He lapsed into silence for a moment, then looked back to Dale with another question. "How have you spent the last few years?" he asked. "Tell me a little bit about your background."

Dale looked him squarely in the eye. Her gaze never left his as she spoke. "I graduated from U.C.L.A. with a Bachelor of Fine Arts," she told him. "But all that really meant was that I had taken a lot of art history courses, which in the real world means very little. I was lucky enough to get a job in Maurice Goldman's office. He's the curator of nineteenth- and twentieth-century paintings at the Los Angeles Museum of Fine Arts."

"Maurice and I are old friends," Kenneth interrupted. "He's in here at least once or twice a year. Good man. Did you work directly under him?"

"I reported to his assistant, Pat Shore."

"If she's anything like the rest of them she kept you running errands, safely out of Goldman's sight."

"She's not," Dale corrected him. "She let me sit in on meetings. I worked with collectors and the Patrons' Circle. Toward the end she even let me put on an exhibit, my responsibility start to finish."

"Did you get much exposure to restoration and authentication?" he asked. "We do our own valuations here. That sort of experience would be invaluable."

"We had an extensive department at LAMFA. I won't pretend that I'm an expert, but I was down there once or twice every week. I know what to look for, and I know who to ask."

Kenneth nodded his satisfaction. "Why'd you leave?" he asked.

"One of man's basic motivations," she admitted. "Money. After I'd put on my solo exhibit I got a new title, Second Assistant, but no raise. I was offered a job at a private gallery, a dealer whose clients had been in to see us from time to time to donate works to the museum. I don't know how he could tell I was ripe for the picking. But Mark Rasten could. He offered me a job at twice my salary, and I went for it.

"Of course that wasn't the only reason," she added. "It looked as if it would be a new, totally different sort of experience, too."

"We understand the financial motivation here at Fraizer's," Kenneth assured her. "We're in the business to make money. We expect our people to think that way, too."

"The time at the gallery was well spent. I learned a lot there. At first I did a lot of cataloguing, and I researched hoping to find new material from the artists he was already carrying. Once I realized he'd been specializing in nineteenth-century also-rans I gave up and started exploring the younger artists in the Venice area and downtown on my own time." She warmed to her subject as she spoke. She wasn't so much pretty as she was striking, with dusky golden skin and elongated limbs. Her slim stalk of a neck made her stand out like a model. Her cheekbones were sculpted, ending in a blunt plateau under her large eyes. She could almost have been Egyptian, until you came to those surprising pools of clear blue. They lighted up now as she continued.

"I found the contemporary art more challenging and more interesting," she told him. "Everything I needed to know about the major artists in the nineteenth century and earlier had already been recorded in the history books. But these young people were creating history as I watched. The books had yet to be written. The pages were still blank. I spent every waking hour when I wasn't at the gallery looking at new exhibitions, going to other galleries. I began to find out that I had a decent eye, that I could distinguish good from bad. I started tracking the prices of some of the artists I really liked. And after I watched them go up, I managed to convince Mark Rasten that the way of the future for his gallery was in contemporary art. Since it's relatively low priced it has a wide audience. Collectors who are just starting out can afford it. Finally he agreed. I worked hard on it. Mark had gotten caught up in the idea, and to his credit he let me do it my way. He gave me a chance, and in turn I worked my ass off. I gave press interviews and gave him every ounce of credit. For the last five years I've done everything there is to do in a small gallery. And now that I look back on it, it was a good training ground."

Kenneth smiled at her as she wound down. "Do you know anything about the auction business?" he inquired.

"I went to them on a pretty regular basis in Los Angeles," she told him. "We always looked at auctions as a good way to track the market value of our artists. As to the inner workings, I'm not too well informed, but I could learn. I'm a quick study."

"What makes you think you'd like it? It's not all glamour. For every minute of glory up there on stage there are hours of drudge work. A few good things come our way because of our reputation, but not many. Mostly we have to solicit. Not obviously, of course. But social contacts have to be maintained, sometimes with people you'd rather not know. And personal relationships with dealers and collectors and curators. There are lunches with the bankers and attorneys who are in a position to give you the good estates when they come up. Finding your sources and getting enough merchandise for a sale takes lots of imagination and legwork. And I don't mean just major sales. We have sales every week. Then there's the cataloguing and research. And the monthly newsletters. And the press to be handled and flattered. And the appraisals and paperwork."

"I warn you, Mr. Fraizer," said Dale, laughing as she held up a hand to stem the flow of his words, "you'll have to try harder than that to discourage me."

He listened with interest as she continued. "I might as well confess that I came to your auction yesterday. From the moment I arrived I felt it. The electricity of the crowd. Their anticipation waiting for that ivory hammer to fall. The momentum building from piece to piece. It was like watching a bullfighter. You held that crowd in your hand until you were ready to make the kill. I've never seen anything like it. How many lunches' did you have to sit through to get those diamonds?" asked Dale with curiosity.

"You would pick the exception to the rule," he said with resignation. "They just walked right into my office. The Maharajah of Mayapur brought them in unannounced."

"I saw a picture of him once," Dale said eagerly. "He was sitting on one side of a scale while his subjects piled on his weight in gold as a tribute. He needed an elephant to carry it off, it was so heavy."

"That was a very old picture," Kenneth informed her. "When the British left, the annual tributes stopped. Not that he ever stopped living like a prince. He's run through almost everything he had over the last four decades. That necklace was just about the last of it."

"He must have wanted top dollar."

"Better than that," Kenneth smiled. "He wanted to negotiate our commission down to half. Told me that Ned Whytson was willing to do the sale for a five-percent fee."

"You had to give in?"

"No. I bluffed him. Offered eight percent."

"And he agreed?"

"Not until he'd walked over to the door and

started to open it. I'll tell you my heart really sank when he started to do that. I thought for sure that I'd lost them."

Dale could hear the sound of typing outside Kenneth's door. They seemed strangely isolated in a world of their own within his office.

"So you see," he said thoughtfully, "I had to earn the right to auction those diamonds. I played the game and won. I risked a commission that could run into hundreds of thousands."

"Who's Whytson?" asked Dale, focusing on a single point from the story.

Kenneth looked startled. "You are a quick study, aren't you," he said to himself thoughtfully. "Whytson's gotten a lot of press lately. He's pretty much dominating the London auction business now. When the aristocracy fell on hard times and had to sell their family heirlooms to pay taxes he taught them how to cash in on their family names. It gave a combination of prestige and mystery to his house. Anything brings more if it belonged to the Churchills or a member of the royal family. No matter how remote. Mr. Whytson's decided to grace New York with his presence now. And we're the competition he's going to have to knock off to do it." He became remote as he thought of it, his attention wandering from the room and from her. Then he suddenly remembered they had been in the middle of an interview.

"He seems to be troubling you a great deal," she offered.

"That's true. He is." Kenneth paused for a moment as he thought of Whytson again. "But that doesn't solve your problem, does it? You know when I told Ronald I'd see you I thought you might even fit in here, sort of a gofer, an apprentice. But now that we've talked I can see you're overqualified for that," he said regretfully. "You're ready to be the assistant to one of our department heads, and then to go on to head a department of your own. But we don't have anything open on that level right now. I don't know of anyone who's thinking of leaving. I can't even tell you to wait until something suitable turns up. You're not in a position to get along without a job, are you?"

"No," she answered, disappointed but forthright. "I need the money. But I am willing to earn the right to work here. Like you earned the right to auction the diamonds. I'm willing to create my own job. Give me a small salary, let me work on one project to prove myself, and then we'll negotiate after you see what I can do. I'll risk the time if you'll risk a little money. Up there on that podium yesterday you courted me. I fell in love with this business. You won't have a harder working employee or a more loyal one."

"What's the project?" he asked.

"An auction of contemporary California art," she quickly replied. "I have the connections to bring it in. I'll work with your people to learn about the cataloguing and the appraisals. I'll pick their brains every step of the way. I think you can pay me, learn about me, and make a profit at the same time. What do you say?"

Kenneth looked pleased. "I say it's worth a try. We haven't had one yet. And some of the SoHo galleries seem to be doing well with the younger Californians. If you can get by on three hundred and fifty a week, I'll give you a bonus if it's a success. At the very least you'll be learning something and meeting the people in New York's golden circle. Now what do you say?"

"When do I start?"

"What are you doing the rest of the afternoon?" he asked.

"Whatever you tell me to do," she answered, smiling.

"I want you to spend it with my son Steven." He passed her a pad of paper, indicating that she should take notes. She wondered if he noticed that her hand had begun to shake as she reached to pick it up. She looked as white as the sheets of paper she was holding.

"Discuss your project with him," Kenneth went on, oblivious to the change in her. "Set a target date for the sale. Have him introduce you to Miriam, the head of the paintings department. And Deborah in P.R. Tell him to explain the terms for shipping and insurance and reserves. Oh, and the cost for having pieces photographed and printed in the catalogue. And the deadlines. That should keep you busy for one afternoon," he concluded.

Kenneth had a reassuring hand on her shoulder as they walked back out to the reception area. "I want you to prepare a letter of agreement between Fraizer's and Miss Kenton," he instructed his secretary. "An employment agreement for the period required to prepare an auction of contemporary California art. She'll be receiving a salary of three hundred fifty a week and bonus at my discretion at the conclusion of the sale. Call Steven," he instructed, "and tell him Dale Kenton is on her way down and that she will require his help." He pointed Dale to the elevator with a kindly smile. "Second floor," he told her. "The third door on the right. But remember," he told her, stopping her long enough to caution her, "we're not talking about a permanent job yet. Just one project. We'll see how it goes, then talk again."

Her footsteps sounded very loud to Dale as she approached Steven's office door. He didn't respond to the first knocks. When the next ones went unanswered she slowly opened it. He was sitting behind his desk, his arms carefully folded over his chest. His face was impassive, washed clean of any emotion. He didn't rise as she walked in, or even offer her a chair. He left her standing there in front of him, exposed and uncomfortable. There was a blank silence in the room as he continued to look at her, examining her more like an object than a person. It seemed to stretch out forever.

"When I heard the name I couldn't believe it," he said at last. "But sure enough, it's the same Dale Kenton." He left her without a response. She had expected shouting, anticipated a scene. Instead he just sat there, looking at her, the expression on his face so cold that she gave in to an actual shiver. He seemed, above all else, to have determined to maintain his dignity. But he couldn't block out the hurt that she saw in his eyes.

"I'm surprised to hear that you want to put in time learning the auction business. You're already so well qualified to be an actress."

She began to tremble as his eyes continued to skewer her relentlessly. She was near tears, but then she looked behind him to the bookcase where his books and papers rested and saw the picture of Katherine that stood there. Katherine's smile looked happy and untroubled. She wore a long dress of a delicate rosebud pink. Ronald stood next to her sharing the moment, looking back at his daughter with a smile that echoed her own. Dale felt stronger having seen it. "I didn't plan it, Steven," she told him. "I thought you'd recognize my name the minute I said it."

"And when I didn't you decided to let me ramble on about my relationship with Katherine?"

"When you didn't I decided to try to find out exactly how you really feel about Katherine," she quickly interrupted. She was surprised to hear that her voice had an edge of anger to it. "She's my best friend. The night before I met you I sat at the dinner table with her and watched her agonize over whether she should accept a grant and go to Paris, or whether she should stay right here and hope that you would marry her. I'm her friend. I wanted to help her answer that question. And now I can. You're not being honest with her."

"You're in a fine position to give me lectures about honesty."

"I was wrong not to tell you who I was. I know that. But that doesn't change the rest of it. Katherine's in love with you, very much in love. She thinks you feel the same way. For God's sake—she's expecting you to ask her to marry you as soon as you've straightened things out with your father. You told me the truth. Can't you do the same for her?"

For the first time his self-control began to crack. "She'll get tired of waiting," he said angrily. "The relationship will dissolve of its own inertia. I don't want to tell her there's no real passion there. I don't want to hurt her like that. I don't want to see the expression in her eyes when she hears it," he finally admitted.

"You're wrong about Katherine," Dale replied quietly. "She'll wait. She loves you. She has for a very long time. You've got to be honest with her."

"What would it accomplish? Make her feel terrible about herself? Is that what you want?" He sat back in his chair. He looked drained. When he looked back up at her his face was drawn and fatigued. "You know it wouldn't have hurt so much if I hadn't actually felt something for you, if I hadn't actually cared. I watched you walk in to Fraizer's yesterday afternoon. I was standing in the corner of the lobby. You looked beautiful, but a little frightened. There was something about you. From the moment you came through the door I wanted to meet you. Once I had, I wasn't disappointed."

"Neither was I," Dale admitted.

He rose from his desk and came to her. There was

a hint of fear in her eyes. He held her chin firmly as he lowered his lips to hers and began gently but insistently to kiss her. He felt the muscles in her neck begin to relax, to soften, as his own passion grew. But she pulled free of him and bolted for the door.

"I'll never do anything to hurt Katherine," she cried. "You've got to understand that." The fright in her eyes had become a fear of giving in to what she wanted.

When she reached the sidewalk in front of the House of Fraizer, she stopped. She felt a nagging little pulse in her left temple, the beginning of a full-blown headache that would probably last through the rest of the afternoon and the evening. People were passing by, talking or hurrying to their next appointments with no sense of the havoc that had descended on her.

Looking down she realized that she still carried the notepad that Kenneth Fraizer had handed her half an hour before. There, in her own neat handwriting, was the list of questions he had told her to discuss with his son. She flung it at the granite wall in frustration. Then picking it up she began to walk home.

Dale took the stairs leading to her apartment by twos. As fast as she'd gotten there, she could see that Katherine had arrived before her and was already standing outside her front door shifting nervously from foot to foot as she waited. She smiled as Dale came into view.

"Sorry I kept you waiting," Dale apologized.

"Don't worry about it. How'd it go with Kenneth? That's the important thing."

Dale wrestled with the locks of her apartment door. Every cell of her body cried out with fatigue. She felt as if she'd been on a two-week forced march. The realization that by the time Steven had talked with his father she might not have a job at

Fraizer's any more didn't help. "I'm not sure. I'll know tomorrow," she told Katherine.

"So tell me about Fraizer's," Katherine encouraged her. She looked wan; her eyes were framed by dark circles. But she still seemed eager to hear about Dale's interview.

"He seemed to like me, Katherine. I think there's a good possibility."

"I know you must have liked Kenneth. He's special. But did you like the house? Did he have a chance to show you around?"

"Actually," Dale answered slowly, "I showed myself around. I went to Fraizer's yesterday and watched an auction."

"And . . ." Katherine asked, sensing that there was more to Dale's story.

"I met Steven. Sat next to him in fact," she said lightly. But as she watched, an odd expression come over her friend's face at the sound of Steven's name. "Are you all right, Katherine?" she asked.

"I'm in perfect health," she told Dale. "I just came from the doctor as a matter of fact. Not an hour ago," she said, checking her watch. She looked composed, but there was an odd undercurrent to her tone. "Was Steven nice to you?" she asked. "He must have been surprised that you showed up there without me. I've told him so much about my friend from California."

"Everything except my name," Dale said softly. "He didn't recognize it."

"But he must have taken care of you once you explained who you were," Katherine said in his defense.

Dale paused for a moment. "Of course he did," she told her. She almost went ahead with the rest of the story, but when she looked into Katherine's eyes she saw a small seed of fear already growing there. Katherine had been insulated, protected, kept naive all her life. A betrayal was bound to hit her hard. Dale decided to wait, to let the information come out a piece at a time, to lead Katherine's thinking into a gradual change instead of bludgeoning her with the truth. Even finding out slowly would be painful, but at least it would leave Katherine free to make her decision about taking the Paris grant with all the facts at hand.

"There's something you're not telling me, isn't there?" Katherine probed. "You can't even look me straight in the eye, can you?"

At the challenge Dale slowly raised her eyes to Katherine's, but quickly dropped them again when she saw the look of distress there. "What is it you're not telling me?" Katherine demanded. "What really happened?"

"I never told him who I was, Kath," Dale admitted reluctantly. She tried to stop it there, but Katherine pushed her on.

"You lied to him?" Katherine asked, puzzled.

"Not exactly. I just didn't go out of my way to make him understand who I was. I thought I could find out more that way. I wanted to help you make your decision about Paris."

"And . . ." Katherine said quietly.

"And I got more than I bargained for," Dale told her. She reached over and took her friend's hand in hers. "Do you want me to go on? Or should I just shut up right now?"

"Tell me," Katherine said. Her voice sounded small and vulnerable.

"He cares for you a great deal," Dale started. Katherine nodded, but didn't look up. She continued to study her hands as they twisted and fretted in her lap.

"But . . ." she asked.

"But he's not in love with you. Not now," Dale added, trying to mitigate the finality of it. "You were right. He is confused. The work. His father. You were right. He's just too young."

Katherine's eyes had begun to fill with tears as Dale spoke. They flowed freely down her face now.

"There's always Paris," she said, taking Katherine into her arms and holding her tightly. It took a moment for Katherine to whisper it in her ear. When she did there was a slight quaver in her voice.

"I'm pregnant."

Dale pushed her back to arms' length and looked at her with concern. She felt her stomach go into knots. Beads of perspiration began to appear on her forehead.

"I don't want him this way. I don't want to force him to marry me. He would always resent me for it." Katherine fought back the tears as she looked at Dale. When she couldn't manage them any more they came out in an uncontrolled flood. "I'm so scared, Dale," she sobbed. "I just don't know what to do."

Dale put her arms around Katherine and held her closely, trying to calm her down. Her whole body was shaking as the muffled sobs continued. "Oh, Katherine," she said as she gently stroked her hair. "It will be all right. Don't worry." But even as she spoke she felt her own fear tighten its grip on her. The more she was around Katherine the more she realized how dominated Katherine was by her mother and how childlike her father had kept her. "You're pregnant," she told her. "But you do have choices."

"Choices?" Katherine replied. "What kind of choices do I have? To have the baby and bring it up by myself? Mother and Daddy would just love that. If I weren't pregnant it would all be so simple. I could just leave, go to Paris, and try to put Steven out of my mind. Mother would be upset. She wants me married to someone first-rate. Dad. Well, he'd like me to take the grant and go to Paris for now. It wouldn't kill him if I didn't marry Steven, even if he and Kenneth are close."

"Katherine," Dale interrupted her. "We're talking about you, not them."

Katherine was silent. When she looked up at Dale her expression was even more troubled than it had been before. "I'm going to abort it." She looked quickly away from Dale, as if she feared she would find disapproval in her eyes.

Dale took her by the hands. "It's a serious decision. One you'll have to live with for the rest of your life. Do you want to give it a little more time?"

"I can't do that," Katherine said. "I might change my mind. Will you help me?" she asked, clinging even more tightly to Dale's hands.

"If you're really sure it's what you want," Dale answered, "I'll be with you every step of the way."

CHAPTER 7

The next morning Dale hurried toward the House of Fraizer. Despite the early hour cabs and pedestrians thronged the streets and sidewalk. She rushed through the side door of Fraizer's, hoping she had arrived early enough to make up the hours that had been lost the afternoon before. She hurried down the hall and raced around the corner.

"Watch it," warned Kenneth as she crashed into his side. He bent down to pick up the copy of the *New York Times* that had flown out of her hand when they collided. As he looked up at her she tried to read his eyes to find out whether Steven had told him or not. They seemed as clear and open to her as they had the day before. Her heart climbed back up to its rightful place in her chest. "Don't forget to read the obituaries," he told her, returning it to her grasp. "Estates to be sold. Don't be shy about going after them."

"I'll remember that," she said, hoping he wouldn't ask her what she'd learned the afternoon before.

"Plus the classifieds. The society section. And the business section," he instructed her. "Got to find out who's making the money to know who can afford to spend it."

He had shed his jacket and was working in shirtsleeves, attending to details that had to be settled in the hours before the public arrived. "Did Steven have a chance to introduce you to Miriam yet?" he asked.

Dale nodded no. The woman who stood at Kenneth's side extended a hand whose fingers seemed as rough and uncared for as their owner. She was an unpolished woman of about forty-five. Her hair was a nondescript brown, interspersed with wiry threads of silver that were thickest at her temples. A cigarette hung from her hand, ashes precariously clinging to its tip. She had the hard-bitten look of a woman who'd worked her way to the top against all odds, without looks or sex appeal or friends in high places to fall back on. Her large hazel eyes studied Dale with intelligence and unspoken challenge.

"Steven's already spoken to me," she said. "He's entrusting you to me for the afternoon. To learn the ropes of the paintings department."

Dale wondered again what was in Steven's mind. He apparently had already done her two favors that morning. "I need all the help I can get," she acknowledged.

Miriam turned back to the paintings that she and Kenneth had been hanging. "Let's finish this," she said impatiently. "I want to get back to my office and make a phone call. I'm working a divorce in Beverly Hills—a contemporary-art couple. Rumor has it that if they can't agree on the division of the collection, they're going to sell. I'd like to catch them early in the morning. Before they settle their differences."

Kenneth smiled. Miriam's dry sense of humor had always appealed to him. He knew she appraised honestly—both art and people. He was curious to hear her opinion once she'd spent a day or two with Dale. "On your way," he said. "Steven's waiting for you upstairs. I told him not to go out before he'd gotten you started."

Dale pressed the second-floor button with trepidation. She was prepared for an argument with Steven. She'd spent half the night tossing and tangling her sheets as she'd imagined the dialogue and practiced replies to his accusations.

His door was ajar, and a secretary was opening two Styrofoam containers of coffee on his desk. "One is for you," he said, handing her a steaming cup. He looked composed, even friendly. "Cream and sugar, wasn't it?" he asked.

"Good memory," she complimented him.

"It seemed important at the time," he parried. The undercurrent of meaning in his voice was so evident that his secretary looked at Dale with new interest. "I'm sorry," he apologized. "That was a cheap shot, wasn't it?"

"Not entirely undeserved," she admitted. "I owe you an apology. I thought that being Katherine's friend, I could get some answers from you and help her out. That doesn't justify my lying to you."

"You could always have told me who you were and then asked the questions."

"Would I have gotten the same straight answers?" she asked him.

He didn't answer. Instead he gave her a small smile. "I think we should keep this between ourselves," he said, indicating Katherine's picture on the bookcase behind his desk with an inclination of his head. "You may have done me a favor after all. I don't want a permanent relationship with Katherine. You just brought those feelings to a head sooner than they would have surfaced otherwise. Maybe I can guide her away from the relationship without hurting her. Then maybe we can try to get together again. I know I went too far yesterday," he interrupted her as she started to speak. "It won't happen again. Not unless you want it to."

It took all of Dale's self-control to hold in the news of Katherine's pregnancy. Under the circumstances it would serve no purpose at all for him to know. "I don't want it to, Steven," she said. "I can't hurt Katherine like that."

"Give me a chance to prove what a nice guy I am before you make that decision," he advised her. "I've already covered for you this morning. My father was in checking on your progress. I told him you'd done brilliantly."

Dale suddenly felt as if she had made a fool of herself the day before, overreacting and rushing out like a child. "He asked me how far we'd gotten on the list he gave you," Steven went on. "It would be a little easier for me to cover for you if I had some idea of what he was talking about," he said, smiling.

She handed him her notes. "Appraisals, reserves, insurance, photographs, charges . . ." he ticked off. "I think we should start downstairs. Bring that," he said as he started out the office door. He pointed to the pad that she had left on his desk. "You'll need it."

Dale found herself straining to keep up. He had

the long-legged stride of a tall man, and she was handicapped with heels. Mistake, she realized. Tomorrow dress for comfort, not fashion.

As they went down the hall they passed office doors at ten-foot intervals. Phones were ringing. People had their heads buried in catalogues and computer runs. Desks and floors were stacked high with objects of all sizes and shapes. Space was obviously at a premium at Fraizer's. "What do they all do?" Dale asked.

"We have over fifty staff experts in various categories of art. Antiques, furniture, silver, stamps, coins, paintings, and prints to name just a few. You'll meet them as you get around. Some of them are doing valuations from photographs that arrive in the mail. Some are researching descriptions for the catalogues. Some are working on getting consignments for auction. You'll have to learn it all," he summarized as the elevator door opened.

"Where are we going?" she asked him.

"I want to introduce you to our photographer," he explained, "and to show you where the storage bins for the paintings are."

Dale shifted her weight to one foot. The other was beginning to hurt mercilessly. She slipped out of one slim heel and wiggled her toes to restore the feeling.

As the elevator door opened they were greeted by a uniformed guard who moved aside to let them pass. "The salesroom may be the arena, but this is what makes it all possible," Steven told her with a sweep of his hand, indicating the space that stretched out before them.

Dale followed his gesture. She found herself looking at a room that seemed to extend for acres. Stacks of china, silver, and antique dolls were piled high in locked cages. Furniture, sculpture, and clocks stood everywhere. To the uninformed eye there seemed to be no particular order in the chaos. She wondered how anything was ever located once it passed through those warehouse doors.

"That's a funny word for it. The arena," she said.

"It's because the salesroom is like the political arena," he explained. "Until the last vote is counted there can be surprises. The stakes are high, and you can play or just watch from the sidelines."

Dale nodded. Put that way it made perfect sense. She followed Steven down the pathways that had been left clear within the collection of merchandise.

"You'll need to get a security pass to get back in here," he told her. "They should have one ready for you in the personnel office on the second floor."

Dale made a note of it. She looked around her with a sense of the wonder of it all. Every object was a piece of someone's life. The victim of a change in tastes, a death in the family, a move out of town, a lost job, or a financial reverse. They all had stories to explain their presence in that dusty, cavernous room. "It looks like I could walk out of here with my pockets full and nothing would be missed," she commented with surprise.

"Don't bother trying," he laughed. "We have a very sophisticated security system down here. You don't see it, but it sees you. And in case you do succeed in getting away with something, it's all insured. We have a blanket policy against fire, theft, and breakage."

"I hope it covers loss. How do they ever find anything down here?"

"Every piece gets a lot number when it comes in," he told her, holding up a numbered ticket that was hanging from a table to their right. "As soon as it's catalogued and the experts have had a chance to make an accurate description of it, we bring it to storage and enter the location in the computer inventory. Nothing's moved until it's sold.

"Come down here two months from now," he continued. "And almost everything you see will have been auctioned. A few things will have been held for special sales, but ninety percent of what's here today will have been sold."

Steven swerved to the left and led her to a door on the side of the storeroom. "We put the photo studio down here where all of the lots are accessible. Usually the photograph is taken before things go into storage, but once in a while we have to reshoot." He knocked as he entered, catching the attention of the photographer.

"Just a second," Dale heard as she spotted him in the center of the room. Phil Jackson, Fraizer's house photographer, was wearing blue jeans. Beyond that it would have been hard for her to describe him, since the upper half of his body was hidden under a black tent that enveloped both him and the top of his camera. In front of him a piece of scrimshaw rested on a table that had been draped in dark velvet. The tusk was beautifully lit to highlight the scene which had been inscribed on its smooth surface. The camera clicked and Jackson emerged.

"Dale Kenton, Phil Jackson," Steven said, introducing them. "Dale's putting together a contemporary-art auction for us," he told Phil. "You should be seeing a lot of her in the next few months.

"I'll give you a price list for the photographs when we get back upstairs," Steven told her. "Once you get the client's O.K., send a routing slip down to Phil telling him the size it's set to run in the catalogue and whether it's black and white or color. He'll shoot the piece before it goes into inventory, then send the transparencies back up to you. If you need to check the paintings again after that," he went on, "they'll be in the bins." He waved good-bye to Phil as he led her out and further into the maze.

Dale halted as they passed a magnificent mahogany breakfront. "It's beautiful," she whistled.

"Late George the Third," said Steven. "It should bring about twenty-five thousand dollars. It's the one next to it that's the real beauty. Early George the Third, signed and dated by William Hallett. That one should bring close to fifty thousand."

She bent to slip the shoe from one of her aching feet. She put it on the floor for a moment, standing on her bare sole and flexing her toes. She picked it up quickly as she felt a shooting pain. She examined the floor, then retrieved a small, brilliant pebble. "You insured for injury, too?" she said, tossing it carelessly into her free hand. She held it up to the light for Steven to see. "You know, it looks like a diamond," she said with astonishment.

"I don't see how it could be a real diamond," he said in an equally surprised tone. "All of the gemstones are stored in a locked vault." Steven took it from her fingers. She felt a small thrill when his hand touched hers. He must have felt it, too, because when their eyes met they both turned quickly away to avoid communicating anything. Rolling it back and forth in his cupped palm he carefully examined it. "It certainly does look real," he admitted, sounding as if nothing had just happened between them. He withdrew a handkerchief from his pocket and wrapped the stone. "Lucky you found it," he congratulated her. "I'll check the inventory listing as soon as I get back and see if it matches up."

Dale turned the mysterious appearance of the stone over in her mind as they walked to the back of the warehouse, but it was forgotten as soon as they arrived at the bins. She got lost in a world whose geography was Jasper Johns, Frank Stella, Louise Nevelson, and Sam Francis. Steven had to shake her shoulder to get her attention. "I told Miriam I'd bring you to her office by eleven," he said, showing her his watch. "We'd better get going."

They walked in on Miriam, her ear glued to the

phone, her hand holding a four-by-five transparency up to the light of the window. She nodded to them to come in. As she replaced the receiver she handed the celluloid square to Dale. "What do you think?" she inquired.

Dale held it up to the light of the window as she had just seen Miriam do. The department head reached over and took it from her hand. "No, dear. Not like that. At least not until you're as old and experienced as I am," she corrected, putting it on a light box to the side of her desk. Dale bent over to see it, picking up the magnifying glass that rested near the illuminated glass. It took her a moment to get over Miriam's remark. It was obvious Miriam looked at her as a young snip who thought that a few art courses and some work at a gallery made her competent. It was equally obvious that Miriam resented it.

"Rothko," she answered. "Probably about 1954. You should be able to get about"—she stopped for a moment to consider—"about $550,000," she decided.

"Well, at least you know something," said Miriam, clicking off the viewing light. Dale was pleased. She had passed the first test. Steven excused himself, leaving the two of them alone.

"We're going to put you in here. At least temporarily." Miriam indicated a corner of her outer office, a bullpen where two assistants were already laboring. "Where I'll be able to keep an eye on you."

Dale looked it over. She didn't have much room, but there was everything she'd need. She'd been allocated a white parsons table, with a gray secretarial chair pulled up to it. Behind it were bookshelves filled with volumes of Fraizer's monthly newsletters and annuals. The most recent volume of *The Best of Fraizer's* rested on the corner of her desk. She had a file cabinet and a large bulletin board. Hundreds of art books filled the shelves that lined every wall of the office. "Great," she said. "I love it."

"It's not the Ritz, but it's all you've got. Now grab your purse," said Miriam, returning to her office for her own, a scarred tote that looked as if it had spent the better part of its life sitting next to her on subway seats. "Lesson one. On-premises valuations."

Miriam walked them briskly out the door, and flagged down a cab. Dale followed her through the back door, barely making it in as the cabby took off. She was thrown onto the seat, landing on a spot of upholstery that had split and curled and hardened to the texture of tempered steel. "This thing's dangerous," complained Dale, watching a run inch its way down one leg. "Not to mention hard on the wardrobe."

"Here's the story," began Miriam, groping in her tote for a cigarette. She pulled one out and began to light it with a battered Ronson. A flame shot three inches into the air. "In five years this thing has never once worked right," she said, tossing it back into the bag with disgust. "Hold this," she told Dale, passing the lighted cigarette over. She examined the strands that hung from the left side of her head, confirming the smell of slightly singed hair filling the back seat was real. "Saves the price of a trim," she said philosophically, retrieving the cigarette from Dale's hand. "We're going over to the Olympic Tower," she continued. "Following up on a cold call that came in this morning." Noticing that Dale looked bewildered, she explained. "An unsolicited inquiry. Someone whose collection we weren't aware of. It wasn't five seconds before I realized that this was one cold call that was red hot. The collector's a Mexican. Name's Huerez. He's living in an apartment in the Olympic Tower that's got to be good for close to a million dollars a pop. He said he needs some quick cash and he happens to have one very liquid asset, a collection of impressionist paintings that is not to be believed. When he started to list them for me I moved faster than the mouth on a Wall Street lawyer. I made an appointment with him within the hour."

"What's he got?" asked Dale.

"Just you wait, honey," said Miriam, enjoying the suspense. "Just you wait and see." Miriam's attention wandered to a spot that she'd just noticed on her blouse. "Damn," she said. "I'm going in to fight for a million or two in art looking like I slept in this outfit. I'd better impress him with my intellect."

"Here," offered Dale, taking the scarf that had been around her neck and knotting it around Miriam's.

"How does it look?" she asked.

"Chic, actually," Dale answered, examining her appraisingly.

"That's what I was afraid of," said Miriam, giving her an abashed look. "Don't tell anyone back at the office. It would ruin my reputation."

Dale was nervous as they rode the elevator of the Olympic Tower. The man who came to the door was small, slender, and dark. The solid-gold Rolex at his wrist winked back light from the large picture window that overlooked St. Patrick's Cathedral. "Senor Huerez?" Miriam asked.

He welcomed them into the apartment. Without a great deal of conversation he deferred to Miriam's request that they view the art. For the next hour they toured the apartment, Miriam dictating and Dale taking notes and Polaroid pictures as they went. By the time they had finished they had listed a Cézanne oil, a group of Degas dancers in pastel, a Signac view of the port of Colliouro, and a Pissarro. The value of those four pieces alone exceeded three million dollars.

Their host brought them back to the living room, where he settled them on a fawn-colored couch of

Italian leather. "As I mentioned this morning, time is of the essence." He addressed Miriam, who answered discreetly.

"I understand perfectly. It normally takes us three to five days to get out a written estimate, but I'll try to get it done by tomorrow morning." Nodding his agreement, he escorted them to the front door.

Miriam gloated as she rode back to the House of Fraizer. "Even better than I had expected," she said. "He forgot to tell me about the Signac and some of the other pieces." Suddenly she was all business. Indicating that Dale should take notes, she began a list of the things that had to be accomplished by morning. "Lesson number two, closing the deal. I want every one of those pieces researched by the end of the day. Historical background. Date. Relative importance in the body of the artist's work. And their provenance, particularly recent owners. We don't want to find ourselves selling anything that's stolen. Start with the Renoir. Try Daulte and Lemoisne for the catalogue raisonné. They should have all the information you'll need."

"Why such a rush?" asked Dale. "I'm not so sure I can finish all that by the end of the day."

"Honey," said Miriam in a patiently instructive tone, "if he cold-called us, chances are he tried Sotheby's and Christie's too. We have to tie him up before those boys get a chance to meet him."

"OK. I'll do it," said Dale.

"The list isn't finished," interrupted Miriam. "I want you to go to Deborah in the P.R. office and tell her to do a mock-up of next month's newsletter. Put his Renoir on the cover. I'll take it over with me tomorrow. Page one stories always have a certain appeal to the ego. And make sure she spells his name right," she said, sitting back on the seat and lapsing into a thoughtful silence.

"Window dressing is what we need now," she

mused as they pulled up in front of Fraizer's. "We need to put together a few other world-class paintings to build this thing."

"Won't that just spread the dollars that would have gone for his paintings?" asked Dale.

"That's not the way it works, honey," Miriam told her as they walked back toward their offices. "There are only a handful of buyers worldwide for art in this price range. A few collectors. A few galleries. A few museums. The more great art we can group on one sale, the better our chances of attracting them all and working the prices up. There are only a few major sales each year. You've got to try to make enough on them to carry you through the slow months in between.

"Here's where I'm leaving you," she said as they came to the viewing room on the first floor. "Wednesday is my afternoon for open valuations. If you need me I'll be down here arguing with people who've brought in paintings that they think of as masterpieces."

Lunch hour came and went without Dale seeing daylight. By five o'clock most of the staff had cleared out. The halls had become quiet, but she was so immersed in finishing the cataloguing of the collection that she didn't hear Deborah close the door behind her.

"Here's the mock-up," said Deborah, standing in front of Dale's table and extending it toward her. Dale took it and inspected it carefully. It looked quite authentic, typeset and colored like an actual newsletter. Dale's Polaroid of the Renoir had been reproduced and mounted on the cover. Two other stories were penciled in below, one featuring a picture of Kenneth Fraizer bringing down the hammer on the diamonds of Mayapur. She remembered that afternoon and the effect it had had on her.

"Does Steven auction as well as Kenneth does?" she asked Deborah with curiosity.

"He doesn't auction at all," Deborah answered. She was a dark-haired girl, probably twenty-five, who ran slightly to the plump side. "Bob Bentley does the usual auctions, but Kenneth works the really important ones. He always keeps that for himself. I'm not so sure he wants to give up the glory."

"Does that bother Steven?" Dale asked.

"He doesn't say much about it. At least not to me," answered Deborah.

"Thanks for the mock-up," Dale said, changing the subject. She found herself growing uncomfortable as they discussed Steven. She reached for the phone that had just started ringing. "Can you hold on for a minute, Katherine?" she asked after saying hello.

"I've got to run now anyway," said Deborah. "Steven said I should give you a rundown on the P.R. we normally do for auctions. Want to get together tomorrow?"

"Perfect." As Deborah left she put the receiver to her ear. "Did you get an appointment?" she asked Katherine.

"Tomorrow. Ten o'clock. Will you meet me there?" Her voice sounded tentative and a little weak.

"Of course I will," Dale reassured her. "I'll be early." She started to hang up, but then thought better of it. "Are you all right, Katherine?" she asked. "Mentally, I mean. No second thoughts?"

"Not enough to convince me I shouldn't go through with it. I'm more frightened of the way that Mother and Daddy might take it than of the abortion," she admitted.

"You haven't told them yet?"

"Tonight's the night."

"They don't have to find out, you know," Dale pointed out.

"Yes they do. Some people might be able to do this without telling their parents. Not me."

"Well, I'll stay home tonight in case you need anything," Dale told her. "Don't be afraid to call." But even as she said it she hoped there wouldn't be any need for her phone to ring.

CHAPTER 8

It's enough to make you give up sex, thought Dale. She watched the nervous fingers of the woman sitting next to her buckle one more cigarette into a lipstick-stained stump. The stale odor of dead butts and burned filters hung over a cheap glass ashtray that was rapidly reaching the point of overflowing. Her eyes traveled to the clock, then back to the troubled faces of the women who squirmed and slumped on the plastic-covered couches that lined the waiting-room walls. The room was clean, but void of personality. The walls, a pale institutional green, were devoid of diversions. Formica coffee tables were overloaded with finger-worn back issues of magazines and arrangements of dusty plastic plants. She stretched long legs out in front of her and leaned back to wait. But there was that nurse again, coming back into the room.

"Are you sure there's nothing I can do for you?" she asked Dale.

"No, I'm fine. Really I am."

"No one I can call?"

"No, really. I'll just keep waiting for my friend."

The name tag read Sheridan. She gave Dale a look that could be interpreted as a cross between kindness and pity. Or maybe it was righteousness. Dale didn't know. Nor did she care. All of her concentration was centered on the single idea of willing Katherine to come through the door. Half an hour late. A little more than that now, she realized, looking up at the clock. Please be all right, she thought. Please be safe.

Nurse Sheridan summoned another patient. On the way out she paused, staring straight at Dale. "Maybe you'd like a cup of coffee while you wait?" she suggested.

"No, thank you," she replied. "Nothing." It was getting increasingly difficult to keep the note of impatience from creeping into her voice.

Nurse Sheridan took another long look. She appeared to be pondering whether she should try to talk to Dale privately. She looked as if she'd heard that friend story so many times before. The minute men heard the word pregnant, they ran.

Dale pushed a long wisp of dark hair from her eyes and studied the other occupants of the waiting room. Beside her sat a worn-looking woman Dale guessed to be the mother of four or five. The woman was studying the pattern on the worn green carpet with a look of defeat. Occasionally she plucked at the sweater which hung over her shoulders, bringing it tighter around her, covering the blot of bruised purple that spread over her upper arm. It was obvious that Katherine had chosen this place because she wouldn't be seen by anyone she knew.

Dale wished she had a Valium. What had started as nervousness was growing into real fear. The clock was creeping with maddening slowness. The door remained closed despite her desperate desire to see Katherine appear. What could have happened, she wondered, to delay her so long? To stop her from phoning. To prevent her from keeping this appointment after she had pleaded with Dale to be with her.

Eleven o'clock. She was sure that Katherine wasn't coming. Reaching down for her purse she started to get up. As she pulled on a coat Katherine rushed through the door, her gray cashmere muffler partially hidden by a gauzy tangle of permed blonde hair. She appeared windblown and tired. Her eyes had the startled look of a deer trapped in a blinding arc of headlights on a back country road. She was ready to bolt.

She thrust wind-chilled hands into Dale's, displaying nervously ragged nails and cuticles that had been worried into a feverish red.

Dale clasped Katherine's hands in hers and looked at her friend with concern. "I've been worried sick about you. You're almost an hour late. That's not like you."

Katherine looked as frail as a child. Her eyes were deep in thought. Dale could practically see the nerves jangling beneath the surface.

"Mother tried to keep me at the house until Kenneth arrived," she explained. "She tried calling him last night but he was out. She got him on the phone first thing this morning. She seems to think he can talk me out of this even though they couldn't."

"You told them last night?" Dale asked. Katherine nodded.

"How did they take it?"

"Mother was thrilled when she heard. She started organizing the wedding before I had a chance to tell her I wasn't going to have the baby. The fact that Steven isn't ready to get married is immaterial to her. She was more concerned with choosing the right caterer for the reception than with whether we'd be happy."

Dale felt sorry for Katherine as she looked at her sitting there, the palm of her hand supporting her chin. She looked so fragile, and the weight of the world was resting on her. "But you didn't let her push you into it."

"I told her I was going through with the abortion this morning. She tried to come with me, but I wouldn't let her. She'd only keep trying to talk me out of it. She was furious when she heard you'd be here waiting for me."

Dale felt her stomach drop as she pictured Betty Bruner's angry face. She didn't understand why Katherine's mother disliked her so, but she knew it was true. "And your father?" she asked. "How did he take it?"

"Pretty much the way I expected," Katherine replied. "He's a practical man. He examines the options. He let me know I had choices, that if I wasn't sure about getting married I could have the baby and bring it home. He loves me so much, Dale," Katherine said, turning to her. The beginnings of tears were glistening in her eyes.

"He's right, you know," Dale comforted her. "It's not the Victorian age. You don't have to be married to have a baby these days."

"It wouldn't work. He means well, but when it came right down to it, when the baby turned into a reality, I know he'd begin to push for a marriage. I won't trap Steven like that. I'm going to have the abortion, accept the grant, and leave for Paris. That's the best way." She looked at Dale, tried to smile, and, failing that, just tried to keep from crying. They both started as Nurse Sheridan tapped Katherine on the shoulder.

"We're ready for you now. Will you please follow me?"

Katherine began to look even more frightened. "Can she come with me?" she asked, grasping Dale's hand.

"I'm afraid not," Sheridan replied with a smile she tried to make friendly and comforting.

Katherine looked at her friend in panic. She picked up her purse and with a shaky hand passed it to Dale for safekeeping. Then she slowly stood up.

Dale's eyes never wavered from her. She realized as she looked at Katherine that her friend had visibly changed. A slight weight gain had become obvious. Even her cheeks looked rounder, healthier, under her worried eyes. She felt a stab of remorse for the life they would be ending that morning.

As Katherine began to walk slowly away, the office door flew open and Kenneth burst in. He looked like a man much older than his fifty-odd years. The fluorescent lights showed lines of worry that seemed to have etched themselves deeply within the space of a few hours. He looked even more stricken when he saw Katherine. Her swollen eyes, with harsh dark circles forming concave outlines beneath them, said it all.

"Why didn't you tell me?" he asked, walking over and putting his arms around her. Without waiting for an answer he went on. "No abortion. I'm here for you now. Come on, Katherine. Let's get out of this place. It gives me the creeps."

Katherine stayed limp in his arms. Her eyes searched his face. She looked like a prisoner awaiting sentence. He glanced away from her quickly and exchanged a look with the nurse, then he grasped Katherine gently by the shoulder and steered her back to where Dale sat. Kneeling by the side of her chair, he took Katherine's hand. "Let's take a walk," he said. "Just the two of us."

Katherine could feel the strength of his arm as he guided her out the door and into the corridor. It seemed to transfer energy to her, conducting it from the reserve he had stored up into her own sapped spirit.

Together they walked into the long deserted hall. Golden sunlight had begun to stream through the windows at its end, bathing the tiles with new life. She could hear the sounds of children behind one of the office doors. Their shrill cries reminded her of the appointment that had been scheduled for that morning.

"You know, your mother called me this morning," said Kenneth, cupping his hand over hers where it rested on his arm, laced through the space between his body and her own. "While I was driving here I found myself thinking about that summer when you had hepatitis. The summer you met Dale," he added, looking at her with a tiny smile.

They walked further down the empty hall. It was as if the two of them were venturing into a void where no other humans would be found. Kenneth stooped and picked up a discarded matchbook and dropped it into an ashtray that stood near the wall. Then he turned to face her. "I'll never forget the sight of you coming off that plane. Your face so thin and yellow as egg yolk against the pillow. I swear you didn't look as if you were going to make it."

"I know," remembered Katherine. "Mom took one look at me in that wheelchair and got hysterical. I was so glad you were there."

"The nurses, and blood tests, and hospital beds. And your mother fighting with the doctors to keep you at home instead of sending you to the hospital. And you, barely able to lift your head off the pillow." He paused thoughtfully. "And yet, you know, I look back on that as one of the best summers I can remember."

"That's a strange thing to say," Katherine told him.

"Well," he said. "I came out to visit with you almost every day that summer. At first I did it because your father wasn't home. He'd done so much for me over the years, I felt I owed it to him. But pretty soon I was doing it because it filled a need for me."

Katherine looked at him, mystified.

"You see, I hadn't had anyone to really talk to since my wife died. Not a woman, at least. My life was the auction house, and then taking care of Steven once I got home. He needed me even more with his Anna gone." Kenneth stopped and gathered his thoughts. "Seeing you so much, it was like having a daughter. One that I could talk to the way I used to talk to her. You were a confidante. And you'd seen so much of the art world, you were wise beyond your years. You had a way of making an old man feel needed. You listened so patiently."

"Oh, Kenneth. You're hardly an old man. And I loved listening to your stories," recalled Katherine fondly. "I can still remember some of the paintings you described to me that summer. The Degas pastel. You got over a hundred and seventy-five thousand for it, didn't you? And the Chagall that the Weintraubs had bought straight from his studio."

"I remember it perfectly," Kenneth said regretfully. "They sent it to Sotheby Parke Bernet instead of to Fraizer's."

They looked at each other and exchanged a smile of genuine fondness. "Can't win them all," she said to him with a small grin.

"I know," he replied pensively. "But some are harder to lose than others."

Katherine looked at him. It was a face she had learned to love so much that just tracing his features with her eyes brought a soft welling of emotion to the surface. She had never felt such trust in another human being.

She should have noticed that though his manner

was warm and soothing, his fists were knotted and tight as if he was using every bit of self-control to hide his true feelings. But his face was anguished. He spoke quickly, not allowing himself the luxury of thought.

"You know, as I thought about it this morning," he said, "I understood what was bothering me so much about all of this. You're carrying a seed that's part you and part Steven. But it's part your parents, too. And it's part me. It's a child that we could all love. You and I could teach it so much, things I wasn't smart enough, or sensitive enough, to teach Steven. And when I think that you're about to kill that— Katherine, it just breaks my heart."

She saw the pain it was causing him, and her eyes filled with tears. It was as if her conscience had spoken to her. He had brought an entirely new dimension to the dilemma that faced her. She looked at Kenneth and was stunned by the impression that he was an older, an original, version of his son. She had always assumed that Steven would mature into a man like him. They were so much alike in some ways, with gestures and facial expressions that were so akin they could have been interchangeable.

"Katherine, can you really kill that child?" Kenneth asked, pulling her to him. "Your son. Steven's son." And she knew that she couldn't. An abortion was just an abortion. But to kill, to break that chain that ran from Kenneth to Steven and then on through her own body. She would never be able to go through with it.

She slowly moved her hands down her body, carefully tracing the contour of her abdomen. The life that was growing inside her wasn't revealing itself yet, but for some reason her thoughts had already become those of an expectant mother. She constantly wondered whether it was a girl or a boy, imagining it looked like Steven, or perhaps like herself. Each day she had become more attached to this baby of hers. "But Steven," she said. "He doesn't want to get married now."

"Katherine, do you trust me?" Kenneth asked. She nodded yes. "Then believe me when I tell you, Steven loves you. He just wanted to be more sure of himself at Fraizer's. He's been going from department to department. He hasn't had a position of real authority. It isn't that he doesn't love you. And you," he said, looking into her eyes until the pain was almost too great to bear, "you love him. You want this baby, don't you?"

"More than anything," she answered, thrusting her hands into his. "Will you be there for me if I need help?" she asked, a quaver of fear in her voice.

"Always," came his soft reply.

Kenneth Fraizer stopped as he got out of the elevator in the building lobby. He leaned back against one of the cold marble walls, and put a hand inside his coat and on his chest, as if he could calm his runaway heartbeat by sheer force of will. Then he went out to the limousine that waited at the curb.

"We're going to the office," he told the driver as he settled himself in the back seat. Several minutes passed before he could bring himself to look at his son, who sat beside him.

Steven looked angry and depressed. "Two weeks?" he asked in a tone of barely concealed outrage. "Don't you think that's rushing things a little?"

"Steven, I'm not going to listen to any more of this," shouted Kenneth in an angry voice. Reaching for the electric control, he sent up the glass window that separated the back seat from the driver's compartment. "You'll marry her and you'll like it, or you'll be out on your ass. She'll make a damn fine wife. Give you a little stability. She understands the world you live in and work in. She'll be an asset to you. And I think you'll find you'll like your position as a married man at Fraizer's," he finished. "Do I make myself clear?"

"Very, Father," said Steven. He felt the old resentment rising up again, the feeling that he was being smothered. Is this my life I'm leading, he wondered for what seemed the thousandth time, or my father's?

It hadn't bothered him much as a child. He had simply thought that they were close, the way a father and son should be. It was a carefree existence. All of his decisions were made for him. His school—Choate. His friends—social and rich. Even the travel and museums that had replaced the sports he had, at first, felt he wanted to try.

By the time he went away to Oxford his life was chafing him like a too-tight collar. He knew he would be contacted by his father's friends and business associates who would be sure to introduce him to "the right people." He sat through boring dinners with men in their sixties and tried to comfort himself with the thought that he was winning his father's approval.

Well, that hadn't turned out to be the case. Ever since he'd come home and gone to work at the house he'd felt stifled. His father's tutelage was conservative. He'd had to master each department in turn. He'd maintained his patience for several years, waiting for the day when his father would begin to give him some of the authority he seemed to guard so closely. It never happened. No decision was ever made without Kenneth's approval, a situation Steven had come to find impossible to abide. He'd thought he had the problem licked. Well, he had, at least until Betty Bruner's phone call. The job that was waiting for him at Sotheby's looked distant now. No way he could afford that gamble if he was going to be responsible for Katherine and a baby. If he didn't like her so much, if he hadn't grown up with her as close to him as a sister, if he didn't truly care about her, he'd have told them all to go to hell.

Instead he sat back, watched the downtown crowds rush by, and prepared himself to say the lines he'd been rehearsing the whole morning. He mentally tried them out one more time. I love you. We'll be married right away.

CHAPTER 9

Dale raced through her office door. Patricia and Ingrid, Miriam's assistants, labored, as usual, over volumes of art history and piles of auction catalogues. Notes were spread over their desks, papers clipped to transparencies and to black-and-white prints of paintings and drawings and etchings.

"Miriam left five minutes ago," Ingrid informed Dale as she reached for the sweater that was draped over the back of her chair. "She said to tell you you're supposed to meet her in Kenneth's office."

"Thanks," said Dale. She grabbed a notebook and a file labeled California Contemporary and was gone as quickly as she had come. She fidgeted during the one-floor ride to Kenneth's quarters. Her discussion with Katherine had gone on for a good forty-five minutes after Kenneth left, long enough to make her late for the publicity meeting that had been scheduled for one o'clock. She glanced at her watch as the door opened on the third floor. Ten after one. She hated being late.

"They're expecting you," said Barbara, Kenneth's secretary, motioning her through the door without a pause. As Dale entered, breathless and slightly off her bearings, four heads turned in unison, then looked back to the worksheets they had been discussing.

"Take the empty chair," said Kenneth, motioning toward a seat to his left. His lips mouthed a silent question, is she all right, to which Dale replied with a subtle nod of her head. "You know Deborah. Fred Taylor is head of community relations for Fraizer's. And I'm sure you've seen enough of Miriam not to need an introduction."

Dale sat down. As she caught her breath Fred finished a report on Heirloom Day. Deborah had explained it to her already. Heirloom Day was the time when Fraizer's opened its doors to the public. People could bring in anything they chose to have authenticated and appraised by Fraizer's experts free of charge. He reviewed the results of the prior Heirloom Day, which had been held one year earlier, then listed the press coverage that could be expected for the one which was scheduled to take place in a few weeks. Dale listened with curiosity.

"How many people are you expecting?" she asked.

"We usually get twelve hundred or so," Fred told her. "We only do this once a year, and, when we do, everyone under the sun brings in family treasures to have them appraised."

"They started lining up at eight A.M.," laughed Kenneth. "We look like the uptown branch of the Salvation Army. They're all carrying things that they hope will make them rich. We see everything from old Lionel trains to grandmother's wedding gown. Porcelains, silver, jewelry, and art. And everyone's dreaming that their family treasure will be really valuable."

"Do you ever find anything worthwhile?" asked Dale.

"Once in a while," answered Kenneth. "Once in a very great while. That's not really the point, though. Heirloom Day is our way of humanizing the auction house. You'd be surprised how many people are intimidated by this place. God knows it looks formidable enough with all those guards at every door. This is the one day when all the barriers come down.

"Attendance has gotten better every year," he continued. "We always get a lot of items for the collectibles sale. Some jewelry and silver. Some art."

"But rarely the real treasure," interrupted Deborah. "I want whoever finds that to give me an emergency call. When that happens, I've got a *Times* front page. Not that I won't settle for a back-of-the-section human interest story," she conceded.

"Enough Heirloom Day," concluded Kenneth, closing a file folder and handing it back to Fred. "You'll get your fill of it before it's through, Dale. I've told Miriam that you'll help her at the paintings appraisal station. I'm not sure you'll find anything for your auction, but it will be an experience you won't forget."

"You're on now," Miriam told her. "Let's hear what you're planning for California Contemporary."

Dale opened the folder nervously. As the rest of the group listened, she reviewed the steps she intended to take to pull the auction together. She would methodically call all of the artists she had worked with during her days at the gallery in the hopes that most would agree to consign one or two works to the sale. It might take argument but she intended to get some of their best pieces, the ones they had earmarked for themselves. She was in the process of contacting the collectors listed in her personal address book. The listing was extensive, the product of almost five years of calls and mailings and attending openings. She hoped to pick up a few pieces of varying quality from them as the days went by. The dealers would prove to be the real problem.

Few of them would be eager to assign pieces to the sale unless they were pieces of marginal value that they were having trouble selling on the Coast.

"We've included your auction in all our general ads," said Deborah, consulting a media schedule for the upcoming months. "*New York Times, New York* magazine, *Avenue,* the *Wall Street Journal.* I think I've picked up enough from you today to write a release and prepare a story for the newsletter."

"Does anyone else have something we need to cover?" Kenneth asked. When the group nodded no, he dismissed them. "On your way," he said. "Except for Dale. I'd like a word with you before you go."

When the door had closed behind them Kenneth moved over to sit next to her on an adjoining chair. "Is she really all right?" he asked. His eyes were so filled with concern Dale wondered how he had managed to hide it during the meeting.

"I think so." She reached over to take his hand in a comforting manner, hesitated when she remembered who he was, but then quickly changed her mind again as the thought of what they had shared that morning came back. "She's acting as if it's the way she wanted it to end the whole time," Dale told him. "I guess it was—she just couldn't admit it since it wasn't likely to happen. She's not so worried now. She trusts you to make it work."

He looked troubled as she said it. "She does trust me, doesn't she?"

"More than her own parents," Dale confirmed. "I can't say that I blame her," she went on when he didn't reply.

"Don't make me out to be a paragon of virtue," he stopped her.

"I won't. But you're about as close as we have at Fraizer's right now," she smiled.

Kenneth studied her closely. A long moment went by before he began to speak. "I want you to know how much you're appreciated around here, too," he said finally. "You've been thinking out this auction of yours like a real professional," he added, quickly attempting to leave the personal behind.

They sat together quietly for a moment, neither knowing where to take the conversation or the camaraderie they were feeling, and both afraid to lose it.

"Why don't you come along to a dinner party with me tonight?" he suggested. "I mean," he corrected himself, "a business dinner. Our hostess may think of it as a party, but for us it's a good way to make contacts."

"I don't know," Dale started to answer. She felt as if her emotions had taken quite a beating in the last few weeks. Every time she ran into Steven it caused another little twinge. Even Katherine, as close as she was, didn't recognize the fragility of the shell that protected Dale's feelings.

Kenneth saw her hesitate. "It's at Madeleine Price's. She has a superb collection of modern art, and she always puts together an interesting group. I think you'd find it entertaining, and productive too. And I really could use the company," he confided. "Every time I go there, she fastens herself to me with a hammerlock."

Dale smiled as she nodded her acceptance. As she walked back to her office a feeling of anticipation about Madeleine Price's dinner party grew with every step. She sat down at her parsons table and looked around the room where she had spent so many hours since she had come to the House of Fraizer.

She reveled in the peace and quiet. Normally she had to contend with Patricia, Ingrid, and Miriam. The chattering and ringing phones were stimulating, but they did make it hard to concentrate or carry on a conversation. When they all left for the day the art department became her personal domain.

She had staked out her territorial rights in a small area to one side of the room. A projector on the corner of her desk was aimed at the wall directly opposite. A space had been cleaned of books and ornaments so that slides could be viewed and studied at will. She had placed a tall cylindrical vase on the file cabinet next to her. A few perfect tiger lilies bloomed above it, brightening the room. She had hung a decent reproduction of a Jasper Johns and a Chuck Arnoldi print behind her. One of John's larger canvases leaned against the wall waiting to be recorded and sent downstairs to the storage bins.

Packing up her papers she thought of the evening ahead. She was beginning to feel a sense of excitement about it. She needed to meet new people, she knew that. She needed to get noticed, to form contacts.

Dale dressed for the evening and then stood before the mirror to examine the results. Stiff circles of gold flurried up from her shoulders like sprouting angels' wings. Metallic lamé clung to her breasts, rib cage, and prominent hip bones, then flared wide to the floor in a wild fandango of glittering fabric. She did a quick half turn, and watched herself swirl and spark from hem to hip with satisfaction.

She was looking forward to Madeleine's dinner party with the same sort of enthusiasm that an unexpected invitation to Carnival in Rio might have produced. Still, she realized that she was becoming nervous about having dinner with Kenneth. It was a rare feeling for her. She usually felt in command of herself during social confrontations, but this job was so important to her she found herself imagining all sorts of disastrous faux pas. She distracted herself by concentrating on her makeup.

Her face was deeply tanned, almost Cherokee

brown. Thick eyebrows winged up over deep-set blue eyes. Her cheekbones were high and angular and she had highlighted them with a rouge of silvered rose. Her lips, normally full and chiseled in appearance, looked even riper painted in a fruity pink. The thick mass of hair that usually hung in a bluntly trimmed curtain on either side of her face had been slicked back in a high, sophisticated roll that curved around the back of her head. One single swoop of bangs had been left swinging free. Now she was the girl so often described as striking.

By the time Kenneth arrived she was feeling relaxed and herself again. He entertained her during the ride to the party with a wildly exaggerated version of Madeleine's background.

Madeleine, as he painted her, had passed through puberty dating older men. She was drinking martinis at the number one table at "21" by the age of eighteen. Her first cigarette was lit by the flame of a solid-gold Dunhill held in the hand of a man who had several. At forty-five she favored restaurants with prix fixe menus and men with the means to provide them.

Kenneth refused to set foot out of the cab until Dale promised to protect him from this potential man-eater. "Let go of my arm just once, young lady," he cautioned, "and you're fired."

Madeleine Price's Park Avenue penthouse had been photographed by so many of the world's leading magazines her circle of friends joked that the flash of strobe lights was beginning to fade the emerald-hued drawing-room drapes. Waiters laden with canapé-covered trays wove their way through the crowd that was moving into the vast marble-floored foyer. The lady herself passed out greetings to her guests as they moved into the living room that lay beyond. She was small, five foot two at most, and she had a sweet demeanor. Large clumps of jewelry flashed at her fingers and neck. She looked pleased to see them, and waved a greeting to Kenneth across the crowded entrance hall.

"What a liar you are," exclaimed Dale. "She looks as dangerous as a lap dog."

"Don't let the sweet exterior fool you," he said. "And don't let go of my arm."

As Dale looked toward Madeleine she realized that their hostess was plowing through the crowd like a battleship running full steam ahead, and that Kenneth was her target.

"Kenneth," she crooned, reaching for his free arm and giving Dale a thorough inspection. "Who's the lovely young lady?"

"Madeleine Price, Dale Kenton. Dale has just come to work for Fraizer's. Contemporary art. I thought I'd give her a treat and let her see your collection."

"How nice," purred Madeleine, looking into Kenneth's eyes. He deliberately broke her gaze and motioned toward the living room.

"Who's here tonight?" he asked.

Madeleine proceeded to list her guests' attributes and possessions with the accuracy of a financial reporter. "The pretty blonde in the black dress—the one with no back," she added cattily, "is Katinka Lambert. She's just married Barney Lambert, the real-estate magnate. They paid three million for an apartment at Seventieth and Fifth last week. You should get him to the English furniture sale you have scheduled for next month."

"I'll keep it in mind," said Kenneth. "You've got a fine head for business, Madeleine."

"I try. I try," she replied. "The Farnsleys are here. In from Houston. She's heading to the Golden Door tomorrow, part of her continuing tour of America's fat farms. Try not to spend any time with her. Boring, boring, boring. Herbal wraps and massages, facials and steambaths. Within ten minutes you know every pore of her body."

"Why do you invite her?" Kenneth asked.

"Henry Farnsley makes up for it," Madeleine explained. "Money does make a man seductive, doesn't it?"

"Who else?" asked Kenneth.

"Ned Whytson is in the corner," said Madeleine, pointing to a sandy-haired man, broad of shoulder and possessing a hearty laugh that happened to be ringing out at that moment.

"The London Whytson?" asked Kenneth.

"One and the same. Here to provide a little competition for you, Kenneth. I think I'll sit Dale next to him at dinner. I've got to get you alone somehow," she laughed as he began to object.

"Well . . . we'll see," he said with assurance. "And don't worry your pretty little head about Whytson's doing me in at this early stage of the game." Looking around the room he perked up. "I see Bill Donovan's here. You'll find him interesting, Dale," he said, turning to her. "He's on the board of trustees of what New Yorkers call the Great Dinosaur of Museums—you know that little place on Fifth Avenue." He laughed. "Has quite a collection of his own, too. Almost as good as Madeleine's. Where did you say you bought that new Nancy Graves, Madeleine?" he asked, fishing.

"I didn't say. Are your competitive juices churning?"

"Maybe just a little," he laughed.

"It's from the Knoedler Gallery. See what happens when you don't call," she teased.

"There's no loyalty," he muttered seriously as he led Dale toward the living room. It was a level lower than the entry hall. At the bottom of four steps two dozen people in tuxedos and evening gowns were milling, glasses in hand. As she began to go down, he put a hand on her elbow, stopped her, and pulled her aside. "Be careful of Whytson, Dale," he whispered to her. "He's been married for the last ten years or so, but he's a known womanizer."

"Don't worry, Kenneth," Dale calmed him. "But thanks for the warning."

"OK," he said doubtfully as they started down the stairs. "Knock 'em dead."

Dale lifted her hem lightly in her fingertips as she walked down. Reaching the bottom she flung it out quickly, with the instinctive ease of an experienced fisherman casting his line and lure. Men on all sides of the room snuck shifty glances from the corners of their eyes. Wives materialized at their elbows, demanding fresh drinks. "When you talk with Whytson," Kenneth told her, "try to find out how far he's gotten with his New York branch."

"Just leave it to me," she said.

Dale and Kenneth drifted toward the center of the room. Soon they were standing directly behind the chair on which Whytson had perched. He straddled it casually, astride one arm with legs stretching out in front of him. She studied him as he spoke. He had entranced the group with his story. They followed the sound of his voice and the motions of his animated hands with rapt attention. Dale admitted she liked him without even meeting him. Most of the men she had seen in Manhattan took their social lives as seriously as they took their businesses, never truly relaxing, constantly weighing down their companions with fidgeting feet and rapid conversation. They laughed so little. Whytson was obviously an exception to the rule. The back of his neck was ruddy and healthy. Next to the pallor that most of his listeners had, the result of lives spent under fluorescent lights and inside city apartments, he gave the impression that outdoor walks and vigorous exercise were as much a part of him as the reddish blond hair that covered his head in a thick, straight cap. His energy sucked in everyone around him, and left them wanting to stay near him.

He didn't see her at first, but she could tell he sensed her presence as his listeners looked up and reacted, then returned their attention to him. He casually glanced over his shoulder and saw her standing there, gold lamé covering her in a gleaming cocoon. Dale looked directly into his eyes, then away from him as if he didn't exist. She did it intentionally, knowing it would make him even more eager to meet her.

Dale threaded her arm through Kenneth's and wandered to the bar. She smiled inwardly. She enjoyed watching men's reactions to her. Particularly men who seemed just a little bit too sure of themselves. From the look on Whytson's face she knew he'd wander over. She could afford to be patient.

It didn't take long. As dinner was announced and she walked toward the dining room, Whytson fell into step by her side. Kenneth separated from her at the door, wandering to the other side of the table in search of his seat. Dale decided to take advantage of Whytson's interest. She was determined to learn all she could about his business, and to learn it before the end of dinner that night.

He followed her into the dining room, materializing behind her to help her into her seat. "Allow me," he said as he drew out her chair.

"Is your accent English?" she asked.

"Is your date Kenneth Fraizer?" he replied in a quick non sequitur. She blushed as she nodded yes. She was grateful for the concealing candlelight. "Then I suspect," he said with a quirk of his eyebrows, "that you already know more about me than the source of my accent." Though he was exquisitely polite, he seemed to enjoy playing with her. He was, she sensed, a man who was accustomed to having his own way. He enjoyed a duel of wits. Not necessarily in a cruel way, but as an interesting challenge. She decided to try drawing him out.

"What do you think of New York now that you've spent a little time here?"

"A great place for an auction business. Even better than I had imagined," he said chuckling. "You Americans are so set on looking like you've had money for generations, you'll buy anything with the word antique on it. And heaven knows we have enough in London to keep you Yanks satisfied." He crowned his comment with a wink to let her know it was all in good fun.

"Won't it hurt your London business," she asked him, "if you ship all the prime pieces to New York?" She was determined to probe until she found out something that would be helpful to Kenneth.

"That's the real beauty of it," he continued, warming to his subject. "You Americans have come to Britain and bought the best we had. It's happened so much that the English are used to paying better prices for pieces that come in from New York than they do for things from English collections. What doesn't sell over here, I can ship back and sell at a premium just because it took the ride. A beauty of a scheme, isn't it?" he said, rubbing his hands together with enthusiasm.

Dale had to laugh. She viewed him with skepticism, but she had to admit he was really quite charming. He studied her with equal interest. Though he looked casual, she pegged him as a man for whom appearances were all-important—the way he looked to himself and, more than that, the way he looked to the people around him.

"And how has your scheme been working so far?" she asked. "You've been open here for how long? A month?"

"Just long enough for my wife to find an apartment here, spend a hundred thousand pounds redecorating it, and skip back to London for the season. Yes, a month sounds about right."

"At least you're helping our balance of trade," Dale laughed. "Unless sales were awfully good your first month. What kind of volume are you expecting on a monthly basis?"

He looked at her with renewed interest, then suddenly began to chuckle, a warm, rich laugh that started in his chest and bubbled out. "You do work for Kenneth, don't you?" he asked rhetorically. "I must apologize, love," he said seriously. "I didn't bring my ledgers tonight. Perhaps you'd like to stop by the office next week and have a go at them?"

Dale acted embarrassed. "I'm sorry," she apologized. "I've just started in this business. I've spent so much time quizzing people at Fraizer's, I guess I forgot to leave the habit in the office."

"New, are you?" he asked.

"I just moved here from California," she told him.

"Lucky you found me your first month out," he said, patting her hand. "There isn't a person around who knows more about the auction business than Ned Whytson. I'd be happy to give you a hand."

She felt herself warming under his touch and quickly withdrew her hand. The reaction was so instantaneous it was startling. She wasn't normally so open to an approach, but then she didn't usually need someone as much as she did now. She'd gotten Steven under her skin, and she needed to forget him. It called for a strong antidote, but her natural caution told her Ned Whytson wasn't it. "I don't think that would work out too well," she said. "I should do my learning with Kenneth, not his competition."

"And who will you be doing your dining with?" he asked, smiling at her engagingly.

As she looked into his eyes she longed to say "with you." "I think they're serving coffee in the living room," she told him instead, quickly pushing her chair back from the table.

123

"I hope I'll be seeing you again," he said, taking her hand in his for a long, lingering moment.

"Before your wife arrives?" she asked as she darted away.

Dale joined Kenneth in the living room and found herself sitting next to Bill Donovan. He was about five foot eleven, and slender in build. His hair was thin and blond, making a transition to silver. His fingers fidgeted with the silver buckle to his western belt. His boot-clad feet tapped the floor in a constant tattoo. Dale found it annoying, but she remembered they were there to make contacts and made an effort.

"Kenneth tells me you have quite a collection of Impressionist art," she said with interest. "Is there any other period that interests you?"

"All great art interests me," he replied curtly.

"Someday if you have the time I'd like to see your collection."

"Do you like the Impressionists, too?" he inquired.

Dale nodded. "I'd have you over tomorrow afternoon, but there's a board meeting at the museum. Acquisitions are on the agenda. I don't want to miss it. Is there something you're interested in acquiring now?" she asked.

"A Gauguin," replied Donovan. "A good one. It's in a Swiss collection and it's going to be up for grabs as of next month. Unfortunately we don't have quite the endowment that the Getty has. There's always a shortage of funds for acquisitions, and there's always an argument about which ones are most important. I have to be there to protect my position," he concluded. "If I don't push it through at this meeting, Sotheby's or Christie's will be sniffing around for it. Or perhaps Fraizer's," he said with a meaningful glance in Kenneth's direction.

"That wouldn't be the one that Samuel Harmon has, would it?" asked Kenneth.

"Maybe yes, maybe no," said Donovan. "And maybe I'll be able to convince the trustees to buy it before you find out."

"Why not auction off something that's not being exhibited to get the funds?" suggested Dale.

"That's a good girl," praised Kenneth. "My protégée," he told Donovan.

"It looks like you've hired yourself a good one," agreed Donovan, rising and excusing himself for the evening.

"I'd like to get going, too," said Dale, leaning over to Kenneth's side of the couch.

"Do you mind if I put you in a cab?" he asked. "I'd like to get a chance to talk to Katinka Lambert before I go and drop a big hint about that English furniture auction."

"No problem, I'll be fine," Dale assured him, thinking for the second time that evening that Kenneth was a master at the auction game. Earlier he had taken her through Madeleine's collection from Ernst to Lichtenstein to Vasarely and had managed to maneuver her up to the Calder mobile just as Madeleine came into earshot. Casually he had told Dale that a Calder of far less quality had just sold for five times what Madeleine had paid for hers just six years earlier. Of course she could get a fortune for hers, he had finished as they walked out of the room, leaving their hostess mulling over the scene which he had so carefully orchestrated for her sake and wondering whether she would be wise to put hers up for auction while prices were good.

Dale slipped out of the apartment after a brief good-bye to her hostess. She was deep in thought as she got into the elevator, looking to the apartment door where Kenneth waved good-bye. She watched the art-deco floor indicator sink slowly toward the lobby. Fatigue was sinking into her body and brain as well.

She gasped in surprise as a hand reached out from behind her and settled lightly on her shoulder. Her initial reaction of terror relaxed as she saw the reflection of a tuxedo, as well as the blurred outline of Ned Whytson's profile, in the polished mahogany of the elevator walls.

"Those things can get so boring," he said. "If it hadn't been for you I would have left hours ago." He seemed sleekly strong. He observed her through casually half-lidded eyes, waiting for her reply. He gave the impression of a cat that was ready to pounce.

"I thought that some of the people were quite interesting," she countered.

"You wouldn't want to have a drink, would you?" he asked, moving to face her, trapping her with his body against the wall of the elevator. He scrutinized her with curiosity.

Despite herself Dale felt a slight thrill of sexual attraction race through her body. Remembering her experience with Steven and the little she knew of Whytson's background, she moved away from him. "Not tonight, thanks."

"Can I at least drop you off at your apartment?" he asked. "I have a car outside."

"That would be fine," she told him. Be careful, her mind prompted her as they passed out through the front entrance of the building and a black limousine moved quietly and automatically out of the darkness to pick them up.

Dale settled into the back seat. For the first time that evening she felt vulnerable.

"You seem nervous," he said, straightening a sapphire blue tie. "Are you?"

"Just tired."

"Relax then. Pretend I'm not even here."

They rode the rest of the way in companionable silence. Dale admitted to herself that she wanted to explore Whytson further. He was a dichotomy, one moment engaging and boyish, the next as mysterious as a dark, possibly dangerous, pool. Not tonight, she cautioned herself.

As the car stopped at her apartment building he got out and opened the door for her. "I'll see you to your door," he said and without waiting for her reply began to walk her in. She turned to him as they reached the entry, thanking him with a polite goodnight and a final, fleeting finger touch. Before she knew what was happening he had her in his arms, giving her a single long kiss. Without a word he was gone.

So much for my rules, she thought ruefully as she watched his powerful figure stride down the front entrance and up to the car, where his driver held the door open, respectfully waiting. Walking to her apartment door she couldn't help but wonder if he would call.

CHAPTER 10

Dale stretched one slim arm across the cluttered surface of the parsons table. She brought a cup of coffee, a dark roast as aromatic as the New Orleans French Quarter on a Sunday morning, to her lips. She'd discovered it in a little Italian grocery on Madison and she'd been addicted to it ever since. The rich brew fueled her on days like this. She'd been at her desk since eight, and the phone had barely given her a moment's peace in the interim. It was glued to her ear now as she sat and sipped, her free hand bringing the cup up and down with methodical regularity.

She waited impatiently, the receiver pressed to her ear. When she got an answer she communicated the message that she needed time with Kenneth right away. Barbara put her on hold for a moment, then returned to the line to tell her that he could see her. She had just started toward the door when the phone rang again. With a look of annoyance she returned to answer it. Her expression cleared when she found Katherine on the line.

"Getting excited?" she asked. "Tomorrow's the big day."

"You wouldn't believe what a madhouse it is in here. Mother's so far gone she might as well be on the moon."

Dale looked at her watch as Katherine raced on with a stream of chatter. "She has Renny coordinating the party. He's been out here every day trying to get some decisions out of her. Ceremony inside? Ceremony outside? I tell him the sculpture garden. As soon as he begins to plan she tells him to move inside because she thinks it's going to rain. She's been arguing with me for days because Steven wants to invite some of the Fraizer employees and she wants it strictly social."

"It sounds crazy but it will all settle down after the wedding," Dale assured her. "We'll have a good long lunch once you get back from your honeymoon."

"Love you," said Katherine.

"Me too. I'll see you tomorrow," replied Dale, rising from her chair.

Barbara opened Kenneth's office door carefully and let Dale in. Kenneth looked up, then continued dictating the letter he had been working on. Dale sat down in front of his desk and waited. Her imagination was captured, as always, by the room. She couldn't help but wonder how it would feel to have an office like that, one that made people respectful as soon as they walked into your domain. It didn't seem to have made Kenneth pretentious. He used it like his own home, greeting visitors and then walking out from behind his desk and joining them on one of the comfortable velvet couches in the corner. A desk is a barrier, he had told her. Use it to good effect, and know that it will put you apart from the people who are on the other side of it. There are times for that, but they're rare.

Dale studied his face as he worked. He looked more tired than usual, weighed down by the responsibilities and problems of the business. He completed his dictation and gave her his attention. "It wasn't so long ago that you came to me begging for a job," he said wryly. "Now you're interrupting me for urgent meetings. You've come a long way."

"I have some good news," said Dale, ignoring his jibe. "Bill Donovan called me this morning. He's convinced the trustees to auction off some of their current holdings to buy the Gauguin. I gave him the idea, so he's giving Fraizer's the auction. What do you think of that?" she finished proudly.

"You're my star pupil," Kenneth told her. "Between this and the paintings Miriam's brought in from Huerez, this could be the year's best art auction. What's the next step?"

"I've made an appointment for Miriam and myself to go over there this morning, but you should call him first. I think he expects us to negotiate the seller's commission. Gave me a long story on how prestigious it would be for us to handle the museum's sale, and that under the circumstances they shouldn't have to pay the usual ten percent. Should I have told him no and just stuck to the rules?" she asked nervously.

"You did the right thing," said Kenneth quickly.

"He's right. It is prestigious for us to handle that sale. Now," he said, smiling at her, "we just have to decide exactly *how* prestigious."

"He's at the museum now," Dale told him. "You could call him and straighten it out before I go over to the meeting with him."

"It's your deal," said Kenneth sternly. "You handle the preliminary negotiations. I'll go over the arrangements you make and give a final approval." He looked thoughtful for a moment. "This is the time when your training at LAMFA will stand you in good stead. You know the inner workings of a museum. You've been there. Use it to your advantage."

"Donovan will be tough," she ventured.

"You be tough, too. Fraizer's stands for quality. It's the perfect setting for their paintings. Here's what you do," he said after a pause. "Ask him what commission he expects to pay. My guess is that he'll come up with five percent. You go to eight. He'll try six, and we'll say yes."

"What if I get him to go to seven," Dale suggested, "and we pay for the catalogue photography, the shipping, and the insurance. Sometimes trustees like to see gross sales figures with just net commissions deducted and no additional expenses taken out. It looks better at their meetings if they can say they maneuvered us into picking up all the expenses."

"Sounds good. But don't push yourself into a corner you can't extricate yourself from. And be careful what he gives you for the auction," Kenneth cautioned her. "They might try to unload a lot of things that have never been hung, things that patrons have donated for tax deductions. As you know, artistic merit is not always the prime concern. Obviously," he added, "we'll sell anything they give us. But if we're going to give this the publicity push it deserves it will look better for us and for the museum if the merchandise is the best."

"Do you really want me to make those decisions?" asked Dale tentatively.

"With Miriam. She knows where to draw the line," he told her. "Better let her do it. And don't get me wrong. I'm sure there will be some very good things, too. Just select carefully."

"There is one other thing that I thought of," she suggested. "We could have the auction at night and make it black tie. We could schedule a late supper by subscription and have the proceeds go to the museum for its acquisition fund. What do you think?"

He considered for a moment. "Not necessary, but contact Deborah and Fred and get the normal arrangements for the P.R. rolling."

"I'll stop back this afternoon and let you know how it went."

Kenneth checked his calendar. Appointments and notes were scrawled in every color of ink imaginable. The handwriting was totally at odds with his own neat appearance. "Don't bother if it's after one. I've got a barber's appointment this afternoon, then I'm going home early. Ivan is coming in this afternoon for the wedding. I want to be there when he arrives."

"Ivan?"

"Didn't Katherine tell you? He's coming in from Paris."

"Katherine and I have been flying in different directions. We managed a five-minute talk this morning, but that was barely time to hear about all the hitches in the plans for the reception."

"Well," Kenneth said with understanding, "Betty Bruner has only one daughter to marry off. It's really been rushed, and between their friends and mine we just couldn't seem to keep it small."

"Who's the mysterious Ivan?" she asked, her curiosity piqued.

"He's not so mysterious, Dale," Kenneth answered.

"And I think you'll like him. Ivan Wolnovitz has been a friend for years. His father and mine had a gallery in Russia. They both fled at the start of the revolution. My father came to New York, his went to London. They always stayed in touch. I may be fifteen years older than he is, but for some reason we've always seemed to gravitate to one another. We don't see much of each other, but our backgrounds are so similar that it feels as if we're much closer than the time together would lead you to believe."

As soon as she heard Ivan's last name she remembered. For a moment she was back in Paris a good six years before. It was so clear she could almost see the rough tweed of Ivan's jacket, and the lively glint of his golden-brown eyes. "I've met Ivan," she told Kenneth. "With Katherine and Ronald. He's still living in Paris?"

"He's a curator at the Louvre now."

"Exactly where I met Katherine!" Dale reminisced. "What department is he in?"

"Wait until tomorrow and you can ask him yourself. He'll be riding out in the car with us. Hurry up," he said, looking at his watch, "or you'll be late for your appointment with Donovan and Fraizer's will be out one auction. Get going."

Dale started toward the door. Her mind was still in Paris, six summers before. Worlds of experience had been lived through since then. Nothing had turned out the way she and Katherine had planned. The only thing that hadn't changed was her long-ago curiosity about Ivan Wolnovitz.

Alone, Kenneth's mind raced as his fingers dawdled, opening and closing a gold-mounted carnelian snuffbox that had been fashioned for Louis XV. The tiny thing rested near the most treasured object on his desk, an enameled gold and silver frame from the workrooms of Fabergé. A miniature of his wife Anna was inside the three-inch masterpiece. Kenneth had insisted that her picture have a Russian frame. It seemed somehow fitting.

What would Anna have thought, he wondered, if he told her that he was forcing Steven into marriage. He meditated on it for a moment, calling back to mind the wise but somehow homey and practical way in which she had approached every problem. She would have told me never to let Katherine find out. That's what her advice would have been, he decided.

He smiled as he thought of the way she would have said it, so plain and straightforward. But his restlessness soon returned. It was good advice, but it seemed too easy, too simplistic to explain the uneasiness he felt in his chest now that Steven's wedding was approaching. There was conflict raging inside him at a time when happiness should have been filling his heart.

Kenneth reached for his phone and buzzed Barbara in the outer office. "Hold my calls for about half an hour. Don't let anyone disturb me." He crossed his arms on his chest and leaned back in his chair in the position he always assumed when he was grappling with a difficult problem. Closing his eyes, he rubbed his hands over them, trying to ease the tension that had been closing in on him since that morning. In solitude now, he looked back to Anna's portrait and began to carry on a mental dialogue with her.

He had tried so hard all those years to make a man of Steven. To make him into someone she would have been proud of. Steven had had all the advantages without having to come up through the same dirt that had stained his parents. He'd groomed him to take over the House of Fraizer one day, the way he and Anna had dreamed it would happen. He was still so young, and just too inexperienced to see that Katherine would make a good wife for him. The kind of wife that Anna had been.

Kenneth put his hands down on the desk. He realized that tears were streaking down his cheeks. He had been talking to Anna as if she were there in the room with him. Telling her why it was too soon for him to let go of their boy. And for those moments she had been with him. She was as close to him in his heart as she had ever been when she was alive. He suddenly felt an overwhelming sense of grief.

He wiped his cheeks, turning the wet rivulets into a moist, salty sheen. He felt unmanly. For all his worldly exterior his emotions were still primitive. He was rough inside, with a lack of finish that had served him well. Too much polish can make a man lose the highs and the lows of pain and joy.

It occurred to him that his grief wasn't for Anna. It had been too many years for that. It was fright, an actual physical wrenching of the gut and clenching of the brain that he was experiencing. He was afraid of being deserted. Steven was going to be moving out of the Park Avenue apartment they had shared for so many years. For the first time in his life he would be truly alone. There was room for the three of them in the apartment, even for four later on. He had toyed with the idea for a day, but then realized how dangerous, even painful it would be for him to spend time around Katherine, watching her and Steven together, in love.

It was terrifying. So much of his life had been devoted to guiding and protecting his son, it was as if some strange sort of umbilical cord connected him to Steven permanently. His life had become focused on protecting and molding the boy. Perhaps he wouldn't have centered so much of his existence around him if Anna hadn't died, he reflected. But that was useless conjecture.

Kenneth looked around his office, weighing and

measuring the value of his life. His gaze moved among the drawings that covered the walls until he found his favorite, the Fragonard that he had picked up at a small auction in Brussels. He felt a brief moment of pleasure as he recalled finding it catalogued as a print, then discovering upon closer examination that it was actually a drawing. His trained eye and his poker face had helped him to get it for a song. Usually the memory brought a smile to his face. Today it gave him a slight chill of fear as it brought back thoughts of those lean days when the profit on one small drawing could make all the difference, could determine whether he and Anna could afford to keep up the social facade necessary to make him appear substantial to potential clientele. They'd made some good friends in those years, but they'd gotten snubbed, too, by good families who found the struggle to make a living amusing. Those snubs had struck deep, reinforcing everything his father had told him, justifying the older man's bitterness at being forced out of his native country, making his mourning for the loss of his station in life real.

With all his successes, Kenneth admitted, he had never managed to overcome that beginning. He had never made that step, that all-important step, into the upper class. It was Steven who would make the transition. Steven who had been properly dressed and sent to the correct schools and taught to think and to dress and to speak like one of the "rich by right" class.

I'm afraid to let go of him, admitted Kenneth. Afraid that he won't be able to carry it through if he's on his own. He needs me to guide him. I've earned us a place, Anna, he said, looking back to the picture that gazed serenely out at him. And now I'm going to make sure that our son will claim it.

Dale's expression was uneasy as she and Miriam rode through the jammed streets that lay between

Fraizer's and the museum. As usual Miriam passed the idle minutes by strewing half the contents of her tote bag over the cab's back seat and rummaging in search of a cigarette. "Hold this," she ordered Dale, thrusting a small Polaroid camera into her lap. Packages of film and flashbulbs followed, until Dale found herself littered with the tools of Miriam's trade.

"So, you've managed to turn a dinner party into a stepping stone," said Miriam with a hint of envy in her voice. Having managed to light her cigarette without setting herself aflame with the infamous lighter, she was quickly becoming wreathed by clouds of tobacco smoke. Dale cracked the window open an inch.

"Kenneth tells me you'll be handling the negotiations," Miriam went on. "This could prove to be a very interesting morning for you." Her attitude reeked of secret knowledge that she would be willing to part with under the slightest urging.

"Why do you say that?"

"Your Mr. Donovan is disliked at the museum, to put it mildly," confided Miriam. "I don't know whether we'll be greeted by smiles or the cold shoulder. The last time I spoke to one of the other trustees your guy sounded about as popular as a tax collector at a bankers' convention."

To Miriam's delight Dale was caught off guard.

"What's his problem?" she asked.

"It seems that the first year he was elected to the board he took it upon himself to organize an aggressive acquisition program. Everyone was ecstatic—they should have been, he was donating enough of his own funds for the program to keep them happy—until they found out that he'd been guiding them to purchase works by two young artists he'd added to his own collection the year before. Every time the museum made a buy, the value of

Donovan's own collection went up. He got a deduction for the donations and his own paintings appreciated. It all came to a head when they'd increased enough to tempt him to sell. Needless to say, he's not totally trusted any more."

"Kenneth didn't say anything about that," Dale said, worry creeping into her voice.

"The other trustees will be watching this sale closely. That much I can assure you," cautioned Miriam.

The cab pulled up to the museum entrance, and as Dale paid the driver Miriam started to make a beeline toward the boardroom and executive offices. Dale had to run to catch up to her. By the time she drew abreast she was panting. She whisked a quick comb through her hair as they reached the trustees' boardroom.

Bill Donovan was waiting for them. He rose to greet them as they were ushered in. Though he was cordial, his look was detached. Resuming his seat he asked the secretary to close the door. His face became even more ill-humored when they were left alone. He cut Dale's attempt at social amenities short.

"We've had a little hitch with this sale, Miss Kenton," he said with irritation. He was plainly as upset as he expected her to be. "My fellow trustees have come up with a request that they neglected to bring up prior to our initial discussion. They've advised the museum staff that it would be premature to proceed with the arrangements until it's resolved."

Dale waited. Miriam sat to her side, looking for all the world like a cat who had just swallowed a canary. Dale felt tempted to reach over and smack the look of superiority from her face.

"The board has decided that they will need a reasonable cash advance against the expected proceeds of the sale. As they see it, since we're de-acquiring these pieces in order to lock up the Gauguin, we should be able to do so immediately. I'm afraid," he continued, looking toward Dale, "that if Fraizer's wants to keep the sale you'll have to find a means for providing interim financing to the museum prior to the auction date."

Dale was caught off guard. Both she and Kenneth had failed to foresee this possibility. Still he had made one thing clear. If she was to maintain her credibility as a representative of Fraizer's, she would have to take the responsibility of shaping the negotiations. She plunged ahead.

"We should be able to arrange something," she said, remembering that back door Kenneth had told her to leave open. "Sixty percent of the low appraisal should be doable, depending upon the total valuation of the lots."

Donovan's expression became sanguine. He was a horse trader at heart, as hooked by the thought of exercising some power over each deal as he was on the final terms that would be decided. And like a good horse trader, she realized, he might have deliberately neglected to bring it up earlier and waited to call her bluff face to face. "Of course we will be charging you interest on the funds from the date that they're advanced until the normal settlement date," she told him.

Donovan looked up with renewed interest and then scowled. It was as if he had heard a call to battle. "I'm not sure that will be acceptable to the trustees."

"I don't know how much I can compromise on that position, Mr. Donovan," Dale told him regretfully. "It's really not my money, you know. It's Kenneth Fraizer's."

"Naturally I don't expect you to obligate him to something that he wouldn't approve of."

"But I do think we might find a little leeway," Dale said thoughtfully. "We'll cut off the interest on the date of the sale instead of on the settlement date. That should save you about a month of carrying charges."

Donovan shuffled through his papers. He looked like a man considering an irreversible decision. Dale held her breath and wondered what her next move would be if he said no. He looked up at her expressionlessly, then slowly began to smile. "How about letting us have the money at cost?" he asked.

Dale drew out the moment, then cautiously said, "I think, Mr. Donovan, that I can guarantee we won't mark up our cost of money to you."

She sat quietly, waiting for him to answer. She had learned from watching Goldman that whoever broke the silence at this point would be in a weakened position. She stared at Donovan, her eyes fixed on his, and said nothing. At long last he extended a hand.

"OK. You've got a deal."

The balance of the negotiations went easily. They settled on the seven-percent commission structure, though Donovan insisted that all the photographs be published in color. When they finished, the icy blue of his eyes had been broken by a twinkle, the result of the satisfaction he derived from driving an acceptable bargain. After he and Dale agreed on a date for signing contracts formalizing the agreement, Miriam asked if she might be shown some of the items which were being considered for the sale. Without hesitation Donovan accompanied them to the museum's storage rooms.

Over a hundred paintings had been stacked in bins to await appraisal and cataloguing. It was immediately obvious to Dale that the museum personnel had never heard of any possibility of the sale's being called off. Each curator had made selections and submitted them as instructed. Donovan had invented a crisis and used it to advantage. He had managed to secure funds for an immediate bid on the Gauguin, and he would be doing it using Fraizer's credit line instead of his own. Though it had been accomplished at her expense, Dale couldn't help but admire his initiative.

"I think we've been had," noted Dale as she surveyed the room that she and Miriam had been left in.

"I considered jumping in and stopping you before you'd committed yourself," Miriam said. "But then I remembered that Kenneth said you were doing the negotiating."

Dale looked at Miriam closely, studying her expression. She realized that Miriam had set her up. She didn't understand why and it made her angry. "You could have helped me out," she pointed out.

"You never asked my opinion," Miriam told her matter of factly. "Besides, honey," she said, quickly giving Dale a pat on the arm, "he got Kenneth down to half a point below Fraizer's cost of funds when he pulled that one on him."

Dale turned away. "Where do we start?"

"At the beginning, honey, at the beginning." Miriam carefully drew out the first of the paintings. An easel had been placed there for them. She balanced the painting on its bottom ledge, adjusted the light and stepped back. Dale focused the Polaroid, produced an impressive flash, then pulled out the film and began slowly waving it through the air in an attempt to speed its drying. As they waited they took their first good look at the canvas. It was a portrait by the English master Sir Peter Lely.

Dale found herself luxuriating in the magical quality of Lely's skin tones. Miriam's voice brought her back to the purpose of their visit. "Do you remember the Lely portrait of Lord Arthur Capel and his wife that was in the National Portrait Gallery in London?"

"The one from Paul Mellon's collection?"

"That's the one. It's not much better than this. With that in mind, what do you think this will bring?"

"I couldn't begin to guess."

"My educated guess is around fifty thousand," Miriam said.

"How can you be so sure?" asked Dale.

"No one is ever sure," Miriam replied. "But the National Gallery's Lely was noted in last year's Sotheby's review at about forty-three thousand. You need to pay attention to things other than just contemporary art," she said. "Luckily I can't afford the luxury of specializing, so I saw it."

Miriam removed the Lely from the easel. Dale was still smarting from the jabs as she reached for the next painting. It was pleasant enough, thought Dale as Miriam reached quickly up to discard it.

"Why so fast?"

"It's O.K. Nothing really the matter with it," said Miriam. "But people are going to be expecting the big names at this sale. South African works like this De Jongh require a certain kind of collector. I don't think they'll be in the audience that night. But this is your baby. If you want it . . ."

"No thanks," said Dale, dismissing it with finality. "I've made enough decisions for one day. The next few are yours."

"Wise move, my girl," said Miriam as she quickly put it back into its place and moved on to the next canvas. Within the hour they had come upon a small Winslow Homer that would surely be one of the featured pieces of the sale. Even Miriam couldn't understand why they had decided to part with a lovely George Luks canvas that turned up later. But along the way Miriam discarded dozens of canvases without a backward glance. By the time they had finished, over fifty pieces had been culled from the original offering.

"Tell them you're saving some for a second auction," Miriam suggested as she looked at the size of their reject list. "You can make this an annual sale for the acquisition committee."

"Something tells me they're planning to buy more than one Gauguin," said Dale. "Too bad they're being so quiet about what it is." She stretched her hands over her head to loosen the muscles that had tightened during a morning of bending and stooping.

"You go on," said Miriam. "I'll be finished here within the hour."

"I think a walk would do me some good," replied Dale gratefully as she headed for the door.

The brisk air that greeted her outside the museum was refreshing. She looked at her watch. It was already twelve o'clock. Too late to pin Kenneth down for a talk, and it would be at least an hour before Miriam would be back at the office and ready to discuss arrangements for the museum sale. She made her decision. It was what she had wanted to do all along, she admitted to herself. She turned toward the corner of Fifth Avenue. Waiting for the light to change she tried to talk herself out of it. Still, she might be able to pick up some scrap of information that would be useful to Kenneth. When the light changed she started across the street in the direction of Whytson's.

If Dale had been asked to describe a building that was the polar opposite of Fraizer's, she would have described the one that housed Whytson's. Its three-story facade faced onto a middle-class residential street in a part of Manhattan that could be called trendy more easily than chic. The building itself was poured concrete, stained a rusty brown and scored with vertical grooves that looked as if giant fingernails had scratched it from sidewalk to roof to relieve what otherwise would have been flat and boxy architecture.

It was the street level that most fascinated her. While Fraizer's presented a facade of dignified stone, polished brass, and uniformed guards to the passerby, Whytson's ground floor was solid window. Pianos, paintings, and rugs could be seen, as well as the reassuring sight of people milling about in lively conversation among the inanimate objects within. The place had a feel of life to it. It invited the casual passerby to stop, take a look, and to enter. Dale walked up to the window and scanned the lots that were on display. She could see that Whytson had made a play for a broad group of clientele, lower in income and less fastidious than the average Fraizer customer. Clever, she thought. He'll build a name where we won't compete with him, then he'll go after our customers once he has a solid base. Beneath his glib exterior there had to be a solid business brain. Despite herself she felt a new respect for him. She was still running his unorthodox strategy over in her mind as she went through Whytson's revolving glass doors.

Dale examined the foyer with interest. She believed the theory that a business was a mirror of the man who ran it, as much a barometer of his taste as a woman's shoes and jewelry are of her.

She glanced at the offerings on the foyer counter. Next to the catalogue for the current exhibition, a sale of Russian works of art, was a variety of booklets intended to explain the auction process to the novice. Books on bidding and on evaluating what was offered. Leaflets on the terms and conditions of an auction sale. All were set in large type and profusely illustrated. As she slipped some samples into her purse she admitted that they would go a long way toward making a beginner feel at home.

She walked into the exhibition rooms. They were as sleek and modern as the building's exterior. She paused before a glass case that held several gilded and enameled Russian eggs. An upholstered bench had been positioned against the wall opposite it. She found an empty spot and sat down. She stared at the eggs that were displayed in front of her. Track lighting had been positioned to bring out the depth of their detailing and the richness of the reds, greens, and blues that had been baked onto their glossy painted shells, but her attention was focused elsewhere.

I wonder why he didn't call, she thought. It had been several days since Whytson had left her with that single, impassioned kiss. By the end of the first one she had admitted to herself that her ego was bruised. When she had gotten up hours ago she had told herself that she didn't want to think about it and had conveniently pushed it to the back of her mind. But here she was, sitting in his auction house. Obviously it was still bothering her. Even more, she confessed, since she had seen the skill with which Whytson was building his operation.

"What do you think?" A male voice whispered in her ear, a voice with the rusty shadings that years of good whiskey and good living etch into the vocal cords. She started in surprise.

Ned Whytson was sitting beside her. He ran one wide, well-manicured hand through his sandy hair. He looked casual and secure and no more surprised at discovering her in his viewing rooms than he would have been at finding a stray penny in his pocket. He had that sense of adventure about him that she remembered and an expression that led her to imagine he could be gentle at times but then rough and coarse at others. It was a quality she found she wanted to explore further, as she told herself that she was there for Kenneth.

"This is a wonderful grouping of enamels," she stammered after a pause. "I've always loved them. I couldn't resist coming over here to take a look at what you'd gotten in."

He watched her with blasé self-assurance as she groped for words. Then he slowly began to grin, and, putting one hand to her shoulder to keep her from drawing away, he leaned over and once again began to whisper in her ear. "You needn't be so embarrassed," he confided. "I was doing the same thing at Fraizer's two days ago."

"You were?" asked Dale incredulously. To her relief his heavy English accent made the act of spying sound perfectly acceptable. "Only a fool would neglect to keep an eye on the competition," he assured her. "I went in at lunch. The proprietor's more likely to be away then, you know," he said, looking up at the overhead clock that now read twelve forty-five. "If I hadn't installed a private dining room on the premises, you would have gotten away with it, too."

Dale started to smile. "You know," she told him, "I almost believe you."

"You should," he said. "I came to New York with the avowed purpose of stealing away as much of Fraizer's business as I could get. Any advantage I can see, I'll take. My dropping in to keep an eye on you is the least of Kenneth Fraizer's worries."

His statements were made in a light tone. But from the straightforward way he looked at her Dale knew he was telling the absolute truth. He had come to New York to win, and if breaking Fraizer's along the way was necessary he would do it without flinching. Still, there was a certain forthright honesty about him that made him say it to her face.

"I think I'd better go right back to Fraizer's and count the paintings," she told him in an equally lighthearted tone. He had captured her imagination. He acted like a man who expected to exert his will over spirited horses and headstrong women. A country-bred man, with a strong body and a flirtatious style. Better yet, he looked safe to her. He was already tied down by marriage vows, and that was just fine. She didn't want any commitments that would eventually be broken, no promises of happy tomorrows and plans for the future that couldn't be trusted. Enjoying the present was quite enough for her. There was only one person she could count on not to disappoint her—herself. She had learned that years ago and slowly built the barricades that now protected her, walls that had now grown thick. Kept in proper bounds Ned Whytson might be perfect. He was both safe and exciting, and therefore intriguing . . . for today.

"I can save you some time," he said, bringing her back. "I didn't take a thing. Look," he said, pulling out the lining of his pants pockets to show her that he was totally clean.

"Very reassuring," she told him.

"Come upstairs and I'll buy you some lunch," he invited. Dale looked doubtful. "No excuses," he insisted. "After all, I just saved you half an hour of counting. I know you have the time." Dale followed him upstairs.

Whytson's private dining room was set to the rear of the building on the third floor. From his vantage point you could enjoy a view of the East River or of a city block. The walls were of cast concrete like the outside of the building, and the room was saved from being gloomy by a tightly woven carpet of natural straw-colored sisal. The small dining table, suited for no more than eight, was of dark green glass with a rugged black stone base. A burst of fresh lilac had been placed at its center, blooming forth from a fishbowl of plain blown glass. The walls were hung with modern paintings and prints of obvious quality.

"My rotating collection," said Whytson as he pulled her chair out for her. "Enjoy them while you may. They'll be gone as soon as we have our next art sale." As he took his seat a uniformed waiter appeared bearing wine and fresh seafood salads.

"He seems to be prepared for two," commented Dale, wondering how often Whytson appeared for lunch with an unexpected female companion.

"Closed-circuit television. It covers the entire building. I flip through the circuit periodically. I spotted you as soon as you entered the foyer. What kept you away from your desk all morning?" he inquired. "Stealing some fabulous collection out of my clutches?"

She started to describe her morning to him, then caught herself mid-sentence as she remembered who she was talking to. "It's not a good idea for us to pick each other's brains," she told him. "No business. O.K.?"

"No problem for me," he told her, passing a basket of French rolls and sweet butter. "But you're probably losing the best teacher you could have found for the auction business."

He's so damn sure of himself, Dale thought as she took one of the crusty brown rolls. Then she imagined how reassuring that could be. Not reassuring enough for his wife, she thought, remembering what she had heard of their arrangement. It was one of the things that intrigued her. She could relate to Ned Whytson without worrying about strings being attached. He wouldn't want anything more than some uninvolved fun. And once he got the New York auction house running smoothly he'd be off to London again.

"Luckily Kenneth Fraizer's already supplied me with a good teacher," she told him. "Miriam Fisher."

"Never heard of her," said Whytson, picking a shrimp up with a swoop of his fork. His manner implied that if he didn't know Miriam she couldn't be any good.

"She just keeps a low profile," she told him, then

went on to relate the full scope of Miriam's abilities. The more she talked, the more she enjoyed it. He seemed attentive, even prolonging the description by asking rather pointed questions about Miriam's abilities and background. By the time she had finished she'd painted the picture of a paragon.

"So, I'm not the one in a million," he admitted with a boyish smile. "But I can still teach you a thing or two about New York restaurants. How about dinner tomorrow?"

Lunch had passed quickly and the conversation that had begun with such problems had become easy. Still, she felt a nagging fear of betraying Fraizer's. She had gone there to scout the competition, and she probably should have left it at that. But thinking back to the longing Steven had produced in her she knew she needed a distraction right now, someone who could be tender to her, who could give her gentle strokes and relieve some of the terrible loneliness that she'd felt since she'd arrived in New York. She made herself shrug off the fear, the feeling she was making a mistake.

"Business is off limits?" she asked him.

"I promise."

"Perfect," came her reply.

CHAPTER 11

Sophie Ableman was purring like a kitten. The faint bluish glow of a television screen on the other side of the room silhouetted her head. Her hair was in moist, streaked strands that clung together and fell in a disheveled tumble over her face. Her expression was a study in sensual gratification. She gave out a little moan as educated hands played with her feet and then worked their way up to her heavy, dimpled thighs.

"Mrs. Ableman." The voice of her masseuse timidly interrupted the fantasies she usually fell prey to at about this point in every hour session. "Your maid wants to speak to you."

Sophie Ableman looked up to see Terry's face hanging over the massage table where she was spread. Her slitlike Oriental eyes betrayed neither approval nor disapproval of her employer's sprawled and sheeted body. The low tones of the "Today Show" droned behind her. Sophie turned it on every morning to hear the news of airplane accidents, bombings, and economic disasters that had occurred in the hours since she went to sleep. It always made her feel so grateful for the way her own life had turned out.

"The caterers will be here at four," Terry summarized. "The flowers are arriving at five. The man Mr. Ableman sent around is here waiting for you."

"Thank you, Terry," Sophie replied. She'd been so caught up in thoughts of the evening to come, a black-tie dinner that she had carefully orchestrated so that she could wear the Mayapur Diamonds, that she had completely forgotten about the guard. "Tell him I'll be about an hour."

Terry padded out of the white-on-white bedroom to convey her employer's message.

Within the hour Sophie had summoned the guard from the kitchen. He accompanied her down in the elevator and into the chauffeured car that was always at her disposal. What good would it do to have the diamonds if they just stayed in a vault at the bank, she asked herself as the driver cut across Fifth heading for the Chase Manhattan branch at

410 Park. Tonight everyone would be able to see what Joseph had bought for her—her latest trophy on display. He really did think of everything, she preened, looking at the guard out of the corner of her eye and trying to determine whether he was carrying a pistol under his jacket. But he was right, of course. Only an idiot would run around Manhattan alone with five million in diamonds in her purse.

Sophie always felt a special pride when she entered the bank where her account was handled. The Ablemans had come a long way, she reflected.

Well, she thought as she went into the vaults and gave the girl who had come in to meet her the key to her safe deposit box, Joseph was certainly a special customer. Twenty million in deposits alone. Not to mention the kind of money his department stores borrowed.

Her heart took an extra little lurch of pleasure when she removed the black box from the drawer. She just opened it for a minute to refresh her memory of the size of those diamonds. She closed it quickly and replaced the safety box in the vault without as much as a peek at the rest of her collection. Her private guard had a ready hand at his coat front as they left the bank and began their drive to Smythson's on Fifth Avenue.

At Smythson's the pair were greeted by a slender-looking woman who was seated behind a Regency desk. She alerted Richard Smythson, and Sophie took a seat in one of the small private viewing rooms to the rear of the main salon. Within moments Richard Smythson was there, a man in his early fifties whose graying hair was thinning a little, but whose warm smile and gracious manner were strong enough to endear him to both husbands and wives.

"You have them out of the safety box?" he inquired.

"For the first time. Joseph even sent a guard," she said. "I'm so excited about wearing them."

"Well, we'll get them cleaned for you right away. Can't have them looking shabby on their first trip out," he said, taking the well-worn black box from her hands. "It's a magnificent set," he admitted as he looked at it. "There's certainly not another one like it in the world. You're a lucky woman, Mrs. Ableman."

Sophie acknowledged the wisdom of his statement with a nod.

"I'll take them upstairs to be cleaned now. Do you want the guard to come with me?"

Sophie hadn't thought of that, but it made her seem important. "My husband would insist," she told him. "You know how cautious he is."

"And right he is," said Smythson as he excused himself. "We'll only be a few minutes."

As the two men left the salon Sophie rose from her chair and began browsing through Smythson's showcases. Once she'd satisfied herself that they didn't have anything to compare to her own diamonds, her thoughts flitted back to the party.

She imagined the expression that would be on Doris Buttle's face when she got one look at those diamonds. Despite herself Sophie had begun to smile as Richard Smythson came back into the room. He walked toward her hastily. The expression on his face was grim. "Could you come upstairs with me, Mrs. Ableman?" he requested politely. "There's a problem we need to discuss."

Sophie began quizzing him without cease on the way up, but he just replied in hushed tones that it was best discussed in private. "I've already contacted Mr. Ableman," he added. "He'll be here any minute."

Richard Smythson seated Sophie in a chair in front of the desk in his private office. Her jewel box was on its surface, flanked by a small black machine with a dial and a metal-tipped probe.

"Any time that jewelry is brought to us for cleaning or repairs," he told her, speaking in a voice that was even more quiet than his normal soft-spoken manner and gesturing to a weathered man who was seated in one corner of the office, "Dennis takes a loupe to it. When he looked at your ring he couldn't quite believe what he was seeing, so he tested it with the diamond probe." Smythson indicated the black box that was sitting on his desk.

"The light dispersion wasn't right," Dennis told her. "It looked like the sort of spectrum you'd get with a synthetic. I have made mistakes before," he quickly admitted. "But not this time, unfortunately."

"So we used the diamond probe," Smythson continued, keeping his voice deliberately calm as he addressed himself to Sophie, whose expression was one of pure confusion. "It distinguishes diamonds from diamond substitutes in a matter of seconds." Holding up the jewel box he gave a bewildered shrug. "I'm sorry to have to tell you this." He paused, then told her the rest. "They're not real, Mrs. Ableman. They're cubic Z."

"You told me in Kenneth Fraizer's office the day before the auction that these diamonds were all at least D flawless," she insisted. Her voice had risen to an hysterical pitch.

"They were," said Richard. "They've been switched. It's just the larger stones. They didn't bother with the smaller ones, but all the major diamonds in the necklace and the large stone of the ring have been tampered with. You can see the tool marks on the prongs that are holding the stones in," he said, offering her the necklace with a loupe. "The substitutes have been cut well enough to fit in the same setting where the originals were sitting, but the grooves where the prongs bend over the top of the stones look like they've been opened and reclosed. I'm sorry, Mrs. Ableman," he said definitely. "But this isn't the necklace we examined in Mr. Fraizer's office."

Joseph Ableman arrived at Smythson's within minutes. His response was more to the point than his wife's had been. Dialing Fraizer's number he managed to get Barbara on the line.

"I don't give a shit if his son is getting married," he roared. "You find Kenneth Fraizer and you tell him to call me. Someone can damn well find the man." Then sitting down on the chaise in Smythson's office and putting his arms around her, he began to comfort his wife.

CHAPTER 12

Dale spent the early part of Saturday morning in bed. She'd opened the drapes, letting the crisp clear light of the best part of the day flood into her room. The wide bed was strewn with papers, brochures, and booklets. She'd brought home a full week's accumulation of marketing materials and advertisements from other auction houses. A five-day collection of the *Wall Street Journal* was cracked open too, underlined in strategic places with transparent yellow marker. I'm looking more like Miriam every day, she chided herself as she put her street-stained bag into the bedroom closet and temporarily out of sight.

She took a long shower, then carefully put on makeup and a suit of teal-blue silk. Katherine kept wandering into her thoughts as she dressed. She hoped she was doing the right thing. For a moment she thought of Steven, but to her relief Whytson's face intervened.

Racing around the apartment she tracked down stray earrings and a blue bag, and within five minutes she was walking out of the building's front door.

She looked up and down the block, sure she would spot Kenneth, then she realized Ivan was standing next to the limousine at the curb. He looked much the same as he had in Paris; the years hadn't stuck to him, hadn't changed either his face or his figure. When he saw her approaching he greeted her with a smile. "You're not going to run away this time?" he asked lightly. She nodded no, grateful that he'd gotten it out of the way so quickly and gracefully. "We'd given up on you," he said. "Kenneth just sent me to come and get you. He's a bit nervous today, as you might imagine." He leaned down and gave her cheek a light peck and a strong male scent of cologne followed.

"Let's not keep him waiting," she said, starting for the car.

"Ivan's reintroduced himself?" asked Kenneth, sliding over to make room for the three of them on the limousine's roomy back seat.

"He certainly has," she said, sitting up straight and pushing a few wisps of hair away from her face. The three of them quickly fell into an animated conversation that continued unabated as the outskirts of Manhattan slipped by their windows and the car passed into the relatively rural environs of the North Shore of Long Island.

She stayed silent as Kenneth and Ivan played an artwork trivia game that left her amazed with the extent of their knowledge. One of them named an artist, the next one gave the date of his birth, the next the names of his father and mother and the town where he was born. It went on in ever smaller circles as they alternated in supplying the name of the street where his studio had stood, a list of his pupils, his favorite restaurant, the name of his dog, the color of the hat of the woman in one of his most obscure paintings, what he had ordered for dinner on the night of his death, and his mistresses' married and maiden names. It was obvious that they relished testing one another; they couldn't have enjoyed themselves more if they'd been given a round-the-world cruise for two.

Dale joined in as they exhausted their knowledge of a German expressionist, Helmut Schmidt. "Did you see that one of his paintings sold for $850,000 in London last week? That's a new high for him, isn't it?"

Kenneth looked at her approvingly. "Been reading *Art News*? Good girl." Of course she had been reading. He knew she would. And as usual, he thought, Dale had absorbed it all and was asking for more. Since she'd arrived at Fraizer's he had been schooling her. He had taken her to parties where eager hostesses had dragged out the family silver or asked guests to get up from the Louis Quatorze dinner chairs so that Kenneth could give an estimate of their worth on the spot. He had taught her to look for potential, but hidden, damage in valuable works of art. At every step she had repaid him with her total attention. He wasn't normally a vain man, but he couldn't help but feel flattered. He had to admit she was giving him a good deal of pleasure.

"That's a big jump in value for Schmidt," said Ivan.

Dale looked thoughtful. "The German expressionists have gotten a lot of press lately. Maybe someone thought he'd get in while the commodity was hot and unload it at a profit as it moved up."

"Too simple," said Ivan. "When you're dealing with six-figure art you've got to look below the surface. There's usually a hidden agenda. It might be ego. It might be a rivalry between dealers or collectors. And it might, as in the case of this particular painting, be a simple attempt to bump up the prices for the artist."

"Fill in the blanks," said Dale.

"It's not so very complicated. I think that Max Albers has been busy," said Ivan. "Schmidt's widow decided to sell the bulk of the paintings that he'd held for himself while he was alive. Max and his gallery got them. Of course when you're sitting with thirty or forty works by the same artist, you can't help but devote some thoughts to getting his prices up. Max took the quick way. He placed a few of Schmidt's paintings in some very visible auctions and made sure that they went for new record prices. Auctions are always more public than individual sales. So he was sure the word would get out."

"Wasn't that a gamble?" asked Dale. "The world could just as easily have seen them sold for record lows."

"You're not that naive," Ivan suggested. "Albers planted a shill in the audience. First the shill made the genuine bidders think they had a fight on their hands. Everyone loves to win, you know—that's why it's so important to do your homework before you go to an auction. To know the comparative prices and to set a limit on your bid before you get auction fever. Then the shill jumps in to make the buy if the bidding doesn't take the price high enough. Albers had everything to gain, and only the price of a commission to the auction house to lose."

"Isn't that unethical?" asked Dale, looking to Kenneth.

"Strictly against the rules," he told her. "But it's as hard for an auction house to prevent a dealer from buying in his own paintings as it is to stop them from ringing."

"Ringing?" she asked.

"When a group of dealers band together at an auction sale and agree ahead of time which of them, and it will only be one, will bid on each important painting—that's ringing. If it's a sophisticated group they'll have a contact at the auction house that will let them know what the reserve on each painting is so that they can meet it without taking the bidding any higher. That way they're never bidding against each other. Since there are so few private buyers who play in the high price range, it's a great way for them to keep the prices down. And it's almost impossible for an auction house to detect ahead of time."

"Not that there was much effort in this case," said Ivan, his face a study in disgust. "The Schmidt sold at Whytson's London branch. And as we both know, our friend Ned has never taken great pains to be an ethical policeman within his own house."

"Isn't it a little risky to make accusations like that when you don't know the facts?" she demanded. To her surprise she found herself defending a man she barely knew.

"I don't need to know the facts. I know Whytson," said Ivan, lapsing into silence.

"By the way," she said, deliberately shifting her attention to Kenneth. "I had lunch with Whytson yesterday."

Kenneth looked startled, but his expression quickly changed. "That's right," he said to her. "I did tell you to try to pick his brain. But you be sure to edit your conversations with him so he doesn't get any information about our operation." He paused for a moment. "Find out anything interesting yesterday?"

"Nothing more than what can be seen on the surface by spending an hour in his offices. But I did come away with the impression that he's determined to succeed in New York. No matter what it takes."

"Keep after him, Dale," Kenneth encouraged her. "I imagine you'll be able to find out more in a few hours than I could in weeks."

Ivan looked from Kenneth to Dale, disapproval clear on his face. He leaned back in his seat and began to study the landscape outside. The three of them drove on without conversation for several minutes.

"How's Celeste?" Kenneth finally asked, breaking the silence.

Ivan paused, then answered. "We're still involved. Wonderfully involved, I must say. I just wish I could persuade her to move out of London and come to Paris with me. I feel like we're on planes more than we're on the ground."

"She'll come around," Kenneth reassured him.

"I hope so. I love everything about her except her damned refusal to move to Paris. I really crave spending more time with her, maybe even making this relationship permanent.

"Speaking of changing residences, where are Steven and Katherine going to live after the wedding?" Ivan asked. "It must have been hard for them to find an apartment on such short notice."

"They're going to be living with me," Kenneth answered. "At least until after the baby is born." Dale noticed he grew pale as he said this. She attributed it to nerves. It was only natural for a father to be nervous on the morning of his only son's wedding.

"Are you sure that's going to work out?" Ivan asked. "Starting a marriage is difficult enough as it is. Especially with a baby on the way. But with one more in the equation? Well, you know what happened when my father told me not to move out of his house," he laughed. "I went to Paris and put the

English Channel between us within the week. It wouldn't work for me, Kenneth. But then Steven's not me."

"Actually, he suggested it," Kenneth told him. "And in some ways he's right. The apartment is so large I'd just be rattling around in there by myself. And it will make it easier on them not to have to worry about starting somewhere from scratch while Katherine's pregnant." He sounded as if he were trying to convince himself. Kenneth added softly, "I must admit Steven and I argued about it quite a bit before I agreed." He stared straight ahead, and then methodically straightened his tie as they approached the high wrought-iron gates that marked the boundary of the Bruner estate.

Acres of green hillocks rolled out before them like mounded velvet gathered up by nature into softly sculpted handfuls. Above them a circular driveway crowned the entrance. To its side catering trucks had crowded into the space that led into the garage area. Frenzied waiters and cooks carried trays and ice buckets and dishes through the side entrance as the first flurry of limousines, carrying family and close friends, pulled up to the front door.

Dale was impressed, as always, by the size of the house. Still, she wasn't awed. She had grown up around money in Hollywood, a town where Mercedes were more common than houseflies. She had rubbed shetland shoulders with cashmere-clad schoolmates and come home unscathed by jealousy. She had shared their tennis courts, swimming pools, and sports cars. Movies were made to be seen in their private screening rooms. Like a bank teller she had grown accustomed to the touch, the feel, the very odor of money, as well as to the knowledge that its benefits would only rub off on her for a matter of hours or, at most, days.

They entered a foyer already jostling with the

family and friends. The Bruner dining room was almost unrecognizable under the flowers and candles and heaps of food that were being assembled. The long tables that lined the walls were covered with woven willow baskets filled with crudités and fruit. Cheeses stood on graduated Lucite platforms, flanked by ice-filled bowls cradling crystal containers of caviar. Platters of pâtés and pasta salads lined the front of the tables. Fresh oysters and crab legs and lobster had been arranged on icy mounds. Warming plates were being readied. And to one side of the room the cake, a six-layer construction of raspberries and marzipan and lacy white frosting, waited for its moment of glory. To one side white-coated waiters poured champagne.

Within minutes Dale learned firsthand how colorful the Bruner gatherings could be. They were a huge and noisy clan with a marvelous variety of friends. Ronald Bruner appeared to be an island of calm in the roiling crowd. He grasped Dale's hand with affection, then putting one finger to his lips for silence he motioned for her to follow him out of the room and into his study. He breathed a sigh of relief as he carefully closed the doors behind them. "I'm glad I was able to sneak you away," he told her.

"Sit down." Ronald motioned to a comfortable linen-covered chair. "I wanted to show you what I'm giving Katherine today," he said, reaching to the desk where his correspondence was normally scattered. As he walked back to Dale his hands held a small bronze sculpture.

She recognized it immediately as an Archipenko, probably from about 1916. It was a fine example of his work, a loving study of a woman combing her hair. "It's beautiful," she said. "I know she'll love it."

"That sculpture means a lot to the Bruners," said Ronald. "It's the thing that brought us together with Kenneth Fraizer, and with Steven, in the first place.

If it weren't for that sculpture, Katherine might never have met Steven."

"How did it happen?" asked Dale.

"It was one night in May," answered Ronald, "at least twenty years ago. I went to an auction at Fraizer's, took one look at that Archipenko and fell in love with it." As he held it in his hands, its warm bronze patina glowing, Dale could understand why.

"The bidding was tight. But I got it," Ronald said with a satisfied smile that betrayed his determination to possess the things that he considered beautiful. "After the auction I went back to speak to Kenneth Fraizer. That Archipenko is just one of a series that were cast in different sizes; I thought he might have a handle on where the rest of them were.

"He was on his way out the door but he invited me to come back to his apartment and finish the conversation. It wasn't too long after Anna had died, you see, and he had to get home to be with Steven. I took one look at the two of them alone together in that hulk of an apartment and decided to adopt them into our family. It's gone on that way for years. And this," he said, reaching for the sculpture that rested in Dale's hands, "was the catalyst that started the whole thing."

"It's a wonderful gift," said Dale. "I can see how much it will mean to Katherine to have it."

"It will remind her of all the years that she and Steven spent growing up together," nodded Ronald.

They sat silently for a moment, both caught up in their own thoughts of the wedding that would take place that afternoon. It was Ronald who spoke first.

"I want to ask you a favor, Dale," he said. His eyes were intense. "This marriage isn't getting off to the easiest start. It will need all the help it can get. I know that when you told Katherine about your conversation with Steven you did it to help her. But I beg you now not to say anything ever again that will remind her of it. You wouldn't be doing her a favor. It would only cause problems."

"Don't be ridiculous," said Dale, reaching up to take Ronald's hand. "I would never do anything like that."

The study door opened a crack, and then further once Betty Bruner confirmed that she had found them. She looked directly at her husband and said, "We have guests waiting for you. I think you should be there to greet them." Then she turned on her heel without speaking a word to Dale.

"Come on," Ronald said, helping Dale to rise.

Kenneth knocked tentatively on Katherine's bedroom door. When he didn't get an answer he pushed the door open a crack, then stepped into the room. He saw Katherine standing before the full-length mirror at the entrance to her dressing room. She was looking directly at her own image, but her expression was so far removed it seemed as if she wasn't even aware of the cloud of white tulle and fresh gardenias that was reflected back. "What are you thinking?" Kenneth asked in a hushed voice. She glanced up at the sound of his voice, as alarmed as a sleepwalker awakening in strange terrain. "How long have you been there?" she asked.

"I just walked in. I hope I didn't startle you."

"Don't worry, Kenneth," said Katherine, attempting a smile that emerged somewhat feebly. "You know how glad I am to see you."

"I brought you something," he said, sitting on the edge of Katherine's bed. He withdrew a small black leather case from his jacket pocket and held out its contents to Katherine. "Something borrowed," he smiled, extending a choker of cultured pearls to his future daughter-in-law. "They were Anna's."

Katherine beamed. Kenneth rose and stood behind her. Carefully she slipped the catch of the pearls closed, fastening them over the high Victorian neckline of the wedding dress. They stood together in front of the mirror observing the effect. He couldn't help but marvel at the loveliness of the picture Katherine presented. Her dress demurely covered her arms, shoulders, and neck with delicate layerings of white lace. The waist nipped in with a V that dropped from her hip line to slightly below her waist. A skirt formed of layers of frothy white tulle burst forth below, stopping just under Katherine's knee in the front, then dropping gracefully to a floor-length train that followed her as she walked. Her legs were covered in lacy white hose that blended into simple white satin slippers with tiny heels.

"You're just beautiful," he said. "As if you didn't know that already."

Katherine surveyed her image. "It doesn't show, does it?" she asked, running her hands over her stomach. Her voice trailed off as she waited for his reply.

It came in the form of a large hug. Releasing her, Kenneth grasped her by the shoulders and turned her back toward the mirror. "No," he replied. "It doesn't show. Look at yourself. You're beautiful."

Katherine greeted his statement with emotion. She felt such tenderness for this man. Her eyes began to fill with tears. The message was clear. She was frightened.

Kenneth held her by the shoulders. "Katherine," he assured her, "you're going to make a wonderful wife, a wonderful mother. There isn't a doubt in my mind. Remember how much we all love you. I'll be there for you, no matter what."

"I'm just not sure I'm ready," she said, her voice quavering as she looked up.

"But it will be wonderful to have a baby," said

Kenneth, a note of longing slipping into his own voice.

"I don't even feel grown up," Katherine told him. "Someone has always paid my rent. Now it will be you. I've never had to worry about where I'm going to live, because I've never had any choice. Someone else has always paid my bills. All I've ever carried is one cute little phrase—charge it to my father. Now I'm going to be responsible for so many decisions. Not just for me, but for Steven and for a baby. I'll be in charge of two other lives. I don't know how to do it," she said. Her voice began to crack and tears welled up in her eyes.

Kenneth pulled her close to him and held her until her trembling began to subside. Grasping her by the shoulders he looked into her frightened face. "It's going to work," he said in a comforting voice. "Of course it will. You just have the pre-wedding jitters. It happens to every bride. But if it's any comfort to you," he smiled, wiping a tear from Katherine's cheek, "I'm told that the groom is usually shaking at twice the rate. If Steven's late walking down the aisle," he joked, "it's probably because his hands were trembling too hard for him to tie his shoelaces."

For the first time Katherine's familiar grin washed over her face. "Maybe you could do it for him," she kidded. Instead of answering, Kenneth kissed her quickly on the cheek and turned to go.

The wedding ceremony was as beautiful as an Impressionist still life. Katherine had willed good weather, and nature had decided to cooperate. Rows of white chairs had been arranged in the garden. The Bruner sculpture collection could be seen silhouetted to either side, adding a bulky dignity to the arrangements of white roses and Phalaenopsis orchids that wove their way up the poles of the simple white arch under which Katherine and Steven were to say their vows.

Dale could feel the sun warm her head as she walked down the steps of the veranda toward the aisle that had been left between the groupings of chairs.

She stood watching with the rest of the crowd as Kenneth and Steven walked down the aisle. As Ronald Bruner came down the aisle with Katherine on his arm all faces turned to look at the bride.

Dale breathed a sigh of relief. Katherine walked confidently. Her head was held high. That strong, dimpled chin of hers thrust forward. Her eyes looked unwaveringly ahead. Her arm rested lightly on her father's. She moved as regally as a princess. Her eyes revealed a hint of doubt as her father stooped to her cheek for a tender good-bye kiss. But she quickly recovered her composure and moved calmly to Steven's side.

Dale was soon caught up in the solemnity of the wedding. It was over before she knew it. Or perhaps it just seemed that quick because her mind had floated away into its own private dreams. That ceremony left Dale feeling strangely empty and alone. She could hear the happy murmurings of the crowd as the music broke out and the couple moved back down the aisle toward the steps of the veranda. The crowd flowed up the stairs behind them, hurrying to give their congratulations to Steven and Katherine and to the Fraizer and Bruner clans. In the confusion that followed, Dale slipped down the stairs to the sculpture garden. I just need some time to myself, she thought as she walked toward the Rodin near the corner of the tent.

She stood behind the tent, half hidden from the view of anyone who might be passing on the veranda overhead. Her fingers moved mindlessly over the polished surface of the Rodin. Her eyes stared out over the closely cropped grass. Within moments Ivan came into her line of vision. He was moving directly toward her, she realized, proceeding inexorably with her as his goal.

"Up to your old tricks?" he asked as he approached her.

He cleared up Dale's confusion with his next sentence. "Katherine's told me all about how she met you in the Louvre. Putting your fingerprints all over the Winged Victory, remember?"

Dale quickly withdrew her hand from the Rodin, then laughed at the memory. "Too bad it wasn't you who found us instead of that guard. You're a curator there now?"

"I didn't take the job until last year. Six months after I met you I decided to open a small gallery in Paris, not dissimilar from the one my father had in London. I struggled with it for a long time. When the Louvre offered me a spot the decision wasn't hard. The gallery wasn't doing all that well. I love to travel. Geneva, London, New York was all I needed to hear. Besides," he grinned, "it gave me a chance to get back at the dealers who'd been competing with me for years. They've never had a tougher curator to get by," he chuckled. "Or so they say."

"Wasn't it difficult giving up a business you'd spent years on?" Dale asked, thinking back to the pangs she had felt leaving the gallery in California.

"It might have been more difficult if it had been doing better," he admitted, dismissing the subject.

"I realize it's been a long time coming," she said, phrasing her next words carefully, "but I want to apologize for acting like such an ass that day I met you in Paris. It was a difficult time in my life."

"I did worry when you went tearing out on me like that," he admitted. "I called Ronald and he assured me you were all right. And then you left so quickly. . . . But come on," he offered. "We can walk through the garden. Ronald won't mind if you manhandle his collection."

Dale watched his back retreating. He was a fine-looking man, she conceded. And there wasn't much she wanted to do at the reception. She certainly wasn't in the mood to deal with a crowd. She traced Ivan's footsteps through the velvety grass.

"Come here," he ordered, pausing by a David Smith sculpture. As she approached him he reached down and picked up her hand, placing it inside one of the large metal tubes that were part of the work. Slowly he guided her through the interior of the steel. "Feel the weld seams?" he asked. "It looks perfectly smooth on the surface. But if you explore a little you can find how Smith got there." He held her hand for a moment longer, running it back and forth through the hidden recesses of the piece, explaining its construction to her as he did. Finally he brought her hand back out and placed it on top of the polished steel strut that was closest to where they stood, his own hand coming to rest on the same flat surface.

"So," he said, "you're working for Kenneth now. What do you think of him?"

"I haven't known him very long," Dale protested.

Ivan quickly interrupted her. "Let me ask you an easier question. What do you think of Fraizer's, of the auction business?"

"It's exciting," she answered eagerly. "I love it more than anything else I've ever done. I thought I had the world by the tail when I was working at the museum, but this is better. Something new is always happening. It may be a painting hitting a new price ceiling. It may be working with a new collector. Even the Heirloom Day that's coming up looks like fun. There's an energy level I didn't find at the museum. In a way it's a little frightening, though."

"What do you mean, frightening?"

"It's competitive. That's not so bad. I'm used to that. The gallery business is, too. But the auction business is a little tougher for a woman. It's been the territory of high-powered men for too long. They see a woman coming in and they put on an air of gentility. Still, they can't completely cover up the fact that it's a cutthroat business."

"Don't let them frighten you," Ivan told her. "They look powerful on the surface, but most of them are as insecure in their own way as you are underneath. They're just people. Once you understand that, it's easy to deal with them. Even better, it's fun."

"Too bad you're not here to give me lessons. You're just staying for the wedding?"

"I'll spend an extra day or two with Kenneth. We hardly get a chance to see each other anymore. I think he could use someone to talk to right now."

"I got that feeling in the car," she agreed.

"Dale," Katherine called. She was standing on the veranda above them, silhouetted against the afternoon sun. "We need you up here. They're about to do the pictures."

"I've got to go," Dale told him. "It was good talking to you again."

"And you too," he agreed. As he watched her go up the stairs he admitted he found her interesting. Even the way she had retreated into the garden to be by herself after the wedding ceremony seemed somehow in character. He couldn't allow himself the luxury of taking it any further, he reminded himself, thinking of Celeste. But her words had affected him. He realized that he envied her. His job offered prestige, but the excitement she described, that just wasn't there. He wondered if it ever would be. Or if he'd just have to go on trying to find his excitement through other parts of his life.

CHAPTER 13

Here's to the man who invented the long hot bath, Dale told herself as she slipped languorously into the warm soapy water. The fragrance of scented oil enveloped her as the liquid rolled over her lean brown body. She looked at her reflection in the flickering light from the candles she'd brought into the tiny cubicle New Yorkers called a bathroom, amazed at how even the most mundane place could be transformed by their subtle light. They don't hurt my mood, either, she told herself as her mind wandered back to Katherine's wedding and to the concern she'd felt for her friend, who'd looked so nervous at the start. Dale soothed herself by remembering Katherine's later look of composed contentment as she and Steven departed in a rain of rice.

I wonder if I'll ever be able to let go of myself that completely, she asked herself, to trust one man to be the center of my universe. A sense of loneliness came over her as she realized how far from that point she still was. She tried to think ahead to her date with Ned, but Kenneth's parting shot came back to her. Be careful, he'd reminded her as he closed the limo door.

Careful, she thought. If only he knew. She needed a man in her life, true. But she wasn't ready yet to give up control—not to Ned or to anyone else. The pain was still too deep, the scars too raw. She quickly stood up and turned on the overhead shower, letting a blast of cold water bring her back to reality.

Ned was punctual to the minute. Breathing heavily from his run up the stairs, he handed her a bouquet of white tulips. "Didn't think you were the red rose type," he explained.

"And I didn't think four flights of stairs would do you in," she returned.

His laughter was infectious. "I took the liberty of booking us a table at my favorite Italian place," he told her as she put the flowers in water. "Hope you don't mind."

"What's it called?" she asked him.

"Mi Giardino."

"I haven't heard of it," she said. "Not that that means anything. For a small island, Manhattan certainly manages to have a lot of wonderful little places hidden away."

"It certainly does," he agreed.

Ten minutes later their cab pulled up in front of one of Park Avenue's most imposing apartment complexes. "This *is* hidden away," she commented as they walked through the lobby. There was no sign of a restaurant on the entire ground floor.

"It's in the penthouse," he explained. "Great view." Kenneth's words of caution slipped from her mind as Ned guided her into the elevator with a fleeting touch on her shoulder.

"Mr. Whytson," a butler greeted them as he answered the door. "Back already." Dale walked into an apartment that was the mirror image of the man himself.

"This is your place, isn't it?" she asked. He confirmed her suspicion with a smile.

"I don't share your sense of humor," she told him angrily, starting toward the door. "And I don't appreciate being lied to." She was glad Kenneth wasn't there to witness the scene. She could have kicked herself for having forgotten his advice.

"For heaven's sakes," Ned said as he grasped her hand to halt her. "I didn't mean to upset you. I do have a stupid sense of humor—you're right. But I didn't lie. We're exactly where I said we were going. Mi giardino—my garden," he told her, leading her through the living room to a greenhouse terrace beyond, where a table for two was set and waiting. "And my cook does fix the best Italian food in the city. Forgive me," he pleaded, "for thinking a little quiet would give us a better chance to talk, a better chance to get to know each other. I haven't tried to rape you yet," he pointed out. "You have to admit that."

She could see that he was on the edge of another of his infectious laughs; it made it hard to think of him as threatening. She suddenly realized that she had overreacted, and felt a little foolish. "And you'd better not try to," she cautioned with mock severity. The mood lightened with her words.

Dinner passed quickly. She didn't know whether it was the food, a rich osso bucco that lived up to its cook's reputation, or the heady red Italian wine that seemed to reappear in glasses the moment they were empty. He was attractive, she admitted as she looked across the candlelit table. He had a strong streak to him, always in control of himself and of the situation. Still, at times there was a boyish quality that showed in the sparkle of his eyes and the quirky way his mouth turned upward as he tried to stifle the ready laugh that always seemed to be lurking just below the surface. The mixture of qualities was appealing. A thought of her other Italian dinner, the one she had shared with Steven, intruded. For the smallest second she felt the unfairness of being deprived of someone she had wanted, then quickly chastised herself for her selfishness toward Katherine.

"That's an awfully nice Gainsborough sketch," she told him as they sipped tiny cups of espresso that had appeared after dessert. She tipped her head toward a study for a portrait that was hanging on the wall beside them. She deliberately broke their eye contact as she did; the physical, sexual energy between them had heightened to a point that bordered on uncomfortable.

"There are some other wonderful pieces here," he said as he took her hand between his. "Would you like to see them?" She paused for a brief moment, savoring the warmth of his firm grasp. Every argument against it flashed through her mind, but his warm grasp won out.

"Yes," she answered quietly.

"The Reynolds," he pointed out as they went through the living room. His arm had wrapped itself comfortably around her waist. She found it difficult to concentrate on the Peel in the hall.

"The entire Royal Academy," she managed to get out as he led her further into his apartment. The bedroom loomed ahead.

She struggled for a moment as he nestled his face in the hollow of her neck. Then she made her decision. He was married. He was safe. He wouldn't expect any commitments from her, nor she from him. And God knows he was just what she needed right now. Kenneth's cautions, Whytson's wife, English artwork . . . they were all pushed away in the totality of that need.

She put her arms around him. They stood that way for a time, then he gently lifted her and carried her to his bedroom. The soft glow from the fireplace warmed his face as he placed her on the bed. He quickly stepped out of his clothes, throwing them carelessly to the floor.

He grew hard just looking at her. Still, his kisses were slow. His fingers stroked her body with no sense of urgency. She could feel how gentle his touch was through the slinky silk of her dress.

He freed her buttons. His mouth moved over her breasts, to her stomach, to her garters and stockings. He loosened them, then slowly swept them to the floor. He never stopped whispering to her, whispering that she was beautiful, whispering that she excited him, telling her in barely heard words that he had wanted her from the moment they had met. He lifted himself to his elbows and gazed at her. Long shapely limbs stretched out like a banquet, waiting for him to feast.

He was as gentle in his lovemaking as he was strong in business. "I'm yours, Dale," he whispered. "Here to please you." He held her hands still while he pleasured her. He played with her feet, stroking them, taking her toes one by one in his mouth until they were relaxed. He moved up to her calves, licking the back of her knees, and was rewarded with low cries of pleasure. When he moved to her inner thighs with little love bites she begged him to enter her and struggled to release her hands, but he held them tightly.

"More," he whispered as he moved between her legs, his tongue quick and hot. She was ready to explode, and still he teased, stopping, then repeating the motion with his tongue, each time a few minutes longer. A trail of wet saliva mixed with her own juices. Her body glistened with sweat. Her head tilted back, a look of abandon and pleasure golden in the firelight. Her hands dug into his thick shock of hair as she came.

Ned moved himself up, his body even with hers. He held her hands tightly, and as he entered her, thrusting deeply into her, her fingernails dug into his palms. His own passion grew into a reckless search for satisfaction as he felt her respond to him. His tongue probed deeply into her mouth as his body locked into hers, making them one. They were joined in a rising rhythm that led their desire to heights where it exploded with sudden force.

Later they lay side by side, neither saying a word as they let the world outside their own appetites come back into focus. The fire had died down, leaving them floating in a velvety darkness. Dale sensed him beside her without seeing him. She wished that she could look into his face, that she could confirm the things her instincts were now telling her. Despite his power, his aggressiveness, his will to succeed, she thought, he was a lonely man. As insular as she was herself. His need for her was as great as her own for him. Each for their own reasons, and what did it really matter what they might be? That magical quality called chemistry was there for both of them. It was enough.

CHAPTER 14

Kenneth and Ivan walked into the front hall of the Park Avenue apartment. The click of their heels rapped an announcement of their return to the empty hall. Kenneth replaced the keys in his pocket silently, then, turning toward Ivan, he smiled sadly. "It's not the sort of space that's hospitable to one person. It's the acoustics. Everything seems to echo when you're alone here."

Ivan put a comforting hand on his friend's shoulder. "They'll be back in two weeks."

"I think I'm looking forward to that. This place is out of proportion for a single man." Kenneth looked over Ivan's shoulder into the vast living room with its eighteen-foot ceilings. "You just try spending some time here by yourself. It turns depressing." He quickly shook his head, as if to do away with the thoughts that were lurking inside. Then he started toward the circular staircase that led up to the second story. "Let's go upstairs. We'll be more comfortable."

An ornate iron and brass banister led up the stairway, then circled the walkway above. Looking over it as they walked, Ivan realized again that all had been left exactly as Anna had placed it nearly thirty years before. Even the light that came from the polished brass sconces on the paneled walls seemed to filter from under satin shades into air that was laden with the thick dust of memories.

Kenneth opened the double door at the end of the walkway. Some lights had been left on and, though it wasn't necessary, a fire had been laid and lit in the library. "Sit down," said Kenneth, motioning Ivan to a comfortable high-backed chair. "Some brandy?" he asked.

Ivan nodded yes, then leaned back as Kenneth went to pour. His eyes scanned the library. A fine Oriental rug showed a well-worn path between the chair where Ivan sat and Kenneth's desk next to the window. His eyes wandered back to the fire, then to the mantelpiece above. A Degas painting hung over the fireplace. Looking at it, Ivan allowed himself to think about the frightening period when both Kenneth's father and his own had fled from Russia. Morris Fraizer had carried four paintings—a Degas, a Cézanne, a Monet, and a Matisse. His own father wrapped just one canvas around his body under his shirt. It was a Gauguin that Kenneth's father had insisted on giving to his close friend before they left.

It was sold within the month. The money fed Ivan's father and family until they were established in London. His father had reinstituted himself in the world of art. And later, he had taught his son to follow in his footsteps, and he had reminded him as well, through the years, that they owed their very existence to Morris Fraizer.

"I'm glad you're here," said Kenneth, standing

over him and holding out a snifter generously filled with cognac. "It was good having you share this day with me. I think fate's taking a hand in keeping us together."

"I hope you're right about that," said Ivan, swirling the viscous brown liquid and watching it stick to his glass.

Kenneth studied Ivan closely. He was soft. Not physically. There he was all sharp angles and muscles. Tracings of clearly visible veins outlined his hands and his fingers and forearms with no protective layer of fat to disguise them. He could see the pulse beating regularly even as he watched. It wasn't Ivan's body that was the problem. It was his soul.

It was easy for Kenneth to recognize the signs. Until five years ago that might as easily have been himself looking out on the world with an accommodating smile. He'd been noncombative. He'd rarely objected. He had above all tried not to think, because it was then that the fear set in. And the more he had repressed it, the more the fear had infected him.

Ivan had it too. Kenneth was sure of it. Ivan had watched his father buckle under to Whytson, and to all the other Whytsons of the world. And he'd never acknowledged that it was happening or fought back, because that would mean admitting that a threat existed. He'd kept the terrors inside, he'd let their icy fingers wrap themselves around his heart until there was only a cold void where real feeling should be. Ivan needed a way to recognize the dread and work it out of his system, and Kenneth believed he could give it to him.

A good friend helps you through the rough spots, thought Kenneth. Even pushes you into them if necessary. He was determined to put Ivan into the kind of situation that would force him to release feelings he'd been walling up inside himself since he was a child.

"I've got a problem, Ivan," he said suddenly. "And I need your help. Come with me." As they reached the end of the hall Kenneth stopped in front of a door. He pulled a key from his pocket and, without ceremony, let themselves in.

Ivan looked around him. The space was small. Just room to stand, to take five or six steps in either direction, to sit. A monk's cell of a room, which might once have held a small bed and a nightstand and a bureau at best.

Kenneth reached to his left and turned on a light. Overhead several small floodlights snapped into life. Ivan realized that they had been carefully aimed at a grouping of drawings and paintings that hung on the otherwise vacant walls. Kenneth played with the rheostat until they were bathed in a glow that brought out their fine old shadings, then motioned to Ivan to take a seat in the room's only chair.

Standing in front of Ivan he partially blocked his view of a charcoal drawing which hung on the wall that the chair was facing. Still, Ivan had seen enough of it, the heavily knotted muscles of the horse's rump, the strong shoulders and forearms of the rider, his thighs straining to keep his mount under control, to tag it as a Delacroix. His curiosity was aroused. "What is this, Kenneth?" he asked.

"It's my own private collection," he said, sounding a bit odd. "I've never shared it with anyone before. What do you think?"

Ivan got up to take a closer look at the artwork. He circled the room slowly, giving each piece a few minutes of his time. They were uniform in quality, each and every one of them a potential museum acquisition. And yet he couldn't find a common thread to link them. Neither style nor period nor subject matter had provided the collector with his philosophy. It was a confusing grouping—one which he didn't yet understand. Something about them wasn't quite right.

Each piece was carefully lighted and labeled with a tiny plaque. Each one had a single date and price. He completed his survey of the room and returned to the point at which he had started. Moving nearer to the Delacroix he read the inscription—August 3, 1980, $729,000.

"What's this date, Kenneth?" he asked.

"That's the date I bought it," he said, revealing no particular enthusiasm. He seemed emotionally dry, hollow inside like a sunbaked sponge.

Ivan didn't know what to make of it. He turned back to the drawing. He looked at it for several moments, then walked away from it and back to where Kenneth had remained standing.

Kenneth watched him, rethinking his own strategy.

"You know, I remember that Delacroix," Ivan said suddenly. "Herbert Stanford bought it, didn't he?"

"I will forever trust your mind to retain details, Ivan," said Kenneth. "Stanford did buy it."

"Didn't he donate it to the Cleveland Museum of Art?"

"He did," Kenneth confirmed.

"But how did you get it back?"

"The curator told Mr. Stanford something very interesting about this Delacroix."

"What?"

"It's no Delacroix," said Kenneth calmly. "It's a forgery. Mr. Stanford demanded his money back. I gave it to him. And he kindly gave me this," Kenneth said, motioning to the drawing, "as a souvenir."

Ivan was silent for a moment as the startling realization of what Kenneth had told him sank in.

"But, Kenneth," he protested, "if he donated it as a tax deduction he must have held it at least a year. Your own catalogue says that a lot has to be returned within twenty-one days if it wasn't as represented. With that amount of time to accomplish it, it's entirely possible that the substitution was made after the drawing left Fraizer's."

"It wasn't," said Kenneth wearily.

"But how can you be so sure?" demanded Ivan.

"Two reasons," he replied. "First, I've known Herbert Stanford too long to think that he'd do something like that. After all," he added, "he is worth upwards of three hundred million. And secondly," he said after a pause, "six other forgeries have turned up at Fraizer's during the last year and a half. Works of art worth over fifteen million dollars. Works we've authenticated prior to sale."

Ivan's expression was one of shock.

"Every one of those clients has gotten a full refund," Kenneth told him. "The buyer of a lot can return it to us in the same condition it was in at the time of the sale and get a refund if the item, when considered in light of the descriptive catalogue entry, is a deliberate forgery. That's what our catalogue says. That's what they did."

"I've never heard of any of these forgeries," said Ivan quietly.

"Neither has anyone else in the house other than Steven. I've repaid all of them out of our own funds."

"Your insurance company wouldn't pay?" Ivan asked. "That's outrageous."

"We've never filed any claims," Kenneth told him. "The minute we do the insurance carrier will call in the police. Given numbers like this they would have had an army of detectives swarming over Fraizer's. It would be the worst kind of publicity. And at the worst possible time. Steven has persuaded me, and I do agree with him, that given Ned Whytson's move into New York we can't afford that kind of bad press. People would just stop buying at Fraizer's if they knew this sort of thing was going on. So here we are. Still secure in the eyes of the public, and teetering on the brink of personal bankruptcy."

Ivan bridled at the mention of Whytson. "Who could be doing it?" he asked.

"I've become increasingly convinced that Fraizer's has become a target for someone who wishes to bring discredit on the firm," Kenneth replied. "For over a year I've been trying to find out who that person is," he continued. "Who possibly could devote this amount of time and attention to destroying the business it's taken me decades to build? This amount of time," he whispered, "to destroy me."

"Kenneth, you make it sound as if someone is conducting a personal vendetta against you instead of embezzling the way they would from any other business."

Kenneth looked at Ivan appraisingly. "Sometimes I do imagine that they want to discredit me personally. Steven's more rational about it. He thinks that Ned Whytson is behind all this—working with someone on the inside at Fraizer's of course—and that it's nothing more than a way to keep us disorganized and defensive while he moves in on the New York market.

"Some days, when I'm feeling very philosophical," Kenneth went on, "I think that it's not any person that's doing this—that actually it's fate pulling me up short because my motives aren't right any more. I went into this business because I loved beautiful objects. Art, the product of another man's inspiration, always offered a moment's relief from the ugliness that was around us. People might do mean-spirited things. The world might have a nasty edge to it. But every time I'd look at a Rembrandt, or a Turner, or even a simple molded plate it would let me believe, if only for the shortest period of time, in the innate goodness of men."

Kenneth took a few steps over to the east wall of

the room. He stood near the painting that was hanging there, looking more through it than at it. He touched the frame, running his fingers over the gesso scrolls that had been gilded and carved. "Somewhere along the line as Fraizer's grew," he said quietly, "my goals changed. The profit became more important than spreading and preserving the art. I began to want the money, because I knew I could use it to make the business larger, to take it back to Europe. To let them know that while they might have forced my father to leave once, they couldn't keep the Fraizers away forever. I guess my dreams got selfish."

"And so," he sighed, smiling strangely, "maybe I'm not being cheated by life after all. Maybe I cheated myself when I started to think that the beauty was just something to be used."

"You can believe in both, Kenneth," Ivan reminded him. "Art and profit aren't mutually exclusive, never have been. We wouldn't have had a Renaissance, a da Vinci or a Raphael, if the Italian princes had joined you in that sentiment."

"That's just what I wonder now," he said sadly. "Whether I do believe in art any more."

"What can I do to help you, Kenneth?" Ivan asked him.

Kenneth leaned forward eagerly. "You can come to New York and help me to investigate this! I need someone inside the house. Someone I can trust. Someone who knows art and knows people. I need you, Ivan."

"That would mean leaving the Louvre, Kenneth. I can't do that."

"Hear me out before you make that decision," Kenneth insisted.

"Don't you think it would be more logical for Steven to help you?" Ivan replied. "He knows the house better. And he has so much more at stake than I do."

"Steven can't start questioning the staff in detail for the same reason that I can't. It's too obvious. But if you're new here, you're a different story. Your questions can be interpreted as a simple desire to learn."

"Are you sure that's the only reason you don't want Steven to work on this?" Ivan asked him. "I sense more than that going on between you."

Kenneth looked reluctant to confide more. "Steven and I have a disagreement about the direction the house will be taking in the future," he admitted. "I want to expand, to take Fraizer's international. I want to put our name over doors and in catalogues in as many countries as I can, and neither this nor anything else is going to stop me.

"I can understand why Steven wouldn't have the same feelings about expansion that I have," said Kenneth, shaking his head regretfully. "Especially not now when he's about to have a child."

Ivan interrupted. "Don't tell me he doesn't understand what an important thing this is to you. I can't believe that."

"Understanding is one thing," replied Kenneth with a small smile. "Commitment is another."

"I'm not privy to your financial statement, Kenneth," Ivan spoke up, "but after listening to what you've had to pay out to buy in those forgeries, I have to wonder about your timing. Your bank account can't be too flush these days."

"We ran through the company's surplus capital six months ago. As of this morning we started drawing down my personal account, too."

"This morning?" Ivan asked. He was beginning to understand that he had been brought to this room for a reason. Kenneth didn't answer. Instead he reached into his pocket and slowly extended a black leather box. Ivan took it and put it carefully in his lap. It rested lightly on his thighs. He touched it, not knowing if he wanted to open it at all.

It had been crafted from the finest kidskin, leather so thin and soft that it clung to the square form of the case it covered without a single awkward seam or fold. It showed the signs of age, spots where its deep black surface had been scuffed to a lighter gray, places where snags had left small craters in the leather's smooth surface. But the royal arms that had been stamped onto its cover still remained as deep, rich golden lines. They had obviously been filled with a generous portion of gold leaf by an owner who had no concern for the cost. Ivan hesitated, then opened the small container. He recognized the Mayapur Diamonds immediately.

"The buyer was in to see me early this morning," explained Kenneth. "His little visit cost me five million."

"This ends the debate about expanding into Europe for the time being, doesn't it?" said Ivan.

Kenneth looked at him curiously, his head to the side. "That's a very calm and collected response, Ivan. Do you know many people who lose five million in one day?" There was a pause, and Ivan put his hand on Kenneth's shoulder. "I'm sorry, Kenneth."

"The expansion is something I have to do," said Kenneth firmly. "God, I was explaining to Steven this very morning. It seems as if I'm trying to justify it to someone every minute now. A man wants to build, Ivan," he said emphatically. "To have something permanent. You'll understand that better once you're older, once you have children of your own. But for now just think of it as giving some meaning to your father's escape from Russia—of making your own life more meaningful. You can't forget your beginnings. I may live on Park Avenue, but I haven't forgotten the Lower East Side. You have a past to make permanent, too."

"But whatever you do," protested Ivan, "if you build Fraizer's in a dozen cities—it's still so small. Don't you see that?"

"No, I don't see that, Ivan. Besides, you know how many times over the years I've talked to you about taking Fraizer's international." Ivan acknowledged this with a nod.

"The time is now," Kenneth told his friend. "A location's available. Three floors. Across the street from Sotheby's on Bond Street. There couldn't be a better place to open. Or a better time to make a dent in the London market. Whytson's over here trying to run his New York operation. We could sneak up on him before he knew what was happening."

"I don't know, Kenneth—" Ivan started, but Kenneth interrupted.

"Are you happy in Paris, Ivan? I know you're still learning about the Louvre, but are you enjoying it?"

"Like everything else, Kenneth, it has its fine moments and its lesser ones."

"But you're still there," Kenneth pursued.

"It was important to establish my own identity after my father died," explained Ivan. "The Louvre's done that. People rarely connect me with the gallery any more."

Kenneth reflected on his friend's answer, then he looked up, stared straight into Ivan's eyes, and barked out three direct words. "You're a coward," he said, dismissing him. "You chose not to run your father's gallery only because you're afraid you wouldn't be able to make a go of it. With all your experience you couldn't make your own go either, because you're afraid to commit to anything, afraid to take it seriously. What would happen if you did and then you lost it? The same thing that happened to your father? So you retreated to someone else's business—the Louvre—instead."

Ivan became suddenly erect in his chair. "Are you planning to manipulate me into working with you? It won't work, Kenneth. I refuse to be goaded into it. There will have to be a better motivation for me than that."

Kenneth leaned forward. It was the opening he had been waiting for.

"It would give you a chance to even the score with Whytson," he said quietly. It was his closing argument. And as he had anticipated, it made Ivan pause. "You don't have to give me your answer this minute," he said, leaning back in his chair.

"But what would you tell your people here?" Ivan asked him. "How would you pass me off?"

"I'd like to be able to tell them the truth," Kenneth said. "That's the other thing I wanted to talk to you about tonight. I'd like to tell them I'm going to open a European operation, and that you'll be heading it. I mean it, Ivan," Kenneth said, seeing his friend's amazed expression. "We'd be partners, and I can't think of a better partnership for either of us. What do you think?"

"It's a bit much to digest with no warning," Ivan answered. His thoughts went back to that afternoon, and the pleasure he had seen on Dale's face when she talked about the auction business. He'd envied her having a job that she looked forward to every day. "I'll compromise with you," he said finally. "I'll take a sabbatical from the Louvre to work on the investigation. We can use your story about my heading the European operation as a cover. It will give me plenty of freedom to spend time in New York, ostensibly going over the figures and learning your business. But for now I'm not sure about doing anything permanent. Let me have some time to think it over."

"I'm pleased, Ivan." Kenneth rose and clasped his friend's hand in his own.

"Let's just take this one step at a time," Ivan cautioned him.

"Good," Kenneth agreed. "You could start by looking at that Bond Street location I'm considering. Can you stop there on your way back to Paris and see how the space is broken up? You could send me back the figures on it. I need them to do the estimates on what it's going to take to open the London branch."

"That shouldn't present a problem," Ivan agreed.

"And you'll give the permanent offer plenty of thought?" Kenneth persisted.

"I will," Ivan told him. "But not right now. Right now I'm just going to bed."

After Kenneth saw Ivan to his room, he returned to the library. He sat down behind his desk. He felt tired, too tired. His conversation with Ivan had drained him. He'd been hard on Ivan, intentionally so. It had hurt him to watch his friend suffer, hurt him terribly. But in his heart he knew that it was necessary. He hadn't expected Ivan to throw everything over on a whim. But he did seem to be seriously considering it. He'll think it over, and he'll accept, thought Kenneth. It will be a union that will benefit both of us.

CHAPTER 15

Kenneth stood at his window watching Fraizer's doorman give one last swipe to the brass plate that read The House of Fraizer. It threw back the glow that twenty-five years of burnishing produces when combined with the welcome sunlight of a mild winter morning dawning over Park Avenue. Last night's rain had washed away a day's worth of New York City soot. Sidewalks that were as gray as morning yesterday gleamed with renewed purity.

The doorman twirled on one spit-shined heel and returned to his regular spot by the door, as Kenneth looked down and surveyed the lineup that was waiting for Heirloom Day. It snaked out below him, stretching from the front door and around the corner until it disappeared from sight.

Normally Heirloom Days made Kenneth feel secure, confident, and very much at peace, reminding him of how many times this tradition had been repeated since he started the House of Fraizer. Today he was in a state of turmoil.

Barbara knocked cautiously before walking in. She'd been with him for nine years, and knew him well. Each day at nine she entered like clockwork, carrying a small tray on which she balanced a cup of water and two bottles of pills. The cup had been made by Ilja Iwanow in Moscow in 1745. The pills had been purchased at The State of Your Health on 57th Street the week before.

"You know what time it is," she said, extending the tray to him with a smile.

"I can't possibly thank you enough," he teased, thinking it was easier to take them than to argue with her.

He accepted the vitamins with a counterfeit smile, and as she turned her back, he reached into his pocket for the Mylanta. It was the fourth time that morning. His stomach was a hydra, writhing in twenty directions.

He picked up Anna's picture. What would she have thought, he wondered, if he told her that he had written a check for close to five million dollars and gotten nothing tangible in return. He stood up from his comfortable Recaro chair and walked to the console behind his Louis XV desk, the product of the workrooms of P. A. Foullet. His hand slid over the beautiful bronze of Neptune that Giovanni da Bologna had created so many years before. He prayed for a God of his own to come to his rescue.

He could picture the afternoon of the jewelry auction as clearly as if it were occurring, just now, before him. When he had purchased the Mayapur Diamonds, Joseph Ableman had been speechless with excitement. He had taken them with him, unwilling once they were purchased to have them out of his grasp for even a moment.

It was the seventh counterfeit of the year. It brought the total Fraizer's had repaid to over fifteen million. It was a staggering amount. He could no longer afford to continue to pay for these fakes. If the upcoming fall paintings auctions didn't do well, his plans for expansion would be no more than an empty dream.

He walked aimlessly about his office. It mystified him. He no longer slept at night, lying instead on a bed whose sheets were twisted and tortured before dawn.

Their security was tight, but obviously not tight enough. He had moved to call in a private investigator after the second, third, and fourth forgeries, but had discussed it with Steven. Discussed . . . you could hardly call it that. There had been arguments, debates. Each time they had agreed to continue to quietly pay off the forgeries. Each time they were reminded of their battle with Whytson's, the bad press that they couldn't afford. The damn public was so fickle as it was that adverse publicity could turn the small edge Whytson was working for into a very big slice of Fraizer's business.

But reality now had to be faced. Kenneth's single remaining resource was the Degas with which his father Morris had fled Europe so long ago, the last of the four paintings that had been their family's life blood, and Steven's suggestion was that he sell it. Kenneth sat at his desk and closed his eyes in a futile attempt to block out the present, only to have the past, like a series of tintypes, run itself before him.

He remembered the Cézanne that had paid for his father's first year in America. The Matisse that had financed Morris's first small antique store. And the Monet that had been sold so that he could open Fraizer's. But most of all he remembered the promise he had made to his father when Morris finally agreed to let that Monet go and give his son a start. He looked again at the Degas as his father's words echoed in his memory.

"These paintings, Kenneth, have been the foundation of my life in this country. They are the only heritage you will receive from me. The only link you will have with your past. And your only reminder of what kind of man your father was. If we sell this Monet, you must give me your oath that the last one will never go. It will be your heritage." He paused, letting the import of his words be felt. "Think about it, Kenneth. Hard and long. Don't give me your answer now. But know that if you make me that promise, the two of us together will open Fraizer's on Park Avenue, make those uptown thieves pay through the nose."

Kenneth waited for two days before going back to Morris. He could have given him his answer that night, but he knew his father, and so he waited. His vow was given.

So much of value lay in the past, thought Kenneth, that it stripped every nerve ending raw when he argued with Steven over the sale of the Degas which remained. He despaired of making him understand—his boy who had no memories that extended beyond the protected existence of the Park Avenue apartment where they now lived—that such intrinsic value could be attached to a single material object. There was no way, he realized, that he could break faith with his father and their history. Morris Fraizer had been a survivor. He, too, was being put to the test. He looked to the Degas leaning against his couch. He had brought it to the office firm in his resolve to have it appraised and to put it on the block if necessary. But looking at it here he knew he couldn't. Every fiber of his being cried out against it.

CHAPTER 16

Dale sat in her office relishing the early-morning silence. The quiet was a contrast to the frenetic pace of her days. Without phones ringing she was able to catch up on correspondence and lay out her plans for the day. She added her signature to a sales contract that was being forwarded to a California collector, sealed the envelope, and dropped it in her Out basket.

Almost nine, she realized, checking her watch. The scheduled starting time for Fraizer's annual madhouse. She was looking forward to Heirloom Day. Everything she'd heard indicated that the anecdotes the day produced were enough to keep the entire staff talking for months to come.

Lines of hopeful treasure brokers had already filled the sidewalk in front of the Park Avenue door by the time she'd arrived that morning. The crowd carried bags of all shapes and sizes. Unmarked shopping bags lined up next to trendier bags from Bloomingdale's. There were large grocery bags from Dean & DeLuca and smaller bags from Martha's Fifth Avenue store.

"Hope you have on your comfortable shoes," said Deborah, sticking her head into the office. A notepad was clutched in her hand. A camera dangled from her neck.

"Thanks for reminding me," said Dale. She shook off her dressy boots and reached to the shelf behind her for the sturdy walking shoes she had learned to keep on hand. Deborah, waiting for her to finish, looked wan and strained, despite the enthusiasm she had in her voice.

"You know, you're not looking so hot," Dale told her. "Is something wrong?"

"No, I'm O.K." Deborah's smile looked forced.

"I don't think so," Dale said after looking at her again. "Have you been sleeping?"

"Not as much as I'd like to," Deborah admitted.

Dale sat down. She still wasn't sure that she liked Deborah, but she looked so sick. Maybe she just needed someone to show an interest in her.

The discussion was more than Dale had bargained for. By the time Deborah was finished she had given Dale a blow-by-blow description of her latest affair, of the man who had jilted her, and of the fact that she was pregnant. It was as if she hadn't another friend in the world, and was totally unwilling to give up the one she had just found. As much as Dale sympathized with her, it was draining.

"Have you talked to him?" she asked sternly.

"No," Deborah answered, avoiding her eyes. "But I haven't given up. Things have a way of working themselves out. This will too. Let's drop it," she said to Dale. "You don't want to be late for your first Heirloom Day."

Dale followed Deborah into the main gallery. Every seat was taken. People had lined up in the standing room against the walls. The excess piled out into the reception area. At the information tables that had been set up in the foyer, Fraizer employees battled to keep up with the flow, answering questions and distributing numbers to keep the line for appraisals orderly.

Experts in various categories had set up tables on the stage in front of the main gallery. Every few minutes a potential client got up from one of the tables and filed off the stage to their right as another number was called and someone else hurried up the steps. The young and the old displayed their treasures. Girls in their twenties carried in unwanted wedding gifts. Senior citizens brought in bits of their past. Blue jeans sat next to polyester. Haute couture rubbed elbows with the street.

Despite the pep talk that Kenneth had given to Dale and the other appraisers the week before, she was taken aback. When the economy is iffy, he had told them, people get concerned. They want to know what they own and how much they might get for it in a pinch. Fraizer's Heirloom Day is the time when they can find out. You'll be exhausted by the time it's over, he had told them, but you'll be stimulated, too. You have to be on your toes every minute. There's no such thing as junk. Diplomacy is the key word. The market for grandmother's wedding pictures might not be here, but it wouldn't do to tell their owner that and have a public-relations day turn into a source of resentment. When in doubt break the news in the kindest way possible. Remember, he had finished, if we find one real treasure, it will have been a smashing success.

Dale stood at the back of the room taking it all in. She overheard a blue-haired little lady at her elbow instructing the young man who sat beside her.

"When you're my age, dear," she told him, "everything is an antique. This dish was in my mother's house from the time I was a child. It must be worth a fortune by now." Her listener cradled a large ceramic piece in his lap as he nodded along to her story.

Dale felt her heart going out to the old woman. She hoped against hope that the plate was worth something.

The young man smiled as he held his own prize out for his companion to examine. It was a velvet-lined gold box, intricately patterned in a design of flowers and leaves. "I bought it for my fiancée, but now that she's changed her mind, I think I'd rather have a trip to Bermuda."

Dale smiled to herself as she walked toward the stage. As she approached Miriam she heard her giving a fifteen-hundred-dollar estimate on a small Bonnard drawing to a graying man in his fifties. He seemed thrilled. "Where do I sign to have you sell it?" he asked.

"Read this carefully," said Miriam, handing him a long printed form. "It's our contract. It tells you what our commission structure is, and what other charges might be levied against you. I have a sale coming up in about ninety days that would be just right for it. We'll tag it and keep it in inventory until then."

The man quickly scrawled a signature on the contract without pausing to read it. Miriam handed him his copy as a receipt and sent him on his way. Giving the Bonnard to one of the warehouse men who stood to the back of the stage, she prepared to meet her next potential customer.

"Why don't you walk through and get a feel for the whole thing," she told Dale. "Then come back here and give me a hand. All hell's going to break loose today. I can feel it."

George Winslow, the head of the Enamels Department, was appraising collectibles at the next table. The woman sitting across from him was in her middle sixties. She was neatly dressed in a gray flannel suit and a pillbox hat that bespoke another era. "Young man," she said to him with a flirtatious smile. "You're in for a big treat. Just wait until you see what I've brought you."

"Good," said George smiling back at her and reaching toward the mammoth candy box that was sitting on the table in front of her. "Now I want you to know that I've been collecting these for a very long time," she said, suddenly protective of her mementos. "Probably since before you were born." Her hand clamped down on the box, keeping it from George's grasp. George took one look at the lace-gloved fingers that quavered on its worn lid and retreated.

"May I look at that?" he asked gently.

"Of course," she said. "That's why I'm here, isn't it?" Slowly she lifted the box's lid. Lovingly she handed him a few of the valentines that lay, in hundreds, within its compartments.

Dale struggled to stifle her laughter as she watched George master his urge to chuckle and proceed with his composure intact. He spent several minutes examining the valentines, carefully turning them front and back. Finally he looked up, respect in his eyes. "They're so beautiful." He paused, as if fighting strong emotion. "And they're filled with such sentimental value. I would never forgive myself if I took them away from you."

She looked him straight in the eye. "You're quite right," she said, holding her head high. "For a young man you're very bright. I think I'm going to write Mr. Fraizer a nice note about you," she said, extending her gloved hand to him as she rose.

"Thank you, ma'am." George gave Dale a wink as

they watched the woman's back retreat. Dale leaned over and whispered in his ear. "Will you be my Valentine?" she asked. George gave her a playful slap on the backside and sent her on to the next table.

Dale walked toward Harvey Singleton, the head of the Silver Department. A young girl in her twenties sat across from him, her mother's Austrian tea service in her lap. She spoke in the hushed sort of whisper that is normally heard in libraries and reading rooms. She told him how faithfully she polished it each week. He strained to hear her, leaning across the table as she confided that she hated the idea of selling it so, she could hardly consider doing it. "Unless, of course, it's worth a fortune," she finished.

Harvey handled himself magnificently as he told her that she was right; the set was so special it deserved to remain a family treasure.

Dale's attention wandered back to George. She saw that he was speaking intensely to the elderly man who sat across from him. She walked back to his table and stood behind him as he examined a doll. Its face and hands were of fine bisque china, colored in a delicate white with peachy cheeks flushing under large brown eyes of lustrous glass. It was clothed in a long satin dress and a velvet cape. A tiny feathered hat perched on its red curls.

"It's a Bru doll," explained George to the man who sat across from him. "They were made in Germany in the nineteenth century. It should bring anywhere from five to twelve thousand," he told the man.

"You're kidding," the gentleman exclaimed.

"No. It's the established price range for these dolls. They were all handmade. They're relatively rare."

"My God," said the man, smiling. "This was my grandmother's. There are two more in the attic."

"Are they all in such good condition?" asked George.

"Oh yes. One is still in the original box."

"If I may respectfully suggest, sir, leave this one with me now. We'll tag it and give you a receipt. Then let's set up an appointment for you to come into my office next week and bring in the others. We can make all the arrangements for a sale, if you would like."

"That's wonderful," he said. "Just wonderful. I never thought they were really valuable." He signed the contract, took his receipt, and walked off the stage grinning from ear to ear.

Dale walked back to Miriam's table and took the chair next to her. "Shall I just watch?" she asked.

"No way," Miriam told her. She reached for her cigarettes and her lighter, and pulling the hair back from her face gave Dale the go-ahead. "You're going to get your feet wet. You can handle the woman that's on her way up here now."

Dale gave her a careful evaluation as she approached. She was in her early forties. She looked sophisticated, thought Dale regretfully. She hoped that the woman was bringing her something worthwhile. She didn't seem the type that would be satisfied with a story easily if Fraizer's didn't want her property.

The woman sat down across from her and began to speak with self-assurance. "My mother passed away last year," she said as she started to take the brown wrapping paper from a foot-square package. "She left me this. It's not really my taste," she explained. "What do you think?"

The paper stripped off, she handed a lovely colored-pencil drawing to Dale. It was protected by nonreflecting glass. The nameplate at the bottom of the frame read Moulin de la Galette. It was signed by Théophile Alexandre Steinlen. Dale breathed a sigh of relief. The drawing was good. She looked at it carefully, then began to tell its owner of its background.

"Steinlen was a contemporary of Lautrec's. He was an illustrator during that period. Their styles are very much the same, though Steinlen never reached the same status as Lautrec. However," she added, "he has been acknowledged as a fine illustrator. Do you have the provenance on this?"

The woman looked mystified.

"I'm sorry," said Dale. "Do you know where your mother got it?"

"Oh yes," the woman replied. "It's from the Hammer Gallery. But she bought it quite some time ago," she apologized.

"They'll still have the records on it," said Dale. "With the provenance you could get two thousand, maybe twenty-five hundred for it."

The woman looked amazed. She began to reach for the drawing with a new air of respect. Before she could get it back into its wrapping Miriam spoke up.

"Would you like us to sell it for you?" she asked eagerly. "We could tag it now, give you a receipt, and put it into the sale that's coming up in about ninety days."

"That would be fine," said the woman, handing the drawing to Miriam.

Dale completed the paperwork. She felt like a fool. She'd been so pleased at finding a good sketch that she'd forgotten the real purpose of the day. As the woman left, Miriam looked at Dale.

"You were right on target with that estimate," she said.

"Right," answered Dale. "And I almost blew getting us the consignment."

"You won't make that mistake again," said Miriam, dismissing it with a wave of her hand. She looked up, and did a double take as she watched Michael, the head of the Jewelry Department, at his table. He was situated across the stage. "It looks like that boy's got himself a winner," she said, nudging Dale. "Go over and see what's happening."

Michael was deep in conversation with a woman in her mid-fifties who was exquisitely dressed in a black suit with a sable fling thrown casually over its shoulder. Dale recognized the quality of the fur, though the styling was at least ten years old. A small gold box sat on the table before her. It was a fine Swiss oval, enameled in four colors. A maker's mark, a crowned DMG, was evident on the bottom of the box. Michael was tracing it out for her with his forefinger as he spoke.

"A conservative estimate is about sixteen thousand," he said.

The woman reacted with glee. "That's wonderful," she exclaimed. "I have an entire collection of them at home."

"A collection of these?" asked Michael.

"Well, yes," she said, smiling shyly. "You see, my late husband traveled a lot over the past forty years. Everywhere he went he tried to find a little something for me. Some jewelry, you know. And he always brought them to me in these wonderful boxes. I liked them almost as much as the jewels. So I saved every one."

"I've already had to sell the jewelry," she said, shaking her head regretfully. "He died several years ago, you see. And I did think these might be worth a little something. But so much," she said with amazement. "I never expected them to be worth so much."

"I'd be happy to come to your home next week and inventory them for you," said Michael. "We could discuss which auction might be most appropriate for them."

"I would appreciate that so much," she said, handing him an engraved at-home card. "Perhaps on

Tuesday. If you could just call in the morning and confirm the time."

"With pleasure, Mrs. Richmond," said Michael, looking at the card. "I look forward to seeing you again."

It left Dale astounded. She hadn't realized that people could have possessions that were worth so much without realizing it. She put a hand on Michael's shoulder. "That was wonderful, Michael," she told him.

"It certainly was," he said, looking up. "I have a November sale of objets de vertu, and those boxes will bring in a tidy sum. I'm dying to see what else Mrs. Richmond might be hoarding at home."

"What do you think her husband did?" asked Dale.

"I don't know," Michael replied. "But I will by the time I leave her house next Tuesday."

"Is that why you offered to go to her house?" asked Dale. "To see what else might turn up?"

"You're learning, Dale," said Michael as he gave his attention to the next person who approached.

CHAPTER 17

Kenneth propped up the square of white cardboard on his desktop, using his bronze inkwell as a makeshift easel. Then carefully, almost sacramentally, he folded back the flap of thick paper that protected it.

"It's got a real feeling of solidity," he said with satisfaction. "I like it. What do you think?" he asked, turning the board toward Ivan, who was sitting in front of his desk.

Ivan reached over and took the board from Kenneth. He studied the logotype that had been rendered in color and mounted there. FRAIZER'S INTERNATIONAL stood out in a classic serif type that might have been carved in marble. The effect was intentional.

"If I didn't know better I'd think Fraizer's International had been around as long as Westminster Abbey," he assured Kenneth as he passed the board back over his desk.

"Think you'd like signing your name on that stationery?" asked Kenneth.

"I told you yesterday, Kenneth, don't count on me. And don't rush me," said Ivan, a note of irritation creeping into his voice. "I'll take on the investigation and look over the London property for you. As for being the head of Fraizer's International, I want some time to think it over."

Kenneth held up a hand to stop Ivan's complaint and smiled. "I know. I apologize. It's just that I feel so strongly that it would be good for you as well as being good for Fraizer's. Let's just drop the subject for now and go over those figures," he said, indicating a summary of Fraizer's requirements for their London facility. "Then I'll give you this file to take on to your meeting in London."

Ivan looked down at the coffee table where Kenneth had spread out his sheets of paper. Columns of figures ran from top to bottom. Square footage requirements for office space, galleries, salesrooms, and storage. Estimated sales figures by month for the first year of the branch's existence. Projected overhead and salaries. It all looked well organized.

"If these figures are anywhere near accurate, your London branch should be a break-even proposition within the first year of operation," Ivan commented.

Kenneth continued to look at the table. His hands played with the papers he had spread out so carefully on its surface. Then he looked up and gave Ivan a direct and unwavering look. "I agree," he said. "This should be a very profitable branch for us if we're able to get through our problems and salvage enough cash to give it a fighting chance during the start-up phase." He paused and watched as Ivan continued to scan the typed sheets of projections. He appeared to be carefully considering something before going on. "Of course it would have an even better chance with you running it."

"You're like a bulldog," Ivan told him. "I already have a life, Kenneth. A position. Friends. A certain amount of prestige. It's taken me a while to get there. It hasn't been easy. It's not something I care to just throw over at your whim."

"We can set up the international operation as a separate corporation," Kenneth pressed on. "You'll own a percentage of it. I realize you're considered an important man because of your position at the Louvre," he admitted. "That you get a lot of attention and compliments. But are you going to be satisfied with having your ego stroked ten or fifteen years from now? Is that going to be enough for you? You need something more solid than that. Something you can build for yourself. And Fraizer's International can be it."

"You're pressuring me, Kenneth," Ivan interrupted impatiently. "You're pushing too hard."

"I just wanted you to have all the cards on the table while you were considering it," Kenneth said quietly. "So you would give it a fair chance."

"It's an attractive offer," was all Ivan would concede.

Kenneth leaned over the table and reached for the sheet that outlined the space requirements for the new branch. Ivan withdrew into his own thoughts.

Then he interrupted Kenneth, who was beginning to explain the physical layout of the projected branch to him.

"I think it would be helpful if you gave me a more specific idea of how you think this investigation should be pursued, Kenneth. I can stay over in New York for the next day or two. Where would you suggest I start?"

"First find out everything you can about the people within Fraizer's who might be involved. Use the London branch as a cover. You can tell them you're trying to determine the type of staff you'll need in London. The demands that will be made on them. That sort of thing. I'd start with the head of the Jewelry Department, Michael Edwards. That's where the trail is hottest. He's down at Heirloom Day this morning," Kenneth remembered, looking at his watch. "You could have a free run in his office. But try to get over to London very soon to look at the premises that are being offered. That will establish your cover and at the risk of setting you off again, I would appreciate it if you'd give us some help on the London art auction we have scheduled in two months. It will be our only introduction in Great Britain until we get the permanent offices open. I want it to be done right." Kenneth smiled as he said it. "Even if you do turn the permanent position down, your ability to get back and forth between Paris and London quickly would be a big help to us until I can find someone else to head the operation."

"I'll only do that if you'll give me some backup, Kenneth. Someone who can finish the job if I decide not to come over permanently. I can't just go flying off from the Louvre every few days if I go back there."

"Who?" Kenneth asked.

"How about Dale?" Ivan offered. "She's probably picked up enough knowledge of the business to be of some help to me. She seems bright enough. Do you trust her?"

"She didn't start here until recently. She still has more ambition than knowledge," Kenneth pointed out. "Still, there's no way she could be involved in the forgeries—she hasn't been here long enough—and she doesn't have a specific assignment once her own auction is finished. I suspect she'll jump at the chance."

"But I will have to tell her about the forgeries," Ivan cautioned him.

Kenneth thought for a moment, remembering the lengths to which Dale had gone to try to be honest with Katherine. "Do it," he told Ivan. "She may be inexperienced, but I'm confident she's honest. I trust her to exercise discretion about this."

"Then it's settled."

"Almost," Kenneth interrupted. "Tell me something. I got the distinct impression on the way out to the wedding that you two don't exactly hit it off."

"I'm afraid I was young and arrogant when I first met her in Paris and she was even younger. Even then there was something that seemed withdrawn and closed about her. I probably could have handled it if I'd met her today. I couldn't then. I'm still not sure we can ever be real friends," he admitted. "But I am going to need some help, someone who's here in New York while I'm in London, someone who's in a position to follow up on things and report back to me."

"All right," Kenneth agreed. "I'll ask her how she feels about it."

"I think it would be better if you let me do that," Ivan suggested. "Why not send her down to Michael's office to talk to me?"

Dale stepped off the elevator into the familiar hodgepodge of Kenneth's outer office. Barbara looked up at her immediately. "He said to send you right in when you arrived," she said, motioning toward Kenneth's office door.

Kenneth continued writing as she stood before his desk. "Wait on the couch, Dale," he instructed. "I'll be with you in a minute."

Dale started toward the couch. As she walked over, the sheen of a painted and varnished square of canvas caught her eye. Curious, she went over to where it leaned against one of Kenneth's ceiling-high bookcases.

Dale knelt in front of the canvas. It had to be one of the finest Degas she had ever seen. He had captured a fleeting moment during a dance rehearsal when the air was heavy with perspiration and the dancers collapsed onto benches like fallen flowers. Tendrils of moist hair curled at their necks. They stroked sore feet, still bound in scuffed satin toe shoes. Crumpled tutus were being straightened and ribbons retied while the dance master, insensible to their collapse, rapped his stick on the exercise bar against which he leaned to call them back to attention.

She felt those familiar acquisitive stirrings, the desire to take every truly interesting work of art she had encountered and spirit it off to have and to hold as her own.

"There are going to be some rumblings in the art community when this goes on the block," she murmured. "What do you think you'll get for it?" she asked, looking over her shoulder.

"It's not going to be auctioned," he replied quietly. "Not while I'm alive. I'm as likely to auction off Steven. Or my photographs of Anna. Or the grandchild that's about to be born. It would be like selling my father's dreams. I just brought it in to be cleaned," he finished. "It usually hangs in my library."

"I envy you," Dale told Kenneth, looking back at

the painting. "Can I borrow it once in a while?" she teased.

"No," he said with a sentimental smile. "You can't."

She realized that he was in no mood to joke and decided to keep quiet until he told her why he'd called her in. Suddenly she had a feeling that she was about to be let go. To be told very nicely, but finally, that there would be nothing further for her to do once the contemporary auction had been held.

"How's your auction coming?" Kenneth asked her.

"Great," she answered with a burst of enthusiasm. "There's something I want to show you this morning. A surprise."

He looked interested. "What is it?" he asked.

"Well, it's blue and it's white and it's about three feet tall and two feet wide." She waited for him to venture a guess, but instead the preoccupied look came back over his face. "It's a Sam Francis," she bragged. "I managed to get it for the sale. It's the best thing we've gotten yet. Should go for at least thirty-eight thousand. Are we in time to have it photographed for the cover?" she asked, throwing one more query into the silence that had engulfed him.

"Absolutely," he smiled. "Now would you drop this off in the Jewelry Department?" he requested. "Give it to Ivan. You'll find him in Michael's office."

Dale inspected the small manila envelope that he handed her. It was about the size of a matchbook and was unlabeled, a fact that made it particularly intriguing. "What is it?" she asked.

"Your diamond," Kenneth said. "The one you found the first day you were here. Steven gave it to me. He did a search through the records, but he couldn't match it up with anything. I'm hoping that Ivan will be able to solve the mystery. I want you to tell him how you found it."

"If you can't find the owner you could always give

it to me as a bonus," she suggested. "Finders keepers. Isn't that how it goes?"

"I don't think a girl like you is going to have to rummage through Fraizer's lost and found for her diamonds," he said. "Before you know it some nice man will be giving you one of your very own."

Dale didn't react for a moment, then she gave him a playful smile and said, "And you'd be out one protégée!" But the fun had left her face by the time she walked back out to the reception area.

Ivan quickly finished looking over the desk in the entrance to Michael's office. He moved on to the inner office, then stopped as he stepped inside. His heart was beating too rapidly. He wasn't accustomed to sneaking, and the idea of being caught at it was upsetting. He stood quite still and gradually brought himself back under control, then he moved over to Michael's desk and began riffling through papers to see if he could spot anything out of the ordinary. It all looked commonplace enough. Correspondence with potential and current clients. Copies of Gemological Institute of America reports that had come in that morning. A blueline proof of the catalogue for a minor upcoming sale. He hesitated for another long moment, then, steeling himself against the worst, sat down in the big leather chair and began to open the desk drawers.

The shallow top drawer was mundane enough. Paper clips, rubber bands, stationery, and staples. There was chewing gum and an aerosol-spray can of Binaca. A notice from the public library about an overdue book. His life can't really be as dull as all this, he thought. At least for his sake I hope not.

He closed the drawer and went on to the deeper one beneath it where a series of file folders stood in a neat row. He scanned their tabs quickly. Old estimate letters. Sheets of sales prices from past auctions. He had almost given up hope when he spotted one that looked promising—bills paid, personal. He was disappointed to find nothing of interest there either. He got up and crossed over into the small side office where Michael kept his holding safe, his equipment, and the file cabinet that held copies of evaluations. Let's just see what he had to say about the Mayapur Diamonds, Ivan thought as he pulled open the top drawer and reached for a file.

Dale put the small manila envelope into her jacket pocket. She felt its sharp corner, the small lump of the single small stone inside. That diamond again, she thought. It keeps turning up. She ran a quick hand through her hair and then started toward Michael's office.

The corridor was deserted, temporarily devoid of both visitors and staff. Everyone was down in the melee of Heirloom Day. She walked the length of the second floor, then stopped at the door to Michael's office and knocked. Getting no answer, she opened it and looked in. The room seemed empty. She started to close the door and go back to her office, then thought better of it and slipped inside. She was startled by a shaft of light across the desktop. When she looked up she saw Ivan silhouetted in the doorway between Michael's office and the small anteroom where his equipment and temporary safe were housed. "My God," she said with relief. "You startled me. When I didn't see you here I thought you must have left."

"I was looking for some papers Michael was supposed to have ready for me," Ivan explained.

Dale looked at him appraisingly. For a moment she accepted the story without thinking, but then something clicked inside her head.

She sat down in the chair behind Michael's desk. She reached out and pulled the chain of the desk lamp. It was a classic bookkeeper's lamp, brass with a glass shade. The thin light it produced washed them in a greenish glow the color of seaweed. She studied Ivan long and hard in the murky dimness. "What are you really doing in here?" she demanded. "Kenneth told me to meet you here."

"He didn't tell you anything else?"

"Just to give you this." She handed him the envelope. Opening it he emptied its contents on to his open palm. The single stone shone brilliantly.

"I found it my first day here. I was in the storeroom with Steven."

"Have you any idea where it came from?" Ivan asked.

"Should I?"

Instead of answering her Ivan handed her the catalogue for the Mayapur auction. "My guess is that it would be a perfect match for one of these," he said, pointing to one of the medium-sized diamonds near the clasp at the back of the necklace.

"What are you talking about?"

"They're fakes," he said, pointing to the necklace. "Just like fifteen million dollars worth of the merchandise that's gone through Fraizer's during the last year. Someone here is systematically stealing from the house."

A look of shock crossed Dale's face. She took a deep breath. She became even more disturbed as Ivan related the whole story to her.

"So," she said as he finished, "Kenneth had the clue in his hands all along." She appeared to be lost in thought for a few moments, her fingers kneading the small diamond as some inner turmoil wrinkled her brow. It was a familiar feeling that had come over her. That sensation of surprise that strikes when all your foundations erode underneath you. It was no stranger to her. It reminded her of the day her father had abandoned them. Dale fell wearily back into the chair.

Why did a kind of dry rot always turn up in the places that were most important to her? The places she was building her life around. At least this time she had found out the truth quickly, she thought. At least this time there was a chance to get out before the whole house of cards fell down around her. She looked back up at Ivan. "So, you're trying to find out who's doing it?" she said.

He nodded, not feeling any more of an answer was necessary.

"Where do I fit in?" she asked, visibly pulling herself together. "You must have told me all of this for some reason."

"I need your help," he said simply. "I'll be back and forth to London helping Kenneth work on a new location there. We need someone here in New York who can keep looking into this while I'm gone. I can't handle the whole thing alone. I'm not going to lie to you, Dale. It could be dangerous. People do strange things when this amount of money is involved. We can't afford to have anything go wrong, to have any obvious trouble. Fraizer's reputation is at stake."

Dale didn't answer immediately. She weighed her words carefully before she spoke. "I don't think I'd be any help to you, Ivan. I don't have any experience in this sort of thing. The truth is, I'm not even sure I want to get involved in something like this. It would mean spying on all the people I'm working with. I don't like it. And they'd figure out something strange was going on soon enough. None of them would trust me."

"Except Kenneth," Ivan pointed out. "You'd not only have his trust, you'd have his appreciation as well. It would solidify your position at Fraizer's. You wouldn't have to worry about whether you'd be here after the contemporary sale. That would be a foregone conclusion. He'd owe it to you, Dale. And if there's one thing I know, it's that Kenneth's loyalties are of the highest order."

Dale sank deeper into her chair. It hurt Ivan to see her looking so confused. "Don't you realize how terribly important this is to Kenneth?" he asked her. "This mess could destroy him if it's not brought to an end." He looked at Dale as if having her work with him was the most urgent thing in the world. She remembered how difficult it had always been for her to turn down her father when he'd put things that way. She hadn't been able to do it then, and she couldn't do it now.

"Just tell me where to start, Ivan," she gave in.

"Well," he suggested, "you've been here longer than I have. Do you have any idea about who might be behind this?"

"Obviously you're giving Michael Edwards some consideration," she pointed out, referring to the fact that Ivan had been going through his office.

"Tell me about him," Ivan probed. "How long has he been head of the Jewelry Department?"

"Five years," Dale answered. "He used to be at Smythson's. He left and came over to Fraizer's when Richard Smythson, Sr. died."

"Got any feelings about him?"

"I think he's honest," Dale answered. "Nothing out of the ordinary seems to have happened since he's been at Fraizer's. He left Smythson's on good terms. I don't think he needs money, either," she added. "I heard that when he came over to the house Kenneth made a deal with him that gave him a percentage of the Jewelry Department profits every year. It's a pretty extraordinary contract. But then he came into the operation knowing almost every buyer of major jewelry in the world on a first-name basis. They'd all done business with him at Smythson's at one time or another. There aren't that many buyers for major pieces out there, you know, and they tend to follow the dealers they know."

"Anything else about him I should know?"

"You might ask Deborah to show you the publicity file on him."

"You could get her to show you the files on all the department heads, couldn't you?" Ivan suggested. "There's no telling what might show up in those."

Dale picked up the pad from the top of Michael's desk and made a note of it.

Ivan realized as he said it that this might be just the sort of thing that would tip the forger off to the fact that Dale was involved in the investigation. He felt a few pangs of uneasiness as he thought about it, but then he reassured himself that from what he knew, this wasn't the profile of a violent individual. The forger was a cerebral criminal, one who was more likely to try to mislead than to strike out physically. "Where are you planning to keep those notes you've been taking?" he asked Dale. "I don't want you to leave those lying around the house," he cautioned her.

She dismissed his fears quickly. He could see she was beginning to get caught up in the excitement of the chase. "Who else?" she asked herself. Her pencil drummed restlessly against the pad she was holding. "It's tough to say. You can only see the surface of the people here," she pointed out. "Most of them seem to get so totally immersed in the house they don't have a life of their own any more outside it. Look at Miriam," she volunteered. "It's almost as if there's a big void where her personal life should be. A blank space. She keeps to herself so totally outside work it's not natural."

"Maybe she's the victim of some secret vice," Ivan chuckled. "Coke? Heroin? Seriously," he went on, "she's spent so much time around collectors it's not inconceivable that she's developed a few expensive tastes of her own. Maybe she just doesn't want to call attention to them at the office."

"I don't think so," Dale disagreed. The drumming

of her pencil grew rapid as she thought. "Deborah," she exclaimed, quickly jotting it down. "She's been seeing a married man. She's quite secretive about it. Maybe that's because he's the outside contact." She looked pleased with herself. She was beginning to enjoy the game. "Who else could profit from the forgeries?" she asked.

Ivan shifted uncomfortably, as if he were reluctant to share some piece of information. "Out with it," Dale ordered. "We can't work together if you hold back on me."

"Kenneth could use the money," he answered in a subdued voice, "to finance the expansion of Fraizer's. It seems strange that he's so set on going ahead with it now, especially with the cash drain these forgeries have caused. He's thought about expanding the operation for ten years. God, I'd wager he's talked to me about it at least a dozen times. But there's never been an urgency about it. Not the kind of urgency that would demand he press forward under these circumstances. It's almost as if he has an obsession about expanding Fraizer's. And if that's the case, who knows what lengths he'd go to see it accomplished."

"That's a terrible thought, Ivan."

"I know," he agreed. "I feel bad even bringing up the possibility. Forget I said it," he ordered her, dismissing it with a wave of his hand.

She started to say more, but they heard the sound of footsteps and voices coming down the corridor. Ivan looked at his watch with alarm. "They must be finished downstairs. We should get out of here fast," he told her.

Dale ripped the top page off the pad and carefully replaced everything on Michael's desk exactly the way they had found it. Ivan clicked off the lamp, and they hurried out.

The morning sunlight seemed artificially bright to

Dale as they left the dim office and came back out into the hall. It was almost as if a new day had dawned. It wasn't until she reached her own door that she remembered to confirm the date of Ivan's return. "When will you be back?" she asked him.

"I hope in about three weeks—but for now let's call the Ablemans. I want to talk with them before I leave."

CHAPTER 18

Dale trailed Ivan out the front door of Fraizer's. "Looks like it's going to be another wet one today," he said, buttoning his overcoat. "Want to risk it, or shall we take Kenneth's car?"

Dale looked up. The sky was an empty, leaden gray, the kind that might open up at any moment and send people scuttling for doorways and cabs. "How far is it to the Ablemans'?" she asked.

"Just to Seventy-second and Fifth," he said, knotting a camel's-hair muffler around his throat. It fluttered gently against the tan of his overcoat as a faint, but definitely chilly, breeze hit them.

"Let's try it," she decided. "The walk will feel good, and if it starts to rain, we can always catch a cab."

Ivan jammed his hands into his pockets and, shrugging his shoulders up against the cold, started walking toward Fifth Avenue.

"Tell me about the Ablemans," requested Dale. She was struggling to button her own coat while she matched his brisk pace.

"He's from the department store family," explained Ivan. "He's a big spender himself, and what he doesn't buy, one of his friends is sure to be bidding on. That's one reason why Kenneth settled with him the same day he came in." She seemed attentive. He was glad he had asked her to come with him. He turned into a doorway to the right of them. An immaculately uniformed doorman inquired as to their business, then reached for the house phone to check with the Ablemans' apartment. Dale pulled a mirror and a brush from her bag, and did the best she could to restore her hair.

It always amazed her to see how insulated the rich could remain. They didn't have to see everyone who came to their door, or answer pestering phone calls. There were always layers of people wrapped around them to protect them from the real world.

"They're expecting you," the doorman confirmed. "The elevator's to your left."

They walked to the mirrored cubicle, and gave the elevator operator their floor number.

After a short ride the door slid open, and as the operator stayed it with a white-gloved hand, a slender Oriental housekeeper dressed in dove gray motioned for them to follow her. She turned her back on them and started across the foyer without waiting to see if they were following.

The white bow of the housekeeper's apron bobbed a good fifteen feet in front of them at the other end of a hall that was hung with a collection of small, but good, Impressionist drawings. White cuffs winked at the woman's wrists as she motioned them into the library beyond. She left, then reappeared bearing a heavy silver set of pots and accessories that she placed on the coffee table between them. "Mrs. Ableman will be in in a moment," she informed them.

Dale sank back into the corner of the couch as Sophie and Joseph Ableman entered the room.

He had a kind but aging face. Next to him his wife looked light and fluffy and insubstantial.

They both listened intently as Ivan introduced Dale as his assistant, then apologized for asking them to repeat what they knew of the events leading up to the substitution of the Mayapur diamonds. Ableman recited his story slowly, pausing judiciously before answering each question to be sure that he had his facts straight. It rapidly became obvious to Dale that he was a thorough businessman who let no detail escape him either in his ordering of things or his observation of them. His purchase of the Mayapur Diamonds had been no exception.

"Are you sure the diamonds you bought were the ones you inspected?" Ivan asked after Mr. Ableman had finished his detailed description of everything that had happened.

"I'm not enough of an expert to know that for certain. The only thing I knew was that they had been left in the care of Kenneth Fraizer for the period between my inspection and the sale. I never questioned their authenticity."

"What happened after the sale?" Ivan asked. "Who carried them off the stage? Could the substitution have happened then?"

Ableman was silent for a moment. He tactfully reached for a cigar from the humidor that rested on the coffee table. "It was Mr. Fraizer who carried them offstage," his wife interjected. Ableman clipped the end from the cigar, then studied it carefully.

Dale felt discouraged. She had been hoping against hope that it could be shown there was a reasonable possibility the substitution had occurred outside the Fraizer premises. It was obvious now that that wasn't the case.

The sky looked nearly black as they hit the street. The air had become so laden with moisture it was hard to draw the line between the threat of rain and an actual drizzle. Dale looked at Ivan inquiringly, sure that he would flag down a cab, but he thrust his hands into his pockets instead and strode down the street in the opposite direction to Fraizer's so lost in his own thoughts he didn't notice her hesitation. She closed her coat, then ran to catch up with him. They walked side by side in silence for a minute, their long legs matching stride for stride, and then she began to ask him the questions that had occurred to her while they were in the Ableman apartment.

"How much do you trust him?" she asked, referring to Ableman.

"Totally," Ivan told her.

"You know there are two ways we can go about this," Dale explained. "We can take the things he's told us for granted. Like the guard. We could skip checking with Brinks, to make sure that the guard was one of theirs. Or we could double check every little detail of his story."

"I trust him," Ivan told her. "Kenneth's done business with his family from the time Fraizer's started."

He put his arm around her shoulder to steady her as they came to the corner of Fifth and Central Park South and were hit once again by the wind that always seemed to whirl there on days like this one. Dale felt his breath quicken as the stiff breeze lifted the skirt and hair of a girl who had been walking in front of them. She didn't know for a moment whether it was the sudden sight of legs or the slight warmth from her own shoulder that caused it.

"We'd better make a run for it," she told him. "I think I just felt a drop hit my head."

They looked for a cab on Fifth Avenue. When one didn't appear they ducked into the shelter of Doubleday's. Art books and novels were piled in stacks in the windows behind them, their colorful covers offering a contrast to the bleak picture outside. Ivan spotted a passing teenager and promised him a ten if he found them a taxi. Then the two of them huddled in their small dry spot while they waited to see if he was successful.

"I think I should talk to the people who designed Fraizer's security system."

"That's Manhattan Security," Ivan told her. "I checked with Kenneth on that. If you want to go over there while I go back to the house, I'll make a phone call and tell Mr. Crown to expect you. He's the one who worked on that system."

"That's a good idea," she said as the boy came back with the cab. She ran a hand through her hair, shaking the drops of dampness from it as she spoke. Polished red fingernails through long black strands that clung stubbornly to their lacquer. Ivan caught himself watching them instead of listening to what Dale was saying, and had to struggle to recreate the questions she'd just directed at him.

He pulled the door open and they flung themselves onto the clammy seats of the cab's interior. Then they swung past Fraizer's to drop him off, and he directed the cab on to Church Street and the Manhattan Security office.

Thomas Crown stood to greet Dale as she entered his office.

"I appreciate your seeing me on such short notice," Dale said as she took a seat in front of his desk. "Did Mr. Wolnovitz explain why I wanted to meet with you?"

"Yes. Kenneth Fraizer explained that you were doing some refurbishing at Fraizer's. Would you like a general explanation of the system? Or should I get into the details?"

"I'd like to know as much as possible. I'll just disregard what's not of use to me."

"All right," he said. "Why don't you move your chair over to this side of the desk." He opened a manila file folder, extracted a set of blueprints, and spread them out in front of him. Then he began to outline the alarm system for her, pointing out the location of its various components on the plan.

217

"The perimeter of Fraizer's—by that I mean all the windows and the exterior doors—is wired into a sound system. If the alarm is tripped while the system is activated, a bell sounds on the premises. This system is also hooked up to our office, and to the police computer. As a result, three separate alerts are triggered when the system is tripped. Simultaneously, floodlights which are mounted on the roof of the building, as well as all the building's interior lights, come on."

"But the activated alarm can be turned off from outside the building, can't it?" she questioned.

"The perimeter alarm can be turned off with a key, either at the side entrance of the building, or at the front door," he agreed, indicating both locations on the blueprint.

"Does the system record it when that happens?"

"Fraizer's doesn't. Some of the more advanced versions will, but Fraizer's doesn't include a time slot. We recommended that one be added, as well as a number of other features that would update the entire system, but no action has been taken on that yet. We summarized our recommendations in this report," he said, handing her some Xeroxed sheets, "and submitted them to Mr. Fraizer quite some time ago."

"May I have a copy of this for my file?" she asked.

"No problem. I'll give you one before you leave."

"Well," she suggested, "there must be more to the system than just a key."

"Of course there are weight and motion sensors in the storerooms. A computer system at the entrance to the jewelry vaults. And closed-circuit television cameras in the office and sales area."

"No cameras in the storage areas?"

"I'm afraid not."

"Mr. Crown, I'm not a security expert. But this doesn't seem very sophisticated to me."

"You're quite right," he agreed. "The system was put in twelve or fifteen years ago. Security has come a long way since then. Let me take you through our recommendations and you'll have some idea." He read down the list quickly. "Voice ID cards at the entrance to the vault areas, as well as at the perimeter doors. That's a system in which a locked steel door opens when a magnetic card is inserted and you announce your name and a personal ID number," he said, looking up at her. "The number is changed every month, and the voice ID is a definite credential. It can't be forged—no two imprints are the same." He flipped to the next sheet of the proposal. "New floors should be installed, pressurized to the point at which the application of one ounce of pressure will trip the system. TV cameras in all the storage areas as well as in the entrance. That way the guard sitting in the reception room can see the entire building on mini screens at the front desk. There's more," he said, closing the report, "but those are the highlights."

"Maybe I can talk Mr. Fraizer into letting us include this in our new plans," she said, taking the report from him.

"You should," he told her. "Fraizer's has been lucky so far, but that can't continue forever. But I should warn you, he seemed quite adamant about not making the expenditure for a new system when I spoke to him about it previously. Let me get a copy of the cover letter for you as well," he said, starting for the door.

"No need," she told him, rising to leave. "I'll be calling you back if I make any progress with Mr. Fraizer."

She found herself in the damp back seat of a cab for the second time that day. It all seemed to her to come down to that twenty-four-hour period between the inspection of the stones by the Ablemans and Richard Smythson, and the auction late the next day. That indicated the forger was someone who could count on consistent access to the vaults since there wouldn't have been time for a second try if someone interfered with him. Not only that, it would have required several hours of uninterrupted time with the jewels.

The security system nagged at her. It would have seemed so logical for Kenneth to have updated it as soon as he read Crown's report. She couldn't help but think that if she were an outside investigator—someone who didn't know Kenneth as well as she did—the superficial evidence would lead her to the thought that he'd been masterminding the thefts himself. He had the opportunity. He hadn't bothered to update the alarm system. He had the motive—he clearly could use the money for the expansion he was planning.

But she wasn't someone from the outside. She did know Kenneth, she'd spent time with him, learned from him; it was inconceivable to her that he could be behind the forgeries.

She shook her head. If she'd learned one thing that afternoon, it was that she and Ivan faced an incredibly complicated situation. Despite her worries she felt an edge of excitement sharpening in her as she thought about the possibility of solving the mystery at Fraizer's—and the pleasure she would see on Kenneth's face if she did.

CHAPTER 19

Ivan picked up his carry-on bag and quickly walked through Heathrow. He hailed one of the tall black taxis that waited in front of the airport, checked his watch to see if he had time to drop off his things at

Celeste's in Belgravia before going to his appointment, and decided against it. "New Bond Street," he told the driver as he settled into the back seat. The cab pulled quickly away from the curb.

He felt disturbed and saddened. So much had been dredged up. In a matter of a few hours Kenneth had managed to pull out memories that he had pushed below the surface for years. More than memories, actually. Forebodings and fears that were lurking like shadow figures in the back of his psyche. There was so much he wanted to forget, and Kenneth didn't allow him that luxury.

His mind began to work over Kenneth's problem like a terrier worrying a bone. He couldn't just dismiss it. Kenneth had bared his soul to him in his attempt to convey the urgency he felt. For that reason alone it deserved his honest attention.

Was he really happy at the Louvre? He knew, as few of the people who surrounded him in his professional life did, how hard he had to struggle to keep his energy level up for his work there. When he accepted the position it had been everything he was looking for. It took him out of London and let him blank out memories of his father, their gallery, and that last sad fiasco with Ned Whytson. Kenneth had implied that he had just run away, making everything his father had tried to build meaningless with a single act. The suggestion had angered him at first. It seemed unjust and unfeeling. But as he spent time thinking about it, he admitted that he might have been too easy on himself. Leaving had been the painless way out. He had known even then that the position at the Louvre wasn't a whole life. It had been satisfying to him in the beginning because he didn't have to think. But the shame that Kenneth had stirred up in him had remained lurking underneath the placid face he presented to the world. He had to admit that the clues were there all the time if he had only cared to acknowledge them.

Then Katherine, with her marriage to Steven, had brought the other thing to mind. He knew he was the kind of man who would never feel complete until he was secure within the cocoon of a marriage and a family. Thinking of Katherine brought a rush of strong emotion to his heart, and a thought of Celeste to mind. His love for her was presenting certain problems. She was a strong, passionate woman. She often intimidated him by her very certainty about how she wanted her life to proceed. She was appealing and intriguing, but she never took great pains to prove her love for him beyond the mere fact of making herself available to him. At first it had lent her an air of mystery in his eyes. Lately it was beginning to bother him.

That was the most obvious appeal in Kenneth's offer, he admitted to himself. If he finished the investigation in New York and then moved back to London to open the first European branch of Fraizer's, it would simplify his personal life. And yet something made him hesitate. If Celeste wasn't willing to be in Paris with him—if she wasn't willing to live anywhere in the world with him, how could he ever count on her? He wondered how deeply she cared for him. Was it merely the fascination of a long-distance romance? Their times together were always heightened by the fact that one or the other of them would be leaving in a matter of days or hours. That's fantasy, he told himself. Not the reality of living.

"We're here, sir," said the cab driver for the second time.

"Oh, I'm sorry," said Ivan, rousing himself with a start. He got quickly out of the cab. He had time to make a quick survey of the street, he thought, looking at his watch—to renew his acquaintance with the various shops and their brand of clientele.

New Bond hadn't changed, he told himself with satisfaction as he strolled its neat sidewalks. It had always been one of the plushest shopping streets in London. He paused as he passed by his favorite, Asprey's. The store had been catering to the esoteric whims of the affluent with ivory-bottomed mustache cups and Georgian-silver sweet trays for so many decades there was nothing you couldn't find there. Further down was the wonderful Piaget store where he had gotten the watch he was wearing today. It was as much the epitome of the carriage trade as Fifth Avenue or Madison in New York; it was certainly the sort of atmosphere that Kenneth could be successful sharing.

Strolling back toward the vacant building, he spotted a harried-looking man getting out of a taxi at the same spot where he had debarked minutes earlier. "Mr. Travis?" he asked, walking up to him and extending a hand.

He followed him into a foyer that measured around twelve by fourteen. It was small by Kenneth's present standards, but certainly sizable enough for British expectations. A nicely aged staircase with a fine mahogany railing led up to the second floor. A small elevator with wrought iron and brass decoration stood next to it. "Three floors?" asked Ivan.

"And a basement as well," said Travis, unrolling the plans. Ivan studied them quickly to get an idea of the layout. "Can I get a copy of these?" he asked.

"My pleasure, Mr. Wolnovitz."

"Shall we start with the basement?" suggested Ivan. "If there's not enough storage area we have a problem."

"I think you'll find it quite suitable, sir," Mr. Travis encouraged him.

They climbed into the small elevator, and dropped a level. To Ivan's surprise the basement seemed to run under the width and breadth of the two adjoining stores, as well as under the building they were touring. "This used to be one parcel with the stores on either side," explained Travis as if reading his mind. "When they were divided, the storage area remained with the center property."

When they concluded their tour of the property half an hour later, Ivan congratulated himself on time well spent. The location was excellently situated. New Bond Street attracted a native stream of well-to-do clients. It was sure to be supplemented by visitors from Claridge's, which was just a few short blocks away on Brook Street. But what made it even more desirable was the fact that the building had large rooms and storage areas. The room that could be converted to the main sales room was large enough to hold four hundred.

Ivan thanked Mr. Travis for his time, then he walked a few blocks down New Bond Street and turned left on Brook. He needed a cup of tea before going to Celeste's, and he had a notion to call Kenneth from Claridge's rather than from her house. He still wasn't sure whether he should let her know about Kenneth's offer. Or should he try to get her to prove herself, to see if she would agree to move to Paris to be with him? What he wanted was a relationship that would endure. But the sinking feeling he got in his gut when he tried to phrase his request that Celeste move to Paris made him doubt she would do it.

His mind went on to the other complications of Kenneth's offer. He felt safe in Paris. Safe from being thrust into the path of Ned Whytson. Protected from thinking about what the man had done to his father. And shielded from having to come to grips with his heritage.

If only he could count on Celeste to understand and to help him through the difficult time that a move might cause. He sat thoughtfully. His left hand mindlessly stirred cubed sugar into his now tepid tea. White toast sat cooling in the silver holder. His waiter, an elderly man of about seventy who had spent a lifetime in Claridge's service, saw his customer's mood and tactfully refrained from going to his table. Finally Ivan made a decision—he would tell Celeste.

He found he felt rather good. He was eager to call Kenneth once he'd had a chance to make a more thorough review of the figures. It was likely to be a short call. Kenneth would be happy with the results of this morning's meeting. Still, he'd have to wait a few hours until it was a decent time in New York to reach him. He could count on Celeste to amuse him until then.

CHAPTER 20

It was pouring as his cab pulled into Lyall Mews. Puddles glistened on the worn cobblestones and deepened the colors of the three tiny houses that shared the whimsical old alleyway.

Celeste's was the nicest of the three. It had been the stable of the main house until the turn of the century when an enterprising relative of the original owner had decided to convert it, as the English put it, to a "quaint Mews house."

Ivan quickly paid the cab driver and darted under the shelter of the second story that overhung the back door. He pulled the string of the old-fashioned copper bell that hung next to it, and in a moment the door swung open, slowly revealing the inquisitive face of Charles, the houseman.

"I expected you at the front door, sir," Charles reprimanded. He was totally attuned to the formalities that class differences make incumbent, and often shook his head in disapproval at the casualness with which Ivan flouted them.

"It's pouring, Charles. Why should I track up the parquet floors when I can as easily come in here?" He indicated an expansive kitchen and pantry in which the curving copper bars of the original horse stalls had been preserved and incorporated into the decor.

"Whatever you say," Charles answered.

Charles's attitude never failed to peeve Ivan. He somehow always managed, without ever saying anything directly, to make it sound as if Ivan was only one of a series of suitors who regularly turned up at their doorstep.

Ivan followed Charles into the library, where a fire was laid. The scent of burning pine gave an appealing, outdoorsy flavor to the room. Celeste was waiting in its warmth. He seated himself next to her and grasped one of her small, white hands in his own. He loved the fragrance of her, he thought as he began to nibble on the small ear that peeked out from under her blonde curls.

"Darling, I'm so glad you're here," she told him, and she did seem truly pleased. "There's a nice bottle of Montrachet chilling in the bucket on the bar."

The fatigue that had settled in on him lifted. "Let's take the wine upstairs and have a little nap before lunch."

"My dear sir," she said, jumping up and heading for the kitchen. "I do think you should spend the day in bed. A lovely idea, too, I might add," she said, looking back over her shoulder as she went to tell Charles to hold lunch. It's amazing, he thought. Just sitting next to her makes me feel more alive.

They climbed the stairs slowly. He followed her into the bedroom, the heavy silver wine bucket cradled in one arm. She put the two crystal wineglasses she had been carrying on the nightstand next to the bed and took the bottle from him to open it. Charles had brought the cork almost out of its neck with a corkscrew, then left the tip of it in to keep the wine from splashing as they carried it. She grasped its protruding top in her hand, and slowly extracted it with one of the most suggestive rotating motions he had ever seen. He took one sip, then began to undress her, lingering over each piece of clothing as he went, letting his hands stroke her breasts as he slid buttons from buttonholes, running his fingers inside elastic as he pulled it free. He could feel her nails on his skin as she unbuttoned his shirt and then deftly unfastened the buckle of his belt and released his zipper. He lay naked on the bed as her hands and her tongue began their magic.

Celeste moved on top of him, letting the soft parts of her body submit to his own hard outlines. Her breasts relaxed into him, then sprang back into their original fullness as she rolled over and left him behind. She cupped the bowl of a wineglass in her hand, took a large drink from it, then returned. As he opened his lips to kiss her, he felt the liquid slip in, all the richer for the slight warmth it had gained in her mouth. It was a game that they played. She said it was the only way she ever really enjoyed drinking, the best way to bring out the bouquet in any wine. He loved taking it from her mouth into his own, and letting it slip in languid little swallows down his throat. Often at dinner parties he would look across the room at her as he raised a glass to his lips and a secret smile would unfold on her wonderful rich mouth as she realized what he was thinking.

He took her breasts into his hands and began slowly caressing them. She had large areolas that grew darker and changed from buttery roundness to tense points as he sucked them. His tongue traveled down her stomach, stopping momentarily when he reached the point below her navel where a fine line of downy blonde hair divided her body into symmetrical halves. As he traced the shape of her inner thighs with his mouth, he could feel himself grow hard. That adamant throbbing, that would only be eased with his entry into her, began.

He reached that magic spot of hers that was so wet he could never have enough. She was playing with him, taking little love bites along the length of his body, covering him with moist reminders of the distance her tongue had traveled, in much the same way he had covered hers just minutes before.

When he thought he would explode she rolled on top of him. Sitting on his rigid cock she put her legs on either side of his chest and began riding him as if he were a wild bronco. Each time his body began to buck with her motions, following her rhythm, she would pull away from him, then slow her teasing until his heart eased down from the breakneck pumping she had caused. Then, as he began to relax again, she would push him into her and ride hard on him. His hands finally trapped her waist, forcing her to stay, guiding her forcibly up and down, up and down. She gave him his way until he was so ready he felt on the verge of bursting, then sensing his impending climax she pulled away from him, freeing herself. The pleasure and pain of it was almost too much for him. She knew how to keep him like that, hard and pulsating.

Celeste turned over and made a trail of saliva up his stomach, over the taut muscles that carved their firm outlines on his rib cage. She moved her nuzzling face underneath his arm where she knew the skin was smooth and sensitive to the touch. He lay quietly, his eyes closed, and gave in to the delicate torment of the sensations she produced.

When at last he raised himself on top of her, throwing her legs high onto his shoulders to clear a pathway for his body to thrust deeper and deeper into her, she moaned the litany that was so exciting to him. Her words were fevered, demanding. "Now. Please now, Ivan," she begged. "Give me those juices now." With a final, near-hurting attack on her he gained the limitless release she always gave him.

Later, lying still on top of her, the quick throbbing of her flushed pink body linking her to him like two musicians in perfect time, he felt an unbearable desire to become one with her. His lips next to her ear, he whispered, "My God, Celeste. I can't stand having this be a weekend love affair. We've got to talk."

"Don't you feel good?" he heard her whisper in return.

"Wonderful," he told her.

"Let's not talk right now," she replied in a small voice, as she fell into a peaceful doze.

Ivan leaned back against the bed pillows. He reached to the nightstand on the side of the bed opposite hers, and fumbled in the dim shadows for the pack of Gitanes he had taken out of his jacket pocket that morning. He had smoked them since moving to Paris, and had grown to love their strong odor, almost heavy enough to have been a cigar. He took a deep drag, savoring the taste. He smoked so infrequently, perhaps two or three cigarettes a day, that the pleasure was always fresh for him.

He watched the glow of the ash move steadily down the thin cylinder of tobacco as he wondered once more about Celeste, who was asleep beside him, her blonde hair scattered like soft straw on the pillow, her porcelain face showing an innocence that fled when she was awake. She was by nature a lady in the living room and a whore in the bedroom, and the difference seemed to have become even more dramatic since they had been spending less time together. He would have been lying if he said he didn't like it, but she so obviously enjoyed making love and being made love to that he wondered how she managed during the times they were separated. It was possible, and he liked to think true, that she remained celibate. He glanced furtively at the small leather date book that lay on her nightstand, resisting, but barely, the urge to open it and see what she had been up to while he was gone.

He drew back the curtains far enough to let him watch a thin stream of light bathe her streaming hair on the pillow. She looked up drowsily, caught him watching her, and favored him with a slow, sleepy smile.

"Darling, there's something I want to ask you."

"Oh, Ivan," she said, looking up with a wounded expression. "No more about Paris. Please. Let's just have a relaxing few days without quarreling."

"It's not about Paris, Celeste. It's about London."

She looked suspicious, then intrigued.

"You know how close I am to Kenneth Fraizer," he went on. She nodded to acknowledge it. "It seems he wants to open a branch in London."

"How grand," she said excitedly. "We'll throw a party for him. Do tell him I'll arrange it, Ivan. Won't you?"

"Perhaps you could give it for me, instead," he told her, smiling. She stopped and looked at him with surprise. "I just looked at some property on New Bond Street for him. He asked me to do a workup on the location. He wants me to run it, as well," he added. "It would mean my moving back to London permanently. It could change everything for us." He saw her confused look, and decided to make things absolutely clear. "We could get married. Have a few children. Even share the same tea cozy when we've gone round the bend," he said, teasing her.

He saw the sudden panic on her face. It flashed there for the briefest moment, then was gone. But in that transient instant her eyes had darkened and her light had gone out. Even as he watched her, fright was replaced by that big wide smile that photographers so loved. But the hesitation had been there, and it had hurt him. Not that he would ever be able to acknowledge that to Celeste. She liked strong men. And even now she was searching for a gracious out for both of them.

"Darling," she said tenderly. "That's so terribly exciting. You know how I would adore it if you were with me. But you should think this over very carefully. After all, you were so terribly unhappy in London after your father died. For your sake, darling, will you be happy here?"

He had poured his soul out to her. He had imagined she would be happy to have him moving back to London. Perhaps not ready to make a move into marriage so suddenly, but at least pleased that they could be together with enough consistency to decide what they really wanted to do about their relationship.

"It's just an idea that's been thrown out for discussion," he said casually. "No decisions made. If I do move back we should go slowly with one another. Give each other a bit of freedom. After all, we've both become so accustomed to maintaining our separate lives. I'm not so sure after all that I wouldn't feel impinged upon. I was a bit hasty," he said, smiling at her.

He could see the muscles in her face relax. Her mouth became full and ripe once again. They had passed over a difficult stage and things were still intact.

He knew it was the beginning of the end. He hadn't even looked seriously at another woman in Paris. He had been hopelessly in love with her. Now it was painfully obvious to him that it was a game she had been playing with him all along. His commitment to her had never been returned.

He watched her as she dressed for supper. She was so engrossed in the task of matching her lipstick to her nails, of arranging the folds in her skirt to blossom perfectly from beneath the wide belt that cinched her waist, she never noticed him. The past years with her had been a fantasy, he admitted. Always making plans for a fleeting day or two. Meeting here or there, then turning and running from one another. One conversation had wiped out any illusions he might have had, and laid down a new set of ground rules for them both to abide by.

He thought back to the dream he'd had the night before. His father had been hanging a new front door on their London townhouse. It was a deep green door, the color of a worn dollar bill. He had been centering it with care, assuring himself that it swung clear and perfectly when it was opened, that it closed solidly when he swung it shut. He was straining to finish his task. Every time he went to work on it again, another group of partygoers arrived and Celeste, who was waiting inside, pulled the door open to let them in. The sound of shouts and laughter always followed them, leaving his father alone on the stoop working at his task.

Thinking back on it, Ivan felt a terrible emptiness. Perhaps Kenneth's right, he thought. My heritage and family do mean a lot to me—more than I've been willing to admit. I toyed with accepting Kenneth's offer in order to get Celeste. It's her rejection that's let me see why I should take it.

CHAPTER 21

Dale opened the door to the Paintings Department and realized that someone sat waiting in front of her desk. The woman had her back to her. As she leaned into the path of the window, light from the winter sun filtered through the buildings to burnish the foxbrush of red hair that swirled around her face in the light breeze from the radiator that stood against the wall. Then she sat back and let one slim leg cross over the other, and began to mark time with an impatient beat of her foot. Dale walked around to the other side of the desk and found she was looking into Katherine's face.

"Your hair," she said. "I didn't recognize you."

Katherine let a little smile escape her, happy to have fooled her friend. "They did it for me in Cannes. What do you think of it?" she asked.

"You look like a Renaissance Madonna," Dale told her. And in fact she did present a combination of rosy pinkness and the bright reddish hair of Northern Italy that Raphael could easily have painted. "I'm so glad to see you."

"I thought I'd start shopping for the baby's layette. It would be more fun if you'd come with me."

Dale jumped at the idea. "A perfect excuse to skip lunch. New York's already given me an extra five pounds. But maybe you'd like to go with Steven instead," she suggested.

Katherine paused, measuring her words. "No," she said, "I think I'd rather have someone to talk to."

They emerged to a cold, crisp day. They were lucky enough to find a cab dropping off a fare in front of Fraizer's and they grabbed it. "Saks Fifth Avenue," Katherine told the cabbie. "Fiftieth and Fifth."

"Lady," he complained, "I know. Do ya think you're the only fare who's ever gone there?"

"If you know it so well," said Katherine, regaining the upper hand, "why don't you get us there? We're late as it is."

Dale smiled to herself as he stepped on the gas and sent them both rocketing back into their seats. She still had to get used to New York cabbies. They were a breed unto themselves. Still, he did manage to weave in and out of traffic and to cross Fifth Avenue against the red light with the speed and accuracy of a well-aimed bullet. "Let me get it," she said to Katherine when they pulled up.

She handed him four dollars and told him to keep the change, then felt like kicking herself. Overtipped again. She could tell by the smile on his face. I must waste ten dollars a week on that, she told herself.

"Have a nice day, lady," the cabbie said as she got out.

"Sure," she replied, glaring at him as if it was his fault and slamming the door with the aplomb of a true New Yorker.

She followed Katherine through the first-floor crowds and up the escalators to the eighth floor where they emerged from chaos into the peaceful world of the infants' boutique.

"Where do you begin?" Katherine asked, bewildered.

"With a salesgirl," Dale suggested, equally confused. "Are you free?" she asked the pleasant-looking girl behind the counter. They explained that they needed a layette for a firstborn, and she bustled away to put some things together. As she waited Katherine started fingering some of the tiny sweaters that were lying on the counter.

"They look so small, don't they?" she asked, holding a yellow one up to her face. "It's frightening. Babies are so dependent on you. A whole new life that will be shaped and molded. So much depends on the input you give them."

"Don't forget the genes, Katherine. Yours and Steven's are pretty good." At the sound of Steven's name, Katherine put the sweater back on the counter and sat down. She didn't respond to Dale's comment.

"What went on in the south of France?" Dale asked, looking down at Katherine. "You came home a week early, didn't you?"

"We never left the House of Fraizer behind," Katherine said softly. Her eyes as she looked at Dale threw off a sadness that pierced the heart. "First, Steven hated the idea of Kenneth's having made all the arrangements for our honeymoon. He didn't say so, but I could tell. Then he called back to the office and found out that Kenneth had sent Ivan into London to look over some property he was considering for a branch office. You'd think someone had set off a bomb. Nothing would do but that we come back from Europe right away. If he gets this crazy whenever Kenneth does something that he disagrees with, I'll spend my life feeling more like an arbitrator than a wife."

"It could be just an isolated incident, couldn't it?"

"It's possible," Katherine conceded. "Steven did have some cause to get angry. Kenneth is making a major decision about whether to open a branch in London. The location is important, and he usurped Steven's right to be consulted about it. Everything that was wrong between them before seems to have grown since we got married. Steven couldn't be more contrary. Once Kenneth got interested in the baby, Steven didn't seem to care about it any more. It's like he's deposited his seed and he doesn't have any more responsibility for it. I don't know whether he's caught up in work, or just trying to avoid me. Or maybe," she said slowly, "he's having an affair."

Dale felt her stomach turn over. "That's just silly, Katherine," she told her. "You've only been married a few weeks. It's your imagination. You're feeling insecure."

"I know," said Katherine.

Dale looked at her closely. She could tell that Katherine was still keeping something to herself that was even more upsetting. Her hands played with ends of her long woolen muffler. "There's something more, isn't there?" Dale asked.

"Dale," she said with resignation, "the real truth is that Steven just married me to get ahead. He thought his father would give him more responsibility if he did it. He as much as told me so himself. Well, Kenneth hasn't. It didn't work out that way. Steven knows he's made a bad bargain. He's keeping it, but he's taking his disappointment out on me."

"Don't even say that," Dale told her. "It's your imagination."

"No, it's not," Katherine told her. "Please don't try to calm a supposedly hysterical pregnant friend. He got angry with me after the phone call to his father. I tried to tell him we could still go to London, still look at the location, and he blew up. Said he was my husband and that I should be defending his interests, not explaining Kenneth's. It all came out then."

"Well, I think he's out of line," Dale said in a tone of outrage. "Getting married isn't a direct line to heading a business. Where was it ever written that marriage means you do better in business?"

"Maybe Kenneth built up those expectations," Katherine said. She looked down at her hands as if they held the secret to her problems. "I don't really mean that. But it seems so empty, Dale," she said, looking back up and into her eyes. "No love, no caring. If only I hadn't married him."

"Steven's ego needs a little gratification," Dale suggested. "It appears as if he has a high opinion of himself, but it's never been backed up by approval from Kenneth. Sure, he seems immature at times. Who wouldn't if he'd never had a chance to make his own decisions?"

As Katherine listened to Dale she dared to hope. Her child was going to be born, and it was going to be born legitimate. She knew in her heart, despite the things Steven had told her, that he had been pushed. All in all, he seemed to be handling it well. It would grow on him as they went along and made adjustments. Her own parents were like that, not wildly in love, at least not that she had ever seen, but happy together. Their relationship was solid. Hers would be too. It was up to her to make a go of it, at least to hold the thing together until their child was born. And maybe, just maybe, he would learn to love her as well. "Maybe the baby will help," she said hopefully. "Maybe it will settle him down. Make him feel better about himself."

"They've been known to do that," Dale said kindly. The salesgirl reappeared, her arms filled with tiny undershirts, baby blankets in soft shades of pink, blue, and yellow, and doll-sized nightshirts. The furrow that had appeared on Katherine's forehead slowly eased as she fondled the tiny clothes.

Dale picked up one of the baby blankets. "This is going to be one lucky baby," she told Katherine. "You're going to make a wonderful home for this little one."

"Steven thinks that Kenneth is going to spoil him," Katherine told her. "That he'll take over his grandson as his own personal charge. Yesterday he told us that we should use the entire third floor for the baby and the nanny. Then when he's older we can turn it into a suite for him."

"Sounds interesting, but what if he turns out to be a she?"

"He wouldn't dare," Katherine told her. "Kenneth's too set on a grandson."

Talking about it, Katherine touched her stomach with an air of wonderment. "You know," she said, "I can't quite believe I'm going to be a mother. I used to hear women talking about how they would do anything for their children, and I used to wonder why they would say that. But I understand it now. This little being that is growing inside me is dependent on me for everything—its very lifestream. I don't think that can stop once he's born. I think that will go on forever. Not his dependency, of course, but his getting some of his inner resources from me. I want to give him so much, Dale, I really do," she said seriously.

"Oh, Katherine. You're going to make a wonderful mother!"

"It's good to talk to you," Katherine told her. "There are some things that I can't seem to say to anyone else."

"Don't you think you should start by trying to talk them out with Steven?"

"Easier said than done," Katherine told her with resignation. "He's away so much I spend more time with his father than with him. I wonder how Kenneth will feel about living alone in that huge place if we move out."

"Still, you've just gotten married. Don't you think you should have a little more privacy? Besides," she added, "I have a hunch that a man like Kenneth wouldn't have to be alone for long."

Katherine felt uncomfortable as she listened to Dale talking about Kenneth. An actual physical tension took hold of her. She felt herself being tugged in two different directions, and the muscles at the back of her neck tightened up. She wanted to change the subject. "What's been going on with you?" she asked Dale. "Have you met anyone interesting?"

It was Dale's turn to fidget. She took tighter hold on the soft blue blanket. Finally she looked up and in a somewhat embarrassed tone told her, "Ned Whytson. I have been seeing Ned Whytson."

Katherine looked shocked, then stern. "Dale," she cautioned, "be careful. He's married. And he's had every woman in London."

"I'm not in London," Dale replied in a sulky voice. "I'm here."

"I wouldn't give a nickel for his reputation here, either," Katherine told her.

"Please stop," Dale protested.

"No, I won't," Katherine persisted. "Ned is your competition. You really can't count on him not to take advantage of the situation. He doesn't have the reputation of a man who accepts defeat gracefully."

"I know," Dale told her. "Ned keeps telling me that himself. He is so direct about it, so willing to admit that he will do anything to win; it actually makes me trust him more." Dale stopped, unsure of what else to say.

"You can't go on seeing him. What if Kenneth finds out? He's a stickler for loyalty."

"But I did tell him," Dale rationalized. "At least about our first lunch."

"He didn't know it was going to go on," Katherine quickly rebutted. "He thought you were just doing it to get information."

"I was," Dale protested. She suddenly sounded frightened. "It's not my fault Ned turned out to be interesting. He's bright. He's in a perfect position to give me solid information about the business I'm trying to get ahead in. And I really need this job—need to earn a place at Fraizer's. I can't afford to lose it right now."

"Maybe if the California art auction does well?" Katherine suggested.

"I think it will," Dale told her. There was enthusiasm in her voice for the first time since they had started to talk about her personal life. "I've knocked my brains out on it and I finally feel like I've gotten it under control. We have eighty-odd lots, and some of them are really good. They're all in the storage bins, tagged and catalogued. The catalogue was mailed this week," she added, reaching into her purse and handing one to Katherine. "I've been carrying one with me ever since they arrived. I have to keep looking at it to believe this is really happening."

"Sam Francis," Katherine whistled, looking at the cover. "Not bad."

"Thanks to Ned," Dale told her. "He had a lead on it and told me about it."

"The man is generous to a fault," Katherine commented. She wasn't about to keep the note of sarcasm out of her voice.

"Not really. It's from someone he hasn't been doing business with for years. They had a run-in in London a few years ago over something or other. Ned thought that if he couldn't have it I might as well reap the benefits."

"Promise me you'll be careful around him, Dale," Katherine said, suddenly serious. "I don't want anything to happen to you."

The salesgirl returned and placed piles of small, soft towels, washcloths, and receiving blankets on the counter. "It looks like so much," Katherine exclaimed.

Dale looked at the lovely pastel array. Her own circumstances weren't so pretty. Being involved with someone like Ned assured her she wouldn't need any of this. It left her with a sad, empty feeling. Did she really want to go through the rest of her life alone? She pushed the thought to the back of her mind. She could do only what she was strong enough to handle, regrets wouldn't change that. Still, she wondered what it would be like if she allowed herself the luxury of a real relationship.

"I promise," she said quietly.

CHAPTER 22

Miriam closed the door to her private sanctuary. It was a strangely Spartan, monkish cell. Every piece of furniture was mismatched and at least as worn as her broad wooden desk. The walls had started as white, but had discolored over the years to an uneven yellow. White squares showed up against panels that were otherwise blank, souvenirs of some former owner's decorating in a place where no art now hung. She picked up the stack of work that waited for her and settled herself behind her desk. She started by giving a cursory examination to her correspondence. It largely consisted of requests for valuations. The letters came in all shapes and sizes. There were Polaroids and transparencies and an occasional page from an exhibition catalogue. None were particularly distinguished. She decided to turn the whole mess over to one of her assistants.

Under the general inquiries she found a few order bids for the upcoming paintings auction. They were the first to arrive, quick responses since the catalogues had just been sent out that week. She transferred them into the file folder to be picked up and entered later that day by one of her girls in the outer office.

There was some assorted personal correspondence at the bottom of the folder, then a thick set of sheets that she had ordered from the World Art Market Conference—copies of the talks that had been given there that year. She usually managed to get there herself, but when this one was scheduled in Los Angeles she had decided to skip it.

She flipped through the mimeographed pages. Her eyes sped over the front page of a talk to collectors by Henry Hopkins from the San Francisco Museum of Modern Art. "Think of history, and what your local institutions might need," she read. She let out a quiet little chuckle. Good advice, Henry, she thought, tapping the paper.

Hopkins's words rang true. The museum sale that they were about to conduct had some fine works that were being divested when their only crime was one of not fitting into the taste and the plans of the institution's trustees. She was hoping that collectors who were involved with other museums would come forth to pick them up. She had gone to the trouble of seeding some carefully placed catalogues in cities whose museum collections might be ripe for some additions. She knew she would get attendance from the dealers. They loved selling art that had been in museum collections. Divested or not, it still carried a special patina of respectability that made it simple to place.

It promised to be a lively crowd, one that might bid high. With any luck the night might push her figures to a new high, right into bonus territory, where she would begin to collect an override on every dollar that came through the door of the Paintings Department.

As much as she hated to admit it, it was Dale who was responsible. She had gone after Donovan, and he had responded by directing his energies into the divestiture sale as if it were the only thing in the world he had to occupy his time. Dale might still be wet behind the ears, but she'd managed to be in the right place at the right time and she'd pulled it off. When Miriam thought of all the years she'd put in herself, and the hours she'd spent cultivating every known collector in New York, it didn't seem fair. Still, the overrides, if any, would be coming to her. It was only smart business to try to overcome her resentment long enough to make this museum sale pull in the top dollars she knew it would. She opened her door and, spotting Dale at her desk outside, asked her to track down Deborah and to report with her on all the information they had on the museum sale. Within minutes Dale was sitting in front of her, though Deborah still hadn't arrived.

"That Deborah," said Miriam, reaching for a cigarette from the pack on her desk. She lit it, inhaled deeply, and filled the crammed cubicle with a hazy cloud. "Always knows it all, but never there when you need her. Do you think they're using her to test some new industrial glue?" she asked suddenly. "Her ass seems to be permanently fastened to her chair."

Dale began fanning the smoky air.

"You really should slow down to five packs a day. You're going to kill yourself with those things."

"Too late," said Miriam philosophically. "I went in for a checkup last week and they told me my lungs had turned as black as my heart." She glared at Deborah as she rushed in, and pointedly looked at her watch. Then she leaned back in her chair, stared at the wall, and drummed her short, unpolished fingernails on the desktop. "Deborah," she said finally, "have any press releases gone out on the museum sale?"

"They went out last week," Deborah answered, relieved to hear that Miriam was concerned with something she had already taken care of. "Dale worked on them with me. I think we're getting good coverage so far. The *New York Times* picked it up for next week's Sunday section. I thought you would have seen them," she said, handing copies of the releases to Miriam. "I assumed Dale had shown them to you," she added, looking pointedly in Dale's direction. Miriam reached into her purse and drew out a crumpled pack of cigarettes. She tried to light one with a book of matches that looked as if it had been dunked in coffee and then dried out, and failed. She continued striking matches fruitlessly, then tossed the whole mess in Deborah's direction. "Light one for me while I look this over," she told her as she picked up the press release. Deborah scratched matches over the wilted cover with no luck, then tossed them into her lap in despair as the sound of Miriam's "Oh shit" resounded through the tiny office. She didn't know what she had left out or forgotten, but she did know that Miriam had been coming down on her so hard lately it had begun to hurt.

"Maybe it's my fault," Miriam said as if talking to herself. "But shit, Deborah," she said, turning toward her, her face creased and angry, "instead of playing up the museum's paintings in these releases, you've made a big deal of the fact that some of Donovan's personal paintings are going to be auctioned. He's got his share of enemies—in the art world and out. He's alienated every quality dealer in the country. His fellow museum directors, too. Using his name in conjunction with the sale may hurt us. There are dealers out there who will come for this sale for the same reason they would want to attend a public hanging. And I don't mean just one or two of them."

"Look, Miriam," Deborah responded, "you and Dale gave me all the facts to work with. Including the information about this sale being Donovan's brainstorm. Sure I know Donovan," she admitted. "I know he is a big collector. I know he buys here, too. Why didn't you say when we met that you didn't want his name mentioned? When I wrote the first draft I went over it with Dale—per your instructions."

"I know, Deborah, but do I have to go over every little comma?" Miriam asked, the anger rising in her voice.

"No, you don't, Miriam," Deborah shouted back.

"But you might just edit the facts before you give them to me. I'm not a mind reader, you know, and the man does spend money here. Big money. In your department, I might add."

"Miriam," Dale interrupted. "I feel this is my fault. Donovan added several of his own paintings to the sale. You know that. They photographed well, and their provenance was perfect. I figured that they made the museum's paintings look even better."

"It's done," said Miriam, throwing up her hands in defeat. "You'd better let me know everything that has been happening around this sale, and I mean everything."

Dale looked back at her, at a loss as to where to start. "Do you have a list of the catalogues that have been sent out by special request?" Miriam prodded. Dale nodded and handed it over. Miriam scanned it quickly, then gave a negative swing of her head. "Have the dealers you've spoken to shown more interest in this sale than we expected them to?"

Dale thought carefully before answering. "Just the opposite," she replied. "Particularly considering the fact that we have a lot of important paintings in this sale. You remember you asked me to follow up with some of the majors from Europe? Find out when they were coming in and if they needed help with theater tickets or dinner reservations or anything else like that?" Miriam nodded yes, but didn't say anything.

"Well," Dale continued, "I've been on the phone for the past few days and it appears that a lot of the people you gave me aren't coming at all." Miriam's silence was reminiscent of shell shock. At length she took a deep breath and turned to Deborah. "And you?" she asked. "Anything unusual happening in your department?"

"We've gotten a lot of calls from the press," she

told Miriam. "But I would expect that with this group of paintings."

"Any calls about Donovan?" Miriam asked.

"There was one," Deborah remembered, "specifically asking about Donovan's paintings."

"Ladies of the auction world," Miriam said, straightening in her chair and addressing them in her best women's group tone, "I think we have a problem on our hands, and I'm not sure how to unload it."

Dale looked bewildered. "My dear," Miriam said, looking directly at her, "you are about to get your initiation into the real world. I have a strong hunch that a ring has been formed for this sale and I am not referring to ring-around-the-rosy."

A deep sigh escaped Deborah. "Miriam," she asked, "are you sure?"

"How can you ever be sure of something like that?" Miriam asked her impatiently. "It's just that the ache at my temples tells me it's a good bet." She closed her eyes and rotated her fingers in small, tight circles at the sides of her head. As Dale watched her, she remembered her drive out to Katherine's wedding with Kenneth and his little lecture on ringing. She had never imagined it would come home to roost so quickly. She couldn't help but wonder whether it had been set up deliberately as one more complication in the troubles the house was having, and, if so, whether Deborah's submission of the articles with Donovan's name was as inadvertent as it seemed.

"I had better see Kenneth right away," said Miriam. She opened her eyes slowly as if the sight of her office and the two of them sitting there was painful to her. "You might as well sit in on it," she told Dale grudgingly. "It's your sale too." She stood up abruptly. As much as she would have preferred to speak to Kenneth alone, her sense of fair play told her Dale had every right to be present since she had been instrumental in arranging the sale. "Would you like to come too?" she asked Deborah.

"Not necessary," replied Deborah quickly. She remembered the old adage about killing the messenger who brought bad news—she had seen it happen too often in the business world. "Just fill me in later."

Dale was silent as she followed Miriam to Kenneth's office. She felt her own inexperience as never before. Donovan had simply struck her as a likable pirate—one who would negotiate until he had exhausted the last shred of advantage, then keep the bargain he had struck. Now it seemed the very mention of his name was enough to trigger underground machinations. She felt naive, and yet it was worth remembering that Miriam did know his reputation and even she had forgotten to take it into consideration. No one is infallible, she thought as they got the signal to go through Kenneth's door from Barbara. You just had to be one step ahead all the time.

She looked toward Kenneth's desk, saw it was empty, then spotted him sitting on the couch in the corner. Steven had pulled up a chair opposite him. It appeared that they had been interrupted in the middle of a private conversation.

"To what do I owe the unexpected pleasure?" asked Kenneth.

Miriam answered him. Her voice was somber. "There's no way to say this except to go directly to the heart of the matter. I think the museum sale is about to be ringed. Too many of the dealers aren't coming in. I think they've chosen a few to do the bidding. They've made up their minds to kill their competitive urges and to keep down the prices on Donovan's paintings."

"Ringed?" asked Kenneth. Both he and Steven began to speak at once. Miriam silenced them, then began to explain what had come up during her meeting with Deborah and Dale. She told him that she felt Donovan in particular was being set up for major losses. She knew that Donovan was not a friend to Kenneth—his abrasive nature had rubbed all the Fraizers the wrong way. But the museum had, in and of itself, symbolized so much to Kenneth over the years that he might not want to risk a scandal that would ultimately attach itself, at least to some degree, to its name. When she had finished, Kenneth sat quite still for some time, then he slowly framed his thought out loud.

"OK," he said, "let's say the major dealers have already decided among themselves how they're going to divide Donovan's paintings between them. They may already have designated the ring members who will be doing the bidding on behalf of the group. That would explain why some of them aren't bothering to come in for the sale. Not only will Donovan be left with a fraction of what he would have made if the dealers weren't in collusion, Fraizer's will be facing a lower sales total and lower commissions than we had expected." Miriam looked him square in the eye as he outlined it. "A result that will be bad for profits, as well as for prestige. Let's go over the list and the probable selling prices," he ordered.

As Miriam rattled off the information, it became apparent to everyone in the room that the group Donovan had personally entered in the sale stood to bring in as much as twenty million. Kenneth began pacing the room. His eye caught the Fragonard drawing opposite his desk, then the picture of Anna that stood on the console behind it. He continued to walk the floor, glancing behind the desk from time to time, then he spoke tentatively at first. "Well," he said, "we negotiated the commissions on all sides with the museum as well as with Donovan. Steven, get the calculator. Let's see what we're up against."

Steven quickly punched in commission figures as Kenneth fed him estimates of the probable selling prices of each picture. Then he returned to his desk, turned to his son, and asked him, "What's the total?"

"We stand to make over a million in commissions on Donovan's paintings," he replied curtly. Kenneth looked over to Miriam. "It's sketchy evidence," he reminded her.

"I know," she admitted, "but it's one of those hunches that just plays." Kenneth nodded, acknowledging her gut feelings.

"I don't think there's much we can do about it at this point," Steven interrupted. "The catalogues are out. We already have order bids in on some of those paintings. The sale is only three weeks away. Even Miriam admits she could be wrong."

"It would be nice if I were," Miriam said from the corner. She had settled on one of the couches and was weeding through the cigarette box on the table looking for the strongest smoke in stock as she spoke. "But I'm not."

"In essence you seem to be saying that we should just keep quiet about our hunches and proceed with business as usual," Kenneth said to his son. Something cold and brittle had happened to the tone of his voice.

"Well," said Steven hesitantly, "yes. That is what I think."

"Miriam?" Kenneth asked.

"Even if it is ringed they'll probably only try to steal Donovan's paintings. We'll still get full price on the museum's works. And while what we do get for Donovan's might not be as high as it would have been otherwise, it will still add a lot of volume to the house, not to mention to my department. Look, Kenneth," she told him, "I'm as upset about this as you are. I was counting on this sale to reach some new highs. I'm still not in bonus territory for the year."

"So what you're both saying is that we should keep quiet about it," Kenneth summarized.

"He's your client," Kenneth said, looking at Dale. "What do you say?"

Dale felt suddenly exposed. She had been sitting quietly, more an observer than a participant. She knew she was a beginner, the morning had certainly made that clear to her. She wasn't sure how much her opinion was really worth, and she was apprehensive now that Kenneth had decided to press her for it. She tossed a strand of black hair back from her face in the nervous gesture that had become so familiar to all of them, then pulled herself to the fullest height she could muster and spoke as boldly as possible. "I think he has to be told," she said. "They are his paintings, after all."

"Dale," Steven started. His voice had an overtone of impatience to it.

"I'm sorry, Steven," she interrupted. "I can't help it. I know the catalogues are out. The sale obviously has to go on. But I think that in all fairness the man has a right to the same information that we have. Tell him. Then let him make the decision."

"That's not our job," Steven shouted in irritation. "Our business is to sell, not to determine who is buying."

"Steven," Kenneth's voice barked out sharply. He motioned his son toward the couch where Miriam was already seated. Then he came around to the front of his desk, leaned his tall frame against it, using his spread fingers as the fulcrums that balanced him, and gazed out at the three of them. Kenneth looked older to Dale, the creases that were traced from his nose to the corners of his mouth more craggy than ever. Or perhaps it was just the light that made him look as if he had grown suddenly aged, for when he spoke his voice seemed as vital and vibrant as ever.

"I want to make it perfectly clear to all of you," he said strongly, "if you have had any doubts on this point, that if you ever hear of anything that may damage a client, no matter how small, it must be communicated to that client immediately." Steven started to speak, then quieted as his father's raised hand indicated he hadn't finished. "If you must cheat someone, cheat me. Pad your expense account. But as long as I'm alive and the name of my father, and your grandfather," he added, looking to Steven, "is over this door, we will not cheat the public. It's the way your grandfather did business when all he had was a little store on Broome and Greene, and it's the way I still do businesss today. Donovan is part of that public. Better informed, perhaps. Smarter. Maybe even dishonest himself. That's Donovan's problem, not mine. As far as I am concerned, he deserves to be protected every bit as much as the rest of them."

"You're going to tell him," Steven said flatly.

"I'm going to tell him what we know," Kenneth confirmed. "The choice is his. I am also going to tell him that there will be no penalties if he chooses to withdraw the paintings."

Steven started up in his seat, incensed. "At the very least," he said quietly, the effort he was making to keep his voice under control apparent, "we should charge him twenty percent commission on the reserve. It is standard practice in the business. Objects that are pulled after the catalogue is published demand some payment. It is not our fault that he's hated."

Miriam nodded. She knew Kenneth was right in forewarning Donovan, but she wanted those sales figures in her column. To his credit, Steven had a valid point. There should be some charge if the paintings were pulled.

Kenneth didn't notice. He had walked over to his son. He looked at him with disappointment in his eyes. "Won't you ever think ahead?" he asked. "Can't you look past the short run? With you it always has to be what's good for today. You can't exercise patience with me. You will not exercise it with Donovan. He'll be back. He'll let us auction the paintings later, and more of them."

Steven's face took on a look of disgust. "Donovan will do whatever is best for himself at the time," he told his father. "Don't kid yourself."

"Donovan will pay us back," Kenneth said firmly. "That's one thing you have to understand about this business. Our profit and loss may be based on figures, but we get those figures through people—their judgment of us and ours of them. We deal in objects, that's true. But more than that, we deal in relationships with the people who buy and sell. It's true we need the money," he said to Steven. He had lowered his voice as if this was something that was to be shared just between the two of them. "I am as acutely aware of that as you are. But if Donovan withdraws the paintings more or less on my recommendation, I can't expect him to pay a penalty as well. He will bring them back later," he said, reassuring his son. "Don't worry."

Steven looked back at his father without another word. It was obvious to Dale that he had decided to give in without any further fight. Still, he took it so quietly, she had to acknowledge she found it odd.

"Barbara," Kenneth called as he walked over to the door and opened it wide, "call Bill Donovan and ask him to come by today or at the latest tomorrow. Check my calendar and choose a time. Tell him it's important."

CHAPTER 23

Dale left Kenneth's office in Miriam's trail. The older woman slammed through his reception room at record speed, leaving Barbara with her half-finished good-bye still hanging. She rammed the elevator button with a passionate jab strong enough to floor a middleweight. As its doors opened she crashed in and turned around to see Dale still standing in front of Barbara's desk, hesitating to follow her. "Are you coming or not?" she asked impatiently as she began to fumble in her jacket pockets. Dale slipped in behind her, treading carefully. "Got a cigarette?" Miriam asked.

"You know I don't smoke," Dale answered.

"That's the trouble with you people from California," she complained in a heated tone. "No damn vices."

Dale decided to remain discreetly quiet. Instead, she concentrated on the meeting that they had just left. "Dropping those paintings from the sale will be pretty rough on you, won't it?" she asked. When Miriam didn't answer, she went on, "But you did the right thing. Telling him, I mean."

Miriam stared at the elevator wall as if she could see through it and right into Donovan's mind. "He'll pull them," she said in disgust. "I really wanted those sales to boost up my figures for this quarter. Damn it anyway." Then she looked back at Dale, as if she was just remembering that she was there. "Of course I did the right thing by telling him. It's just that I never figured he'd call Donovan and suggest that he withdraw the group. Not that your opinion helped much. The next time Kenneth asks you a question like that, I wish you'd remember that I'm still the head of the Paintings Department, and that information, and *opinions*, should go through me first before you deliver your own judgments." The elevator doors opened at the second floor. "Well," said Miriam as she started back to the office, "it should be an interesting conversation. I wonder what the infamous Bill Donovan will say when he hears about this." Dale followed her out and strode quickly to catch up with her.

"Now that you have lost your bonus you might as well forget that nice little Renoir sketch that's waiting downstairs for the sale," Dale joked, trying to lighten Miriam's mood. Miriam looked at Dale strangely. "Come on, Miriam," Dale went on, "you can't fool me. I saw the way you looked at it when it came in. If it had been a quart of ice cream you would have devoured it before the guy who handed it to you had time to blink. You liked it all right."

"It was nice enough," Miriam agreed, "but I wouldn't have spent the bonus on it. I don't own any art. Not one piece."

Dale looked at her, shocked. "Surely you don't expect me to believe that," she said. "Your whole life is art."

They had reached their department. Instead of answering, Miriam reached for the door and opened it to let them in. She walked straight through and into her private office. Dale followed her in. Miriam looked at her, as if her glare would be enough to get her to clear out. When Dale refused to budge, she went on.

"The paintings that come in here," she said, motioning toward the stack of transparencies and prints that littered her desk, "I look at them as dollar bills. They mean nothing to me in and of themselves. No more than the piece of paper that a dollar is printed on. It's what stands behind them, the bullion, that makes them worthwhile to me. In this case, the amount of bullion that people might be willing to pay for them."

"I don't believe you, Miriam. I've seen the way you look at some of the things that come through here."

"It's a game to me, Dale. Just a game of how much I can get for them. How can I covet the things that come through here?" she asked with emotion in her voice. "I'll never be able to afford the best of them. Not if I got a bonus every other week. So I don't let myself get infected with the bug of wanting. I can't let myself."

"Oh, Miriam," Dale said. There was sympathy in her words. It was like watching Tantalus, tempted for eternity with the sight of the things he wanted most dangling just out of reach. Miriam was showing a vulnerability that Dale hadn't seen before. Still, she couldn't stop her mind from working, from wondering. Miriam was protesting, but maybe too much. If she really were out to hurt Fraizer's, pulling the Donovan paintings and depriving the house of the commissions that were attached could be one way to do it. Was it real? Or was it just the sort of diversionary tactic that a clever thief would use? Dale made a mental note to remember this conversation and to make it a part of the notes she was planning to share with Ivan in a phone conversation later that week.

"Sure, I cared about them at first," Miriam went on. Her voice was softer than Dale had ever heard it. "The paintings. The prints. I loved them all and I couldn't let go of anything. If a Picasso came in, I wanted it. Could I afford it? Never. So I had to sell it. Obviously I had to sell it. And each time I had to deliver one of them to the buyers, I resented handing it over. I found myself looking at these strangers as thieves. Had they been looking at this painting every day for weeks? Had they been loving it? What right, I would ask myself, did they have to take it? To take my painting. That's when I went cold turkey. Sold everything I'd accumulated. Started smoking instead. I haven't bought anything since," she concluded. She gazed across the desk at Dale.

Dale returned her look without really seeing her. It had occurred to her as Miriam talked that there was another possible motive for Fraizer's forgeries. One they hadn't considered yet. One that would make it immeasurably more difficult to find the thief, because it was one that wasn't tied in to logic or financial gain. It was altogether possible that there was someone else in the house who loved art too much to give things up. If that were the case, the stolen pieces might never have been sold at all. They might be resting somewhere, stored until the day the thief deemed it safe to take them out and look at them again. How can you possibly find someone like that? Dale asked herself. His gain would be as invisible as a soul's longing to own beauty. She realized that Miriam was staring at her.

"I'm going out," Miriam said. "If anyone asks, just tell them I'm out. Maybe forever," she muttered over her shoulder as she went out the door.

Dale sat down at her desk. She studied the wall opposite her without really seeing it. Her mind was still with her conversation with Miriam. She constantly found herself amazed by the vagaries of human nature. So little was as it seemed on the surface.

The office door budged a crack, then swung fully open. Steven came in. "Mind if we talk a few minutes?" he asked.

"Not at all," she answered, as he sat on the edge of her desk. One leg swung clear. The other touched the floor, balancing him on his precarious perch.

"I couldn't help but overhear you and Miriam in the hall. She really raked you over the coals. Don't pay too much attention to her, Dale. She's just feeling threatened right now."

"By what?"

"By you," he told her.

Dale looked embarrassed. "But that's foolish. She hasn't any reason to feel threatened by me. She's got years of experience on me. I just felt I had to tell Kenneth what I really thought. Just as you did. I'm sorry about what happened in there, Steven."

"Just another meeting of Fraizer and Fraizer," he said lightly. "Nothing out of the ordinary." She looked back at him seriously, refusing to acknowledge the carefree tone he was using.

"I realize it's none of my business, but perhaps if you had stood up and fought a little harder. . . . You had a good point this morning. I agreed with you. At least with half of what you were saying," she corrected herself. "Kenneth was right in telling Donovan. You must see that it wouldn't have been ethical not to. No more than knowing about a robbery ahead of time and keeping it to yourself would have been. But the other part, the commissions, you were right there. If Donovan chose to pull the paintings, he should have been asked to pay Fraizer's a commission. Why weren't you more insistent?"

Steven looked at her and sighed. "Dale," he said. His voice sounded tired and strained. "It's so much more complicated than you know. I'd been meeting with my father for an hour before you got there. Arguing like blazes over his sending Ivan to London in my place. And about something else, as well."

"Still, don't you think you should have stood up for what you believed?"

Steven's eyes riveted her. His face had gone perceptibly paler. The conversation, which had flowed so easily just minutes ago, ground to a standstill. "You do get points for tenacity, don't you?"

"I'm sorry," Dale apologized. "Let's just get off the subject."

"I've got to run anyway," he agreed. "I'm meeting Katherine for lunch."

The unfinished conversation left the room with an incomplete air, she thought as she toyed with the thin gold chain around her neck. She wondered if he had been able to come to grips with his problems with Katherine yet, and knew as soon as she thought it that he would never tell her. The sudden ringing of the telephone broke the silence of the room. Dale picked up the receiver. As she did so she looked at her hands with dismay. They were like neglected stepchildren. Her cuticles bordered on the objectionable. Her light flesh-tone polish was chipped and peeling at the ends of her nails.

"Would you hold for Mr. Whytson?" a voice asked.

She stretched out her feet as she waited and ran into an obstacle under her desk. She ducked her head to see what it was, then remembered the pair of walking shoes, sturdy low-heeled loafers, that she'd brought in and left there. Lately she'd found herself on the stairways more often than the elevators, but then lately she'd found she was always pressed for time.

She took a quick look at some order bids that had come in that morning, then put them in a folder in the bottom drawer of her desk to be worked on after lunch. It wouldn't do to have them sitting out in the open; like all blind bidding, a certain amount of secrecy was required to make it work.

"Hi," she said as he picked up the other end of the line. Ned's voice sounded cheerful enough, but then it always did. If you were to read him on the surface you would think his moods never varied further than the distance between euphoric and merely happy. "You're sounding very chipper."

"Why shouldn't I be?" he asked playfully. "When I have the most beautiful girl in New York on the other end of the line. It's enough to put even the average man into a frenzy. And as you might recall, I'm not the average man."

Once again she found herself feeling guilty about the way her relationship with Ned was growing. If only she had told Kenneth she was seeing more of him. Well, it was her private life, she reminded herself. She wasn't mixing any business talk into their evenings. She had a right to see who she wanted.

"You do have your peculiarities, I must admit," she answered.

"Now, now. Don't run on with compliments. At least not during office hours. What if I pick you up around seven and you continue your train of thought then?"

"Sounds good to me."

"Dress for dinner and the theater. I'm feeling expansive today."

Dale hung up the phone.

Damn him anyway, she thought. From the way he had spoken, carefully choosing each phrase before he used it, she could tell he had something up his sleeve. She'd find out what it was soon enough. Tonight wouldn't be the night. His voice had told her that he would have his guard up. But soon, she told herself. Soon.

CHAPTER 24

Steven helped her down the front steps to the door, which was below street level. Katherine walked past the painted iron jockeys that stood, waiting at the entrance, to serve as hitching posts for carriages that would never appear again.

Sheldon Tannen met them at the door and ushered Steven to a table after a friendly welcome. Legally, "21" was a public restaurant, but for decades the Kriendlers and Berns and Tannens had run it like a private club. There were no written rules for what made you acceptable, but money, social position, and fame were a help and sometimes even those weren't enough if you arrived with too much liquor under your belt.

They were seated on a banquette on the left-hand side of the room downstairs. Their table was within easy eyeshot of the kitchen. Waiters hurried in and out of the swinging doors with covered plates that smelled of steak or bay scallops.

Steven signaled to their captain. The man was at their side in an instant. "A dry Bombay Martini for myself," he said. "A glass of Chardonnay for the lady. And a bottle of Pouilly-Fumé for the table in the corner."

"Very well, Mr. Fraizer," the captain replied, disappearing as quickly as he had surfaced.

Katherine looked over to the corner table. Two men were seated there, one tall and fair-haired, the other short and silvering. "Who are they?" she asked.

"They own a company called World Banknote," Steven replied. "They have just started a corporate collection, a large part of which came from our last prints and paintings sale. I'd like to see them back with us for Dale's sale next month."

"Maybe we should make it champagne," she said.

"Overkill," he answered. He pulled the bread basket over and reached for one, a paper-thin slice of brown bread that had been crisped with a coating of cheese. "You always have to know where to stop. Give too much, people get suspicious. Think they've given you too much profit and you're making it up to them. I've never seen a bottle of Pouilly-Fumé make anyone nervous. That's what I call a good wine."

Katherine smiled, then declined as he handed her the bread basket. She was too pleased at the chance to have lunch with him, and perhaps a good talk as well, to feel very hungry. He reached in and withdrew another slice of toast. "Dear Katherine," he said. He reached for his glass. Small beads of water slid down its side as he raised it and downed it in one gulp. He gave the captain one of those silent signals that are understood in every country around the world, and the man padded off to get him another.

He looked at her, hating himself for using her as a pawn in his chess game with Kenneth. But it seemed like the only possible way of getting through to his father. His wife and his father had gotten closer since the wedding, while he and his father had seemed to pull further and further away.

He reached for his glass and then for a menu. "I know this by heart," he said. "It's always the '21' burger for me. What about you? The sole?"

"Sounds fine," she told him. Her eyes caught his, flashing hopefully. "I'm glad we have this time alone," she told him. "It hasn't happened often enough since we got back."

He took her hand in his. "You're right," he told her. "There hasn't been enough time. The problems in the business . . ." He cut himself off suddenly, as if he didn't want to go on. "I realize it's caused some problems with us. I'd like to talk them through, to iron them out."

"What's happened at Fraizer's?" she asked, suddenly concerned. "Tell me," she insisted.

"No," Steven told her, trying to lighten the mood. "I want to keep you happy now. You can share the worries later. There'll be plenty of years for that.

261

Right now I want your mind filled with good thoughts."

"You make me feel useless," Katherine said. "I promised to share the good and the bad."

They sat in silence for a few more minutes, as the captain brought their lunches. He placed the burger, smelling richly of sirloin and nutmeg and Worcestershire, in front of Steven. Katherine tried to get him to talk again.

"I'm serious, Steven," she repeated. "You can't cut me off from the negative things in your life and expect that we'll understand each other. It just won't work."

He considered again, and then decided he had no choice. Sneaking a sidelong glance at her, he was caught for a moment by the absolute purity of line that could be traced from her cheek, softly, rounding, then flowing into her small chin. He had an urge to reach out and touch her, to run his finger over those gentle curves, an urge that was difficult to resist. He almost felt as if he were in love with her. He considered carefully before deciding to continue.

"I am going to tell you some things," he said, "that can't be repeated to anyone. Do you understand?" She shook her head yes. "Promise?"

"Promise? Steven, I'm your wife."

"I'm not quite accustomed to that yet, Katherine," he said, taking her hand in his. "Sometimes I forget that I have someone on my side now.

"Over the past year," he told her, "we've had several major forgeries turn up at Fraizer's. We've paid them all off, to the tune of millions in cash. Father told me about them and we reached a decision to handle them ourselves, to use our own resources, rather than alert the insurance companies and suffer the bad publicity that would bring on. What is worrying me now is the report on the expansion location Ivan sent back from London this week. I have to agree," he admitted, "the figures look good. Father is very intent on expanding into Europe. I can't seem to make him realize that our cash flow won't take the strain right now."

"Steven, I don't know what to say," Katherine said as he finished. "Now I understand why you've been so preoccupied. My anxieties seem so petty. You've been carrying so much—you and Kenneth."

He looked at her fondly. Despite his bad news a warm glow had flooded her face. "It's good to have you to confide in," he told her.

"I wish I could do more."

"Having you to talk to is enough," he assured her. They both sat quietly and sipped their drinks, thinking their separate thoughts.

"The truly frustrating part for me," he told her, "is that there's a simple solution. If only he weren't too stubborn to accept it." Katherine looked interested. It was all the encouragement he needed to go on. "We could take Fraizer's public. It would solve our immediate cash problems—make up the outflow that we have had to pay to buy back the forged pieces. Better than that, it would give my father the funds for this European expansion that seems to be such a mania with him."

"It sounds like a wonderful idea. Have you checked it out with anyone? Anyone in the financial community, I mean?"

"I've been discussing it with Herb Phillips for six months now. In fact," he admitted, "it was his idea initially. I sort of stood back for a month or two while he tried to persuade me."

"He really thinks it can be done?"

"From the general information I've given him about Fraizer's, he thinks he could produce an underwriter if Dad would give the okay."

"Have you discussed it with Kenneth?"

"I'm not sure I'd call it a discussion," he replied. "I suggested. He lectured."

"Lectured? I don't understand, Steven."

"Well," Steven told her as he signaled for another martini, "he started with the family loyalty lecture. 'Three generations of Fraizers have worked to build this business,'" he intoned, mimicking his father in one of his more serious moods, "'your father, and your grandfather before him, and now you.'" Steven's voice had become deliberately droning, as monotone as a recording that had been repeated and repeated until it no longer made any impression on the listener. "'We were forced to leave our country in shame. It's a blot on our name that we're still working to cleanse. Going public is fine for families that are sure of themselves and their roots. As to the Fraizers, we have to restore our name before we can afford to give it away.' Frankly, Katherine," he said, resuming his own voice, "I think his respect for tradition has given him a blind spot when it comes to the idea of a public offering."

"And you want me to talk to him?" she suggested, suddenly realizing where the conversation had led.

"I need your help, Kath. I need you to talk to him, to make him see the light. There isn't enough cash to expand to London, not without a public offering. It's a dream he'll have to postpone if we don't raise some cash."

"I don't know, Steven."

"He'll listen to you, Katherine," Steven insisted. "There's no one he's closer to than you. Tell him we don't want our child robbed of its future," he said, gripping her hand tighter.

Katherine felt deflated, though the resentment that was creeping into her thoughts might not be justified. She was Steven's wife, and he had every right to ask her to help in something like this, something he believed in. He looked at her for what seemed like endless minutes. His face was kind. He was obviously trying to anticipate her answer. She was grateful for the semi-darkness of the room.

How could she possibly try to change Kenneth's mind about something he held so dear, a belief in family and tradition that had guided him for so many years? She didn't know how to answer Steven, she just knew that she couldn't try to change Kenneth's mind about something that was so important to him. It was the very essence of all that he believed in.

"I don't think Kenneth will change his mind about his personal values for me or anyone else," she said softly. "I think the only answer for all of us is to solve the mystery of those forgeries, and to do it soon."

CHAPTER 25

Herb Phillips stood at the windows of the Phillips Building, which fronted on Fifth Avenue. He took another sip from the coffee mug in his hand. He was in the building, without exception, by five-thirty in the morning. By the time most of his executives made it to the office, he had accomplished the greater part of a day's work and was ready for his nine A.M. workout.

He enjoyed the view, especially after the dark hours of dawn had passed into the bustle of the waking city. He never felt the time he spent watching the crowds was wasted. He prided himself on his ability to identify with the mind of the average Joe who might buy a hundred shares of a new issue, as well as with the wholesale traders who had snapped them up by the thousands.

The morning promised to be an interesting one; the call he had been expecting from Steven Fraizer had finally come. Figures were ready—financials on the House of Fraizer. His friend hadn't promised anything definite, but his words had hinted that anything was possible.

Herb felt the tingle of nervous excitement that signaled the start of every new project for him. The idea of taking an auction house public was an interesting one. There was no doubt about the glamour and romance, the entire mystique that surrounded those houses in the minds of the public. He put down his mug and started toward the club on Central Park South.

A black Cadillac sedan pulled to a stop in front of the New York Athletic Club. The chauffeur was out within seconds, holding open the back door. Steven emerged quickly. His dark blue suit fitted his body as neatly as a kid glove slipped over pliant fingers. His shirt was a patterned white-on-white jacquard, on which a striped red tie rested in colorful contrast. His shoes were polished to a high gloss that reflected everything around them, but his facial expression was blank, sending nothing back to the people who looked into it. Only his jaw, set and rigid, gave a clue to his state of mind.

His gloved hand carried a briefcase that had been crafted in the Paris workrooms of Hermès. He gripped it firmly. In it he carried a folder in which the financial situation of Fraizer's was summarized. The contents had been carefully prepared. He counted on them to resolve a number of his problems. The only thing he had failed to include was any mention of the forgeries and their negative impact on Fraizer's cash flow.

He walked quickly through the paneled lobby and got into the elevator that would take him to the athletic facilities. He was changed within minutes. Hanging his clothes, then carefully placing his briefcase in his locker, he went looking for Herb, who as usual had beaten him in.

He could hear him grunting as he lifted, each rep eliciting a louder whoosh of air as it was finished than the one that had come before. He saw him reflected in the ceiling-high mirrors before he rounded the corner and could be seen himself. Herb was a large-boned man who would quickly run to fat if he let his body have its way. He dedicated himself to the struggle against it with the same determination he brought to business. Every day he pushed himself harder, reveling in the burning, aching pain. Steven stopped and studied him in the mirror while he took a few seconds to compose himself. This meeting with Phillips was an important one. They were contemporaries, classmates at Choate who had played basketball together, crammed for exams together, and gotten drunk together. They had stayed close, even when they reached the age where they found themselves sudden rivals for the same girl. They had a lot in common, two sons of respected fathers who had taken small companies and turned them into larger ones. There had been no doubt in either of their minds that the two of them would make those companies larger still. Herb had. Steven couldn't deny that, not even to himself, though it made him more acutely aware of his own slow start. He took a deep breath and walked into the weight room.

Herb looked up from the bench press. Sweat beaded on his forehead and ran down his face. "How'd the honeymoon go?" he panted.

"It went," Steven replied. He walked to the pulleys that were nearest to Herb's bench and pushed the pin into the blocks of iron at forty pounds. It hit with a small clang that rang out clearly. The room was empty, aside from themselves. He picked up the leather grips. He began to pull, slowly moving his arms back and forth, letting the weights settle and click at the end of each motion.

"Don't let them drop like that," Herb advised him, as much a perfectionist in his workouts as he was in his business. Steven pretended not to hear him, but it grated on him. The rivalry that neither of them would admit to was constantly slipping out in one-upmanship that more often than not bested Steven. "Heard that Allen & Company may be doing the new I.C.G. underwriting," he said casually. "Thought you were close to those guys in Detroit."

Herb lifted, then settled his weights once again. "And I heard that Ned Whytson is telling everyone that you'll fuck anything that walks if it can get you a piece of the business." He carefully placed the weights on the bench in front of his bent knees and stood up.

"Only if it's walking on two good-looking legs," Steven corrected him. "And when I show you the figures I brought with me this morning, you will see just how much business I'm good for and thank me for it." His arms were beginning to glisten moistly. He continued to pull.

"What's the bottom line?" Herb asked. He'd have hours to look over the figures later. He wanted to have some rough idea of what they were talking about before he began any discussions with Steven.

Steven dropped the pulleys. The weights fell back with a loud clash. He moved to the bench that Herb had just left. "Roughly two hundred million dollars in revenues and twenty percent pretax profits," he told him. He picked up the weight that Herb had put down, tested it, then removed ten pounds from each end and lay down on his back. "Of course, that's confidential. Only our accountants have seen those figures. I haven't discussed this idea with anyone but my father." His voice sounded unusually reserved. His sentences had become clipped.

"Steven, I'm not a fool," Herb said impatiently. "If those figures are accurate, and if everything else holds up, you shouldn't have a problem in the world taking Fraizer's public."

Steven stopped straining at his presses, sat up and pushed his hair away from his face. Herb could tell that he was excited. He'd had a habit, since the time when they were young, of running his hands through his hair whenever the anxiety of wanting something really badly overcame him. It seemed to be the only way he could hold on to himself once the fever caught him. He wasn't conscious of it, and he didn't do it often, but, when he did, Herb read him like a book.

"Come to the steam room with me. You're not doing shit with those weights anyway." He tossed Steven a towel and led the way back to the locker room. "Fraizer's has always been a family-held business," he said mildly. "Why would Kenneth want to go public now?" He spoke slowly in an attempt to relax Steven. He knew from past experience that nervous people never really listened and he didn't want to waste his time.

Steven answered quickly. "He's wanted to take the house international for a long time," he told Herb. "Europe and Asia. London was to have been the first branch.

"Frankly, I never thought it would happen," he went on. "He's talked about it for so many years it stopped seeming imminent. That changed as of last week. He's found some property on New Bond Street and come up with projections that look pretty favorable." He hesitated for a moment, then went on. "Frankly," he confided, "I'm not entirely in favor of it. I'm not sure I want to stake my entire inheritance on this. It's a big financial spread, but I can see that it's a reality. The next best thing is to spread the risk."

"Taking it public will do that for you," Herb confirmed. "It's a pretty typical move for a company that wants some capital for diversification or expansion."

"That's what we figured," Steven said. His tone was beginning to even out. He had stripped off his warmup suit and thrown it into the gym bag in his locker. He wrapped a towel around his waist and, holding it with one hand, set off for the steam room at Herb's side.

"If it's your estate you're concerned with," Herb pointed out, "you've got to remember that once the stock is publicly traded it's probably going to up your taxes."

"That's one of those good news-bad news stories I'll be happy to deal with when the time comes," Steven laughed. "Give me an idea of what will need to be done to get this accomplished."

Herb opened the door to the steam room and set the timer. He climbed up to the top step and slowly spread his towel out over the hot tiles. "Look, Steven," he said, "none of this is going to be a problem. Just relax."

"I am relaxed," he said, running his hands through his hair. His features looked soft, almost blurry, in the moist air. "Let's hear some facts about this."

"All right," said Herb. "In order to do a fully registered offering with the S.E.C., you'll need audited statements for the past five years."

"No problem," said Steven, ticking it off on his mental list of things to be done. "Price Waterhouse has been doing our statements for years. They're very thorough." Even as he said it he was beginning to think about how he might conceal the outflow of funds that had paid for the forgeries.

"Then there's a due diligence review," Herb went on. "The underwriter will be conducting a full-scale investigation including all aspects of your business dealings plus a check on the principals of your company. That will probably mean you and Kenneth, maybe a few others. You'll have to be prepared to disclose everything that could be material to an investor's investment decision, which essentially means everything about the company and yourselves. You and Kenneth may think of it as personal business; the S.E.C. won't. Going public is just that—going public. The company and its operations will be under the scrutiny of the underwriters and their counsel."

Steven felt faint for a moment. He couldn't seem to pull in enough oxygen to fuel his brain. He didn't know whether it was the hot air that was searing his lungs, making every tiny capillary strain, or simply fear. The forgeries could mean the end to this. Luckily there wasn't another living soul who knew about them other than Kenneth. Damn it! He remembered he'd told Katherine about them. He'd just have to contend with her if the situation presented itself. The only important thing was never to reveal they had taken place. Whether the company remained in family hands or went public, that was just the kind of publicity they couldn't afford. Beads of perspiration covered his face. He reached for a corner of the towel that was hanging around his neck and wiped it, then spoke, trying to control his voice. "The Fraizer name is respected. So is the company. I don't think we'll find anything the S.E.C. would be concerned about. This should certainly put Whytson in his place," he said, changing the subject, then warming to the idea.

"Perhaps," said Herb, "but it carries disadvantages with it too. I wouldn't be your friend if I didn't point them out to you. You'll have shareholders and directors looking over your shoulder, checking on salaries and perks and transactions between the company and management. They'll scream bloody murder if sales go down. Nothing is sacred any more. It becomes a time-consuming process that you'll have to live with forever."

Steven shrugged. "So we'll live with it. How much do you think we can raise?"

"We'll sell shares for a multiple of earnings. A company like yours . . ." He thought for a moment. "Maybe ten times earnings. I'll have a better idea of how the stock will price out when I've had a chance to review the financials. There are other factors that might influence it."

"Give me a time frame, Herb. How long is this going to take?"

"You have to know all of this today, buddy?" Herb looked at the clock that hung just outside the door to the steam room. The black numerals were ghosted into shadows by the mist that clung to the inside of the door. "My secretary will think I've died if I don't get back soon."

"Just give me a quick idea of the timing," Steven asked. "Then I'll send you back into the world."

"At best we've got three or four months of work ahead of us. And that's optimistic," Herb said. He climbed down from the steps and walked to the door. He opened it and then held it for Steven. "You're looking a little pale. Are you feeling all right?"

"I'm fine," Steven told him. "But maybe you were right. This was a lot for one morning. I feel like my head's been put through a sieve."

They stood side by side as they dressed, barely exchanging a word. Steven finished first, and excused himself, nervously running his hands through his hair once more. Still, as he left the room, Herb noticed that he walked with more dignity than usual. His head was held high, his steps sure.

Amazing what the thought of power can do for a man, Herb reflected as he knotted his shoelaces. He looked at the bench where Steven had been sitting. The fact that he'd never discussed this meeting with Kenneth was obvious to Herb.

It was probable that Kenneth would still hold the controlling shares of Fraizer's if the company went public, but in the course of restructuring the business, Steven's position couldn't help but be solidified. Herb had known for years that his friend would rather be admired by his father than accountable to him, and this might just accomplish it. He had ambition, that was obvious. But did he have the fortitude to carry it out? Kenneth Fraizer wasn't a man who would be talked into something he didn't want. At any rate, he thought as he pulled on his jacket, we share the same goal. He wants to take the company public. I want to execute the deal. At worst it should be an interesting scenario to watch as it plays itself out.

CHAPTER 26

"So they're going to ring me, are they?" Bill Donovan leaned back in his chair and stretched his legs out. He gradually started to smile, and his small, even teeth clamped down on the Monte Cristo that hung from his lips. He looked around Kenneth's library, studying each painting, each vase and ashtray, at length as if he had nothing better to think of, then looked back to the two men who were sitting across from him. "This may just be the most entertaining thing that's happened to this boy in an age." He continued to puff away for another minute as he waited for the surprise to subside from their faces, then he casually dropped a large ash into the cloisonné dish at his side.

"I don't think you understand, Mr. Donovan," Steven spoke up. "What my father is trying to tell you is that you stand to lose a substantial amount of money if you auction your paintings now."

"Do I look like a halfwit, son?" Donovan asked. His voice had begun to take on the smooth Texas drawl that always surfaced when he was doing his wiliest thinking. "One thing I am a bona fide expert at, I assure you, is anticipating the ways a man can lose money and sidestepping them as fast as I'd give the slip to a rattler."

Kenneth leaned forward, making the space between himself and Donovan more intimate. "One thing I'd like to make totally clear is that as far as Fraizer's is concerned, you can withdraw your paintings from the sale with no penalty. We're not in the habit of fostering unethical business practices, either directly or indirectly."

"I wouldn't withdraw the paintings now if you paid me to," Donovan chuckled. He leaned back and took another long draw of his cigar. His face was wreathed in a grin. "That would just spoil my fun. What I'd much rather do," he said, sitting up now and speaking in an alert and definite tone, "is give them enough rein to see if we can fool them into running with it. And when they do," he said, winking at Kenneth, "we'll just steer them into our corral."

"Not having been in Texas myself," Kenneth said, looking somewhat bewildered, "I'll just have to take your word that will work."

"Has in the past," Donovan said, looking abstracted.

"Mr. Donovan," Steven asked him. He too was looking confused, if a bit relieved. "Are there any precautions you would like us to take? I'm not sure what we can do, but if there is anything you can think of, let us know."

"Only one thing you can do," Donovan said, starting to rise. "Start loading up on smelling salts down at your place." He took a last swallow of the port that was on the table at his side as he stood there. "In case any of these boys have faint hearts. I'll be going now," he said, reaching for his coat. He looked directly at Kenneth. His voice was serious, his accent totally gone. "And I do thank you for telling me. I know you didn't have to."

Kenneth and Steven stayed where they were when he left. Each of them sipped his drink wordlessly. "Well," Kenneth said at last, "I'm not sure what he has up his sleeve, but I'm glad I'm not on the side of the opposition."

"You don't get to be president of a conglomerate like his without being a fighter," said Steven. They lapsed into silence again, each caught up in his own thoughts. "Is that part of the reason you want to branch out?" he asked his father after a moment or two. "That sense of winning? Of having been a better man?"

Kenneth cradled his glass in cupped hands as he considered his answer. "It's much more than that, Steven. I've tried to find a way to explain that to you for so long. To Ivan, too, though I think from the sound of our last conversation that I may just be beginning to get through to him."

A hot flush colored Steven's face. There always seemed to be an implied criticism of himself in his father's approval of Ivan. He resented every word of praise that was spoken about him, and always had. He started to reply, then heard the sound of Katherine coming down the stairs. Her steps sounded heavy, measured. She had been tired lately, glad of any excuse to lie down. He felt more constrained than ever from discussing things with her. He even found it hard to talk to her about the baby anymore, his guilt at having placed her in this situation had become so great.

She cautiously opened the paneled door, looking in before she entered to make sure that they weren't still discussing something sensitive with Donovan. Then she came into the room, her smile taking them both in. They got to their feet, emerging from the identical chairs that flanked the fireplace. Kenneth busied himself arranging the couch for her, while Steven rang for the butler. They both missed the moment when it happened.

As she walked into the library her stomach went into a spasm that stopped her short for a second as it knocked the breath out of her. Though she wasn't aware of it, the color drained from her cheeks. As quickly as it had come, the pain passed. She decided not to say anything. She didn't want to spoil their evening. It was so rare that it was just the three of them together quietly doing nothing.

The warmth of the flames that leaped in the grate felt friendly and kind as she settled herself on the couch. She leaned back, catching her breath as unobtrusively as possible. "Are you comfortable there, dear? Do you want a pillow against your back?" The concerned voice was Kenneth's. He leaned over her, offering a round needlepoint cushion.

"Thank you, Kenneth," she said gratefully as he slipped a cushiony pillow against the small of her back.

"I remember Anna carrying her favorite little back pillow with her wherever she went when she was pregnant with Steven. It seemed to help her quite a bit." He smiled affectionately at Katherine, and then turned back to his son.

"I'm sorry, Steven. Where were we?"

"We were talking about the expansion," he replied. He spoke calmly. He'd decided to pass over the hurt he was feeling and go on as if nothing had happened. "I was going to tell you I've given the expansion a lot of thought. I'm willing to go along with you now. I think we should do it."

"What caused this?" Kenneth asked curiously. "I thought your opposition to it was set in concrete."

"The figures that Ivan sent back were better than I anticipated. We might not find a location as good as this one again. And I'm beginning to understand a little better," he added quietly, "the reasons why you want Fraizer's to be recognized and remembered, now that we have another generation about to join us."

Kenneth didn't answer. His eyes were focused on the flames before him. The only sound was the crackling of the wood as it caught, then burned. He cupped his glass in his hand as the amber liquid warmed by the fire. The emotions that were welling up in him were almost too great to contain. He felt as if a fond but futile wish were being fulfilled. He knew from their last conversation that Ivan had begun to understand the importance of creating something and leaving it in the care of future generations. It was a natural course of events, though not one that seemed to come naturally to Steven.

"But I worry," said Steven. "Maybe that's part of being a father, too. I flinch every time I think of going out on a limb with our finances the way they are right now. It's not fair to Katherine," he said, indicating his wife who lay on the sofa beside them, "or to the baby."

Katherine was silent. She knew immediately where Steven was headed. She had thought about their luncheon conversation for hours, and had finally realized she couldn't, or wouldn't, help Steven try to change his father's feelings. The realization that Kenneth's desires and dreams were that important to her was frightening.

"I know," said Kenneth. His voice sounded choked. "I just try to have faith that everything will work out if I do what I know is right."

"Dad," said Steven. He looked eager now, his eyes bright and focused. "That's just not good enough for me. There's too much resting on my shoulders. I have had some talks with Herb Phillips. He thinks we would have no trouble taking Fraizer's public. He could put together an underwriting that would net us a lot of cash," he said eagerly. "And still let us keep controlling interest in the house."

Kenneth reached to the table by his side, picked up his glass, and brought it to his lips. He couldn't still the trembling in his hand that made the liquid shimmy inside the glass walls that contained it. He felt sad, spent in every cell of his body. Fraizer's had always been a family business. If he had his way, it would be run by Steven some day and hopefully his son's son. He thought of Steven selling the business and felt as if the Cossacks were pulling at his guts. He couldn't face the idea of going public with the company unless it was the last resort. He turned to look at Katherine and found his gaze was being returned. Intuitively he knew that she would understand what he was about to tell Steven. If only he could frame it in a way that wouldn't seem like a personal slight to his son. It was the long term, the future of Fraizer's and of the family, that they had to think about. He hoped against hope that Steven would some day realize that.

"You have such promise, Steven," he said kindly, "and you're so quick to throw it away. I won't agree to going public now." He looked at his son's face, and saw the cloud of pain that was settling on it. "Once you give up control of your business it's just a matter of time before they'll find a way to take it all away from you. You'll have no business and you'll have no work. All you'll have is an engraved certificate you can trade for cash."

"Theoretically that's fine, Father," Steven said. His voice was strained and angry. "But it doesn't solve the problem of all the cash that's been lost. Not to mention the cash we don't have for new offices. Especially if another forgery shows up and we have another hemorrhage of cash out the back door."

"God willing we won't have any more forgeries," Kenneth answered. "God willing we'll be able to keep our heads above water until after this New York painting sale and the annual fall sale in London. Steven, I have no doubt that we could go public, but it's not something I'm anxious to do. It's to be used only if all else fails, and I don't think that will happen."

"Well," said Steven. He sounded resigned. "We'll know soon enough, won't we. The fall painting sale is in three weeks. If we don't make at least three million on that, the decision is out of our hands."

"If we don't make three million on the New York sale," Kenneth agreed, trying to placate him, "I'll start talking seriously with Phillips about your idea. If the London sale is bad, too, we may, unfortunately, have to move forward with it."

Steven resumed sipping his drink. He'd lied to Herb Phillips about the extent of power he wielded at his father's company, but he felt as if his title in life was "son of." Son of Kenneth Fraizer. Son of the man who owns Fraizer's. He wanted so much to be president of a public company, even if his father did retain the title of chairman of the board. He finished his drink and excused himself, leaving Katherine and Kenneth alone in the library.

Katherine lifted herself on one elbow. "I'm sorry, Kenneth," she said.

He raised his head and looked up at his daughter-in-law. She had matured so much in the few short months that she had been married. She had grasped the focal point of his short but heated discussion with his son. At all costs, Fraizer's had to remain a single unit. It couldn't be sold off to an uncaring public interested only in making money. Fraizer's was more important than that. "Lie back," he said. "You look tired." He smiled fondly as he groped for memories of his years with Anna. "I remember when we were planning Steven's room. She wanted to surprise me—to find a special crib for him. She was looking for an antique."

Katherine's eyes traveled to the small picture frame where the soft face of Steven's mother gazed out at her. As always the mention of Anna's name triggered thoughts of the two of them, Kenneth and Anna, together. She looked at him and wondered what he had been like as a husband, a lover. Had he been as tender, as gentle and giving as he was now? Or did he have the selfishness of youth, the demanding side that Steven was showing now? She thought she knew the answer. People don't really change. They're the sum of their past experiences. The foundations of their personalities are laid early. They may continue to build upon them, strengthening what's already there. But they rarely tear them down and start over.

"You do understand, don't you?" he said.

"Yes," came the reply, so soft he barely heard it. "Tell me, Kenneth, what do you think of naming the baby Anna if it's a girl?"

"You don't have to do that," he told her. His eyes were glistening, on the verge of tears.

"But I want to," she said.

"And Steven?" he asked.

She was surprised to realize that she'd never discussed it with Steven. It was like so many things between them, put off until later. She tried hard to bury that, to keep it from depressing her day to day. But now she had to struggle with it since it had been thrown up to her. "He hasn't made up his mind yet," she started to say, but the pain seized her again. She put her hands across her stomach, as if to protect the baby. Kenneth was at her side immediately.

"Come," he said, placing a supporting arm behind her. "Lie down. Stretch your feet out." He helped her to adjust herself. "You should stay off your feet more, Katherine," he said. The concern in his voice was obvious. "I'll see to it that your breakfast is brought up to you in the morning so you can stay in bed a little longer."

"Did you treat Anna this delicately too?" she asked him.

"Oh, yes," he said, smiling. "I was forever trying to get her into this position."

They both laughed. It seemed to clear the air. She stretched out languorously, finally relaxing. A faint smile still lingered on her lips as she looked up at him.

Their gaze locked and held for a moment, both savoring the total peacefulness that they seemed to bring to one another. He reached out and softly stroked her hair. If she used her imagination it would be easy to pretend he was her husband. Her heart skipped a beat at the thought. It seemed suddenly peaceful to her. Enveloping. Kind. She found herself longing for it. But perhaps that was just the pregnancy. Maybe she needed that warm nest to curl up in for the moment.

She stirred, suddenly troubled by the fantasy that seemed to have taken over her mind, and sat bolt upright. He reached out to her, imagining that the pain had come on her again, and instinctively reached out to hold and comfort her. They stayed that way for a few minutes, not a word passing between them. Suddenly she moved away. Their eyes locked for a moment, then looked away, embarrassed. It was as though time were standing still. Finally Kenneth broke the silence. "You had best go upstairs, Katherine," he said quietly. "You need your rest."

CHAPTER 27

Dale stood in the wings, to the left of the backstage area. Now and then a worker hurried in carrying a painting, carefully counted his way through the lineup of art that had been arranged numerically to follow the catalogue designations, placed it, then raced away.

She was nearly bursting. Each time a well-wisher came by, a department head or assistant congratulating her on the job she'd done putting it all together, she felt a little more ferment, a little bit more anxiety about her debut.

She clutched the catalogue like a lifesaver in the choppy seas of her emotions. It was thin, only a third the size of the listing for the major auction that would follow hers. Its cover was buff, as plain as a simple slab of limestone. The block printing at the bottom of the page read simply Fraizer's, with the date underneath. A photograph of the Sam Francis painting was centered on the page, giving it a feeling of substance and strength.

She flipped through the slick white pages. She'd been through the book so often she had it as good as memorized. They were all there. Sam Francis. David Hockney. Ed Ruscha. DeWain Valentine. Even Tony Lamm, one of her own California discoveries. It had taken a lot of work, but she'd finally gathered enough pieces from the West Coast to justify calling it Fraizer's first California Contemporary sale.

She'd grown to love each one of them during the time they'd spent in her care. She reached a Diebenkorn, one of the stellar attractions of the sale. It was from Ronald Bruner's collection. She was sure Katherine had convinced him to put it up for sale because of her. It was one more thing that she owed the Bruners. One more on a long list.

Dale turned and saw that Steven had been watching her.

"Excited?" he asked. He moved to the line of paintings that were ranged behind the stage curtain like soldiers waiting for inspection.

"Petrified," she answered. She watched him as he inspected the paintings one at a time. He looked as if he were assigning a value to each one as he went, and for some reason that made her nervous.

"I put the total sales at somewhere between three-quarters and a million," he announced. "At least fifteen of the paintings you brought in should top thirty thousand, and just between you and me," he confided, "my father is prepared to give you a bonus once you top the five-hundred-thousand-dollar mark. In short, you're in the money."

It was what she'd worked for these months, agonizing over pieces that were promised and lost, adding up order bids as each day's mail came in.

She looked happy as she returned to the side of the stage and looked out into the room. It was four-thirty. People were wandering in in twos and threes. The salesroom was beginning to fill. An hour ago she had felt like someone who was giving a party to which no one would come. The feeling was slipping away from her with each new prospective bidder that sat down.

They were young, she realized, much younger than the clientele that normally frequented Fraizer's art sales. Kenneth should be pleased; they'd managed to tap into a new market. She looked out over the sea of faces, searching for any recognizable friend, and spotted Katherine standing near the front of the room. Katherine had been watching her count the house, and was now smiling at her in a knowing way. She looked tired. Still it was like her to show up to offer moral support. As she watched her crossing toward the stage, Dale realized that her destiny, then and now, had been set the first day they met.

"It's your day," said Katherine. She reached up over the edge of the stage and clasped Dale's hand in her own. "I talked to Kenneth a few minutes ago and he said there were quite a few people on the phones waiting to bid. Not to mention this," she said, sweeping the crowd with her hand. "You're going to do really well," she encouraged Dale, "I just know it."

"Come on up here with me and watch from the side," Dale invited her. "I want to be able to see their expressions as they bid."

Katherine slowly and carefully climbed the steps to the stage. Miriam joined her, aware that the buzzing that was now filling the room meant the sale was about to begin. They stood on either side of Dale, who was clenching her hands with an anxious gesture.

"Where's Kenneth?" she asked, suddenly worried that her mentor would miss the sale. Then her eyes opened wide as he walked to the podium.

"He wanted you to have every advantage," Katherine said. She put her arm around Dale and gave her a big hug. "You know no one can auction as well as he does."

"Well, I'll be damned," Miriam said. She took a long, careful look at Dale. "He certainly never held the hammer at my first sale."

Dale felt the barb and began to apologize. Then she stopped. She wasn't going to let anything spoil the next hour for her. The crowd grew still as the tote board that hung over the stage flashed on to record the bidding in four different currencies. She took Katherine's hand, and grasped it so tight her knuckles stood out as white knobs against the tan of her skin.

Two of Fletcher Benton's works went, then a Ruscha. As Kenneth started on a Billy Al Bengston, she saw the magic he was able to create. He started the bidding at fifteen hundred, and quickly worked it up to four thousand by playing off a woman in the third row and a man who was seated behind her. Dale was sure it was going to be sold at four thousand, and it appeared that the bidders agreed; they were silent and still. Then she saw Kenneth look directly at the woman in the third row. It was the kind of look that said, "Lady, you're making a big mistake if you don't go up," and within the space of a second her hand shot up and he called forty-two hundred. "I have forty-two hundred," he called again. "Do I hear forty-four hundred? Once, twice," and the hammer went down at her price as one of the runners went over to her to record her number and name.

One by one the gouaches by Sam Francis, the sculpture by Robert Graham, and the pastels by Diebenkorn were brought on stage and sold. One of her favorites, a pencil sketch of the Cairo Museum by David Hockney, came up next. She remembered how thrilled she had been when she received an order bid on it for $25,700 from a doctor in Palm Beach. He'd attached a handwritten note instructing that every cent of the bid be used without any further consideration; he was determined to have it for his collection. She was certain he'd get it. Miriam had set a high estimate of twenty thousand for it.

Kenneth opened the bidding at five thousand, and then quickly took it to ten. In a matter of seconds it rose another six thousand. Seventeen came from the back of the room. Quickly it shot up to eighteen. Bids from the phones took it to nineteen, then bids from the floor took it to twenty thousand. Kenneth had an order bid of twenty-two at the podium. "Do I have twenty-four thousand? Do I have twenty-four thousand? I have twenty-two," he said finally. "Going once, twice, at twenty-two." The hammer went down.

Dale was pleased. The order bid from Palm Beach had obviously been successful, and her doctor had managed to pick up the drawing that he was so set on without going the full extent of the $25,700 he'd committed.

The next series of pieces was gone in what seemed like five minutes. The Fletcher Benton sculpture. A Chuck Arnoldi piece constructed of three branches. An Ed Moses and a DeWain Valentine. She looked at her watch. It seemed impossible that an hour had elapsed since the sale began, but the evidence at her wrist was definite.

"Dale, I do think you should be proud of yourself." Miriam's voice sounded sincere.

"I don't know," Dale demurred. "None of the heavy hitters showed up—the big dealers."

"That will take time," Miriam told her. "You hit your figures. That's enough to expect from your first sale."

Dale looked around the room. The podium was deserted; Kenneth had left it as unobtrusively as he'd appeared. Art Department assistants sat at a table in the front of the room, making arrangements for payment and shipping with the purchasers of the art. Steven stood at the bank of phones to the side of the stage where phone and order bids were handled. He was deep in conversation on one of the phones. He looked upset. She saw him turn his head, and when he found her eyes he hung up and walked over to her at a brisk pace. Concern was written on his face. He took her elbow and tactfully steered her away from Miriam and Katherine. "Take a walk with me for a minute," he said in a hushed voice. His words weren't audible to the other women. He reached the front row of chairs and motioned for her to take a seat next to him, then, leaning over and speaking in a near whisper, he began to quiz her.

"Have you ever heard of a Dr. Melvin Olsham from Palm Beach?" he asked.

"Sure," she answered. "He's the one who sent in the order bid on the Hockney. Kenneth sold it on his bid from the podium."

"His order bid wasn't at the podium, Dale," he told her. "Apparently it wasn't entered in the list of written bids."

"That's impossible," she protested. "I time-stamped it myself when it came in. Oh my God," she said. Her hands flew up to her face. "What if I left it in my desk drawer after I stamped it."

"You can't expect to get an order bid executed from your desk drawer," he replied, stating the obvious. "It wouldn't matter if the bidding had gone beyond his bid, but as it turned out, by rights he should have gotten the drawing. To make matters worse, he's already called to find out what the closing bid was."

"Oh," she said, barely able to contain the tears that were welling up behind her eyes, "he must be furious."

"I promised him I'd call him back after I looked into it. Frankly, I don't know what to tell the man."

"Maybe we should ask Kenneth to handle it," she suggested. She felt totally depressed. It was the kind of mistake that was impossible to correct. There was only one Hockney drawing, and there was no way to re-auction it. "The doctor might feel more satisfied hearing it from the owner of the house."

"It's been my experience that there are certain types of mistakes that my father has a hard time forgiving."

"Oh, Steven," she said hopelessly, "it was so stupid of me." She turned away so he wouldn't be able to see the struggle she was having to control herself.

"Hey," he said, handing her a handkerchief, sure that a flood of tears was on the way, "you've had a lot to absorb. Three months ago you'd never worked in an auction house. And now you've already put on your own sale. It's a miracle," he concluded, "that you didn't have more screwups."

"Are you sure Kenneth shouldn't be told?" she asked him.

"I'll take care of it," he said. He placed his hands on her shoulders in his most reassuring fashion. "It's a lesson you'll never forget. As far as I'm concerned, that's what counts."

"Just what I intended to do." The voice came from over her shoulder. Dale turned around, and found herself looking into Kenneth's eyes. He placed his hands where Steven's had been a moment before and gave her shoulders a proud squeeze. He looked happy, even proud. She felt dishonest looking at his open joy. "Congratulations. You've had a real success," he told her. "Something you and Fraizer's can feel fine about." Dale tried to answer, and found herself mumbling confused sentences. He mistook her stammer for modesty, and kindly changed the subject. "Come on," he told her, reaching for her hand. "The real wolves will be arriving for the main auction within the hour. We need an experienced hand to help us get ready."

CHAPTER 28

The night had turned crisp and clear. A handful of stars blazed like lighted pinpricks in the sky. The temperature that had been in the fifties during the day had dropped to forty by seven, bringing out sables and mink along with the throngs of chauffeured cars that pulled up in front of the House of Fraizer. Women in wonderfully tailored Adolfos emerged, flashing brilliant smiles for the score of photographers that milled in at the entrance. Some held copies of the catalogue that read *Important Paintings;* these were important people, too, each one concerned with getting a proper seat for the sale, each one carrying an ego as big as his bankroll.

It would be a full house. They'd known that for days now. Miriam lingered near the front door, greeting key collectors and dealers as they came in and then turning them over to Dale, who escorted them to their seats.

She felt ragged. The effects of her order-bid blunder still weighed on her. Not telling Kenneth about it had left her uncomfortable. She continued to turn it over in her mind as she settled people in the salesroom. There was a huge crowd, and they were all beginning to look identical to her. She knew she should be more alert, but she couldn't seem to get her spirits up again.

As she walked back from the salesroom to the large foyer she spotted a woman who succeeded in catching her attention. She was tall and slender, and had apparently arrived alone. Her face wasn't familiar from the society columns, nor was she a recognizable part of the international art scene, yet she was an impressive figure. She wore pure white, a draping dress of jersey that clung to her figure and flowed in a capelike effect down her back. There was a wonderfully contrived turban on her head, below which two huge brown eyes and a mouth, boldly painted as a cheap neon sign, flashed out. A woman that showy was memorable and Dale didn't remember her, though a sense that she was familiar continued to nag at the back of her mind.

The woman crossed the lobby, and commenced a struggle with the girls who were seated at the door to the salesroom to screen and register bidders and spectators. Her attempt to secure a seat proved futile. She cast her big eyes up at the ceiling, then she swept the room with a glance that searched for any other possible way to get in. Her eyes caught Dale's as they reached the door, and showed a momentary flicker of recognition that immediately faded. She continued to hold her glance, her expression a silent appeal. Dale walked over to her. "May I be of some assistance to you?" she asked.

"It appears I have arrived too late to secure a seat," the woman replied. Her expression was coy, the sort of flirtatious entreaty that usually works better on men than on other women. Still, Dale had the feeling that she was a buyer, not a spectator. She made a snap decision to give her one of the half-dozen seats that had been held back for the use of the house. "Follow me," she said. "I think I can take care of you." The girls at the desk looked up, trying to decide whether she was exceeding the bounds of her authority. Dale decided to move quickly, before they could protest.

She passed across the foyer and into the packed salesroom with the woman at her side. She could feel the eyes of the other spectators follow them down the aisle. An awareness of the woman's presence spread quickly and evenly through the room. The woman's eyes stayed straight ahead, never wavering to either side. She seemed accustomed to the attention she received. "Thank you," she said as Dale seated her in the front row. Her accent seemed Latin—Portuguese, perhaps, though not quite distinct enough to be definitely recognizable. As she looked into the woman's face Dale had another strong feeling of déjà vu, but she still couldn't recall where they'd met.

She walked back up the aisle and stationed herself at the back of the gallery. Miriam moved quietly to her side, where she proceeded to check on the pivotal dealers and collectors who had arrived.

"There's Jarvis McLeash," she told Dale. She pointed to a man in the third row. His constant companion, an effete young man in his twenties, was seated beside him.

"From London," Dale said, ticking him off on the list of calls she had made for Miriam earlier that month. "Where are Rodney Trump and Syd Adler?" she asked. Miriam pointed to the two pacesetters of the New York art scene. They were seated cheek by jowl in row eight, their friendly, but definite, rivalry apparent in the courteous way they were treating each other.

They spotted Charles Groder from Geneva within eyeshot of McLeash. He looked as businesslike as ever, his catalogue opened to a page of notes that had been written with Swiss precision. At Dale's request Miriam searched the audience for Bourgineau of Paris. Just as she was about to decide he was missing, she spotted him in the front of the room telling Bob Bentley, Fraizer's head auctioneer and the man who would be holding the hammer for the sale, the silent signals he would be using during the evening and the identities of the other spectators who would be making bids on his behalf.

She turned to the other side of the room, where she caught the eye of Senor Huerez. It seemed years since the day she and Miriam had raced over to his apartment trying to tie up his collection before Sotheby's and Christie's sniffed him out. He bowed his head slightly in her direction, then returned his attention to the stage. Behind him, in the right-hand corner of the room, Kenneth stood in his favorite spot. It was a vantage point from which he could see every bit of action and interplay as it occurred. He flashed her a big smile and a thumbs-up sign, then signaled for her to join him. She looked to Miriam, who merely shrugged and motioned her away.

Bob Bentley stepped to the podium and rapped for silence at precisely seven P.M. The click of the tote board, its signs for pounds, francs, dollars, and marks snapping back to zero, sounded loud in the hushed room. Two workers emerged from the wings, carrying a large oil painting which they placed on an easel in the center of the stage. They arranged themselves on either side of it, carefully balancing it between them. Bentley looked to his side, making sure that it had been positioned and that his bidders had seen it. Then he raised his hammer and his voice rang out in the room. "Lot number one," he called. "An oil on canvas by the French painter Jean-Baptiste-Camille Corot. Dated 1845. The bidding will start at thirty thousand dollars."

For the next half hour momentum built. Bentley ran through a series of relatively minor works, teasing the crowd, working their excitement to a fever pitch in advance of the major works of the evening. Then he brought out the Cézanne from Senor Huerez's collection, a tranquil village scene in muted tones of yellow and green. The audience became attentive. Bentley's voice was distinct and strong. "The opening bid is $200,000," he said. Then he quickly moved into the auctioneer's litany, that fast singsong that seems to have no clearly defined beginning or end. "I have $300,000 on the right. $325,000 on the telephone, $350,000 from the gentleman on the right." All heads turned trying to get a glimpse of the man he was referring to, but there was no way to tell where the bidding was coming from. "$400,000 to the lady front center," he said, pointing to the woman in white who had raised her paddle with a cool nonchalance that could only be the product of years in the auction room. Dale congratulated herself on her intuition. The bidding stayed fast and furious. $450,000 came in on the phone. $500,000 from the woman in white. "Do I hear $520,000?" Bentley pleaded. "Do I have $520,000?" nodding to the gentleman at the right of the room, and received a negative nod. "Last time. Do I hear $520,000? Once. Twice," and he knocked it down.

Dale looked behind her and found an easy smile on Kenneth's face. Miriam had been right on the money; the painting had hit its high estimate. "Damn, she's good," he said to Dale before he turned his attention back to the stage. She felt a light tap on her shoulder. Senor Huerez had joined them after the hammer went down.

"I hope you're pleased," she said.

He shrugged, the mannerism of a man who had trouble admitting he was happy. "Who wouldn't be," he said. "The figure is exactly what was predicted."

A minor Renoir, a red-chalk sketch of a nude, sold for $25,000. Senor Huerez's Pissarro followed. It was only a matter of minutes until the price reached $300,000. It was sold on a phone bid. He tried unsuccessfully to stifle a satisfied smile. Dale gave him a broad grin in return.

You could feel the excitement build. If they'd been at a prizefight the emotion would have broken out in stamping feet and wild yells. Here, people limited themselves to silently raising paddles and hands as the bidding went on, but anxiety was beginning to show in their faces.

Dale scanned the audience. The evening was going well. No ring had surfaced; if one had been formed they were exercising amazing patience. She caught sight of Miriam near the girls who were on the phones and gave her a thumbs-up sign. She got a blank stare in return, then Miriam turned her back and focused her attention on the stage.

One of Donovan's paintings had been carried on, an especially good Cézanne. Apples the color of new spring grass flashed out in a lifelike imitation of reality. "What do you think?" she asked Kenneth quietly.

"The night has just begun," he whispered back. "Remember, it's Donovan they want. If anything's going to happen, it should start now."

The Cézanne had a low estimate of a million, a steep price, but not too much for that particular painting. The bidding started at $200,000 and moved rapidly up to $750,000. McLeash took it to $800,000. "We may have been wrong," Dale said, looking to Kenneth, who didn't seem so easily convinced.

As quickly as it had accelerated, the bidding stumbled to a halt. McLeash was the only dealer bidding. A man in the back of the room followed him up to $850,000. McLeash gave his signal, raising the bid to $870,000. "Do I have $900,000?" Bentley asked. "$900,000, ladies and gentlemen?" No response from the audience. "Last call," he said reluctantly. "$900,000 once? Twice?" And the hammer went down at $870,000.

The disappointment on Bentley's face was apparent only to those who knew him. His mouth had tightened, indicating he was upset. He'd lost his bidders $130,000 below the painting's low estimate. It had gone just $30,000 over its reserve. He had been forewarned; his instincts and training told him it was

294

time to do something. He caught Kenneth's eye and got the signal that he'd been waiting for to take things into his own hands. It was obvious that unless they received competition on the lots—which didn't seem to be forthcoming from the audience that was there that night—Donovan's works in the auction were going to be split between the dealers in the ring at low prices.

"It looks as if Miriam was right, Dale," Kenneth said quietly. Though his words were whispered in her ear she found herself looking around the room, afraid that someone might have heard them. She sought out Bill Donovan in the audience. He looked sanguine. He might as easily have been on his way to a picnic as sitting in the salesroom taking a shellacking. "I think he's in for it," she agreed. She could feel her stomach begin to tie up in knots. "I don't understand him," she admitted. "We go out on a limb to warn him, and he does nothing but sit and watch it happen. What kind of masochist is he?"

Two more of Huerez's paintings followed. The Chagall went to the woman in white. A small Signac was picked up by Syd Adler. Then the last of Donovan's showpieces was brought center stage and spotlighted. There was a stir in the audience as the Monet was positioned. It was a view of Waterloo Bridge, one of a series showing the London landmark at differing times of the day, that the artist had painted from his window in the Savoy Hotel. Bob Bentley took a deep breath and squared his shoulders. There was determination on his face. He started the bidding at $250,000.

A phone bid brought it to $300,000, and Syd Adler came in with $325,000. The woman in white brought it to $350,000. Adler met her and topped her with $375,000. Another buyer phoned in a bid of $400,000. Adler beat it with $425,000. He had the look of a man who wasn't, under any circumstances, going to let the painting get away from him. The ring had obviously chosen him to be their buyer. He managed to bluff the competition, and the bidding came to a standstill.

Undaunted, Bentley continued to pull bids from the audience. Only a skilled eye would have detected the fact that one came from the chandelier on the salesroom's ceiling, the next from a pillar at the left side of the room, and that yet another was pulled out of thin air. His moves were so fast, his attitude so certain, that the novices in the audience were convinced. He banged his hammer down at $470,000. The painting was carried offstage, bought in by the house.

Well done, thought Kenneth. At least Donovan has his painting back, even if he does have to pay us a commission. Or maybe we can just offer to include it in our annual sale in London, Kenneth decided. And only charge him for auctioning it once. He mentally totted up Donovan's losses for the evening. The paintings he had left in the sale had sold just above their reserves. It seemed like a fiasco to him, but when he looked in Donovan's direction, the collector sat calmly, a look of total peace on his face.

The final painting to be presented on center stage was a Renoir portrait of two girls reading. Dale couldn't imagine why the museum had decided to sell it; it was the pièce de résistance of the sale. The room crackled with new electricity as the painting was positioned on the easel. Bill Donovan, who had been leaning back in his chair to this point looking somewhat bored, suddenly sprang to life. It made Dale wonder if he were planning to join the bidding. It seemed unlikely. He'd put some of his best Impressionists in the sale. He clearly wanted to weed them out of his collection.

The bidding started, moved to a million, then jumped in increments of $100,000. Donovan came in at $1,800,000. Even Kenneth looked surprised. Dale glanced toward the stage in time to see Miriam exclaim, "Well, I'll be damned!"

The woman in white came in at two million, with a smile as big as her bid. Neither she nor Donovan were trying to hide their bids; in fact, each was flamboyant about them.

The Paris dealer, M. Bourgineau, came in at $2,300,000. The rest of the room had dropped out, somehow knowing they were about to witness a cockfight. Donovan's determination was legendary. The other major dealers must have given Bourgineau some kind of signal and instructed him to play Donovan up and make him pay a sizable premium. He smiled as the lady in white took it to $2,400,000. She might be an unknown quantity, but Donovan wasn't. If he wanted that painting, they were going to make him pay dearly.

Bob Bentley stood straight and tall at the podium. His face had begun to relax as he scanned one bidder, then another, searching for silent signals. To his surprise the bids were made openly. The only thing surreptitious was the eye contact between the dealers that was becoming increasingly active as they watched Donovan being played up to $2,500,000 by Bourgineau. They sensed their opportunity to even the score with this man who had outbid them on important acquisitions so many times before. As the bidding flew up over the painting's high estimate, they fought to suppress their smiles.

Kenneth was bewildered. He couldn't understand what Donovan was up to. He knew only too well the value of the Renoir. It was good, that was certain, but it wasn't as good as a Renoir that had sold earlier that year for less. He looked to the front of the room, where Charles Groder, the Geneva dealer, was sitting complacently. His hands were laced over his stomach. He was the image of a man who had just finished a perfect meal and settled down with a fine port and a Cuban cigar.

Bourgineau's confidence seemed to increase as he saw his every bid topped by the woman in white. At worst he could count on her to take the painting off his hands if Donovan unexpectedly dropped out. Her bid of $2,700,000 tempted him to move to $2,800,000. He was confident that Donovan would come in at $2,900,000. He did.

The room was hushed as Bob Bentley said, "Do I have three million?" Without a moment's hesitation the lady in white raised her paddle. She seemed to enjoy the spirit of the game.

Bourgineau went to $3,100,000, imagining every dollar of the inflated bid coming out of Donovan's wallet. He pulled his paddle out of the air, licked his lips, and waited for Donovan's response. Nothing happened. The only sound in the room was Bob Bentley's voice, clear as ever, saying, "Do I hear $3,200,000?" A look of panic crossed Bourgineau's face as the woman in white nodded no, then stood up to leave. She started up the center aisle, reached the row where Donovan was seated, and paused. "Against you, sir. Do I have $3,200,000?" Bentley asked, focusing on Donovan who gave him a negative nod, stood up, linked arms with the lady in white and began to lead her from the room.

Bourgineau's face registered disbelief. The look on Charles Groder's face changed from contentment to the stricken expression of a man who's just learned he has food poisoning. The hammer went down at $3,100,000 to a round of applause. The audience turned to Bourgineau, expecting to see the elation of a winner. He looked as if he'd just lost his mother. Adler and Trump stalked up the center aisle, their faces blank, their minds toting up the extent of their loss and the amount each one of them would have to ante up to make it good.

Donovan stopped by Kenneth's side. "That's one painting those boys will remember for a long time. I don't think they'll be trying that little piece of work on me again," he chuckled. The woman in white smiled with him as Donovan put his arm around her. "You haven't met Constance Richmond, have you?" he asked Kenneth and Dale. "It's about time you did, don't you think?"

"She can bid for me any day," Kenneth said enthusiastically. "I'm just sorry you left some of your own paintings in. I'm afraid you've lost a little tonight."

"I had to know if they were up to their old tricks," Donovan said. A wide grin creased his weathered face. "There wasn't any way to tell unless I left a few of my things in there. I think that last Renoir taught them a lesson. As I figure it, they lost more on that one than they gained by ringing me. It should make headlines tomorrow. You should thank me," he said, giving Kenneth a playful punch on the shoulder. "It will do wonders for Fraizer's reputation."

"They're going to have a hell of a time reselling it at that price," Kenneth agreed.

Donovan shrugged. "Listen," he went on, pulling them all into the circle of his arms. "I've had my cook fix up a late supper. I'm counting on you to join us. Both of you," he said, indicating Dale. Miriam wasn't included in the invitation. "I'll even throw in a look at the Bill Donovan collection," he added.

Miriam took a long look at Dale, who was standing at Kenneth's side, then she turned without uttering a word and walked away. It was obvious to Dale that through no fault of her own she'd made an enemy. She considered going after her, then decided to leave it until the next morning. She looked to Bill Donovan, who was waiting for her decision. "That's a collection I definitely want to see," she told him. As they started toward the door she pulled Kenneth aside. "Don't you think Miriam could come, too?" she suggested. "She's worked harder than any of us on this."

"I do," Kenneth confirmed. "But it's not my dinner party, and it's not my place to extend invitations."

Dale gave a parting look at Miriam who was sitting in one of the now-empty gallery chairs. She wasn't sure whether it was the fact that Kenneth had personally handled her auction or the exclusion from the invitation to Donovan's that hurt Miriam most. But she felt in the pit of her stomach that something negative would come from this night.

Miriam was the kind of woman who had gone to work when other females were still trying to get into college and snare a husband and a permanent home. She'd given up a lot of her life to make it. The one great passion she had left was her work, and she was suddenly being given the sense that her professional recognition was eroding.

Miriam had been with Kenneth in the early years. He'd confided in her fully, using her to replace both business partners and wife. She'd been treated as an equal, not patronized, and she'd worked through the ranks enjoying a camaraderie with him that seemed to have faded as the house grew.

She must have felt like nothing more than another employee, Dale worried. One more social-security number with a salary after it at the end of every year. As they walked out of the salesroom Dale could hear the rasp of a match as Miriam lighted one more cigarette. It sounded as crisp as old rifle flints being struck by a firing squad about to do its duty.

CHAPTER 29

The last lock opened with a key. It was deadly quiet inside the chain-link cage where Fraizer's major paintings were stored. The only light in that black space was the pinpoint beam of a flashlight. It was swinging back and forth within the stacks methodically, searching.

He peered into the dark, straining to distinguish the outline of the stacks of paintings the tiny tape recorder had guided him to.

He listened carefully, then pulled a painting from the stacks. He walked to the far corner of the room, pulled up an easel, and assembled it quickly. Then he brought a clip-on light out from his pocket, attached it to the easel and plugged it into a wall socket behind him. He carefully placed the painting on the easel. A diffused wash of light illuminated the Monet of the Waterloo Bridge that had been on Fraizer's stage just a few short hours before.

The view had been painted at twilight, the hour that Monet had so loved. The small light brought out subtle changes in the purples, mauves, and deep-sea greens of the London scene. A low whistle emerged from the man's lips.

I haven't seen this since '65, he thought, when they auctioned it at Christie's. Got about fifty thousand for it then. It was sold again in '78 for over a quarter of a million.

He lifted the canvas and placed it on the desk. His respect was apparent in the way he cautiously moved it. He removed a plastic Ziploc bag from his pocket and laid out the tools of his trade. He picked up one of the shining surgical knives and examined it closely. It had been sterilized so that no residue from anything else would get mixed up with the pigment samples he was about to take.

He spent the next five minutes removing tiny paint flecks, putting them between small glass slides. He tagged them and catalogued them for use in mixing pigments, referring back to the painting in front of him. Then picking up a camera with infrared film, he made photographs that would show him the different combinations of metals and dyes that had been used to create each color. Finally he applied a thin rubbery resin to the canvas. He let it dry for fifteen minutes.

The silence of the room became oppressive. The emptiness grew into a tangible, palpable thing. He imagined he could hear his heartbeat ringing out. It was gradually getting faster and crazily staccato. He touched the resin lightly. A few more minutes and he could clean up and pack it all in.

He peeled the resin off cautiously. He was holding a record of the painting that would let him duplicate its brushstrokes. He traced the contours of the canvas with his fingers to make sure there was nothing left on it.

He worked efficiently, carrying the painting back to the storage bins and sliding it into the same place where it had been housed before, then picking his tools up and replacing them in his bag. He threaded his way through the storage rooms to the alley behind the house.

It was expected in six weeks. Not much time but enough for a professional like himself. He put the tape recorder back into its spot over the door, then walked away, as much a stranger to his employer as he had been when he started his little adventure.

CHAPTER 30

Donovan leaned forward and selected a walnut-brown cigar from the humidor being offered by his butler. He examined it appreciatively for a moment, then clipped the end off with his polished white teeth.

He settled back into one of the slim Italian lawn chairs that were grouped beneath the greenhouse's pitched glass roof. Aromatic smoke began to curl up and over him, ascending toward the glitter of stars that could be seen through the glass panes above.

"Pre-Castro," he informed them.

"That's one thing technology hasn't improved," Kenneth confirmed, sniffing a mate to the one that now drooped in Donovan's lips.

"So's that," Donovan countered. He pointed to a large Rothko oil that hung directly inside the veranda doors.

Dale looked through to where it hung, bathed in a soft golden light that seemed to make it shimmer in the quiet of the living room, though she knew it was standing still. "It looks like you've been collecting forever," she said.

She thought back to the brief tour of the penthouse they had been treated to when they arrived. It boasted all the accoutrements of the best old New York apartment buildings—high ceilings with moldings, a foyer as large as most people's living rooms, and shining parquet floors. But the walls were the true treasure chest. They were a banquet for the eyes. A collection of drawings by Ed Ruscha and David Hockney had been hung against their soft ivory surface extending the length of the entrance hall. The paintings overshadowed everything else.

Oils by Milton Avery and Helen Frankenthaler hung side by side in the dining room. A Morris Louis spanned the length of the room. Dale had felt as if she didn't need any dinner; she just wanted to feast herself on these modern masterpieces.

"You might say I've been collecting all my life," Donovan agreed. "Anything beautiful."

"Not to mention companies," Kenneth added.

Donovan glanced in his direction. "I grew up dirt poor. I sure didn't want to die that way. I adopted a method of operation early on. When I want something, nothing stands in my way. And I mean nothing."

"Morals?" Kenneth smiled.

Donovan replied with an enigmatic look, but no direct answer.

"If he had them they wouldn't have been ringing him like that," Dale teased. "I hear they reserve that kind of treatment for very special cases."

"Don't be so sure," Donovan cautioned. "They did it to William Randolph Hearst back in forty-one. If it's good enough for him, it's good enough for me."

"He was one of my father's first customers," Kenneth told Donovan.

"He got you into the business. And in case there's any doubt about it," Donovan told him, "I'm the one who will help keep you in it." He lifted his glass to Kenneth. "I drink to you," he said. "We've had our differences, but you've always been a gentleman. I'm in your debt. Remember, you can call it in when you need to."

"Knowing you as I do, it's a comfort to think that you're in my corner," said Kenneth, returning his toast. "Otherwise I'd have to spend my time worrying about you buying the house right out from under me. Just another jewel in the Donovan crown."

"Probably," Donovan agreed philosophically. "Some of us have that old killer instinct. Some don't." They sat silently for a moment, each enjoying the view of the city below them, each caught in his own thoughts. "Take your friend Whytson," Donovan went on. "There's a man with an instinct for survival. He's been to my office twice this month. Didn't have much trouble coming to the point on either occasion. He's ready to cut the commission to me on the buy end and the sell if I begin sending my paintings through his sales." He studied his glass meditatively for a minute, waiting for Kenneth to respond. Kenneth watched Donovan's face, but said nothing. "Of course I told him I'd be staying with Fraizer's," he said finally. He'd been cheated out of granting Kenneth a favor since it hadn't been asked for. "But I thought you should be aware of his tactics."

"I appreciate that, Bill," Kenneth said. His voice seemed as calm as the expression on his face. "He's tried that with a number of our clients. With some it has worked, with others it hasn't. I don't think it will affect us in the long run. Still, he's trying his damndest, I'll tell you that. There aren't all that many of us who are willing to go to such lengths to succeed."

"How about Dale?" Donovan suggested to Kenneth. Dale felt a hot flush rising in her cheeks. She felt like a commodity, being discussed in her absence. She was glad the room was dark. "What she knows about art isn't a spit in Miriam's bucket. But that didn't stop her from coming after me and the museum. Did it, Dale?" he asked, smiling at her.

Kenneth looked at her appraisingly. Light from the apartment building opposite them shone onto one side of her face, etching the pure lines of her cheeks and large eyes. She still had that look of naiveté, but there was more to her, something Donovan sensed that he had missed.

"Call me old-fashioned," Kenneth said, "but I still

don't think Whytson's way is the right way to succeed."

"Maybe you're right," Donovan said. "There was an item out of London on the financial wire service yesterday. Whytson's going to be doing an additional stock offering later this month. The way new issues are dying right now he wouldn't be bringing his stock out in this market unless he really needed the cash. Maybe he won't be around long enough to give you a real run for your money."

Dale missed Kenneth's reply. All that registered was that Whytson needed money. Did it really make any sense? After all, if Whytson had been profiting from the forgeries as Kenneth had suggested to Ivan, he wouldn't be hard up for cash. Unless, of course, he'd been secreting the art or the money instead of putting it back into his auction house. That didn't sound like Ned. The way the world looked at him—the fact that he was viewed as a success today—was of more importance to him than how he'd survive in the future, at least that was Dale's conclusion. He'd no more hide away the money while his business became a failure than resign his position as president and go to work in the stockroom. The only other possibility was that it was a grudge match, a deliberate attempt to break Kenneth simply for the fun of seeing him go down.

"I think I'll excuse myself for a moment to go to the ladies' room."

"Let me show you the way," came a soft voice at Donovan's side. The lady in white, elegantly wrapped in an ivory kimono that blended into the walls so perfectly that she might have been part of them, rose gracefully and led Dale into the living room.

"You know," Dale said, "I have the feeling we've met somewhere before. But quite honestly, I can't recall when or where." Her eyes wandered around the rooms and halls of the apartment as they went, picking up small details that she had missed the first time through.

"We met during Heirloom Day," the woman told her. Her smile went inward, shining on a secret she had been holding inside the entire night. "One of your appraisers did me quite a favor by letting me know that my old jewelry boxes were worth sixteen thousand apiece. So you see," she told Dale, "I owed Fraizer's a favor."

Dale stopped, bewildered. She planted her feet on a Heriz runner, and refused to go on before getting some answers. "How does Bill Donovan come into this?" she asked.

"We've known each other for years," the woman explained. "He bought my late husband's company. Ran it up ten times in value, too, I might add."

"Donovan strikes again," Dale shrugged. "He bought you out cheap."

"Yes," she agreed, "he did. But when Gerald died Donovan explained to me what he intended to do with the company and offered me stock options. He's made me very comfortable with that move. Not rich, but comfortable."

Dale thought back, remembering the sable fling and the life of money and success it denoted. Donovan was a complex man, one with a sense of fairness despite what he said.

"The powder room is this way," her companion said.

By the time they returned to the terrace, Dale had begun to feel the effects of the long day. Her body was begging to go home, her mind cried out for sleep.

"Kenneth," she said, "would you mind terribly if we made it an early evening? I think the day's just caught up with me."

Kenneth arose solicitously. "It's been delightful," he said to both Donovan and his companion, as he made the excuses for both of them.

"Do you always feel this good the day of an auction?" Dale asked as they settled into the back seat of a cab. "I feel as if I've just conquered an entire country."

"Usually," Kenneth told her. "I've been giving some thought to what happens now that your auction is done," he went on.

"Do you have any ideas?" she asked tentatively.

"I do have an idea for the short run," he told her. "Want to hear it?" She nodded silently and he went on. "I'd like to send you over to London next week to join Ivan. He's making arrangements for the painting auction over there next month. I was thinking of sending you over there as his assistant. You'd stay for a few days next week and get the feel of it, then come back to New York to do follow-up work for him in our main office. Of course, you might have to go back and forth a few times, as well." He waited for her reply. It was important for him that someone with some experience, even experience as thin as Dale's, get over there as a backup for Ivan. As happy as he was that they'd managed to save Donovan from some losses, his own bottom line was still shaky. He had to admit he'd feel better if he didn't have the forgeries hanging over his head, and letting Dale handle some of the auction details to free Ivan up to get totally involved in the investigation seemed to him to be the fastest way to accomplish that.

"London? Oh, Kenneth. That sounds wonderful." The memories of her first and only trip to Europe rushed back. Going as a representative of Fraizer's would be excitingly different.

"Not too wonderful," Kenneth cautioned her. "There's a lot to be done over there. All the arrangements for an auction coming up—some of it petty detail. Make no mistake, you'll be learning start to finish how to handle an off-premises auction. It's quite different, even more demanding. No detail can be overlooked because no systems are in place.

Phones, security, insurance, press. Ivan will be keeping you very busy."

"I don't doubt that." She'd become accustomed to Ivan's demands in the short time she'd worked on the investigation with him. As civil as he could be on most occasions, his manner of asking her to do something occasionally came out more as a command than a polite request. It was a tone that Mark Rasten had accustomed her to, but for some reason it grated more when Ivan used it. She couldn't put her finger on the reason, but her irritation with it had steadily grown. She hoped they could make it through days of close contact without blowing up. That caused her a moment's hesitation. But then she looked at Kenneth sitting next to her. In repose his face looked lined, worried. She felt suddenly disloyal for putting her own concerns in front of the good of the house. "All right. I'll go," she told him. "But there's something I didn't tell you earlier this evening," she said, hesitating. "You may not want me to once I have. I forgot to turn in an order bid," she hurried on. If she got it out quickly she wouldn't have a chance to change her mind. "The client was furious. It was all Steven could do to calm him down. I hope we haven't lost a good customer. It was all my fault," she finished, looking at him. All the shame she felt at her mistake was obvious in that look.

Kenneth didn't answer for a moment. He seemed to be looking inside himself, back to the time when he was starting, raw in the business.

"I've gone over it a thousand times," Dale muttered. "I still don't know how I could have been so careless."

"How did you handle the client?" Kenneth asked her.

"We told him the truth," Dale said. "That was all we could do."

Kenneth took a deep breath, then leaned back in

his seat. He looked satisfied. "When you face a problem head on and deal with it," he said, "it usually works out. That was my mistake with the forgeries. I didn't deal with them directly. I just hoped they would go away. It was obviously a vain hope. Just give me the details on this screwup in the morning," he went on. "Enough so that I won't be caught looking stupid if it comes up. And don't feel so bad," he said, studying her downcast face. "You've come a long way. No one's perfect."

To her surprise it had been easy. He hadn't been angry at all, just understanding. It occurred to her that she might as well get it all out—her growing relationship with Ned Whytson, too. It bothered her more and more that she hadn't told Kenneth about the amount of time the two of them were spending together. It had grown in proportion, and the sooner Kenneth was aware of it, the better she would feel. "There's something else," she said. "No more, Dale," he said, holding up his hand as if to ward off bad news. I've had enough for one day. No more bad news until the morning."

CHAPTER 31

He heard her cry out. The sound was clear and sharp. In the stillness of the night as he twisted between his sheets, he heard his name being shouted. It was a cry for help. Kenneth grabbed the robe at the foot of the bed and ran through the hallways. There was no mistaking where it was coming from.

The door to Steven and Katherine's bedroom was open. She was sitting up. A hysterical keening came from her lips. He looked at the bed. He saw blood, pools of it, spreading red and alive underneath her. "Oh my God," he said. It sounded like someone else's voice, like a voice coming from far away. He looked at the clock. It was three A.M. Then he reached for the phone and punched "O" for operator.

"Help is on the way," he crooned as he stroked her forehead and hair. He tried to comfort her without moving her. Somewhere he'd read that you shouldn't move a person who was bleeding. "They'll be here in a minute and everything will be all right." His eyes returned to the empty sheets beside her, the spot where Steven should have been.

There is nothing quite so lonely as a hospital in the early-morning hours. The corridors are inhabited by scrubwomen, wearing the resigned look of the overworked as they pull ragged mops from pails of dirty water. Among them, sitting on chairs or pacing the halls, people keeping desolate, frightening vigils are scattered.

Kenneth hunched forward on a molded plastic chair. His back was short with pain, the muscles tense and knotted. When he rubbed his hands over his itching eyes his head became filled with darting sparks of light that told him how tired he really was. He prayed silently, first and foremost that Katherine would be all right, and then for the baby. He had placed a call to her parents, who were on their way now, and he had told the maid to wait up and to send Steven over as soon as he appeared. Damn him, he thought as he painfully lifted himself and began walking the space between her door and the end of the hall. Where could he have been?

He came to the end again, and turned, pushing

off for another lap. He counted the green linoleum tiles as he paced off the first few steps, then he saw the doctor standing outside her door and began hurrying his strides. He had the cheerless look of a man who's just been cheated. Kenneth knew without asking that the news wasn't good.

"I'm sorry," the doctor said. His face looked tired over his hospital greens. "We did everything we could. It was too late. The baby's gone."

Kenneth leaned back against the cold enameled wall. One hand went to his forehead, supporting his head which seemed suddenly to be falling forward dangerously. "How's Katherine?" he heard a voice say that must have been his own.

"She's resting," the doctor said. Kenneth didn't hear the rest of his words.

"As long as Katherine is all right, there will be other babies," was all Kenneth said.

She woke when the noon light was already making inroads into her darkened room, breaking through in thin elusive beams that slipped between the slats of the venetian blinds. She had a moment of confusion, then her eyes adjusted to the light and she could pick out the shapes of a bedside table, a water jug, and, hanging slightly above her, a bottle that appeared to be connected to her by a series of tubes and tapes. It all came back to her. She waited, afraid to do it, then she took the chance and put her hands across her stomach. Her eyes became blank, staring up at the ceiling. The tears began to form and then slowly, one by one, to run in endless streams down her cheeks. A low, strangled moan gurgled in her throat, the sound of a she-animal robbed of its purpose.

"Katherine, I'm so sorry," he said. "I was at the office. Going over figures. I should have been with you." The voice came from the dim void to the left of her. She turned her head and looked carefully and realized that it was her husband.

"The baby? Is the baby all right?" she asked him, though she already knew the answer.

He sadly nodded no. He was over her now, his face close enough for her to see the swollen pockets of flesh under his eyes, and the lines that fatigue had brought on. She remembered then. He hadn't been there.

"Please leave," she said. "I don't want to talk to you now." She rolled over on her side and pretended she had fallen back to sleep. He waited for a moment. She could feel his eyes searching her back, looking for the answer to her feelings about him. Then he turned and quietly left her room.

She had always thought that she loved Steven, but, as she listened to his steps retreating, the reality of her feelings over the past years became suddenly clear. It was as if losing the child had forced her to shed the lies she'd used to mask what was hidden in her subconscious all along.

It had been a mistake, a horrible mistake. She had married the wrong man. As she thought back she realized that all the wonderful memories of the Fraizers she treasured were of Kenneth. Their time together when she was sick. His coming to her when he learned of her pregnancy. All through the years their communication had been honest, forthright, and easy. She had talked out so many things with Kenneth, things she didn't even talk to her parents about. She'd projected the whole thing on to Steven—the strength she felt around Kenneth, his gentle and caring manner, his tenderness. And she'd managed to fool herself for so long. But then came that night when Kenneth had reached for her on the couch, the night when she had started to imagine what it would be like if she were Kenneth's wife. It had all seemed so real.

She lay there in the dark, the tears beginning to stream down her face. "Oh, God. I'm in love with Kenneth," she whispered softly into the empty room.

* * *

It was dinnertime when she woke again. They had taken out the IV while she slept. The smell of meatloaf being taken to the rooms was in her nostrils. She lay back, not hungry, and pretended she was still asleep, but the flutter of her eyelids, the little waking motions in her face, had alerted him. Kenneth sat by her bed, fresh from the office, the thin veil of concern on his face subtly changing the set of every feature. There had been time by then for her to think about things, and to understand what she had to do. When she looked at him, she knew that she was right.

She studied his face. He was an older—an original—version of his son. That was the source of the problem. She had always assumed that Steven would mature like him. They were so much alike in some ways, with gestures and facial expressions that were so akin they could have been interchanged from one man to the other. It wasn't Steven's fault. It was an injustice she had inflicted on him.

Kenneth leaned down to kiss her hello, and the mere closeness of him was painful for her. "You're looking better," he lied. She knew her face was washed clean of color and she looked tired and weak. She began to smile knowingly.

"You're just trying to make me feel better. You always do."

He smiled back, acknowledging it. "I may have exaggerated a little," he conceded. "Because I care about you."

"I know you do," she told him. "I've counted on that." A look of distress clouded her face. "What I've finally realized in here is how much I care about you, too. More than I've admitted to myself," she added quietly. She looked straight at him as she spoke, the struggle that was going on within her clearly evident on her face. "Ever since I moved in with you I've used you to fill every need I have—not physically," she added quickly, "but mentally. You've been the one I've

314

gone to, the one I've listened to. I've cut Steven out, or, I should say, we have. It isn't right, Kenneth."

He studied the blanket as he sat on the side of her bed. He looked like a patient who's just been given the bad news he's expected, but denied, for months. When he finally spoke his voice was unsteady. "You've replaced a part of my life that I thought was gone after Anna died," he admitted. "I never expected to be able to find someone to confide in again." He carefully skirted the physical attraction that Katherine had already emphatically denied. He started to reach out for her hand, then quickly stood up instead. He began to pace the room, counting the tiles of the floor as his feet went back and forth over them. He looked everywhere but at her face.

"It's had a terrible effect on Steven," Katherine persisted. "When he wasn't there for me last night I blamed him. I resented the office, the hours he spends there instead of at home. Then I realized I've driven him out—we have. I should have understood the problems he's had growing up in your shadow. It can't have been easy on him, Kenneth. Instead, I sided with you when the two of you had a disagreement. I fell right in line with your thinking and left him standing on his own. I cheated him, Kenneth. I cheated him of the support he deserves from a wife. And I think you've cheated him, too."

He walked slowly to the mirror that hung on one wall, and reached up to unknot his tie. It seemed to suddenly bind, to hold him in. He looked into his own face, digging deep as he did it. There was no question, he realized, tormented by the knowledge. He was a father who had sheltered his son, instead of helping him to grow.

He supposed that every man has had that moment of panic when he truly realizes the things that he has counted on as his—the physical strength, the solid business, the position and prestige, in fact his very life span—will be leaving him someday and passing to his son. The first reaction is to struggle, to fight it, to stave it off and preserve the status quo. The resignation comes later. And finally, in good cases where selfishness can be left behind, the pride in the achievements of the young man who will replace you. Perhaps it was time to step aside for Steven. He'd so often spoken to people who said that they would give their lives for their child. Well, tonight he was going to do the same.

"Try to give him more responsibility, Kenneth," Katherine said softly. She'd gotten up and was standing behind him now, her face next to his in the mirror's image. He felt his heart melt with longing as he looked at the two of them there, so close together. "Not just another title. Real responsibility," she went on. "You've got to make him feel as if his opinions count, his advice matters. Before the decisions are made. Not after. Will you do it?"

He looked at the two of them together there for another long moment. He tried to freeze the picture in his mind. "I'll try," he agreed, and, turning, he gently removed the hand she had put around his shoulders.

CHAPTER 32

Bill Donovan looked around his office in frustration. His eyes finally fastened on the light fixture that was hanging over the head of this person who was proving to be such a hindrance to him. He pictured it falling and breaking his skull, cracking it like a fragile eggshell from which a runny bulk of brain would stream—if he had any, that is. Why businessmen were ever foolish enough to invite lawyers into their midst was beyond him.

"We had an agreement in principle on this two months ago," he shouted. The fist he slammed into his desk raised the papers that had been neatly arranged there a good inch into the air. He stopped and held his breath for a few seconds, deliberately bringing his face to an apoplectic purple. Before he could go on, his unlisted private line rang. "Hello," he barked. He sounded like a drill sergeant preparing to rub the noses of some raw recruits into the dirt. His expression mellowed a bit with the answer. He decided to drag the call out and let the man across from him sweat a little. It was one of those moments he loved in deal making, when the bluff had been played and the game could swing as easily in one direction or the other. This time he thought he would come out a winner.

"William, my friend," the voice at the other end said. As he heard it, Donovan's mind conjured up a picture of Lord Henry Balbour. He looked for all the world like one of the English steeplechasers he raised, all wide red nostrils blowing gusts of air as if he were in a constant state of high-strung excitement. "I have an interesting bit of news for you. Are you sitting down?"

"I never sit down," Donovan barked back. "Too much to do to keep this operation running smoothly." He hoped the man sitting across from him was taking note of his tough tone.

"You must have changed since I last saw you," Balbour drawled in a jaded voice. "That aside, I thought you would like to know that the underground network will be offering a rather interesting Monet next month. I just got a call this morning."

"Why haven't they let me in on it?" Donovan asked.

"Because it's yours, dear boy," laughed Balbour. "It's the Waterloo Bridge painting. The one you placed in the Fraizer's sale. That's one good reason not to let you in on it, isn't it?" he asked rhetorically. "Another is that the salesperson is new. Guess you're just not on the invitation list."

Donovan looked thoughtful for a moment. Then he asked, "How much do you expect it to go for?"

"Oh, about twenty cents on the dollar, I should say," Balbour answered.

A sly smile slowly spread across Donovan's face. It couldn't be more perfect. He had hated the idea of parting with that Monet. If the cash situation at the company hadn't been so tight, if oil prices hadn't taken such a crash, he never would have considered doing it. Now it looked as if he would have his cake and eat it too, get full price for the painting at auction, then buy it back at a fraction of its worth. Of course he wouldn't be able to display it, but that didn't bother him a bit. He had already stored away a dozen hot paintings—Renoir, Pissarro, Bonnard, Manet—and one more would just make it better.

His mind slipped into the private room he kept at home, the room he shared with no one else in the world. He enjoyed nothing more than a few hours there. It held a leather sofa, two matching chairs, a humidor filled with his favorite Dunhills, and his private collection of masterpieces. He never would have believed how much hot art there was in circulation, good art, until he got involved in buying it. He certainly believed it now. "When's the auction?" he asked.

"The night of Fraizer's London event," Balbour told him. "But I'm afraid that if you're interested, I'll have to do your bidding for you. It's strictly by invitation."

Donovan felt a moment of irritation at having his fun thwarted. He loved to bid, to see other men give up and buckle. But if that was the way it had to be, he would do it. "Take it up as far as you have to," he instructed. "I'll spend that night waiting by the phone."

"It's done, dear boy."

Donovan held the receiver to his ear for a few seconds after he had gone off, then he turned his attention back to the lawyer who had been watching the entire performance.

"Mr. Donovan," the little man said, "upon reflection I think you may be right. A deal is a deal. I'll draw up the papers and have them on your desk by Monday."

Donovan smiled as only a born pirate can. He started back to work, but something in him balked. He wanted the Monet back, desperately. The cutthroat in him, the one that had built his personal collection, said keep it. Why not, he asked. The only person in the world that you owe loyalty to is yourself. Yet something in him kept remembering that he owed a chit. Explaining it to Kenneth Fraizer might be a little tricky. Nevertheless, he picked up the phone and dialed.

CHAPTER 33

Dale put her head in her hands and rubbed her temples with slow, soothing circles. The glow of last night's auction had worn off quickly once she arrived in the office. She'd scheduled a meeting at ten with Deborah, and there was the mail to get through before that. On her desk was a note from Kenneth asking her to see him in his office at eleven. She checked her watch, decided to use the hour before the meeting going over her notes on the forgeries, and pulled a thin file from the back of her desk drawer.

Her notes looked sparse as she flipped through them. A copy of the security proposal from Manhattan Security. And a lot of blank spaces that needed filling in. She rubbed her eyes, rested them a moment, then stretched and spread the papers out in front of her. She thought back to her meeting with Richard Smythson, and began to write out the details.

There had been a bustling crowd browsing inside Harry Smythson's the afternoon she'd been there, or at least what qualifies as a crowd in an establishment where purchases are counted in tens of thousands of dollars instead of in tens.

She had been shown into Richard Smythson's small, elegant office. Another man, modestly dressed in gray herringbone, was already seated in front of Smythson's desk.

"I've taken the liberty of asking Robert Crowningshield to join us," Smythson had told her. "He's the vice president of the G.I.A. and the director of gem identification in their New York office. He provided us with the written report verifying the authenticity of the diamonds prior to the auction."

Crowningshield's story was simple. He had examined the stones prior to the auction. Since the stones were already set he wasn't able to grade for color and clarity. All he was able to do was to measure each stone to approximate its carat weight, and test it to verify that its substance was actually diamond as opposed to cubic zirconia. He had given a copy of his notes on the examination to Dale.

Richard Smythson was the one who had given her an estimate of the time necessary to make a substitution of stones.

"It's a tricky process," he had told her. "I would guess the measuring would take one to two hours for an experienced lapidary. The transfer would be more time consuming. You'd have to be very careful removing the originals and setting the substitutes. If you damaged the setting in the process there wouldn't be much time to repair it, and it would be quite visible during any visual examination."

"We know that the originals were still in the setting when you examined them," Dale said to Crowningshield. "How were they handled once you finished your inspection?"

"I personally carried them back to Mr. Smythson," he had told her. "Michael Edwards from Fraizer's Jewelry Department was waiting here when I arrived. He had Richard test them once more with the diamond probe, then he took them back to your premises."

Not much there, she admitted.

She started from the beginning again, going step by step with a nursery school simplicity that guaranteed she wouldn't miss anything. "Motive," she wrote. "Money, or destroy credibility of Fraizer's." To her, money seemed the most likely objective. Still, Kenneth had suggested the possibility that someone was doing this to destroy his reputation. It would have to be some disgruntled employee, either past or present. Or Ned Whytson. It doesn't fly, she decided, unless he had someone inside the house working with him. There's no way he'd know about the alarm system or have access to the house often enough, or long enough, without someone from Fraizer's cooperating. She'd have to check the personnel records, and double-check anyone who'd been fired, against Kenneth's recollection. She made a note of it.

"Access," she wrote next. Kenneth had consistent access to the house. But certainly he couldn't be doing this to himself. He hadn't even reported it to the insurance company. He'd paid all the buyers back on his own. No motive there. Steven was in the same position. It was his inheritance. He wouldn't be destroying it. He'd agreed with his father that they should avoid official insurance company investigations, that they should make the repayments out of their own funds. In fact, she remembered, he had argued against opening the European branches because he didn't want to jeopardize his inheritance. There was no logic to considering Steven.

Take the easy path, she told herself. Assume that money is the goal. Then it could be anyone in the house. They could be feeding information to someone on the outside and collecting a considerable reward every time the stolen merchandise was sold, or they could be handling the whole thing themselves without any outside help. It made sense to consider the department heads first. They were more trusted; they'd have a better chance of pulling it off. She made a note to spend half an hour talking to Michael in the Jewelry Department after going through Deborah's files. Start where the tracks are freshest, she told herself.

She checked her watch. Ten-fifteen already. She'd been due in Deborah's office fifteen minutes ago. She closed the file and carefully put it back into her desk drawer.

Deborah smiled wickedly as Dale came through the door. "I'm glad you're here," she said. "I need an opinion. Is blackmail still illegal in New York State?"

Dale looked bewildered until Deborah handed her a photo proof sheet. Bright orange grease pencil circled a shot of Miriam talking to Ned Whytson. They appeared to be engrossed in intimate conversation.

"I don't think it would be a good idea for you to make a big deal out of this. You may just upset Kenneth for nothing," Dale told her. Her mind was racing as she stood there. She tried to avoid jumping to the obvious conclusion. "It's from the Hammer Gallery opening, isn't it?" she asked Deborah. When the publicist nodded yes, she went on. "They were probably just making polite conversation about the paintings."

"I'll tell you one thing. I feel like I've known him too long," said Deborah. "And I've never even met the man. He's smart. I've got to admit that. Came into town and planned all his sales around our auction schedule. One day ahead of us, though. Just enough lead time to eat up the press coverage. Hasn't made my life easier."

Dale changed the subject. "Have you gotten out the P.R. files I needed?"

"I'm running late," Deborah admitted. "Thanks to the efforts of our friend Mr. Whytson. But I can have them for you by late afternoon."

Dale felt her innards tighten with impatience. Then she realized Deborah had no idea of the urgency that was involved. She'd only told her that she wanted to look at the files of some of the department heads so that she would have a better idea of how to put the information together for her own press release bio.

"Then I'll have to work on them tonight. Do you have a key to the alarm so that I can set it when I leave?" she asked.

"No," Deborah told her. "But the guard's always here. He can let you out the front door. Just remember to smile on your way out."

"Why?"

"Because you'll be on camera. The mini-TV monitors are at the front door. I think they keep those tapes in case of emergency."

The TV tape, thought Dale as she left Deborah's office. Why didn't I think of that? Why didn't Mr. Crown show it to me? Why should he have, she realized, answering her own question. He doesn't know we've had any problems. I'll have to think of another way to get him to show it to me. Fat chance the thief signed in and out at the front door, she thought. But any chance is worth following up on at this point.

Kenneth didn't stand when Barbara showed her into his office. She could see the rings of fatigue under his eyes from across the room. "You look exhausted," she told him as she sat down.

"It wasn't an easy night. Katherine had a miscarriage around two this morning."

Dale's hand flew to her mouth. "Oh, Jesus," she said. The words came out like a soft cry. "I have to go to her."

"She doesn't want to see anyone right now. I'd leave her alone. She's too depressed to talk about it."

"Thank you for calling me in to tell me about it. For understanding how important it would be to me."

"That's only one of the reasons I called you in. Miriam met with me early this morning. She's given a month's notice. She's going to work for Whytson."

It took a moment for Dale's brain to absorb the shock. She thought back to the night before, to Kenneth's conducting the contemporary sale and to Donovan's decision to exclude Miriam from his dinner invitation. It was timing, she knew. Perfect timing on Ned's part. Miriam had decided she wasn't appreciated and Ned had stepped in. Or had she had this relationship with Whytson for some time? There was that picture Deborah had just shown her. Perhaps Miriam had been Whytson's contact at Fraizer's? Dale's mind kept shifting the possibilities around in her head.

"Let me talk to her," she suggested. "I think I could change her mind."

"I've already told her to clear her desk and get out this morning," he said. "I don't have any need to keep her around here if she's involved with Ned Whytson. She's been with me fifteen years. She's earned a damn good salary. Loyalty," he muttered, "there's no such thing any more." His voice had been high and clear to that point, but it seemed to fade as the words came out.

Dale felt faint. She'd been warned. She should have pushed Kenneth to listen to her last night. If only she had explained how her innocent effort to get close to Ned and find out more about his New York operation had turned into a personal thing before this news about Miriam had come out. She had to tell him now, and the timing couldn't be worse.

"I tried to tell you something last night. Do you remember?" She felt a chill go through her as Kenneth nodded a preoccupied yes. "It was about Ned," she told him.

"What about him?" Kenneth asked abruptly. She could see the muscles of his jaw grow taut at the mention of his name. She cautiously began to relate the extent of her involvement with Whytson to him, to tell him how safe it had seemed, how easy to control. But as she spoke, hoping for an answer from him, for some forgiving word, he sat frozen.

"He satisfied so many needs for me, Kenneth," she told him, close to tears. Her eyes begged him to help her out. "I was so alone here, not even a good friend to talk to once Katherine decided to get married."

"I don't want to hear about what was lacking in your social life, Dale," he interrupted harshly. "Not when the very existence of Fraizer's is being threatened. You're one of the few people around here who knew what was going on. One of the few who knew Whytson might be behind it. Can you tell me you didn't understand what these problems meant to me and to the future of the house? Of course you can't," he answered himself in a disgusted tone of voice.

"I could tell you I didn't know what was going on here until a few weeks ago," she answered, tears beginning to stand out in her eyes. She made an effort and held them back. "This thing with Ned was pretty far gone by that time." She paused for a moment and searched for the right words. "Kenneth, I'm sorry," she said at last. "Honestly I am. I should have told you before. I know that. I've worked hard to prove myself here. I wouldn't ever do anything to jeopardize Fraizer's. But I didn't know about the forgeries. And even when I did find out . . . well, I didn't think that Ned had anything to do with them."

"That's the trouble," Kenneth shouted at her. "You didn't think. I can't know for sure whether you'll think in the future."

She sat motionless. There were no words that would help.

"And I was going to give you a try at Miriam's job." He leaned back in his chair. "I knew you'd be stretching yourself. But with the backup you'd have gotten from me I thought it might work. Well," he said with finality as he leaned forward and began shuffling through some of the papers scattered over his desktop, "that's the end of that idea. You'll stay an assistant department head. I'll be making the decisions for Fine Arts for a while. You've disappointed me," he said, looking her in the eyes. "Greatly. You've let Fraizer's be compromised by your personal problems. I can't tolerate that. I've got a business to run, and right now I need to know that my team is behind me a hundred percent. If you're willing to start listening to me now"—he paused and waited until she nodded her assent—"I suggest you do an outstanding job for Ivan in London. As for Ned Whytson . . ."

"Kenneth, please," Dale interrupted him. "I feel responsible for Miriam's joining him. Let me try to turn this around. Let me try to use him for a change."

Kenneth waited for her to go on. It was obvious that his curiosity had been piqued.

"I'll have dinner with him tonight. I want to see what comes out when I do the listening and he does the talking."

Kenneth heard a new note of determination, a hardening, in her voice. "Do what you think is best," he told her. He looked up and saw that she was still waiting for his advice. "Well, you haven't listened to me up till now," he pointed out. "Why should I think you'll start today?"

Dale hesitated. Had Ned deliberately used her? Picked her brain to get information about Miriam, and then lured Miriam away? The possibility hurt. She'd always known the relationship with Ned wasn't serious. Still, he'd been able to make her feel as if there was nothing quite so important to him as talking to her. With Ned she'd been able to shut out the rest of the world for a time. At least until today. Now she realized why he might have been making such an effort.

Winter had arrived early in New York. Outside Dale's window the drops of rain that had been falling began to turn to snow as the temperature fell below freezing. People below scurried to escape the oncoming storm. She put a record on the stereo, a loud one that disguised her mood.

The chill came through the front door with him. His cheeks had been turned icy by the wind. His lips, as he pressed them on hers, seemed dry and chapped, sapped somehow of the moist life they usually conveyed to her. Or perhaps it was her mind that was playing tricks, not the elements. He unwrapped his muffler, removed his topcoat, and tossed a pair of cashmere-lined leather gloves onto the coffee table. He came to her and tried to snuggle his head into the crevice of her neck, but she held him at arms' length, studying him.

"Here," she said, reaching for the topcoat that still hung in the crook of his arm, "I'll hang that up for you. Fix some drinks for us. I called the King Dragon and ordered in. They'll be delivering in about an hour."

Ned smiled as he walked toward the makeshift bar. It was the right sort of night to eat in. Mad dogs and Englishmen might be mad enough to go out in the noonday sun, but, speaking for one Englishman, he didn't much enjoy slogging through mushy snow. "You always know how to do the right thing," he tossed over his shoulder as he poured himself a stiff Scotch on the rocks and filled a glass with white wine for Dale. "Unfailingly."

"And you?" she asked. "Do you always do the right thing?" He couldn't have given her a better opening line if he'd tried. There was no sense in postponing the confrontation; she wouldn't be able to think of anything else until it had been resolved.

"Of course I do, love," he answered. He turned to look at her from across the width of the living room. "Just come over here and I'll show you how right they can be."

"I'm serious, Ned," she replied, and even from that distance he could see that she was not in the mood to play his games with him. She had something on her mind, and wasn't about to let go until it had come out. It didn't require a genius to anticipate what was coming. Still, he waited, letting her do it in her own way.

"How long have you had this vendetta against Kenneth Fraizer?" she asked.

"I don't have a vendetta with Kenneth Fraizer," he

replied calmly. He tried to look surprised as he crossed the room toward her. "I've told you before, what's between Kenneth and me is nothing more than business. You take your shots however you can, and may the best man win." He sat down in the armchair opposite her and took a deep swallow of the Scotch. He looked over to where she sat. Her eyes were as cold as the night.

"I suppose hiring Miriam away from us was just business, too?" she asked. She crossed her slim legs at the knee, and folded her arms across her chest, like a shield, as she waited for his answer.

"Just that," he replied concisely. He was determined to give her answers to the questions she posed, but to offer no more.

"What I don't understand," she said quietly, "is how you could break your promise to me. What we had together was to stand on its own, business wasn't to enter into it." She paused, waiting for his answer. When he didn't reply she finished it for him. "You betrayed that trust when you hired Miriam."

"Perhaps I'm dense, darling," he said, stopping for a quick swig of Scotch, "but I fail to see the connection. But then I always have been intrigued by the many intricate turns the mind of a woman seems to take."

"You mean you've forgotten that I'm the one who told you about Miriam? The one who went rambling on about how good she was the very first day we had lunch?"

He rose from his chair with the violent motion of a wounded bear breaking for cover. He downed the rest of his drink in a single swallow and deliberately crashed the glass down on the table beside him. His face had turned a nasty shade of red, the color of madness and vein-bursting rage. "Sometimes your stupidity drives me wild," he yelled at her. She felt, at this close range, as if the sound waves were physically buffeting her body. "Are you really so self-centered as to think that you're the only one who knows that Miriam has been the head of Kenneth's Paintings Department for the last fifteen years? The only one who knows how good she is at her job? It's not even your naiveté that makes me so angry," he said, beginning to regain his composure. "It's that you still think so little of me after the time we've spent together. You don't really know me too well," he told her seriously as he went back over to the bar and poured himself another drink. "Or understand me at all."

She looked over to where he was standing and saw the hurt clearly visible on his face. Perhaps she had made a terrible mistake. Maybe she should have had more trust in him. Now she had insulted him, insulted him to the core. "I'm sorry, Ned," she whispered.

He came back over to her and sat down beside her. His expression looked kind as he took her hand in his. "Dale," he said, "long-term employees don't leave their jobs because some new boy in town ups their salary a little. They leave because they're bored or mistreated, most often because they've been bored for years. They go over to the competition because they think it's going to be more challenging. Quite frankly, in Miriam's case, I think she was right. You have to remember that Kenneth and I run two very different kinds of houses. His caters to the establishment. Mine's more eclectic. Miriam's more than just bright in her field; she has avant-garde ideas. She'll make good use of the freedom she'll get with our operation. You can understand that, can't you?" he asked.

Dale sat quietly. She studied her hands, her nails, with apparent fascination.

"She's already doing more with me," he went on. In the face of Dale's silence he felt it incumbent upon him to prove his point. "She's on a plane to Paris right now. I think we may have found a previously unrecorded Picasso."

At the sound of the name Dale looked up at him. There was curiosity in her gaze.

"Now don't go putting yourself on the plane with her," he cautioned. "That was a bit of inside information that I don't expect to have you use against me."

"Couldn't you have at least warned me you were going to hire her?" she asked him.

"A fine idea," he answered, "if I happened to be looking for a way to compromise you. What would you have done?" he asked her. "Given me your blessing while you held the information back from Kenneth? That's the exact reason we made it clear we wouldn't discuss business in the first place. I'm sorry if this has upset you," he said, placating her. "It shouldn't. I assure you Kenneth can take care of himself, and will."

They were interrupted by a knock on the door. As she went to answer it, she turned it all over in her head. He was right; he hadn't needed her to give him information about Miriam. Yet somewhere in the back of her mind she still had the feeling she had been used. She pushed the thought away as she opened her arms to relieve the delivery boy of the large paper bags he was carrying.

Forty-five minutes later there was a litter of Chinese food on the coffee table. Ned poked at the remainders of the beef with green pepper, skillfully steering chopsticks to the pieces that he wanted. Then he picked up a piece of shrimp and, holding it between the V of the bamboo sticks, he brought it to her mouth. "Is there any more hot tea?" he asked.

She reached past him, to the china pot that rested on the corner of the table, then turned toward him to pour. It was then that he grasped her, his hand creeping into her blouse, searching out her breast. His touch was rough, almost desperate. Despite herself she found herself returning it.

His mouth was on hers, pressing with an insistence that told her this was more a demand to be asked into her bed than it was a simple kiss. His hand slid from her waist down to her rump, cupping and cradling quickly. She felt her lips begin to soften and give, accepting, then welcoming, his nuzzling. His tongue had the heady taste of red wine. Despite herself she thought of spending the night in bed with him, his crinkly ginger-colored chest hair brushing against her with the tickly animal feel that always made the difference between women and men seem so clear, and so great, to her.

He had her on the couch now, his hand spreading her legs, his fingers probing as he kissed her, his mouth pushing against her own with a force that pinned her head back on the couch and made her shove against him, frantic that she wouldn't be able to get breath. It seemed to excite him more. He was on her now, his legs spread wider than her own, his body thrusting against her, until the couch began to creak with his motion.

"I can't," she cried, pushing him away forcibly.

"But you are," he pointed out. "Do you think I can't feel what's happening with your body. I know you better than that, darling."

"It's what's happening in my brain that's the problem," she whispered. "If I only knew that what you'd told me about Fraizer's and Miriam is true."

He rolled off her, and sank to the floor, his fingers trailing over her leg as he left her. He quickly stood up and put on his jacket.

"I'm not sure there's a woman in there," he told her as he bent and lightly kissed her on the cheek. The kiss was as casual as the parting of two acquaintances at a party, and as disinterested. He was gone without another word, letting himself out as she lay there near tears.

It haunted her as she packed for London—the fact that he was probably right. She'd proven her loyalty to Kenneth, but she felt like a dried-out husk without an ounce of passion left in her. Oh God, just save me from myself, she thought as the warm, wet stream of tears finally came.

CHAPTER 34

She started to get excited when she saw Hyde Park. It stretched the length of the street to the right of them; a few early snow flurries had mounded against the iron railings where in springtime daffodils grew. Then the Dorchester loomed ahead. Dale leaned forward eagerly. The driver's cheerful "Here we are, miss," slipped her attention as they pulled up to the entrance.

She announced herself at the registration desk, and as they excused themselves to search for her name and accommodations, she turned to take a closer look at the lobby. It was as large as a soccer field. If the ballroom were the same size, it would be the ideal place to hold the annual London paintings auction.

It was tea time, she realized, looking at her watch and mentally adjusting it to the six hours' difference from New York. Waiters in black tails and white gloves were wheeling the sweets trolley from group to group and offering silver trays of watercress sandwiches. The hollow sound of fine bone-china cups meeting saucers of the same mold was clearly audible under the cathedral ceiling. Her mouth began watering at the sight of an éclair. Her eyes followed it as the trolley was wheeled from one table to the next.

"Didn't they feed you on the plane?" She turned, startled at the sound of his voice. Ivan was leaning on the edge of the registration desk. There was an amused look on his face.

"Not like this. How long have you been standing there?" she asked him.

"Only a minute. They called the suite to announce you'd arrived. Thought I'd come down and welcome you. I'd called the airport when you didn't arrive on time."

"We were delayed in New York," she explained.

"Have Miss Kenton's luggage delivered to the Terrace Suite," he instructed the porter. "We have a two-bedroom suite," he told her. "I thought we could use the sitting room as a work area. It should save us some running around time." Then he led Dale over to a small grouping of two chairs with a table that stood next to a flower arrangement the size of a monument. He attracted their waiter with a motion so subtle even she couldn't discern it. He ordered for them easily and surely—tea, sandwiches, sweets, and for Dale a sherry. He kept up a running conversation while they waited, describing the London weather, the appointments he'd set up for the following day, and the work he was turning over to her. Since the sale catalogue was to be printed in New York, he was planning to give her all the information for it so that she could take it back and follow through.

She watched him as he spoke. His movements, his hands and his face seemed relaxed but animated. From time to time excitement came into his eyes, then fled, as quick as the gallop of a racehorse. He'd lost the annoying authoritative attitude which sometimes colored his conversation. She realized now that it might just be a cover for his insecurities, one he didn't need on home soil. She listened as he laid out her London schedule. It was concrete and productive, and he seemed to be discussing it with her more as a partner than as a superior. She felt happier around him than she ever had before.

The waiter returned and arranged their table. They sat quietly for a while, nibbling, each comfortable with the silence. She found she was pleased to be there with him. If her blowup with Kenneth hadn't been on her mind she would have been content. She couldn't shake the sadness that his disappointment in her had caused. It had troubled her throughout the transatlantic flight, and it still did.

"What's wrong?" Ivan's voice sounded friendly and kind. She shook her head. She hadn't discussed it with anyone. "Just the flight. I couldn't fall asleep."

He studied her and decided that she was lying. "It doesn't look like fatigue to me," he smiled. "And I'm an expert."

She started to give another excuse, then hesitated. Maybe it was the lack of sleep, or the disconnected feeling of being in a strange country. Or maybe it was just the warm expression that was on his face as he watched her and waited. She found herself asking his opinion. "Have you ever been involved in a relationship which you thought you could control, only to find out you were being used?"

He was taken aback. The question didn't fit into the context of their relationship. They'd always managed to fence with one another instead of discussing their private lives. "Name a man who won't admit to that," he smiled, thinking of Celeste, "and I'll show you a liar. But I don't think that's what you were getting at. Tell me a little more."

"I made a mistake, Ivan.," she admitted. "I got involved with the wrong man. I'd been warned. He's not particularly liked or respected by some of the people I care about. But the situation suited my needs so perfectly, I ignored them. No, that's not quite right. I decided they were wrong. I convinced myself that I could control things, that he would be different with me because I expected the worst from him and guarded against it."

"The sin of pride," Ivan clucked, wagging a finger at her. "I recognize it well, having fallen victim to it myself from time to time. Why do we always think we're smarter than everyone else?"

"I don't any more. I misjudged the situation. I never thought of using him, and I honestly didn't believe he was using me either. But . . ." She faltered, and it became increasingly difficult for her to get the rest out as she looked into Ivan's face. His eyes, at first so understanding, had turned suspicious. "But he was," she said at last. "And as a result of that, someone's faith in me has been shattered."

"And how do you feel about him now?" Ivan asked. "About this man who was using you?"

He seemed to be able to look through her, through the flesh, the bone, the marrow, right down to her very soul. "It's still hard for me to believe I could have been so wrong," she admitted.

"It's Ned Whytson, isn't it?" Ivan asked. His question sounded like a quiet threat. She nodded yes. "You bloody fool," he whispered to her. "I told you about him the first time I met you. He has no standards, no loyalty. He's just a vulture preying on the vulnerabilities and trust of others."

Anger gave his voice the edge of superiority she hated so much. "Please stop," she begged him. "I never should have discussed it with you."

"The most ridiculous part of it," Ivan went on, leaning across the table until his face was next to hers, "is that you don't have to go to men like Whytson. Grow up," he ordered her. "Take a good long look at yourself in the mirror. You're pretty. Bright, or at least I thought so until now. Warm. If you ever let a man get close to you—a real man instead of some excuse for one like Ned Whytson—you'd find that out. You deserve more, Dale. Honestly you do." His voice had softened. He became more like a friend in those few short sentences than she would have thought possible. He had excused her for her lack of judgment, and he had gone on to make her feel like a worthwhile person, one who deserved to be loved. He'd been angry with her, shown it, then made her intact again.

"Thank you, Ivan," she said. She reached down spontaneously and squeezed his hand. For a moment she wished she could fall in love with him.

"Everyone lets their heart lead their head once in a while," he reassured her.

She looked at him thoughtfully, her eyes urging him to go on. "Yes, me too," he smiled at her. "Mine was named Celeste. She's right here in London."

Dale's heart fell. The jealousy she felt was surprising considering the fact that she'd never even thought she liked him until that afternoon.

"It's gone on for years," he told her. "I kept trying to convince her to move to Paris with me. She kept saying no. I'm sure that if she was really honest with herself she'd admit that she loves me. I know the thought of anyone else touching her still bothers me. But it's not the same as Whytson," he said, suddenly serious. "Kenneth's convinced he's behind the forgeries. Wash your hands of him. Now."

"I know what Kenneth thinks. And as long as I'm over here, I'd like to turn up as much information on Ned as possible. I want to either clear him or bury him, once and for all."

"You'll have your chance tonight," Ivan told her. "We'll be meeting one of my old London buddies, Andrew Russel. He's working for Whytson in London."

He was rewarded by the merest hint of a smile, a slight turning up of the corners of the mouth that suggested she'd gotten by a difficult conversation. It left him with an inexplicable feeling of well-being. "Time to go upstairs. You've just got time to change before we leave to meet Russel," he told her, offering his arm. She accepted it gratefully and let him lead her toward the elevator.

She stepped on the parquet floor of the entry hall of the Terrace Suite. It looked as if it had been there for centuries, aging gracefully, soothed by the gentle rubbings of decades of floor maids. In the bedroom beyond she saw his clothes neatly hung at the foot of the bed on a wooden valet. She drew back instinctively, but he took her gently by the shoulder and slowly turned her to the right. "Your room is over there," he said, pointing to a doorway that offered just a glimpse of peach chintz spreads.

She smiled at herself as she quickly unpacked, amused by her own suspicions. I've been so obsessed with the thought of avoiding a sexual relationship with the men I'm working with I see the threat where it doesn't exist. I've learned my lesson too well, she told herself as she reached for a silk dress she had bought before she left New York. She was eager to put it on. She decided to heed the advice of the salesgirl who had suggested that she wear no more than panty hose under it. She felt the silk flow easily and smoothly over her roundness. There was a sensuous feel to the way it slid around every curve and hollow. She looked at herself in the mirror and was pleased with the effect. She picked up a bag and a coat and went into the sitting room where Ivan was waiting for her. If she had suffered any doubts about how she looked, they were answered by his eyes. He didn't say a word. He didn't have to.

"Ready?" he said at last. Then he offered his arm, and led her away to the Connaught Hotel.

"It's wonderful," she said, looking at the glossy banister that circled above them.

"I used to love to climb to the top when I was little and look down. Dropped a few things on the hall porter's head from time to time, too," he told her. "If you take the time to climb up there you'll see you're standing right above his desk. Always did look forward to Sunday brunch at the Connaught," he chuckled.

She returned his good humor with a warm glance. It tickled her to think of this sophisticated man as a child, though it didn't surprise her to learn that he had suffered from a mischievous streak.

She took a long look around the dining room as they sat down; it was a man's room, full of gleaming mahogany paneling and silver carving trolleys. She turned back, satisfied, and was introduced to Andrew Russel. At first they exchanged polite social chatter, news of new restaurants in London and New York. Andrew brought Ivan up to date on friends he'd lost track of while living in Paris. And then over dinner, Ivan guided the conversation to their real interest, Ned Whytson. "You must be feeling your oats now that your boss is spending so much time in New York," Ivan suggested.

Russel shrugged it off with a disgusted expression. "It's almost more work to have him gone than here," he said. "He keeps changing his mind every minute. Worse than a woman. Oh, excuse me," he said, apologizing to Dale who gave him a sweet smile and said nothing in reply. "But first he has us ship pieces from London to New York to beef up his sales. Good ones. Now he's talking about pulling out of New

York. Of course, this can't go past this table," he warned Ivan.

"We've known each other twenty years," Ivan reminded him. "You must know you don't have to bother to say that. But what I can't understand is why he'd decide to pull back."

"He's crazy, Ivan. You know that. He didn't like anything better than working with Americans when he was in London. Now that he's in New York he says they're crazy. 'The pace of it all,'" he said, mimicking Whytson's rough tones and accent to a "t." "You know the man loves to have his two-hour lunches and weekends in the country," he went on, resuming his own voice. "Thursday till Monday, no less. My guess is that New York's too frantic for him. He thought he was bored with London. Now he's beginning to realize he was merely content."

"But to walk away from a business like that. How can he do that?" Ivan asked.

"He doesn't need any more business," Russel said quickly. "He's made a pile of money, you know. If anything, the New York operation is draining it. Faster than he expected, I'd wager. It's a different lifestyle and a market he doesn't know. I think he'd be glad to be quit of it. But let's drop business and get on to Annabelle's for some dancing," he suggested. He placed his cheese knife on the plate decisively, signaling the waiter that he had finished.

Dale exchanged a look with Ivan that said she'd rather spend the time digesting this new information than dancing. "Another night, Andy," he said, putting a friendly hand on Russel's. "I can see the telltale signs of travel fatigue beginning to creep up on Miss Kenton. I think I'd better get her home early."

Dale and Ivan said their good nights and the doorman whistled them up a cab. The conversation as they drove went immediately to Whytson and the possibility that he wasn't involved in the forgeries after all. The confusion was still lingering when they arrived back at their suite. Ivan kept at it, prolonging the discussion until she felt she would surely fall asleep without ever leaving the sitting room. "I really have to go to bed," she said at last.

Ivan walked her to her bedroom door. She stepped inside, not bothering to lock the door. She reached for a nightgown, then as quickly changed her mind, knowing that the freedom was no risk, and slipped between the crisp white linen naked instead.

She lay there, trying to keep her mind on Whytson, to analyze the new problem Russel had presented, but her thoughts turned instead to the man lying just across the living room in the next bedroom. I've got to be careful, the voice inside her said. I mustn't fall into the trap. He's just the sort of man I could become truly attached to, and that's contrary to my plans. And yet her thoughts were of how it would be to smell him, to touch him. She cradled her arms over her slim body and pulled her solitude around her. It wasn't Ivan's fault that sleep eluded her. For as she saw when the light began to creep through the drapes, the door to her bedroom had never budged.

There was bright sunlight streaming through the windows when she woke the next morning. It took her twenty minutes to get dressed, and then she joined Ivan in the dining room. He spent the next hour outlining her day and his own. He assigned her the London correspondence—making arrangements to have paintings that had been consigned from local owners delivered to the site of the sale and held, and confirming descriptions of the art for a last-minute check of the catalogue copy. The bulk of her day would be spent meeting with representatives of the press, giving them information on the new branch office as well as the upcoming sale. Part of it was set aside for a visit to Whytson's London headquarters. And, finally, she was to check the guest list for the sale night, adding to the list of their regular customers names that had been supplied by one of Ivan's friends with a local public relations office.

"Anything else?" she asked, hoping there wasn't. She'd already filled one notepad. She couldn't imagine how she'd get it all done in time.

"Just one thing," Ivan said. His voice instinctively lowered and became cautious. "It's about our private business. I've talked with Turner over in the restoration department at the museum. I want you to take the Monet over to his office when you get back to New York. He's agreed to authenticate it for us. Keep it locked up," he cautioned. "Assuming it's the real thing. Importing a fake would be the worst introduction Fraizer's could get to the London market.

"Meet me downstairs at four," he concluded as he got up from the table and prepared to leave. "We've got an appointment with the insurance representative from Lloyd's."

The morning and the early afternoon went quickly. He had scheduled her time efficiently, allowing an hour for each press interview, with only a short break in between. She joined him in the ballroom promptly at four P.M. He was already greeting Lloyd's representative when she arrived. The manager from the Dorchester stood by their side.

The insurance man could have faded into any crowd, which was, Dale suspected, just the effect he was working toward. She hoped that her story would convince him; he was just the sort who promised to be smarter than he looked.

It took them half an hour to walk the room, to discuss the dates the paintings would be arriving, and to explain to him and to the manager that they wanted the New York portion of the show to be hung as soon as it arrived, rather than stacked for several days in the hotel storerooms. The Lloyd's man objected for a time. He wanted a day in which his people could check the paintings against the insurance inventory before they were hung. But in the end he agreed, though he continued to complain that it was a bit unusual.

"I'll want six security guards," Ivan told the hotel man. "One in each corner of the room. Two milling in the crowd."

"That's two more than usual," the man told him, checking his notes.

Dale, who had been quiet until now, spoke up. "We're planning on having a Poussin included in the sale," she said as if that explained everything. In fact, it did. Neither the hotel manager nor the insurance man could easily forget the stir caused when an American bought the painting from the Duke of Devonshire's estate a few years previously and announced that he would be shipping it back to the States. English art fanatics, seeing their heritage flowing out of the country, had tried to raise enough money to keep the painting in the country, and failing that had gone to the extreme of chaining themselves to the Sotheby Gallery door to protest its removal.

"That does explain your concern," the hotel manager said.

"Frightful mess that," the insurance man agreed. "It's a pleasure to work with people who make a point of seeing from the outset that nothing can go wrong. Helps to explain why we've never had to pay off a claim for you, doesn't it?"

"You know, we could install mini-cameras at the entrance," the manager suggested. "That way you would have full video of everyone who enters the preview or the sale."

"Good idea," Ivan complimented him. He looked

at his watch, then spoke to Dale. "Go dress for supper," he told her. "I'll finish up here."

The suite seemed lonely when she let herself back in. She went directly into her room and ran a bath. Then she seated herself on the edge of the deep old tub, breathed in the fragrant steam that rose from the hot water, tested the temperature with her toes, and immersed herself.

She luxuriated in the contented feeling she'd had since being here with Ivan. It had seemed to give her a new enthusiasm for what she was doing, almost to make up for everything else that had gone wrong. That didn't seem to hurt so much when she could shift her focus to her work. She quickly ran over the list of things Ivan had given her to follow through on in New York. She would be able to work on the catalogue copy during the plane trip the next day. The rest could be accomplished quickly enough once she was back. Having the Monet authenticated was at the top of the list. I'm going to be more ambitious than ever, she laughed to herself as she quickly soaped, rinsed, and took one of the long terry bath wraps from the heated towel bar. Its warmth felt good around her body. Civilized, these English, she thought, and to her embarrassment her thoughts went immediately to Ivan and centered around some of the totally uncivilized nights they might share. For some reason she had expected him to make a move toward her, almost from the first. Silly, she told herself. It almost sounds as if you're getting interested in him. And as soon as the thought entered her head she wondered if her guard had begun to drop. The explanation is simple enough, she reassured herself. It's obvious he has that Celeste on his mind, no matter what he says to the contrary. And then, without the slightest hint of warning, she realized that she'd begun to cry.

CHAPTER 35

The limousine pulled to a quick stop at the corner before turning down Fifth Avenue, and the edge of the frame bit into her knees with the quick but harmless pressure of a dull knife. She spread her hands to either side of the painting that nestled in her lap, steadying it like the precious cargo she hoped it was.

She moved the painting back a bit on her legs, trying to keep it from cutting off her circulation. Then with one careful hand, she pulled back a corner of the wrappings and sneaked a look at it.

The gray afternoon light seemed to complement its subtle greens and mauves. They appeared as separate brush strokes when she looked at them, only to blend into a subtle continuity of tone, a perfect representation of Waterloo Bridge, when she squinted her eyes, narrowing them to slim violet slits. It was hard for her to believe it might be a forgery. Still, it was one of the most valuable pieces Fraizer's would be shipping from New York to London, and if the thief followed true to form it was just the sort of item he was likely to concentrate on.

"Did you say the south entrance?" the driver asked her.

Dale checked her notes. The south entrance, down the stairs to the basement, ask the guard for Mr. Turner's office. "Would you drop me off as close to it as you can?" she asked, wondering how far she was going to have to carry the painting.

The driver dropped her off in front of a pair of double doors, whose opening was wide enough to accommodate the unloading of a twelve-foot painting, a heroic sculpture, or an Egyptian sarcophagus.

They had all come through the doors of the great museum at one time or another, and doubtless would again. Inside, locked inner doors with a guard station blocked her way, but once his list was checked and her identification verified, the guard brought her in and gave her directions.

The bright green line that was painted on the concrete floor was easy to follow, and so her eyes were free to roam as she went through the halls. Canvases of all sizes had been moved on rolling dollies and were waiting, flush against the wall, for attention. Some were in the process of being cleaned. Others were obviously in need of restoration. There were tapestries, dusty in places, moth-eaten. Small antiquities, alabaster icons, cups and plates of bronze, had been wheeled in on metal carts and left, carefully labeled, outside a number of doors she was passing. She saw Phoenician glass and modern murals, a Calder sculpture and a broken Greek torso. The accumulation grew thicker until it reached a ridiculously jumbled climax in front of a door that belonged to someone who was either an irreplaceable cog in the wheels of the museum's progress or an unbelievably slow worker. She looked up to the plaque and read Milton Turner, Director of Restoration.

He was seated on a high stool with his back to her as she entered. He bent over his workbench with such total concentration that he didn't hear her. She waited for a moment, then cautiously cleared her throat.

Milton Turner faced her with a smile. To her surprise he looked more like a rancher than a scholar. He wore a woolen shirt of rough Pendleton plaid. His feet, in worn Topsiders, were casually hooked around the bottom bar of his high seat. "Have much problem finding us?" he asked her.

"Not at all," she answered. She looked around her, hoping to find a vacant spot large enough to accommodate the Monet. It was beginning to seem much heavier than its actual fifteen pounds.

"Here," he said, taking it from her and walking to the other side of the room. He placed it on a large metal easel, one of four that stood there, and lowered a horizontal brace that locked it into place. "Figures it would be one of the tough ones," he said as he took a closer look at it.

"I'm sorry," she apologized, then added, "What do you mean?"

"The Impressionists," he explained. "The very worst to try and date. Bring us an old master and it's simple. They used a different set of pigments—zinc or lead white instead of titanium, lapis and ultramarine for the blue—things that just aren't sold any more. It takes a pretty dedicated forger to grind lapis for his pigments," he laughed, "and one that isn't worried about time."

"And the Impressionists?" she asked.

"Used the same pigments we use today," he answered. "Almost to a one. There were a few that changed," he corrected himself, "like tin yellow. That went in and out of use over the years. But it's awfully hard to use that as definite evidence of a date," he said regretfully. "For all we know, an artist could have had a tube or two still sitting in his studio during the periods when it wasn't still generally marketed."

Dale looked at the Waterloo Bridge canvas, suddenly seeing it as a mystery composed of colors and chemicals.

"But," he said, "we do still have a few tricks up our sleeves. Want to stay and watch the sorcery? Or would you rather just leave it for a couple of hours?"

"I'm its bodyguard," she told him. "Besides, I wouldn't miss the show."

"Have a seat," he told her, pointing to the second stool by his bench. He picked up a stack of glass slides and some small scalpels, and walked over to the easel. "First we'll X-ray it," he told her as he moved the painting into a small room on the other side of the wall. "The film will let us know where any restoration's been done. We'll avoid those areas when we take paint samples."

"You will be careful with it, won't you?" she asked in a concerned voice.

"We just take the tiniest fleck of paint," he told her. "Just enough to be crushed and tested under the polarized-light microscope for chemical content. It measures their refractive indexes—sort of like their spectrums," he explained. "Then we compare them with the recorded refractive indexes we have on file for the pigments we would expect to find in a painting like this."

"That's amazing," she said. "Is that all there is to it?"

"Not quite," he told her as he continued to work. "We'll take a look at it under infrared and ultraviolet. Sometimes a forger will use an old canvas and paint over it. The original painting will show up under the ultraviolet."

"And the infrared?" she asked.

"That will tell us whether there is any underdrawing. Sometimes a forger won't sketch the canvas first—he already knows the composition because he's spent so much time studying the original."

She wanted to ask him more, but he had become so caught up in the work she hesitated to interrupt him. She sat quietly for the next two hours. At last he looked up to her and smiled. "Looks like the real thing, Miss Kenton," he said happily. "You can tell Ivan to stop worrying."

Dale returned his pleased expression. Both Ivan and Kenneth would be relieved, at least temporarily. But as good as the news was, she realized, it didn't mean that a substitution couldn't still be made before the London auction. "What's the problem?" Turner asked her, seeing her face cloud over with worry. She didn't answer him right away, reluctant to explain fully the problems that had been plaguing Fraizer's.

"Is there anything we could do to identify the canvas?" she finally asked. "Some mark or sign that would let us know later that it's definitely the one you tested?" She stopped, waiting for his reply.

Turner looked at her. A hint of surprise played over his face as he realized what she was getting at. "My good friend Ivan didn't explain the full extent of his problem to me, did he?" he asked her. He didn't expect an answer, and he didn't get one. He thought for a moment, then slowly shook his head no. "It's a tricky problem," he told her. "You've got to weigh the possibility of damaging the canvas against the threat to it. I'd hate to see you put something on the paint itself. Who knows what might happen to it in a year or two. And this isn't just any old painting we're dealing with," he said, looking at the Monet, "is it?

"You could try changing the stretcher bars. Or substituting something out of the ordinary for one of the screws that's in there now," he offered, but, as he thought it over, he rejected the idea. "On the other hand," he corrected himself, "anyone who's taken the trouble to do as good a forgery as I assume you're afraid of is probably going to spot that as well. I'm not sure what to suggest to you," he finally said.

Dale looked around the room with despair. Her eyes traveled over microscopes and chemicals, spectrograms and X-ray equipment, encyclopedias and computers, hardly seeing any of it. They came to rest on his desk, reams of papers and a computer keyboard cluttering its surface. She stared at it for a moment, unseeing. Then her eyes were suddenly alight. "What do you do with the computer?" she asked.

"I mostly use it for cataloguing the results of tests," he told her. "Assembling a record I can continue to use and add to as the years go on."

"Could we use it to record the painting?" she asked. He started to tell her no, but she interrupted him before he could get it out. "There must be some way," she insisted. "Think about it."

"Not with that one," he said definitely. "I can only think of one computer that can do that sort of thing and it's at the Jet Propulsion Laboratory. Ivan's connections might be good enough to get me to make an exception and do some testing for him, but I doubt that he knows anyone at NASA."

"Tell me about it anyway," she persisted.

For the next few minutes he described the process as simply as he could, making concessions for her lay knowledge of the art of restoration. He explained the process of producing a raking-light photograph, using one light source aimed at the painting from a side angle, then magnifying it to show the hills and valleys, the shadows and lights, of its texture and brushstrokes. He told her how they scanned the photograph, using a power spectrum to measure the frequency and size of specific features that occurred in the few square inches they had photographed—the number and length of the brushstrokes, perhaps, or their depth or angle. "Then they run them through a menu of tests," he concluded. "They've concocted over three hundred of them that can date the work or tell you about its creator by comparing it to previously recorded data."

"So let's do it," she said excitedly.

"No chance, Miss Kenton," he interrupted her. "That computer belongs to the government. They've only granted permission to use it for these tests to a few people. The work's so backed up that I've been in line for it for two months on one of my own projects."

"Is your whole future hanging on getting that project done?" she asked quietly. He looked at her closely. "Nope," he admitted. "The only thing that's at stake for me is an article that should have been turned in for publication a month ago. I guess my reputation can survive another month of missed deadlines. I've never been known for speed."

"So you'll try?" she asked.

"And that's all I can do," he cautioned her. "Just try."

The weight of the painting seemed to have been cut in half as she carried it back into Fraizer's. She hand-carried it into the storeroom, and personally placed it in the vault. It was good to know it was authentic. And if Turner succeeded in getting the computer scan done, they could check it again in London before it was auctioned to see if someone had managed a substitution. That wouldn't keep Kenneth from being stuck with the forgery, but it would save him the embarrassment of finding out after the painting had been sold to one of Fraizer's clients. And from what Kenneth had told her, if it was substituted they would have a chance to follow Donovan to the thief.

Closing the lobby door on the horns and shouts that were New York's notion of a welcome, Dale trudged up the stairs to the landing of her apartment. It never ceased to amaze her how heavy a bag of groceries could seem by the time you'd carried it up three flights. She walked down the hall to her apartment feeling flushed, disheveled, and ready for a quiet dinner and bed. She still hadn't left the jet lag behind, probably wouldn't for days.

She looked up and saw Ned Whytson at her door. He was carrying a dozen long-stemmed red roses wrapped in cellophane, and for the first time since she'd known him he looked sheepish and shy.

"How long have you been here?" she asked him. "What if I hadn't come home for dinner?"

"Then I would have spent the next two hours standing here feeling like a blasted fool while your neighbors went in and out staring at me. I was an ass," he said, extending the bouquet. Pastel ribbons trailed behind it. "I was awfully hard on you the last time I saw you. Wounded ego, I guess. I hope you don't mind my coming by."

"Hold on to those until we get inside," she told him, fumbling with the locks. "I'm glad you're here. I wouldn't have wanted to leave it the way we did." As she opened the door to her living room she was thankful that he had come to her place instead of asking her over to his.

"Have some champagne," he offered, pulling another bag out from under his arm. "It will warm you up." She hesitated for a moment, considering whether it was a double entendre.

"I didn't mean that the way it sounded," he said quickly. "How was London? I hope you got a chance to go by Whytson's and check out the competition."

"Don't I always?" she asked, handing him a glass. They clinked in a brief toast. "It's very different from your New York place."

"It is," he agreed. "I've missed it," he added after a moment of silence. "The weekends in the country. The English pace. You people really drive yourselves into the ground over here. You don't know how to live." He sounded so low she wondered if Russel's story had been accurate. "To tell you the truth, I've missed it so much I've decided to chuck New York and move back."

"Who'll run the branch here?" She tried to put the sound of surprise in her voice.

"I'm chucking that, too. I've begun to make arrangements for a final sale here. Anything that comes in after the catalogue is printed will get shipped to London and sold there. That's how I've decided to split the territory," he joked. "I'll take one side of the Atlantic. Kenneth can have the other. Civilized, don't you think?"

"I wouldn't have expected anything less from you," she replied as he refilled their glasses, though the truth of the matter was that she would have. Everything Kenneth had told her had led her to expect Ned to be highly uncivilized. Someone willing to break Kenneth no matter what the cost, even if it required theft and forgeries. At least if he was pulling out of New York she could be sure she hadn't given him any information that was being used against Fraizer's. That lifted her spirits. "What about Miriam?" she asked, suddenly remembering what had caused their blowup in the first place.

"I offered her a spot in London. She turned me down. Says she's too old to learn new tricks at this late date."

"After all those years with Kenneth. Now she's just left high and dry."

"I hardly think I owe her a pension after one short month," Ned interrupted. He sounded irritated. "She made her own choices, Dale. She didn't have to leave Fraizer's. Now she doesn't have to stay in New York. It's business. Strictly business."

"You're a tough man, Ned Whytson," she said, sipping her champagne. She settled further down into the cushions of the couch and stared thoughtfully at her glass. She'd never quite agreed with his business philosophy. She'd simply managed to overlook it. "You follow one line in life. The one that leads straight to what's best for you."

"Let me tell you what I think would be good for Ned Whytson now," he said affectionately. He put his arm around her shoulders and pulled her closer.

"Having Dale Kenton move to London to work at Whytson's. How does that sound to you? I know I'll recover from the disappointment of having to close the business here. But I'm not sure I could recover from having to do without you."

She didn't say a word the entire time he spoke; her thoughts seemed frozen. But as he stopped, it all hit her in a rush. The guilty feelings that her simple need to feel loved without any real involvement had brought on. Her doubts about the way Ned conducted himself. Her anger over the way he had used her to get to Miriam. She remembered Ivan's advice, and the belief he had held out that she might still be able to let the barriers down and be happy like any other woman. She knew what she was longing for now, and she knew that Ned couldn't supply it. The decision about their relationship that had seemed so complicated in London was simple. She wanted to be with someone openly, honestly, with no ulterior motives. It was time, if only she was strong enough.

"I don't want to go, Ned," she told him. She put her hand over his and held it lightly as she studied him, trying to read his reaction. "I guess I used you while you were here," she admitted. "The same way you were using me to try to find out about Fraizer's. It wouldn't work as well in London, would it?"

His expression didn't change. He was on his guard as usual, determined to come out looking like a winner. He carefully put down his glass. "I think dinner would be a little superfluous now, don't you?" he asked as he reached for his coat. When she heard the sound of the lock clicking closed behind him she knew that another chapter of her life was about to begin.

CHAPTER 36

Ivan wished they could move faster. They'd managed to get from Kennedy to the city at a good pace before the cab had bogged down, but now it looked as if they would be stuck in a mass of honking, idling, cursing traffic indefinitely.

It seemed like hours until they reached his office. There was an envelope waiting on his desk. He recognized Dale's writing and tore it open eagerly. She had left him a written report on Turner's authentication of the picture. His first thought was of how pleased Kenneth would be.

He dialed his extension, ready to go upstairs and give him the good news. Barbara was still there, but Kenneth had already left. She told Ivan that Kenneth was making one stop, then going on to deliver some snuff boxes to a client who was staying at the Mayfair Regent. Ivan hung up, then made a snap decision. He'd go to the hotel and hope to spot Kenneth either entering or leaving. The news was too good to waste, and perhaps the two of them would be able to have dinner together as well. There was a lot they had to discuss.

The Mayfair lobby was busy. Ivan walked over to one of the comfortable chairs that flanked the fireplace. He felt exhausted. He picked up that day's copy of the *Wall Street Journal*. The type looked like a hill of ants swarming in front of his eyes. He tried something simpler, a *Time* magazine. Then he stood up and began to pace the lobby, killing time until Kenneth's arrival.

He sensed the commotion behind him before any sound reached his ears. As he turned, the doorman rushed through the entrance, his face ashen. He avoided everyone, looking neither to one side nor the other, as he strode to the front desk and hurriedly whispered something to the assistant manager, who immediately disappeared.

Ivan was drawn there, with the other people in the lobby. They formed a small crowd that, like filings near a magnet, slowly and inexorably moved to the spot of attraction. One man, a white-haired older gentleman, whispered to his wife, "Poor guy. His ticker gave out. Right in front of the hotel."

A chill spread through Ivan's body, from fingers and toes to his guts as he turned and walked toward the door. Please God, he prayed, don't let it be him.

"You don't want to go out there right now." The doorman grabbed him by the arm, but he fought loose. His eyes told Ivan that his worst fears were true. "There's an ambulance on the way," the doorman called as Ivan ran out to the sidewalk. "Just don't move him until they get here."

Kenneth lay there, his face as white as the sidewalk. He looked as if all the blood he owned had been drained from him. He recognized Ivan and tried to smile, then consciousness seemed to slide out from under, wavering like an unsteady bridge that couldn't be counted on.

Ivan felt Kenneth's fingers move inside his own with an impotent squeeze. "They finally got me," he said. His fingers reached slowly up to tap his chest. "Right in the heart. Find out who's doing it, Ivan," he whispered. "Find out who's trying to destroy me."

Ivan nodded a numb yes.

The ambulance ride was a nightmare. They wove in and out of the Manhattan traffic, Ivan feeling every bump and swerve as much as Kenneth. They drove for what seemed like an eternity, though it couldn't have been more than five minutes. The sirens screamed in Ivan's ears like harpies calling Kenneth to the grave. Kenneth slipped in and out of consciousness, and at one point looked directly at Ivan as if he didn't recognize him. His face became ugly at times, a fear of death filling its outlines. By the time they pulled into Lenox Hill Hospital, Ivan felt close to collapse.

He had placed a quick call to Steven, who met them at the entrance and saw his father whisked away by a group of doctors and technicians that were calling out a code blue alert. Seas of equipment began to pour into the area, leaving them stranded together like a pointless island between the waves of activity.

It was suddenly quiet around them. Only an occasional nurse passed by. Ivan turned to Steven as if to speak, but no words seemed to come. There was nothing he could think of that would make it better.

They sat in silence for a few minutes before he spoke. "He's a fighter, Steven," he said. "This is just one more battle that he'll win." As he spoke, Steven broke down and cried.

He couldn't shake the moment when they'd wheeled his father through the hospital doors. He'd looked down at him. He'd seen him ebbing away, and his own star ascending, and at the same time he'd felt the fear that comes when you finally have to take responsibility for your own life.

Perhaps he was most frightened because, for the first time, he saw his own mortality. It was like watching himself dying, his father's life and his own a sort of chain in which when one link drops under the water, the others have no choice but to follow it down. He understood the far-reaching consequences that can follow on any man's most ordinary actions. He had looked at his father's still hands and was now sorry he had ever hoped to pull the reins of power from them, and for that small moment he would have done anything, anything in his power to save him.

He felt faint as he watched the doctor walking down the long corridor toward them. The man's face was noncommittal, his mouth hidden behind a surgical mask, his eyes revealing little more. It seemed to take forever for him to reach them, then bend down to them to reassure them. "It was just heart palpitations. Then hyperventilation when he panicked. He must have been under quite a strain lately. We're going to keep him here overnight for observation," he continued, "then we'll send him home. But I want him to rest and cut down on his schedule for a while—or you really will be bringing him in here with very serious heart trouble."

"Thank you," Steven said, extending his hand to the doctor.

"Thank God," he heard Ivan say beside him.

CHAPTER 37

The temperature outside had fallen to the thirties. Inside the truck depot wasn't much better, though the five- or six-degree difference seemed to be enough to encourage rats to desert the alley trash cans and move into the beams of the ceiling. As he stood inside the door lighting a cigarette, he could hear them, their tiny feet making a noise like the blowing of dry leaves as their nails went scuttling between studs and across the attic floor. The sound gave him the chills.

He looked around the loading dock, then chafed

his hands together, a cigarette dangling from his narrow lips.

"Jesus," he said, "it's colder than a witch's tit in here." Then he was so taken with his own sense of humor, he inhaled the wrong way and went into a coughing fit. He looked around him to see if he had been observed. He had the manner of a redneck who's learned to look as if he has street smarts before he's learned to think with them. He immediately reached into his coveralls for another cigarette to replace the one he had dropped on the floor.

"Get away from that door, will ya," said the other man, the stocky older one. The word Foreman was stitched across the front of his coveralls like bright red markers in a sea of industrial blue. He was Bronx born and bred. If his accent hadn't proved it, his attitude would have. The younger man had decided long ago that the foreman knew his way around the city. He also knew how to make it work for him, or so it appeared from the wad of bills he always flashed.

"Get these things laid out in the van, will ya," the foreman said impatiently. He pointed to the pile of ropes and padded cloths that were stacked on a pallet in the corner of the room. He didn't move himself. He stuck close by the door. The younger man was used to obeying, so he took the things and headed toward a truck that had Artworks Crating and Shipping lettered on its side.

The knock came as he was inside the van. He looked out in time to see the foreman move through the doorway. He slipped out of the van and stood at its side. He waited, stamping his feet in a way that made you think of even colder days. But then he was from Georgia, his blood was thin, and days that seemed normal to any New Yorker appeared to go against him.

Within minutes the foreman came back through the door. He was carrying a single crate. The younger man saw that it was clearly marked with the stamp of the House of Fraizer. An envelope was in the foreman's hand, a thick one that he opened and as quickly closed after letting his fingers ruffle the bills inside.

The foreman looked at him appraisingly, deciding how much it would take to buy him off. The younger man had the beady eyes of a raccoon, always looking to sneak and nab something. One good thing about him though, the foreman thought. He'd come up north with a stringy little wife and two brats. He couldn't afford to make any moves that would lose him his job. It was good to have a man like that, one who was easy to keep under your thumb. The foreman peeled off a single hundred, paused, then followed it with another. "See that one with this number gets loaded first." He pointed to a weigh bill on the side of the crate.

As the young man pocketed the bills, he couldn't help but wonder how many more hundreds had been in the package. Still, the most he did about it was to watch as the foreman took the crate into the truck and slipped it into the space between the driver's seat and the partition that divided the cab from the cargo space. It fit neatly, with perhaps an inch to spare but not much more.

"Ready?" the foreman asked as he pulled a cap onto his head and opened the door to the passenger's seat.

Dale took another sip of tea and looked at her watch. Its face read three A.M.

The apartment already looked deserted. Maybe it was the stack of luggage at the door. She wondered once again whether they had been crazy to try to get everything loaded, then get themselves onto the same plane. They could have sent the paintings ahead the night before. But when she remembered how concerned Kenneth had looked she realized they had made the right decision.

He had looked small in his bed at home. The room was crowded with more flower arrangements than she had ever seen in one place. He had smiled as he watched her looking around in wonder. "At least I've managed to give a boost to the flower industry."

"I don't think there's anyone in the art world who hasn't sent you something," she said, looking at some of the cards. "That must make you feel better."

"I'd feel better if they'd spend their money at Fraizer's instead of on Fraizer," he joked.

She had reviewed with Kenneth all the preparations for the press, the guest list, and the previews that she had made in London. It wasn't easy. Ivan had told her about the conversation he had had with Kenneth earlier in the day. He had never seen him so depressed. Fraizer's had reached the point at which if the Monet was substituted he might not have any way out but to take the house public. The only other way out was to sell the Degas, and Kenneth couldn't bring himself to break the promise he had made to his father.

The sound of the buzzer startled her. She looked around, the reality of the day and the difficulties that lay ahead of her intruding themselves on her.

Steven and Ivan were already at the office when she arrived. The three of them stood downstairs, awaiting word that the truck had arrived. She silently counted the crates that were stacked up around them. Twenty-eight, precisely the number that had been locked away in the vault the night before.

An inventory was in the briefcase she placed next to her luggage. Behind it, in a simple unmarked folder, were Milton Turner's instructions on how to have the Monet photographed once they arrived. To her relief, Ivan had managed to secure a favor from the head of one of London's best museums, who had arranged to have the picture taken and the information sent back on a telecommunicator to the Jet Propulsion Laboratory for an immediate analysis. If all went as planned, they would have a confirmation on the Monet's identity one day before the sale. As the guard came in to tell them that the truck had arrived, she crossed her fingers and prayed one more time, let it be the original Monet. Please.

The loading went quickly. Her shoulders relaxed from their rigid position once the driver loaded the Monet. They had all agreed that it would be safest if they got it in first, then lined the other twenty-seven crates between its sheltered spot and the truck's back doors. When the final canvas was in place and the van's doors closed and bolted, she turned to see that her luggage was safely stowed in the trunk of the Fraizer limousine. Then the three of them climbed in and the car pulled away following closely in the tracks of the Artworks truck.

She sat on the back seat with Ivan. Steven took the jumpseat and traveled sitting backwards. She kept her eyes glued to the truck as it went, half expecting a flat tire or some engine trouble to occur as they traversed the route to the airport.

"Slow it down for a minute here," the foreman said to the young man at the wheel as they entered the Triborough Bridge. "I'm going to need a little time." His foot released the pedals and the speedometer began to imperceptibly drop. The limousine followed their lead, leaving several car lengths between them. As it did, the foreman carefully reached behind him, slipped a panel in the van's divider, and switched the crate that had arrived in their depot that morning with the one that had been leaned against the front of the trailer. Then he slipped the panel back into place. "You'd better hurry it up," he said to the man beside him. "These people have got a plane to catch." There was a satisfied smile on his lips as he watched the speedometer begin its climb back up to sixty.

The same smile was on Dale's face as she saw the last of the crates passed safely up into the belly of the British Airways jet. "Perfect," she said, looking to Ivan. "Next stop London."

CHAPTER 38

"Smile!" Ivan held his hands around his face and focused on an imaginary lens. Steven stopped in his tracks.

"What gives?"

"Video," Ivan replied, pointing to a mini-camera that had been mounted over the door to the Dorchester ballroom. It slowly swiveled as they watched, its omnipresent eye sweeping the expanse of the room. "Lloyd's of London. It was their idea. Anyone who gets near these paintings will be doing it on film."

"Good idea," Steven said approvingly. He looked around the room. Six security guards were already posted. They seemed to be taking their job seriously, two of them standing over the unhung canvases that were stacked against the rolling trolley that had brought them in, the rest of them stationed, one to each wall, with the paintings that had been hung. At the other end of the ballroom, Dale was standing and squinting at a canvas as it was positioned on the wall. Satisfied, she gave the order for it to be put in place.

"Almost finished?" Ivan asked her as he and Steven approached.

"Another two hours, I'd guess," she answered. The strain of the last week was beginning to show on her face. "I think I'm about ready for a bath and some sleep."

"I'll say," Steven teased her, wrinkling his nose.

She ignored him and went on to the next painting, a small Pissarro that had been consigned from a London gallery.

"Let's try it over on the other wall." She turned and started across the room, but before she reached her destination Steven stopped her with a gentle touch on the arm. "Just five more to go," he said. "Why don't you go up and take a nap? I'll stay here and finish up. You look totally beat."

"Thanks a lot," she answered, smoothing her long black hair and pretending vanity. "You certainly know how to make a girl feel good."

"Don't be like that," he told her. "I'll be happy to let you off the hook for a while. Don't worry. I'll watch over everything with an eagle eye. No time out for tea or drinks. Just guarding, guarding, guarding." His voice took on the tired chant of a worker toting a heavy load.

She began to smile. Steven had been a different person since his father's scare. He'd spent the last week working with her, crating and labeling the paintings. There wasn't anything in the preparations for the London trip that had escaped his attention. It seemed as if he had been everywhere.

"You really have been wonderful this last week," she told him. "It's as if you want everything to be even better than he left it when your father gets back."

He looked down at the floor for a long moment, as if compliments were so rare for him he didn't know how to reply. She thought she saw a little tremor in his jaw, but it quickly disappeared and he turned his handsome, clear-cut face to her. "I've never been so frightened as I was when I saw him lying there that night," he admitted. "You know they say that children always take it on themselves when their parents have trouble—arguments, divorces, personal problems. As if they, the children, caused it. I have never felt that way before. Not even when my mother died. But it was all I could think of when I saw him lying there. If he hadn't been doing everything—if I had been carrying my own weight at the house—he wouldn't have been out there."

"Steven," Dale said sympathetically. "You're looking at it all wrong. It's not your fault. You've tried to take on more. I've seen you. It's him. He's always insisted on doing it all himself."

"Maybe," he admitted, "but I still can't help but think it's partially my fault."

"This may sound terrible to you," Dale said quietly, "but it may work out as the best thing that could have happened." She put a friendly hand on his arm to get his attention. "It gives you a chance to show him how well you can do while he's gone."

"Odd," he said. "That's almost the same thing that Katherine said when I told her what had happened and that I'd be going to London in Kenneth's place."

They looked around the walls, which were almost filled now with the paintings they had brought from New York and the ones which had been consigned in London. It was a fine display, with at least a dozen recognized masters included.

"Go on and take that nap," said Steven. "Or don't you think I can handle hanging the last five paintings?"

"Of course you can," she answered. She looked back across the ballroom with the expression of a mother who has just left her brood in the care of an unfamiliar sitter. "Are you sure it's a good idea?"

"Would you go on?" he said, beginning to sound frustrated.

Dale walked into the lobby. She'd been up at two A.M. to watch the truck being loaded. She'd been in the ballroom for the last six hours watching the paintings as they were hung. She'd left them with half a dozen guards, not to mention Steven. And she still felt as if she'd parked them on a street corner and taken a walk. Despite all her precautions she was nervous. Maybe she'd become so obsessed with preventing another theft she'd lost her sense of proportion. She stopped at the front desk and handed some envelopes to the head porter. "Could you post these to New York?" she asked him.

He glanced at the one that was addressed to Manhattan Security. "Would you like this registered?" he asked.

"No," she answered quickly. It was just a request for a copy of the papers Crown had given her during their meeting. She seemed to have lost some of them, and she wanted to keep her file complete.

"Your room number?" the porter asked.

"Terrace Suite," she told him, realizing how much she was looking forward to going up to it and slipping into bed.

The suite seemed huge and empty. She didn't remember it feeling that way on her last trip. She tried to concentrate on the details of the sale, but her mind kept slipping back to Ivan. She rang for a cup of tea, thinking it would calm her nerves, but nothing seemed to help. And finally she admitted that for the first time in years she wanted to be with someone. Not just with anyone for the sake of simply being with a man, but with someone special, someone she cared about and wanted to explore further.

She slowly stirred the tea, wondering when her feelings had changed. She could remember when they'd gone from hostility to friendship. But when had the desire snuck in? She put down her cup and started toward the bedroom, hoping she would be able to get some sleep. She cared more than she had known.

CHAPTER 39

It had become a familiar sight. By eight o'clock bidders had begun to filter into the room, searching for their reserved seats. To one side they'd placed a table and a bank of phones that were being manned by workers who'd been hired to work in the London house. Already they could be heard speaking in three languages, verifying connections to Germany, France, and the United States.

Steven stood at the back of the room, elegant in black tie. Over his head the small mini-camera slowly swiveled in its perpetual half circle, taking in and taping everything that was happening in the room.

Ivan stood to the front of the salesroom, his eyes searching the crowd with the same regularity as the camera's lens. He was the recipient of a constant stream of congratulations, as old friends came forward to convey their best wishes for the new branch office. He accepted them graciously, but with an air of preoccupation. His thoughts, like Dale's, were centered on Lot 20, Monet's Waterloo Bridge.

Dale paced from one side of the backstage area to the other. The festive rustle of her taffeta dress wasn't much camouflage for the concern that was written on her face. She looked toward the phone that had been installed behind the curtains, willing it to ring, willing Milton Turner's voice into existence on the other end of the line. Her throat felt parched and her body too light to be connected to her worried thoughts, and yet a moist sheen of perspiration had begun to spread over her forehead and into the small cracks and crevices of her clenched palms. Turner's call earlier that day had been the worst possible news. JPL's computers had been put on standby to track a satellite flight. He couldn't expect to have an analysis of the picture of the Monet until they'd been released from their priority hold.

She walked forward to where the green velvet curtain separated her from the salesroom in front of the stage. She pulled it back an inch or two and sneaked a secret look at the proceedings. Spectators were settling, almost every chair filled. She sought out Steven's face near the back door. He continued to stare out over the crowd, a worried look creeping into his expression. Dale's heart went out to him. It was obvious that he was suffering regrets because his father couldn't be there. She hoped he'd have cause to look less bothered by the time the sale was over. As the bidding began, she assumed a position backstage next to the phone. Her hand strayed to the table, and lay ready to pick up the receiver when Turner called. She tried to remove her thoughts from the possibility that the painting had been misplaced, and instead concentrated on the sounds of the bidding that crept to her through the heavy velvet curtain. The muffled droning began to sound as caressing as the distant sound of the ocean, as soothing as the crash and retreat of faraway waves.

She had learned by now that every auction has its own pace. The slow building up. The ebbs and flows of excitement. She could sense them tonight without any need to confirm them by looking out and over the crowd. Bids had become more rapid, the auctioneer's tone more urgent. There was a quieter period after that, like a small dip in the stock market adding interest to a steady rise. And then the sounds burst out again in a low key, yet frantic, building to a crescendo.

It felt odd understanding it without seeing it. She would have thought that it would make the auction pass faster, like a long trip spent asleep, but instead each moment seemed to drag out into a protracted piece of time. She was feeling lulled, strangely relaxed and yet alert, when the ring of the phone split the quiet backstage air.

Listening, she felt her heart stop beating at Turner's words. Her throat tightened. But as she hung up, she pulled herself together and did what she had to do. Lifting the hem of her gown, she rushed to the curtain, and pulled it back far enough to look out into the room.

She could see Ivan standing to the side of the room, though she couldn't catch his eye. He was too intent on following the auctioneer and the crowd that watched breathlessly as three among them battled over the Monet that now stood on an easel center stage. She could hear the bidding climb to four hundred fifty thousand and then beyond. She pulled the curtain back farther, revealing her face, frantically motioning to Ivan as the bid climbed another fifty thousand.

At last he spotted her, and knew immediately what had happened.

"It's not ours," she said silently, her lips forming the words for him to read from across the room.

"Do I have $650,000? $650,000, ladies and gentlemen?" The auctioneer's words rang clearly out across the room. $600,000, once, twice," and his hammer came down with a solid bang that neither Ivan nor Dale would ever forget. "Sold," he cried, as a round of applause broke out in the crowd.

CHAPTER 40

The fog was thick as whipped cream. The moisture of it clung to his face as he walked quickly down the street. It settled on his topcoat, surrounding him with the acrid odor of damp wool. He looked neither to the right nor to the left. He had a destination, a very definite one, and didn't want to chance any scrutiny that would let him be recognized later.

The walk took half an hour. He heard Big Ben tolling the time as he turned the corner into a cramped commercial alleyway. Eleven o'clock. He checked his watch, pleased to see that it coordinated to the minute with the hour that was reverberating in the still night air. He looked up, confirming what he already knew. A sign, Balbour et Cie Wine Importers, hung above the doorway where he stood. He glanced over his shoulder and, seeing nothing, walked down the three short steps that led below the street level. He knocked three times on the heavy wooden door, then waited and followed it with two knocks. The door immediately swung open.

He could hear them as he walked between the musty rows of bottles and cases, their voices a muffled guide. He stood outside the door for a moment listening, waiting to hear whether they were talking about him. He welcomed the opportunity to see them before they noticed he had arrived. It gave him a chance to gauge their mood, to venture an educated guess as to which of them would be his biggest rival that night. Then he moved to the doorway and looked in, surveying their expression and their movements.

"Out of uniform, Dimitri?" he said at last. "Or have you finally decided to defect?"

The man to the back of the room, the thickset member of the group, swung around to look at him.

"When in Rome, Baron," he shrugged, "dress like the filthy capitalists." A measured smile slowly creased his face, producing crannies and wrinkles in a reddish skin weathered by untold snowstorms and cold weather.

"I have always wondered, Dimitri," the Oriental member of the group went on, "where you keep them when you get them. Surely you can't be smuggling them back into Moscow. You know how we'd all miss you if you were shot." His hand swept grandly around the room, including the other two members of the group gathering in his statement.

"As if I would ever tell you where my paintings are kept," the Russian replied in his accented English. "I hear a Titian disappeared from the church in Siena last week. One can't be too careful with such thieves wandering around."

"He's right," the Baron interrupted. "I wonder if our supplier had anything to do with that little caper?" he asked, turning to the others. "Wouldn't it be nice if we could include that in tonight's festivities?"

"I don't think the itinerary this week included Italy," Dimitri replied.

"Pity," the Baron said. He passed his empty wineglass to the fourth member of the group, who took it gracefully, and as agilely filled it. "Might I see?" asked the Baron as the glass was returned to him. His hand indicated the bottle which had been returned to the table in front of his friend. It was passed over to him, the green glass still dusty from the decades it had spent locked away in the cellars that surrounded them. "Very nice, Balbour," he said as he looked at the label. "The fifty-six must be going for . . ."

"Around ten thousand dollars," Lord Balbour replied. "If you can find it, that is." He looked back toward the Baron with the satisfied expression that one-upmanship can bring. He'd been buying Bordeaux from the vineyards at the Baron's château for over twenty years. In all that time he'd never let the Frenchman top him in the vintage that he served. Accomplishing that was becoming increasingly difficult with every passing year. The four who had gathered together this evening spared themselves nothing. Each indulged himself in his own particular whim, each could afford to. Be it Tong's girls, the Baron's wines, or Balbour's horses, each bought the best. It was only in the realm of stolen art, masterpieces that could be purchased at a fraction of their cost, that their tastes coincided.

"Any absentee bidders?" Tong asked the group. He was busy estimating the price of the canvas that had called them together. Like all the men who had attended, he'd been there to see the ivory hammer fall at $600,000 during Fraizer's sale. In any ordinary group the stolen painting would be sold for ten to twenty percent of its market value, a discount that reflected the fact that the owner would never be able to put it on open display. But this was no ordinary group. The game between them had progressed so far, they were willing to pay a premium for the mere satisfaction of knowing that the art wouldn't be going to a competitor. It was necessary to bid correctly, and knowing the full extent of the competition was part of the process of reaching a figure that would guarantee success in this very extraordinary sort of auction.

"All the bidders are here," Balbour told him.

Tong looked down at the sheet of paper and the envelope that had been placed in front of him. His mind continued to work in the silence that had descended on them, grinding the facts he had to deal with, the sale price of the painting, the men who were sitting next to him, even finer as he worked toward his decision. He reached for the paper, then withdrew his hand once more, having fallen prey to second thoughts.

It was very simple. Each bidder had one chance. He wrote down the figure he was willing to pay, stretching himself as far as he could since there was no second bid. There was a safeguard for the man who wanted to win no matter what the cost. He could write "open," and pay half again the highest bid that had been made against him. Each of the bidders was accustomed to dealing with large sums, and each of them knew that the money they bid this night would be tied up indefinitely unless the painting could be resold in an equally underground fashion.

"Are you ready, gentlemen?" asked Balbour. He had been assigned to do the honors that evening. He stepped to the front of the room, emerging from the shadows and casually lifting the half-filled glass that was waiting for him to his lips. He rolled the rich liquid around in his mouth as he watched them considering their bids, letting it warm itself on his palate, savoring the ruby aroma that was released as it did. He seemed relaxed, even enjoying himself. He put down his glass and passed among them, watching them prepare their bids. He smiled occasionally, like a spectator at a poker game who knows the hands, and the likely results, before the participants do. He noticed Dimitri studying the others, trying to tell from their eyes how much the others wanted the prize. When each man had finished and folded the slip of paper in front of them, he spoke.

"Mr. Tong," he requested, "would you be so kind as to read your bid?" There was a certain form to these evenings.

Tong opened the paper that he had placed in

front of him, though he didn't have to. "$250,000," he told them.

"Thank you," the auctioneer replied. "Colonel Smolensky?"

Dimitri Smolensky opened the paper with the same plodding slowness that usually marked his progress through life. In this case it didn't take long for the reason to become obvious to the rest. "$200,000," he said. He crumpled the offensive paper and flung it at the wall with the same gesture he might have used to break a fine crystal wineglass after a toast.

Balbour allowed the hint of a smile to play on his lips. He seemed to enjoy the power he exerted during the minutes it took for the auction to finish. "Baron?" he said.

"$255,000," came the quick reply. He opened his bid and laid it out with the others.

"I believe the bid is now mine," Balbour said as he leaned back in his chair. He was feeling quite smug. The Cabernet was an especially good one. He opened his paper slowly, drawing the moment out, then quite softly he told them, "Open."

They came up to him, each in turn, and offered their congratulations in the most civilized possible fashion. He repaid them by reaching into the stonework behind him and withdrawing another bottle of the good red they'd been drinking. It was an easy way to win them back, since the cost would be covered by his profit from Donovan who would be buying it from him. He poured generously into Tong's glass, who nodded his approval. Then he circulated around the room and filled new glasses for the others.

"Just one last formality," Balbour reminded them as he drew out the small black tape recorder that he carried in his pocket. "The English are victorious," he said into it. Each of the other participants confirmed it as they left. Then he carefully placed it on the upper ledge of the door jamb, and let himself out as quietly as he had come.

Kenneth's hand trembled as he replaced the receiver. Bill Donovan's voice still echoed in his ears. His contact had called right on schedule, offering the Monet at $430,000. Delivery had been promised for the next day in New York. The conclusion to be drawn from that was obvious—the painting had never left the States. The substitution had been made before the lots had been shipped to London, probably while they were still in the vaults of the House of Fraizer.

The biggest disappointment had been Donovan's refusal to name his contact. Fraizer would pay out close to half a million dollars without gaining even a name. He felt horribly empty and alone.

He slowly looked around him. He wished, perhaps for the thousandth time, that he still owned the other three family paintings that his father had carried out with him from Russia. It was odd. The closer death came, the more he found he wanted to hold on to the things that symbolized life, his life and his father's.

He ran through it in his mind once again, hoping to find some undiscovered way out. There wasn't any question of his loaning the business more money, he simply didn't have it. It was too late to pull out of the London expansion. In fact, he had to admit that the desire to expand had been burning in him hotter than ever since he had been lying in this small white bed. That left just two other possibilities—sell the Degas, the last of the family paintings, or bite the bullet and go public.

He raised a hand to his forehead, hoping somehow to relieve the pressure that had suddenly gripped it, and as he did he remembered how his wrist had been followed by tubes, metal clamps, and rubber, when he was in the hospital. He had felt like a machine, the husk of a body that had been reduced to the sum of its mechanical functions instead of a person.

It had been that way for his father at the end as well. The memory of it was still vivid in his mind, the old man wasting slowly away while the medical aids, the bottles and gauges and electric connections multiplied around him. Still, the desire to preserve life, if not his own, then the life that would flow on within his son, his descendants, had burned within him. For the first time Kenneth could understand the urgency that had been in the old man's voice when he called him to his side and pleaded with him never to sell their last painting. He felt the same instinctive compulsion to preserve a symbol that would outlast himself.

He wanted to leave two signs, his name, Fraizer, spread throughout the world for all to see and recognize. And a more interior token, a painting that would be held close and cherished by the Fraizers who would come after him as evidence of what they had needed to overcome in order to survive. Going public didn't seem so bad if it let him hold on to those dreams. Especially if he could hold a majority interest in Fraizer's and guide its reputation and the family's destiny. When he looked at it that way, the decision was easy. As much as it pained him he would call Herb Phillips. He thought of letting Steven do it, but then he realized he couldn't let go of the power to make this last decision real.

He lay back on his pillows, his eyes staring blankly at the walls in front of him. To the curious maid who came in and followed the direction of his gaze, it looked like an empty space. But to him it was a Degas, the one that even now was hanging on his library wall, casting a protective shield of family history over him, and helping him to gather the strength to mend himself and face the changes that the future was about to bring.

CHAPTER 41

"Oh, Ivan," Dale said, sobbing. "I tried so hard. So hard." She looked at him, misery in her face, and with a small movement swayed slightly toward him and back. He took it as an invitation and, putting his arms around her, held her until the sobs subsided.

"It's not your fault," he said finally, wiping away the tears with one delicate finger. "No one could have done more than you did."

"It's come at such a bad time, when Kenneth was stretched to the limit."

"You can't think of it that way," said Ivan, gently patting her shoulder as he spoke. "This isn't a thief who's collecting for himself. It's not a vendetta. It's someone who wants money, not art. As simple as that. As soon as Donovan let us know that the painting had been offered for sale, that was clear."

"I guess so," she said as she softly slipped away from his grasp. "I have to go downstairs for a minute," she told him. "I promised a list of the buyers to the front desk. They need some authorization to release them from the storeroom when the new owners show up."

"Do you really have to go now?" he asked her. "Right this moment?"

"I really do," she said, and she looked at him so oddly it was as if she were deliberately running away from the emotion he was showing. He seemed to be toying with the idea of testing her, of telling her how he felt about her before she had a chance to leave the room, then rejected the thought before the words were out of his mouth. "I'll see you in the morning?" he asked.

"Let's have breakfast at nine," she agreed.

She breathed deeply as she stepped into the lift. She had sensed Ivan's growing interest in her. She felt the passion that he was beginning to feel for her and when she most wanted to say yes it grew overwhelming to her. She longed for the safety of him, the idea that she might be able to hide away within his arms while the rest of the world with its troubles and problems went by. But she feared it more.

Anger toward her father rose up in her until it was a choking lump in her throat. She tried to push it down. She had adored him since she was a child. But this time she had to face the fact that she was angry at him, angry and hurt. Angry more than anything else because she couldn't shake the fears his deserting her mother and her had left behind. The fears had taken over her life. They stood in the way of her getting close to Ivan. They left her feeling tired and suspicious and empty.

The lift stopped at the lobby. She walked, preoccupied, to the front desk, gave them the list of buyers, and took back a breakdown of the hotel bill to be reviewed before checkout the next day.

Trying to look at it when she got back to the suite, she was too distracted to concentrate. She left it on the small desk in her room and went to bed instead.

It wasn't any better there. She lay awake for what seemed like hours. Nothing felt comfortable, not the sheets or the pillows or the mattress that had given her such a sound sleep the night before. It must have been two in the morning when the idea clicked in her brain. She was surprised it hadn't caught her attention earlier. She got up, put on her robe, and snapped on the desk lamp. She picked up the hotel bill and her fingers quickly flipped through its pages checking the charges until she found what she was looking for.

It was there, clearly printed in black and white. Nothing definite enough to make her feel comfortable about coming right out with an accusation. But it was enough of a theory to be worth testing. And as she sat there making notes on hotel stationery in the dark hours of the morning, she decided what that test might be.

Ivan was already up, dressed and seated in the sitting room, by the time she awoke. The overstuffed chairs in bright blue and the lighted displays of Staffordshire china made even a gray day like this one seem brighter. A working fireplace had been built into the light paneling of the room, and he had a fire laid.

"I've had a pot of coffee left for you in the butler's pantry," he said. "If it's got cold, just ring the floor waiter. Once you're awake we can go downstairs to the dining room."

"I think we should order up here," Dale told him. "This is one conversation I don't want waiters listening in on."

"In that case," he assured her, "you'll have a typical English breakfast right here in the sitting room." He pushed the electric button that summoned the floor waiter, and ten minutes later a table had been wheeled in, complete with eggs, kippers, toast and fruit, plus flowers and two copies of the *Times*.

After pouring for them, the waiter quietly let himself out the sitting-room door. As it clicked shut behind him, Ivan moved to it and fastened the double locks from the inside.

"I have a feeling we don't want any more interruptions," he said.

She stirred her coffee. "Do you trust me?" she asked suddenly. She looked at him directly, fastening an unflinching gaze on him.

"Yes," he started, then faltered as he tried to decide what else she wanted to hear.

"I mean trust me enough to do something that will sound odd to you without asking for an explanation," she interrupted. "I have an idea who's behind the forgeries," she said softly.

"That's wonderful!" he said, suddenly alert. His entire body moved to the edge of the chair. "Tell me."

"No, I won't," she said, putting up a hand to halt his protest. "It's only a suspicion. Based on gut feel as much as anything else. And a few facts that I might be blowing out of proportion. It's not enough to be certain, and I don't want it to influence your thinking. I want you to go on with the investigation in a purely objective way."

"So why bring me in at all?" he said, sitting back in his chair again. There was something of the hurt little boy in his manner. "Why bother to tell me anything?" He began to fiddle with his tea cup, avoiding her eyes.

"Because I need you," she said. She continued to look at him until he couldn't avoid her any more. When he looked back up and met her serious expression he realized how important the thing she was asking him was to her. He wanted, more than anything else, to help her.

"What do you need?" he asked.

"Those connections you developed while you were at the Louvre," she answered simply.

"All of them?" he laughed. He continued to smile as he leaned back in his chair and waited. She returned the smile for just a second, then quickly became serious again.

"Do you remember the three paintings that were sold by Kenneth and his father to get the house started?" she asked him. He nodded yes. "Well enough to have them duplicated?" she then asked him.

"I think so," he answered, looking a bit bewildered. "Each one has been photographed and reproduced at one time or another over the years."

"Do you know someone over here who could do copies of them for us?" she asked him. "Perfect copies."

Ivan thought for a moment before committing himself. "I think I could call in a few favors from my days at the Louvre."

"Could you get it started before you come back to New York?" she urged.

"I don't think that will be a problem," he agreed. "I have at least a week's work here before I wrap up and go back to report to Kenneth." He paused for a moment before he asked the next question. "But are you really sure you know what you're doing?" he said.

Dale looked at him unflinchingly. "Almost sure," she said.

"All right," said Ivan, returning her gaze. "I trust you." And for the first time in his life, he knew that he did trust a woman. "But do you trust me?"

"Completely."

"Then you're going to have to tell me what's behind all this. I'm sorry," he said, seeing her hesitate, "there are going to be too many people involved for me to just run blind with this."

"So you won't do it for me?" she challenged.

"Of course I will. But you have to be fair to me, too."

She considered, realized that he was right, and began to slowly and methodically explain her plan. A slight smile began to play at the corners of Ivan's lips as he listened.

"As much as I want to solve this thing, I find myself hoping you're wrong," he said as she finished.

She nodded in silent agreement.

"Will you accept some friendly advice?" he asked.

Dale nodded.

"Take a day off before going back to New York. Things may get rough once this plan of yours is in motion. Get some rest now. You'll need it. So do I." Before she had a chance to say anything, he continued. "Why don't we work tomorrow, then spend Saturday at a little place I know outside the city? A relaxing lunch, a walk in the English countryside. You'll love it," he said quickly when he saw her hesitate.

The trip to New Milton in Hampshire took about two hours. The short drive was a pleasant one. Ivan described his first visit there. Though he didn't mention who his companion had been, Dale assumed from his expression that it was a woman, and wondered if it had been Celeste. She began to feel a little irritable, and realized in a moment that it must be jealousy.

They left behind the London suburbs and began passing through villages whose storefronts and cottages had beamed Norman fronts and quaint thatched roofs. They would occasionally cross over small, ancient-looking bridges where the light filtered through the leaves of trees whose thick trunks told of the many hundreds of years they had been standing there. As they reached New Milton and the border of the New Forest they could make out an occasional small deer, a darting shadow within the trees that disappeared as quickly as it had appeared. Soon they reached the long driveway of Chewton Glen.

"What do you think?" Ivan asked her.

She felt an involuntary intake of breath as they approached it. It was a handsome old country house made of brick. Its walkways were built in a series of brick archways whose Gothic detailing brought to mind the quiet corridors of a monastery.

Dale looked out the car window and gasped in pleasure at the sight of the forest stretching out at the foot of the grounds. "Oh, let's walk," she said gaily to Ivan.

They circled the lake, strolling slowly, allowing their eyes to travel at their leisure. Fruit trees had been planted here and there among the foliage. They had shed their leaves and become skeletons, storing up the energy that would burst out as peaches and apples and pears in the next summer's harvest. He spotted a bench under a willow on the bank, and drew her over to it. They sat there peacefully, comfortable in each other's company, as a dozen bobbing geese moved toward them and came to rest in the long lake grasses that were turning brown beneath their feet. It would have been the most natural thing in the world for Ivan to take her hand in his, and yet he didn't. Dale sneaked a glance at him sitting beside her, and caught him looking at her with a gentle smile that made his face seem more alive than anything around them.

"A penny for your thoughts," he said.

"That was the expression before inflation," she told him. "Now it's ten dollars for your thoughts." There was a short silence before she went on more seriously. Bird calls cried out like songs in the quiet air. "I was thinking of how lucky Kenneth is to have you with him right now," she explained. "So much has gone wrong. So much is still going wrong," she corrected herself, thinking about the forgeries. "You go back so far. You must have a bond that's as strong as any blood relation."

Ivan's deep voice broke their next silence. "I've been thinking, too," he said. "But not about Kenneth." It took him a moment to find the right words to go on, a punctuation that was filled with the soft whisper of the grasses that were being shifted by small breezes all around them. Dale's muffler blew up behind her, then settled back on her coat, her long black hair falling over it as it escaped the lifting fingers of the wind. "More about you. I think that behind your professional facade is a woman I'd like to know better. But there seems to be a barrier that keeps me from getting close." He didn't know whether it had been his heart talking, or merely his natural concern for her emotional well-being. All he knew was that behind her careful mask he sensed that he had discovered a woman who needed him to take care of her. Not like Celeste, a woman who kept looking from day to day to make sure she'd picked her shelter in the strongest pair of arms available to her. But one who'd make her choice and would commit herself to stand by it faithfully.

"Oh, Ivan," she said. The sound of a thousand sighs had been compressed into her voice.

Ivan considered, thoughtfully. He took his time, studying her face, trying to see what she was made of inside, as he did. At last he spoke. "What is it? Most of the time you're so eager, so full of life, and yet there is always something shadowing you. I feel as though you keep the real Dale Kenton tucked away somewhere. You pull away just when I mention anything personal."

She looked into his face and found such sympathy there, and such confusion, that she had an overwhelming urge to explain. She found herself talking about it, actually telling him all about her father and the way he had left them.

"He was the one man I was totally sure of," she finished. "I depended on him so. I loved him. And he just left us. It's . . . I guess it's made me afraid of getting too involved with any man." She looked so close to tears that he took her by the shoulders and held her close, cradling her like a child. All at once he found that he wanted to protect her. He wrapped his arms around her as the first tears began to run down her face.

"I can understand how you feel," he said softly. "The only people who can ever really hurt us are the ones we love. And then we begin to hate them, and it's like killing a little piece of ourselves every time we have one of those thoughts. It's easier to just block the feelings out and go on from day to day. Better to feel nothing than to want to destroy. That's why you're still alone, isn't it?" he concluded, as much to himself as to her. "You still don't trust a man to stay with you. You're afraid that you'll lose him if you let yourself fall in love."

She didn't answer. Instead she got up quickly, pulled free of him, and walked away without letting him see her face. It was as if the truth of it, as he finally said it out loud, as he put her thoughts into words, was too painful for her to hear. When she turned back to him her eyes were frightened, her face more vulnerable than he had ever seen it. "Do you think you could get us a room?" she asked quietly. "I need to be held. I need it so very much."

It was half darkened as they came in. Dale pulled the drapes closed, undressed, and slipped under the soft sheets. He went to her and, as he leaned over to kiss her neck, her cheek, he found his senses responding to the strong scent of cologne that clung to her. His face felt warm, every vein beating with a reaction that was an artless, animal yearning that had to be satisfied. He stripped down quickly, then he came through the darkened room to lie next to her.

At first he thought she hadn't noticed he was there. She didn't move or even seem to breathe. And then in the silent, musky darkness he heard her voice saying softly, "Slowly, Ivan." She put her arms around him as his hands searched, stroking the crannies of her body. He was an unselfish lover.

She moved her head slowly down his chest and began to lick at his nipples, catching the sparse hairs in her teeth and gently pulling, moving her tongue in little circles. She could feel the heat rising in him, echoing her own quickening pulse.

He deserted the nape of her neck, and moved his mouth playfully down her throat, then to her breasts, taking first one, then the other and sucking them as if a nectar would come forth and feed his hunger. She was carried away by the most foreign sensation, as if her body had been given over to a force outside herself.

His hands moved down to her inner thighs but his tongue never left her body for an instant. He found the under part of her arm and licked it and his kisses were like little feather strokes. Then he moved between her legs and found that it was already swollen, without a touch. His fingers played magically while his mouth sucked at hers, locking her in place until she found herself crying out for him to enter her.

"Not yet, darling," he whispered. His head moved down her body. He was suddenly licking the inside of her thighs. His tongue darted until she could stand the anguish no longer. She didn't want to come until she'd felt the hardness of him in her body. She brought his head up, catching his full dark hair in her hands, and sought his mouth out with her own. His lean body moved on to her, and he entered her with one thrusting motion. She didn't want it to end. She wanted to have him on her like this forever, deep inside her. He held himself as long as he could, but still the pleasure ended too soon for her.

He lay next to her, turning onto his side and extending into a rangy, languorous stretch. His hands fell limp, almost jointless, over his lean body and onto the sheets. His legs dropped so slack on the bed they seemed to melt into it. His eyes had narrowed to drifting, semiconscious slits.

Dale lay beside him. They stayed that way for what seemed like hours, though she knew it was only minutes. She felt as if she had been sucked into a private bubble that separated her from the rest of the world, protecting her as it did. She could hear the sounds of people outside their room, waiters and maids hurrying about their tasks, but they were in a world separate and apart from hers. She could see out of her capsule, even hear. But while she was inside it she was living in a strange slow-motion world that had detached itself from the rest of mankind.

She took his hand and moved it to that small hillock where the pubic hair began to mound softly out below her stomach. It seemed to take an eternity for her to move her arm far enough to accomplish it. "Can you feel me, Ivan?" she asked softly. It didn't even sound like her own voice. "I'm still throbbing." He didn't answer, but he began to play with her again, long fingers stroking her languidly, then with building speed, until she moaned under the relentless motion and shuddered and was sucked up into another pounding orgasm. She held his hand there as they fell into a sleep that seemed almost drugged.

She had already gotten up when he awoke. He felt a vacant need in her absence. He brought his fingers to his nose, and could smell the faint remains of her fragrance where it lingered on his skin. He could still feel her presence, an aura that she had left behind. And he knew he couldn't hesitate. Perhaps if he went slowly he could be the key to helping her past her fears. Perhaps he couldn't. But he wouldn't dwell on that alternative. He just knew he had to try.

He felt an odd sort of satisfaction as he turned over and watched her looking out of the window, undisturbed in the violet evening light. He felt as if things might just turn out right for them after all. He knew he would be counting the days until he finished his week's work in London and could join her in New York.

CHAPTER 42

It promised to be a cold winter. Thanksgiving wasn't upon them yet, but Dale found New York blanketed in snow when she landed at Kennedy. She was jostled by the crowd as she searched out a cab. It triggered memories of the day she had arrived from Los Angeles and found Katherine waiting for her at the terminal. It seemed like such a long time since they had had a long talk.

The snow was swirling around them, a nearly opaque curtain, as the cab slowly pulled out into the airport traffic. Dale looked at her watch, counted the minutes until her appointment with Kenneth, estimated the time it would take to drop off her luggage and make a quick stop at the office, and realized she was coming up short. "Can't you go any faster?" she urged the cabbie.

He took a long, scathing look at her in his rear-view mirror. Then he stubbed out his cigar with studied deliberation. "Listen, lady," he said in a gravel voice, "I'm not in as much of a rush to kill myself as you are. If you just sit still and stop bothering me, you'll get there." Still, he moved off the highway and started taking back streets that paralleled it. "This make you feel any better?" he asked at last.

"Well, at least we're moving," she conceded. "The traffic is lighter."

"Yeah," he told her. "A lot lighter. We may even get there five minutes earlier. The world gonna change in five minutes?"

She sat in the seat without bothering to answer him. Her thoughts went in the same direction they had followed during the plane ride. Her mind kept clinging to the image of Ivan as she had last seen him, helping her load her luggage in front of the Dorchester. It should have made her happy, but it didn't. Instead she found she had the same sort of feeling that she had always gotten as a child after she saw something she dearly wanted only to have her mother convince her it wasn't practical.

"For a lady who is in such a hurry, you are sure not getting out very fast," the cabbie barked back at her. She realized they were stopped in front of her apartment building.

It was strange to come back into her apartment. It all looked familiar, and yet it seemed as if she had been gone for such a long time. Or perhaps the time had just become longer because so many important things had happened within the space of it. She sat down and began to take a cursory look at the correspondence and memos that she had asked to have sent over from the office. The pile formed an irregular, teetering stack in the middle of her desk. She was glad she'd have the chance to check on things before she went to the office the next day. Most of it was of little immediate interest. She was pleased to see that an answer had arrived to her letter to Manhattan Security. She slit the envelope, planning to include it in the folder on the forgeries she kept carefully hidden in the small desk. She stuck it in the hole punch, preparing to tack it into the file and as she did her eyes rested on the cover letter to the security proposal, the letter she hadn't seen before. She stared at it for a long minute, then nodded her head in confirmation. Any doubts she might have had as she left London were wiped away. She knew now that she had done the right thing in setting her plan in motion. She only hoped she'd done it in time.

CHAPTER 43

Steven checked his watch as he ran up the wide front steps of the Four Seasons. He was ten minutes late. Herb Phillips, a stickler for punctuality, would already be seated in the Grill Room. He would even have reached the point at which he was beginning to look around the room, fingers tapping restlessly on the martini glass in front of him.

He stopped across from the Picasso tapestry and searched the room for Herb. He spotted him in the opposite corner. He stopped from time to time on the way to their table, indulging himself in a little social table-hopping. He was smiling as he slipped into the booth. He smelled like fresh soap and water, and a generous splash of cologne.

"Stop for a haircut?" Herb asked him, looking meaningfully at his watch.

"Nope," Steven answered, ignoring the jibe. "I left the office a little early today and went over to the club for a steam and a massage. Very relaxing. How are you doing?"

"Not as well as you are, obviously," Herb answered sarcastically. "Tell me," he then asked eagerly, "is it on for sure?"

Steven avoided his question. "What are you drinking?" he asked.

"I already have one," Herb told him, indicating his martini. He was known to be a light drinker during business meetings. Being kept waiting had already put him beyond his quota.

"Well then," Steven said to the waiter who stood in front of the table expecting their drink order, "bring me a Black Label on the rocks. A double."

"Is it really on?" Herb repeated.

"What?" Steven asked naively.

"The public offering," Herb said impatiently. "You do know your father called me this morning and asked for a meeting."

Steven picked up the drink the waiter had placed in front of him. He took his time with his first sip. "Nothing like the first drink at the end of the day, is there?" he asked Herb, smiling pleasantly.

"Is it on?" Herb asked again. He was beginning to suspect that Steven had dragged him into a long, liquored dinner for nothing but his own excitement.

"Well," said Steven. He smiled like someone about to bring on an unexpected birthday cake. "I'm afraid the meeting to discuss the merits of going public is off." He watched Herb's face drop. "Because my father has already decided to do it."

The import of the statement didn't register on Herb for a few seconds. Then a grin began to crease his face. "You son of a bitch," he said happily. He raised his glass in a toast, "Here's to Fraizer's and to your future. And let's not forget the fees it's about to generate for Phillips and Company."

"Brutally forthright," Steven commented. "Whatever happened to the excitement of taking an auction house public? The thrill of marketing an unusual business?"

"Oh, that's still there," Herb told him as they ordered dinner. "But we've got a lot of work to do. I always like to remind myself of why I'm working nights and weekends before the grind actually starts."

"So what's the first step?" Steven asked him.

"The first step is for you to hire a good lawyer," said Herb. "When they start the due diligence, they'll be probing into every detail of your business. You'd better look snow white."

"Don't worry," he told Herb. "Just pass the butter."

Their banter was easy and light for the balance of the meal. Herb left Steven nursing an after-dinner brandy in the bar in what appeared to be a mellow mood and started home, eager to get on the phone and break the news to his own father.

Steven finished his drink and paid his bill. The cold air hit him as he went outside, and he shivered involuntarily. He fumbled awkwardly with the buttons of his topcoat as the doorman hailed a cab and realized that he was a bit high. He chuckled to himself a little, pleased about it.

He closed the door of the apartment behind him. It sounded louder than he had intended, a noisy slam that rang out in the quiet midnight air. He maneuvered himself as far as the library. As carefully as he aimed his feet in one direction, they seemed to veer off in another entirely unintended heading. He steadied himself and started the trip to the bedroom upstairs.

Katherine heard him as he crossed the downstairs hall. His heels sounded irregularly, dragging on the polished wood a floor below her. Not that he had woken her. She had tried to sleep earlier, but her thoughts hadn't let her, and so she had lain, alone, through the night while they flitted in and out of her mind like troublesome, elusive shadows.

She blamed herself as much as Steven for the trouble in their marriage, and she had become determined during those days when she lay in the hospital that she wasn't going to give up on it—not yet. Not while the memories of the times that had worked, the times when they had made love and Steven had been warm and giving were still so strong within her. That was when she had loved him most. When he was tender and caring. Those times had been less and less frequent of late, but as soon as she felt stronger, she was going to try to bring that sense of caring and giving back to their lives and their lovemaking. Otherwise, everything would have been a waste, for nothing. The loss of the baby. Everything.

She imagined how it would be the first time. She would try to bring every loving thing that had worked for them before into a single, wonderful experience. He would respond, she knew he would. And it would be the start of a meaningful life together for them. It was too soon now. Now it was all she could do to retain her own peace of mind when she thought of the child they had lost. But later, even soon, she would be strong enough to bring out the tenderness in him again.

He reached their bedroom and came in, shutting the door behind him with sudden, silent care. The room was dark. He stumbled awkwardly on the way to their bed, tripping on the rug, then knocking over a lamp as he reached out to steady himself.

As his eyes became accustomed to the darkness he could see her tousled, sleep-scattered hair. Quickly he began to struggle with the buttons of his shirt, finally ripping it off in frustration and dropping it to the floor. By the time he had begun to take off his shoes, kicking them into the corner of the room, she was wide awake.

He climbed into bed next to her and reached out and kissed the nape of her neck. She relaxed, wanting him to take her into his arms and hold her, wanting him to make her feel secure again, but his actions became more aggressive instead, more forceful. He tried, without foreplay, to arouse her, to mount her and relieve his own tensions, and she began to quietly cry. She had wanted the first time after the loss of the baby to be so special, she had wanted desperately for him to be gentle with her.

"Steven," she begged. "Please. Not this way. I need you, too. But not like this."

It was as if he didn't hear her. She felt him shift his body on top of hers and try to enter her, and she rolled away from him and jumped from the bed.

He reached out, grabbing for her but missing with a total lack of coordination. His fingers caught in the low neck of her nightgown, ripping it with the weight of his body as he fell to the bed. He looked up at her and could see the ripe outline of her breasts exposed by the large tear he had created. He reached for her and tried to force his mouth on her, but she turned her head quickly.

She fled into the hall and ran to the end of the hallway, but when she reached the top of the steps she stopped. Her legs were trembling too much to carry her down the circle of treads to the floor below. Sobbing like a child, she sank to the floor.

As the tears streamed down her face Katherine

tried to get hold of her emotions. She began to realize that she might have made a mistake. Perhaps she should have accepted him on his own terms. Maybe he needed her as much as she needed him—just in a different way. Perhaps it was she who was selfish now, not him. Oh Steven, she thought, what have I done? Have I pushed us even further apart with my own selfish needs?

Katherine gasped as a hand touched her shoulder. She tried to hold her gown around her, clinging to its torn pieces as she rose. She turned and found herself looking into Kenneth's eyes. As she moved toward him, she wept broken hiccoughing cries and let him envelop her in his arms. "Steven?" he asked her. She avoided his eyes, but she nodded her head yes.

Kenneth felt the hair-trigger that had been strung so taut inside him for the past three months snap. His emotions had been hanging in balance, just waiting for the smallest thing, a moment of unguarded fright and a single misguided shot, to set them off. She was shaking, crying uncontrollably. The warmth of her body as it trembled in his arms was almost more than he could bear. "I'll get you a glass of water," he said. "Or, better yet, a brandy."

"No," she said quietly. "Just hold me for a minute." He did, then when her spasms had begun to grow smaller, he lifted her, started down the stairs. He was surprised that he could do it so effortlessly and yet under these circumstances he seemed to have summoned a strength he didn't know he had. "Where are we going?" she asked him as she tucked her head into the hollow of his shoulder and surrendered herself to it.

"The library," he told her, keeping his arms protectively around her. "There's a decanter there." Though he tried to appear calm, inside he too was shaking. He was unnerved by the depth of the need he felt to protect her from his own son. He was furious that Steven had caused her the pain. As they reached the library, he placed her on the deep cushions of the couch, then he measured generously for both of them, then took a glass to her and instructed her sternly, "Drink this. It will calm you down."

She reached out for the glass and began to gulp the amber liquid thirstily. She swallowed without putting it down, as if its biting, burning effect could quench the fear and loathing that was growing now inside her. Kenneth sat on the edge of the couch and put his glass down on the table beside them. He watched her, frightened by the fervor with which she was gulping the brandy. "Katherine," he said. He never finished the rest of it. Instead, his arms went around her. He began to softly touch her face, and then her neck. His mouth found hers, kissing her gently. All the passion that had lain beneath the surface in her came out. It was as though she had never been kissed before.

She put her arms around him, too. Her tongue planted delicate kisses on his cheeks, his eyelids. She wanted to drink in all of him. Her hands found their way to his chest, stroking him tenderly.

He began to kiss the nape of her neck, his tongue caressing, and then his mouth nipping at her with tiny love bites.

Katherine's senses came alive. She pressed her body tightly against his. It was as though it had a life of its own. She opened her eyes and saw Kenneth's finely lined face, so different from Steven's, and yet so much the same. But thoughts of Steven fled quickly as Kenneth's fingers, his mouth, his tongue brought her to heights she had never dreamed possible. Finally she lay quiet under him, not wanting to release his body from her own.

Kenneth tried to speak, his voice so soft she could

barely hear him. "Don't, Kenneth," she stopped him. "Don't say a word. I know what you're thinking. But it's my fault, too." She took his face into her hands, holding him gently as though he were a child. There was no need to say anything more. His eyes spoke for him.

She woke late, still exhausted from the night before. Steven had gone, hours before, according to the staff. She decided to dress quickly and go to his office. She had made a decision, and she couldn't bear to go through the day without acting on it.

Before she went she left a note for Kenneth. The first part was written in a sure and steady hand. It was when she got to the second paragraph, the one in which she told him she was leaving, that her fine script became erratic and the words began to fall apart. She reread it slowly, knowing that Kenneth would understand.

My Darling,

No matter how difficult the months ahead may be, I want you to remember that I've no regrets about what happened last night. You mustn't blame yourself. It was my fault as well.

The only way out of this is for me to leave. It would be torture for us to live under the same roof. It would only make each of us feel more guilty, and come between us in the end.

Steven will need your love and support more than ever now, and most of all, your respect. If I've learned anything during this last year, Kenneth, it's that Steven will never be able to survive without your respect.

Please remember that I love you. Forgive me.
                                        Katherine

CHAPTER 44

Katherine looked outside and dressed warmly after she saw the sun valiantly trying to work its way out to the forefront of an otherwise gray sky.

The ten blocks between the apartment and Fraizer's passed as if they had never existed. She saw none of the people who elbowed by her, none of the shop windows, none of the taxis that honked and swerved. Nothing intruded on her consciousness beyond the thought of Steven and the decision she had made during the early hours of the morning.

Fraizer's doorman gave her his best smile, but she passed by, oblivious. She went directly to the elevator that would take her to Steven's office.

He was looking out the window as she walked in, silhouetted in the morning sunlight. The face that turned to her was tired. He sat wearily down behind his desk, and took some time clearing away the half-empty cups of cold coffee that had accumulated there during the hours he had already spent in the office. Then he looked up at her, the guilt in his eyes more painful to her than anything he could have said, and started to speak. "I don't know what came over me. I'm sorry about last night. It will never happen again. I had too much to drink."

She didn't answer at first. She sat down in front of his desk and looked at him, quietly and at length. "We'll get past last night, Steven," she told him. "We can put it behind us. But I'm not sure we'll get past the next six months or a year, not if we keep living with your father. We have to move out, Steven," she said seriously. "I'm asking you to. It's the only way we're going to make it."

He looked stunned. "I don't understand, Katherine," he said. "Yesterday you were perfectly happy there. Now you have to get out. Not six months from now. Immediately." He shrugged his shoulders in bewilderment.

"Last night brought it to a head. What's been happening to us all along. I can see it now. You're unhappy having your father run your life. You tried to tell me that on our honeymoon and I didn't listen. Well, now I understand. You try to avoid him, and since we're all living together, you end up avoiding me, too. You don't want to see him; I end up not seeing you. It's coming between us, dangerously between us. My mind is made up, Steven," Katherine told him. "We have to get out now." Her fingers played with the knotted strap of the purse that rested in her lap, moving up and down its length and using it like leather worry beads. She felt horrible about the lies.

"Now's not the time," he told her. "Even if you're right, and you probably are. I know I've ignored you," he admitted. "I wish I could tell you that's going to change from this minute on. But with the public offering there's so much to take care of. There are going to be meetings with accountants and lawyers. Kenneth and I will be up to our ears. We'll have to run the house and handle all the details of the offering at the same time. I shudder to think of the hours we'll be keeping. But I promise you," he concluded, "that if you're patient for just these next few months, it will all change. A new leaf," he smiled, holding up one hand in a mock pledge. "A new leaf for Katherine. What do you say?"

"Steven," she said, starting to smile, then losing the glimmer of it as quickly as it had come. "I'm sorry, I just can't," she said. She looked down at her lap, at the purse, instead of into his eyes.

"Why not?" he asked her. "You won't even give me

that much? Not even a few months?" She didn't answer him. Instead she just continued to stare at her lap, nodding no over and over. It wasn't like her; she was usually forthright. Something else was wrong, something more than what they were discussing was lying, slightly rotten, beneath the surface. She finally looked up at him. Her eyes were puffy and swollen from lack of sleep. She looked upset, and yet more definite than he had ever seen her.

"I know this is sudden," she conceded. "I can understand that it's hard for you to make up your mind so quickly. But I can't go back there. I just can't."

"What's the problem?" he demanded, his voice rising in frustration. "You said it yourself. I'm the one who's suffering because of Kenneth, not you. I'm the one who should want out. If I can stand it for the next six months while the underwriting's being done, how bad can it be for you to stay?"

She tried to answer and she couldn't come up with an explanation. But she knew from her reaction, the quick jerk her stomach took at the thought of staying, that her whole being was violently opposed. "I'll stay with Dale for a few days while you think about it," she told him. Her voice was flat. "We'll talk about it again at the end of the week."

"You're being unreasonable. Unless you can give me a better explanation, some reason why I should walk out now, just when things are beginning to work well . . ."

"When do you want to talk?" she asked him. She waited for him to answer, but he didn't, and so she reached down and gathered up her coat from the spot where it had fallen to the floor. "I'm sorry," she said as she walked toward the door.

Katherine walked the streets with deliberate force, pounding her shoes into the pavement until she could feel every step strike the ball of her foot like a blow, sending arrows of pain from her suffering bones through the muscles of her calf, and finally into her brain where they produced a single thought, stop. She couldn't. She had to keep moving, punishing herself until she was ragged. She felt the wet leavings of tears, and let them burn into her skin, the chilly wind etching a chapped track on her cheeks.

She took off her kidskin gloves and let the wind whip at her hands as she crossed Park Avenue and went on. Her fox coat, blowing like a live animal under her wild eyes, looked savage. Her pain was so primal, so close to the source of all pain, it was clearly visible to every passerby.

She turned the corner at Twenty-first Street and almost screamed out with relief at the sight of Dale's building. She took the stairs by twos, ran to the apartment door, and began a frantic pounding. She wanted desperately to get inside before the sobs began.

Dale found her waiting in front of the door when she came home that afternoon. She took one look at Katherine's face, and gathered her into her arms without a word.

"Can I stay here?" Katherine asked as the tears began.

"As long as you want, if you don't mind sharing a bed," Dale answered, stroking her back as Katherine clung to her. "As long as I have a place for myself, there's always room for you."

CHAPTER 45

"I think she's asleep now," Dale said. She pulled closed the screen that partitioned the living room from the bed as quietly as she could. It was odd having Katherine under her care like this; it reminded her of the summer they had flown back from Paris. "I don't think I've ever seen her so hysterical."

"I'm not surprised," Ivan said, looking up from his spot on the couch. "Katherine's always struck me as the kind of girl who holds it all in. Stoic on the outside, while she's shaking inside and just hoping for the best. When someone like that breaks down, they tend to go all the way. And having her mother call here to say you'd broken up her daughter's marriage couldn't have helped."

He sat thoughtfully silent for a minute, then he reached for the pack of Gitanes he had put on the table earlier in the evening and pulled one out. He had some trouble lighting the match. He fumbled with it twice, until finally Dale reached over to the end table beside her, picked up a lighter and bent over to do it for him. His eyes caught hers, the flicker of the small flame between them. Then he sat back and took a deep drag on the cigarette, and held it out in front of him, looking at it like a forgotten friend.

"I don't see you do that very often," Dale commented. "I didn't even remember that you smoked."

"Oh," Ivan told her, "some situations just bring it out."

"Could have fooled me," she laughed. "Especially when I first met you. Cool Ivan, that's what I thought."

He smiled too, more at his own knowledge of himself than at anything she had said. "I don't feel so very cool right now," he told her.

"Because of Katherine?" she asked him. "She'll calm down. Sometimes we all need a good cry. I gave her a sleeping pill. She won't even be able to think about this until morning."

"I know," he said, "it isn't Katherine I was referring to. It's myself."

"What's the matter, Ivan?" she asked. She reached

over and removed the cigarette from his hand, replacing it with her own warm fingers. "Can I help you?"

Ivan looked at her carefully, caught up in one of those male moments when a decision has to be made about betraying some bit of weakness to a woman you care for. He made up his mind to lift the barriers and started to talk.

"Dale," he said, "I feel as if I'm not in control of anything around me anymore. Until I made this decision to join Kenneth I had a job. It was a bit dull, admittedly. But it was consistent. I knew where I was going every morning. Now I'm keeping my fingers crossed that we'll find a thief in time to keep Fraizer's from going under. If you'd asked me a month ago I would have told you I was in love with a girl named Celeste. Now I realize we hardly had a single value in common. What did Kenneth start?" he asked, shaking his head in disbelief.

She looked at him, and as she did she remembered the day she'd first seen him in New York. He'd looked so self-assured as he passed through the crowd of well-wishers at Katherine's wedding. She'd held that picture of him in her mind for months. "You're taking things too seriously today," she told him. "You sound as if you've lost your sense of adventure, and I know that isn't you."

"I can think of a few adventures I'd still be willing to tackle," he said quietly.

"Name one," she challenged him.

"How about marrying you. That would be an adventure, wouldn't it? I do love you, you know," he told her.

She sat back quickly, fading into the plump cushions of the couch. He waited for her answer.

"I don't know what to tell you, Ivan," she said at last. "I feel as if everything I've started is still so incomplete. The investigation at Fraizer's. My work. I don't feel as if I've succeeded at anything yet. And I feel as if I have to. It's important to me."

"Dale," he interrupted her, "those things are all going to straighten themselves out. Even if they weren't they don't have anything to do with whether we should be together or not. The only question that's important is whether you love me or not. And you do," he said, reaching for her hands and looking into her eyes, "don't you?"

She looked away from him quickly. He was right, she admitted to herself. The job, the investigation were excuses. The simple truth was that she couldn't commit herself to him or to anyone yet because the fears were still too great. She wondered if she would ever be able to. "I just can't do it," she told him, hating herself as she did. The words came out as slowly as taffy being pulled.

Ivan watched the interplay of emotions on her face. Eagerness was replaced by longing. "You don't have to give me an answer now," he told her. "In fact, I won't accept an answer from you now," he corrected himself. "I'll think of it as something that's still under consideration. An open-ended offer."

She looked at him wistfully. "I wish you didn't have to go back," she told him softly. "I really need you. Kenneth's going to be so broken up over Katherine's leaving. No matter what she says, I have the feeling that this is a rift between her and Kenneth more than between her and Steven."

Ivan looked troubled as well. "I'm not sure how much I can do from London," he said realistically, "beyond making sure that those three paintings are ready when we need them. That and making sure the London branch is ready for the opening."

"You'll let me know when the paintings are finished? You'll call me?" she asked, hoping for a yes.

"You know I'd like to be taking you back to London with me," he told her as he leaned down to give her a light but heartfelt kiss. "I can't get our last night there out of my mind."

He never finished the words. She turned her body and was enveloped into his arms as naturally as a young bird finding its nest. Her face was buried in the nape of his neck. He began to stroke the soft cloud of her black hair and then the silky neck below it. His hands moved of their own volition. His actions seemed beyond his own control. They searched out the now familiar softness of her skin, easily available to his stroking fingers beneath the silk of her blouse. "Katherine," she said, pushing his hand away.

"Took a sleeping pill," he reminded her.

She looked up to his face and kissed him, softly at first, on the cheek. Her lips moved to his eyes, and then found their way to his mouth. She ran her fingers over his chest. She felt his hair fall over his forehead and into his eyes.

It had started out so innocently, but with each touch of her hands, Ivan's body responded. The emotions and the feelings, the attraction that had been buried for so long sprang to the surface full grown just as they had in London.

Neither said a word as they touched, caressed and explored each other tenderly, and yet when Dale felt him begin to move on her, as he began to envelop her, body and mind, she felt the stab of terror that always came when she sensed she was giving control of her emotions away, leaving herself vulnerable to a man. She had to fight, for a moment, the urge to push him away. Then she remembered how good it had been before.

He looked into her eyes. He could read the hint of fear there, fear of giving in to what she wanted, he decided. He held her chin firmly as he lowered his lips to hers and began to gently but insistently kiss her. He felt the muscles in her neck begin to relax, to soften, as his own passion grew.

His head dipped to her face, then moved slightly down until his cheek delicately rubbed against her breastbone. Though her nipples were hard and ready, he didn't touch them, choosing instead to rub his face teasingly against the soft curve of her neck. She was surprised that he didn't notice the pulse surging in her jugular, since she knew it was causing her whole body to throb. His hair felt slick and icy against her suddenly hot skin. She wanted to hold the length of him close to her in an attempt to lessen the fever. She felt the glow begin—the hazy warm feeling of well-being that she had experienced from the time she was a child whenever she was stroked.

Holding Dale's face in his hands he began kissing her forehead, then her eyes, then the nape of her neck. She found herself responding with kisses, cautiously at first, then eagerly, flicking her tongue over his eyelashes. Taking little bites at his neck. Feeling his body grow harder as he held her, finally kissing her on the mouth, his tongue delicious as it probed its recesses.

He moved to her breasts, withdrawing them one at a time from the skimpy black pieces of fabric that cradled them. He opened his lips, slowly sliding them over the soft scented flesh. He began by licking the entire mound of each, then went on to a sucking and biting that became so excruciating she cried out in pain. She began to unbutton his shirt, to unzip his pants, all the while caressing him, licking him, her tongue playing games on his body.

He was licking her now, his tongue leaving a long, slick trail of saliva from her bosom to the top of her panties. She was frantic to have him go further, to enter her, and relieve the tension that had her helplessly writhing.

His tongue moved slowly up the insides of her

thighs, teasing her. She felt herself growing wet as he became harder and stronger. Every nerve ending was alive. She begged him to enter her.

Thrusting, he mounted her, going deeper and deeper, pounding harshly against her thighs and buttocks until quickly he came in a burst of ejaculations that pulsed through his penis and into her. Her nails dug into his back as he took her to the depths of her passion.

She felt as if the bonds that had tied her were loosened, as if the weight she had been carrying had been thrown aside, if only for a moment. She understood she would have to pick the burden up again in the morning but she pushed that from her mind, replacing it with the look of Ivan's face as it lowered to her, first stopping to dust her forehead with light bird's-wing kisses, then moving down until his lips were on her own.

Afterward, as they lay there in the dim golden light, she studied the way his hand cradled her. She looked closely at his shoulders and chest, where her kisses had been scattered with such profusion, expecting to see some lasting mark. But nothing about him seemed to have changed. Then she realized that the only lasting change was in her. She felt suddenly old, as if she had been shown a fullness of life that she would never be able to hold on to for herself. Oh God, she thought as she lay there in his arms. What am I going to do with myself now? It was still on her mind as she said good-bye to him.

She felt detached as she moved around the living room, plumping pillows and turning off lights. She restored the room to order, then walked cautiously into the dark toward the bed. She dropped her clothes on the chair in the corner of the room, then slipped between the sheets next to Katherine's motionless body. She looked at the outline of her friend's body in the darkened room, trying to imagine what had happened between her and Kenneth. Then she closed her eyes, hoping she would be able to chase the thoughts of Ivan away and get some sleep.

"You're a fool, you know," Katherine's voice, coming so unexpectedly from her still body, startled Dale.

"I was sure you were asleep," she apologized.

"Once in your life. If you're lucky," Katherine whispered. "Once in your life you'll find someone you'll really love."

"Do you really believe that?" Dale whispered back, wondering whether Katherine was thinking of Steven or of Kenneth as she said it.

"Don't be a fool" was all she answered. Then she lay so still she might have been asleep the whole time.

CHAPTER 46

Herb Phillips looked up as she strode through the door. His eyes traveled appreciatively down the length of her deep-red suit, then moved back up to her gray silk blouse, ending their journey on her smile. He was sitting on the couch opposite Kenneth, a tray of Danish and coffee on the table in front of them. Dale came quickly across the room to join them, pulling her skirt neatly down over her knees as she sat.

She looked at them there, gathered to prepare for the first board meeting of Fraizer's as a public corporation, and realized how quickly the time had passed. Preparations for the offering had taken over their lives. Steven had spent long hours with accountants and with Herb Phillips preparing the financial report for the offering statement.

She'd been working more closely with Kenneth than ever before. Katherine's departure was the only subject they both still studiously avoided. The picture that had been taken of her and Steven on their wedding day remained on Kenneth's desk. It added to Dale's suspicion that he not only missed Katherine, but that he loved her as well. It must have left a void in his life, she thought, when she had gone. Still, he never seemed to ask about her, and even cut Dale off the one time she had started to tell him what Katherine had been doing.

"Have something," Kenneth said, passing her the plate of rolls. She picked one out, then passed it on to Herb.

"Here, Kenneth," Herb said after he'd chosen a roll and added it to the array of fresh orange juice and coffee that was already in front of him.

"No thanks," Kenneth laughed. "I already had bacon, eggs, and grilled potatoes at home."

"How you can eat such a big breakfast is beyond me," Herb told him, biting into a roll.

"It comes with age," Kenneth joked. "Like being the chairman and C.E.O. of a public company." He looked well, despite the fact that the first meeting of the new board which would take place later in the day must have been an event that filled him with mixed emotions.

"A very popular public company, I might add," Herb told him, swallowing another piece of roll. He placed an open copy of that morning's *Wall Street Journal* on the table in front of Kenneth. "Sold out within a week, a lot of it in rather sizable block trades. That usually means that the institutional traders have gotten behind it, and the rest of the market tends to follow."

A small smile of satisfaction spread over Kenneth's face. Despite his reluctance to take the company public, he was flattered by the enthusiasm with which the stock had been picked up. It was like a very large and very public vote of confidence after a difficult year. "Let's hope their confidence is justified," he said modestly.

"I have a feeling you're not going to have any problems," Herb assured him. He looked down at the papers that were scattered over the working area of the table.

"We were just going over the agenda for the board meeting, Dale," Kenneth explained. "I asked Deborah to join us this morning and take some notes for a press release, but she is out sick. I thought you might be able to do it and then to coordinate with her later in the day or tomorrow."

"No problem," Dale answered.

Kenneth handed her a copy of the agenda, and she studied it as Herb went on.

"Will all the board members be able to attend?" he asked Kenneth.

"I think they will," he assured him. "There was some doubt as to whether Ronald Bruner would be in town, but he's rearranged his schedule."

The three of them reviewed the agenda quickly. Herb gave Kenneth some instructions on handling the balance of power between the board and the officers of a public company. Then he picked up his briefcase and sped out the door, running, as usual, to another appointment.

"Finish your coffee," Kenneth told Dale. "There's no rush."

Dale lifted the delicate Limoges coffee cup and took another sip. She watched Kenneth as he went back to his desk. The morning light that streamed through the high windows behind him made it difficult for her to read his expression with any accuracy as she spoke to him.

"You know," she said, "for all your forebodings this seems to have worked out well. It may not be what you would have done if you'd had a choice, but, still, you must be proud."

Kenneth tilted back in his chair and laced his hands across his chest. He looked around his office appraisingly, then back to Dale. "If you'd asked me before we did it," he agreed, "I would have told you that I'd walk into my office on a day like this one, and I'd feel like it didn't belong to me any more. But it doesn't feel like that at all. It's like having your fiftieth birthday," he smiled. "Everyone begins to tell you you're middle-aged, but when you get out of bed that morning and look in the mirror, you'd swear it was the same person who looked back at you the morning before."

He reached for the phone and picked up the receiver to cut off the buzz of his intercom. "Send him in," he said to Barbara, sounding pleased. "It's Ronald Bruner."

"Would you like me to leave?" she asked. He held up a detaining hand in answer to her question.

His cheerful expression faded as Ronald entered the office. He could tell immediately that something serious was on his mind. Ronald was normally the consummate charmer, unflappable on the surface no matter how distressed he was underneath. Today his face was drained of color, and he didn't waste any time on a cordial greeting.

"Sit down," Ronald told him. His voice sounded as grim as his face had seemed to be when he came through the door. Kenneth obeyed him without question, sinking down into his chair, tipping it back on its pedestal as he let the full weight of his body fall.

"I thought you considered me one of your best friends," Ronald said accusingly. Kenneth was bewildered by his tone.

"Why didn't you tell me you were in trouble this last year?" Ronald asked him. "Why didn't you let me help you?"

"What are you talking about?" Kenneth asked with surprise.

In answer Ronald simply held out an envelope to him. There was a registered sticker on its surface, and a signature that showed it had been delivered to Ronald that morning. Kenneth took out the letter and scanned it quickly. His look of outrage became unmistakable as he doubled back and read it yet again. The veins in his throat had risen to the surface, his pulse visibly throbbing at an alarming rate, by the time he passed it wordlessly to Dale.

She looked at it, then looked up in horror. "Can they really do this?" she asked.

"They can certainly try," Ronald answered her. "But I'll be damned if I'm going to let them kick Kenneth out of his own company while I'm on this board."

Dale looked back at the sheet of paper that was still in her hands. Its import was unmistakable. A group of dissident stockholders was asking for Kenneth's resignation as president of Fraizer's, and concurrently for his removal as chairman of the board. Their reason for the action was clearly stated. Irregularities in the operations of the house, a series of forgeries, had been improperly concealed. In their opinion, a fraud had been perpetrated on the purchasers of Fraizer's stock, a fraud for which Kenneth, as head of the operation, should be held accountable.

Kenneth punched the intercom button and screamed at Barbara in the outer office. "Get me Herb Phillips," he shouted. "If he's still out at a meeting, find him. I don't care what you tell his office. I want him on the phone, and I want him now!

"This is a bunch of bullshit," he spit out as he waited.

The buzz of the intercom interrupted him before he could go on. "Herb Phillips is on the line," Barbara's voice announced to the room.

Herb's voice sounded unfamiliar over the speaker phone. His usual clipped, rushed sentences were unnaturally hollow. He greeted Kenneth happily, then listened with increasing confusion as the contents of the letter were read to him.

"They can't do this to me," Kenneth finished. His voice had steadily risen in volume as he'd read the letter.

"They may not be justified in doing it," Herb corrected him. "But that doesn't mean they can't. Proxy fights are strange animals. Shareholders always seem to be ready to believe the worst about management if a halfway convincing story is presented. And if what you just read to me is true—if some irregularities in the operation of the house weren't disclosed, they have a good chance of winning."

"So we'll tell them otherwise," Kenneth said simply.

"We can," Herb agreed. "I want to warn you now that we may be in for months of infighting. It will probably take weeks just to trace the real owners of the stock. That list of names you read to me is all corporations. They may even have been formed just to hold this stock. Not to mention the expenses of mounting a campaign to combat them—mailings, publicity, meetings."

"Anything else?" Kenneth asked him.

"Well," Herb's voice echoed out in the room, "the biggest problem we'll face is in the interruption of regular business. There's a distinct possibility that the stockholders will go into court and ask for a temporary injunction that will prevent you from making any business moves until this thing is settled. Those requests are pretty routinely granted in a situation like this."

"How long?" Kenneth asked him. "How long can they hang us up?"

Herb paused again before answering. "I've rarely known them to drag on for more than four or five months," he said, finally.

Kenneth sank back into his chair. His body seemed to shrink. He ran through the list in his mind. They might be able to sustain their New York business, just sustain it, without enjoying any freedom to move or make decisions for half a year. It was the London branch that would suffer. Suffer? That was hardly an adequate word. It would probably go under before it had a chance to succeed.

"I'm not sure we can weather a proxy fight right now," he said at last. His voice was barely above a whisper.

"What was that?" Herb asked.

"Do you think they'd get off our back if I nominated someone else to succeed me before the fight starts?" Kenneth asked him instead.

"It's possible," Herb answered him. "I'd like to get together with the attorneys and the C.P.A.s before I give you a definite opinion on that."

Kenneth sat silently.

"Shall I try to get them together and get them to your office now?" Phillips asked him.

"Do it," Kenneth said abruptly as he hung up the phone.

Kenneth's resignation was greeted by the board with both surprise and concern, but his argument for his decision was presented with such feeling, and his explanation made such sense, that in the end they voted to confirm his wishes. The president and chairman of Fraizer's, he had told them, must be prepared to give of himself not only one hundred percent, but two hundred percent. Particularly during the initial year of its operation as a public company, he must look on it as a twenty-four-hour-a-day job. His first commitment must be to the house. Inventory changes are both enormous and frequent. The operation was attempting to grow worldwide. And, particularly at this point, quality and integrity could never be sacrificed. It takes a younger man, he had said, a man who hasn't been ill, a man in his prime, to rise to this sort of challenge.

Dale's eyes misted as Kenneth rose, his hands hanging at his sides, to make his final statement. "I have given Fraizer's my life," he told them, "but now it's time for me to start doing some living. It is with some regret, but with a great deal of pride, that I request your vote in recognizing my resignation and confirming the appointment of my son to assume my responsibilities as president and chairman of the board." He stood before them, broken inside, and yet sustained by the hope that Steven could still make the company work. In the end, he'd told Dale as they walked out of the boardroom, all that mattered was that a Fraizer stay at the helm, and the unanimous vote of the board had guaranteed that would be the case.

After Kenneth had stood before his friends and business associates, giving away the thing that mattered to him most, Dale had gone to her office and picked up the phone.

"It's time for that shipment," she'd told Ivan when she got him on the line. "And you'd better come back, too."

CHAPTER 47

The first thought Dale had as she stepped off the elevator and into Kenneth's reception room was that Barbara was going to break down. Her expression, normally so welcoming, looked ragged and confused. All of Kenneth's phone lines were ringing.

"News travels fast," Barbara commented as she juggled first one, then another, giving courteous but noncommittal answers, then quickly hanging up.

"Is he free?" Dale asked her, indicating Kenneth's closed office door. "I have to see him. It's important."

"He's left the building," Barbara told her. "He said he wanted to be alone for a while. Then he just picked up his topcoat and left."

"You've got to think, Barbara. Where could he have gone?"

Barbara stared off into space. She had an untypically vacant look in her eyes. Dale walked over and put her arms around the older woman's shoulders. "It will work out, Barbara," she reassured her. "Right now I've got to find Kenneth."

"I'm sorry," Barbara answered. "It's just that everything seemed to be going so well for a change. As difficult as the offering was, Kenneth seemed to have come to terms with it. He actually seemed happy." She looked up, obviously close to tears.

"Does he go anywhere I don't know about?" Dale prodded. "Barbara, this isn't the time to be discreet."

Barbara shook her head. "He is who he is, Dale," she told her. "There's no secret Kenneth has hidden away under the surface. He's a complicated personality, but he's open. Why not ask his driver. He may have taken him somewhere."

"Good idea." She gave Barbara's shoulders another comforting squeeze before she started out of the office. "Don't worry," she said as she stepped into the elevator. "It's all going to work out."

She spotted the driver standing in the foyer. "Where did you take Kenneth?" she asked after crossing the lobby at a near run. She was a little out of breath, but she didn't let that delay her from securing the information she was after.

"Nowhere," he answered, looking a little frightened when he saw the urgency in her eyes. "When he came down he said he was just going for a walk."

"Could you drive me over to the apartment?" she asked him. She started for the car without waiting for an answer. He traded a silent look with the doorman, then followed her to the car.

To her disappointment the butler told her that Kenneth wasn't there. He offered her the use of the library to catch her breath and think out her next move before she went back to the car. She settled herself in Kenneth's worn leather chair in front of the fireplace, something no one ever dared to do when he was in the room. She let herself sink into it, hoping to absorb a feeling for the man, and an idea of where he might have gone, through the pores of its well-aged skins. Nothing seemed to come to her right away, so she let her mind begin to wander. She fought against focusing on anything specific and left room for instinct to take over.

It was the photographs on the mantel that finally caught her attention. There were two of them, one of Steven and Katherine on their wedding day, and a second one of Anna. She realized it was a duplicate of the one Kenneth kept in his office at Fraizer's. The image was precious to him, enough so that he had it in the two rooms where he spent most of his waking hours.

He had reached for it, she remembered, after

Ronald Bruner had left his office. He had fingered the Fabergé frame mindlessly and looked to his dead wife's picture as if he had to explain things to her. "It's all over, Anna," he had quietly whispered. Dale had barely been able to distinguish the words, the sound was so faint. "Everything I worked for. It's not our company any more."

A sadness had risen up in her as she watched him. It returned now as she relived the moment. It was things like that, small gestures and expressions, that always served as a reminder to her of how preciously Kenneth guarded the traditions of his family and his business, and how greatly he still treasured his past. She sat back in his chair. She abandoned any attempt at guiding her thinking, and instead let her thoughts flow in the path that Kenneth's mind might have taken. Within five minutes she sprang up and ran toward the front door.

They traveled through Manhattan. Small snowflakes that had settled like a dusting of tiny feathers in Dale's black hair began to melt as they moved out of the fashionable section of the city and into neighborhoods where people with a look of outer decay and inner hunger loitered outside dilapidated storefronts. The trend began to reverse itself as they reached the outskirts of SoHo. Piled heaps of garbage on the sidewalks were replaced by outdoor flea markets. Shoppers began to appear in Armani jackets instead of torn and fading army surplus gear. Her eyes searched the crowd as they approached the corner of Broome and Greene. The streets teemed with people who were window shopping or heading toward the lofts that they called home. By the time they stopped she had spotted him. He was leaning against the stoplight on the corner. Behind him, set closer to the pavement, a signpost clearly stated the street names that had been the crossroads of his world for all the years of his childhood and youth, the place where his father's store had stood, where he had learned about the business he had grown to love. He looked across the road at the row of ornate metal buildings he had grown up in. A trendy restaurant had replaced their old store. A furniture showroom was in the space where they had lived. And above them, where neighbors had once leaned out and shouted friendly greetings, hanging plants and paintings filled the windows. He didn't see the changes. He saw Anna, frail but beautiful, sitting on the steps. He saw Morris arranging some new find in their storefront window. He saw himself as he had looked so many years ago, leaving their house and walking northward toward the uptown galleries he had coveted from afar. The look of defeat on his face was pitiful. She swallowed hard as she reached for the door handle and stepped out of the back seat. She walked over to him and kissed him on the cheek. It was something she had never done before in the office, but somehow it seemed natural now. Kenneth jumped back, startled at the unexpected touch. She spoke into his ear, trying to overcome the noise of the rush hour traffic. "Do you wish you could start over?" she asked him gently.

Kenneth looked at her thoughtfully, and then slowly shook his head. "If I had it all to do over again," he told her, "I'm afraid it would still turn out the same. I can't think of much I would have done differently."

"That's not enough to heal the wounds, though, is it?" she asked sympathetically.

Kenneth turned away from her and looked back across the street, his eyes searching for some reminders of the past. "The thing that troubles me most now," he said, his gaze resting on the upstairs windows, "is that they might decide to do the same thing to Steven. Do you realize," he asked her, "that

I might walk into the office tomorrow and discover they've decided they don't want any Fraizer in command?" He raised his hand to shield his face as the tears began to silently roll down. Dale took a handkerchief from her purse and handed it to him. "Let's take a walk," she told him. She put her arm through his, subtly steering him through the throng that filled the sidewalks.

She searched his face, trying to judge whether he was ready to listen to her, whether he would pay attention and absorb it. "I think there's a way to get you through this, Kenneth. If you trust me," she said, waiting for it to sink in and for him to react. "I think you may be able to get back the money and the presidency of Fraizer's."

"You're a lovely girl, Dale. I know how hard you've tried. But I think you're in over your head here. Even Herb Phillips couldn't come up with a solution to this."

"Herb Phillips hasn't spent months investigating the Fraizer's forgeries. I have."

"What made me think we could get away with not disclosing them?" Kenneth berated himself. "It was my pride—my stupid pride. I didn't want anything to sully the precious name of Fraizer's. If only I'd understood the consequences. If only Steven had stood up to me and persuaded me to go public with the forgeries."

"The forgeries and the takeover, Kenneth," Dale interrupted. "They're all part of the same package."

"How can you be so sure?" he asked.

"Bits and pieces I've put together. This morning they all began to add up."

"Tell me everything," he insisted.

"Not yet. I need you to play a part in a little drama that's about to begin. You won't be totally convincing if you know the plot turns ahead of time."

"You're sure you know what you're doing?" he asked.

"Totally," she assured him.

"What do I have to do?" he asked her after what seemed an endless hesitation.

"The hardest thing of all," she replied. "I want you to just let me handle it. Go on as if nothing has changed."

He reached into his pocket and pulled out a silver cigarette case. He had carried it for years, using it as a container for his business cards. He turned it over in his palm and read the Kipling quote engraved on it. "Yours is the Earth and everything that's in it, and—which is more—you'll be a Man, my son!" He looked across the street and remembered the morning his father had given it to him. "I'll try it," he said to her, then turned and quickly strode back toward the waiting car.

CHAPTER 48

Dale put down the phone and picked up the clipboard that was being held out to her. The delivery man reached into his coveralls and pulled out a ballpoint pen. "Right here, next to the 'one,'" he said, pointing to the top line of the sheet.

She scribbled her name in the space he had indicated. "Could you break down those crates for me before you leave?" she asked.

The rest of the paintings staff gave a good imitation of continuing with their work, but it was obvious to Dale as she looked out through her office door that Patricia and Ingrid were actually spending their time sneaking glances at the new paintings as they emerged from their crates. She tried to do a little work herself, but her concentration was as bad as theirs. She put down her pen and looked around the office that Steven had decided to give to her.

Every trace of Miriam had been erased. The walls, once the irregular stained ochre of an ancient Roman building, were now covered in a freshly painted white. During Miriam's tenure, the bookshelves had accumulated enough dust to pass for the ignored back corner of someone's attic. They were pristine now, each reference book carefully categorized and lined up in the proper order. Despite the changes, Dale still had a hard time thinking of the office as her own. Every time she closed her private door she was surprised to find that Miriam's battered trenchcoat wasn't still swinging from the metal hook that had been mounted there. She closed the file that she had been working on and walked into the outer office to take a better look at the new arrivals.

Patricia and Ingrid brought out the easels that always stood in the corner of the room. Moving carefully they lifted each canvas, balanced it on one of the stands, then stood back to take a look. Neither of the girls said much for a moment. Patricia gaped at the two paintings as if the ghost of Rembrandt had just walked into her room. "What do you think?" Dale asked them.

Patricia continued to stare at them for a moment before she answered. "Best Cézanne that's ever come through this office," she said. "And the Matisse . . ." she began, though her voice then trailed off as she searched for words adequate to express her respect and fell short.

Ingrid emitted a long, low whistle. "Too bad Miriam isn't here to work on these," she said. "She would have had a field day." Dale decided to ignore it. She could understand how disappointed they must have been when Steven passed them over and gave her first crack at heading the Fine Arts Department.

"I think I'll buzz Kenneth and Steven and ask them to come down and take a look at these," Dale told them.

"Good idea," Patricia agreed. Though neither of them had wanted to suggest it, they both felt better knowing that another educated opinion was being sought. They walked around the paintings, carefully pointed out small motifs that had been overlooked in their first examination while Dale phoned upstairs. They were still analyzing the compositions when Kenneth appeared at the door.

He gave Dale a broad smile as he strode in. "Another first for Fraizer's?" he asked her. "A Matisse and a Cézanne in the same day?"

Ivan walked in behind him. "I think Steven is going to have to up this department's quota," he told Kenneth. "Obviously success comes too easily to them."

"I think that's right," Kenneth agreed as he came across the room. He seemed to accept Steven's new right to make decisions, especially since his son stopped by the office that Kenneth had been allowed to keep to consult with him from time to time. His smile faded as he caught sight of the canvases. He stopped dead in his tracks and, as they watched, the color drained from his face.

"Are you all right?" Dale asked him. She rushed to his side, ready to steady him if necessary.

"My God," was all the answer he gave.

She traded a glance with Ivan and with the other girls, all of them wondering what to do. While they hesitated, he moved closer, reaching out with a tremulous hand and reverently touching the paintings. "Do you have any idea what these are?" he asked them without turning. His eyes stayed locked on the canvases in front of him, his fingers lightly flitting over the curves and scroll works of the frames as he confirmed his first impression.

"Of course," she told him. "One's a Matisse. The other is a Cézanne."

"Where did you get them?" he asked her. He turned around as he did. His eyes had misted with tears.

"They came in from a client in California," she answered softly. She was afraid to disturb the moment, afraid to tip the scales of emotion that appeared to be so finely balanced.

"Fate works in such mysterious ways," Kenneth said so quietly he must have been talking to himself. "With such a sense of irony." He walked over to Ivan and, gently taking him by the arm, he led him over to the easels. "Ivan," he said, his voice thick with emotion, "your father wrapped these very canvases around my father's legs the night that he left Russia. All of Fraizer's grew from these. They are our heritage, the very symbol of our beginnings."

Ivan looked at the canvases more closely. He allowed his eyes to travel, first over the squared-off curves of a Cézanne apple, then through the dappled sunlight of Matisse's Sunday afternoon. He tried to imagine the same images the way they might have appeared in the firelight of a Russian living room so very many years ago. He let himself see them with Kenneth's eyes. He didn't know what to say first, there was so much bottled up inside him.

"I'm so happy for you, Kenneth," he told him. He clasped his friend affectionately by the shoulders and pulled him close. "They couldn't have turned up at a better time."

"You're right," Kenneth told him. He drew back from Ivan, holding him at arms' length. He looked into his eyes, at first fondly, but for the mere shade of the moment at the very last, appraisingly. "Just as I was losing faith, they've come back to remind me that no matter what happens to me, the House of Fraizer will always be."

Dale, who had remained standing in the background while the two men talked, now joined them. "They are beautiful, Kenneth. I had no idea that they had belonged to your family."

Kenneth smiled and nodded. He thought back to the many times he had tried to describe them to Steven, to paint for him in words the beauty of them.

It was at least five minutes before Steven appeared in the office. Kenneth passed the time by recounting the entire history of the paintings to the girls. By the time he had finished, they were as pleased as he was that the works had resurfaced in this almost magical way.

"I think that someone up there wanted you to have these back," said Patricia, pointing toward the ceiling.

"I definitely think He did," Kenneth agreed, smiling at her.

"Wanted you to have what back?" Steven asked from the doorway.

"The most amazing thing has happened, Steven." Kenneth led his son over to the canvases and began to tell him the story of how they had come back. By the time he had finished, Steven was looking at them with an expression of incredulous wonder. "The important thing," Kenneth concluded, "is that we contact the owner right away and buy them back. We can't let them be lost to our family again." As he said it he thought of his father, and of how happy Morris would have been to see the treasures restored to them. "They're so very precious to us."

"Dad," Steven said. He looked at his father with such intensity that it was as if the rest of them weren't even there. "They must be worth at least five million." Kenneth nodded his head in agreement. "Where's that kind of cash going to come from?"

"Obviously not from me," Kenneth said regretfully. "The house will have to buy them."

Steven considered for a minute before he answered. "I don't think we'll be able to make that fly," he said unhappily. "We're a publicly held company now. We can't use five million of the stockholders' money to satisfy personal whims." He saw Kenneth waver, not wanting to accept it. "Dad," he told him, "do you want to guarantee that no Fraizer will run the company?"

Kenneth sat down behind one of the desks in the room. He looked despondent, but then brightened as another thought struck him. "That leaves it up to you then, Steven," he said decisively. "There's your trust fund. You've never had to spend a cent of it to live. We'll negotiate with them. We'll use that as a down payment. We'll set up an installment sale that will let us pay out the balance. That may even work out better taxwise for the owners."

Steven looked dubious. "I'd like to think about it, Dad," he told him. "There are so many other things the cash might be needed for."

Kenneth interrupted him. "How can you even stop to consider?" he asked him. "Your grandfather sold the most beloved things in his life to build this business. These paintings are the reason you've been able to live a life of privilege. These paintings belong to this family, and that's where they should stay."

Steven hesitated. He tried to avoid looking at his father and seeing the unaccustomed look of pleading on Kenneth's face. It was too frightening.

Dale came over and grasped his arm. "Steven," she said, "things are going so well. If the business were doing badly, I could understand your hesitation. But look around you." She swept the room with a gesture. "We should be doing millions this quarter in our department alone. That's not going to go down. Not with you running the house. I only see the volume going up. You can afford the investment." She hesitated, waiting for his reply. "For your father," she finally prodded.

He slowly looked around the room. Patricia and Ingrid had stopped talking and focused their attention on him. His father's eyes hadn't left his face. "You're right," he decided. "It won't be long before we have enough cash to cover a bonus to reimburse me. The risk isn't really so great as long as we run the house well. All right," he agreed. "Talk to the owners and see what can be worked out."

The relief in the air was almost palpable. Ingrid and Patricia began to smile. Steven could see a moist sheen of tears spring into his father's eyes as he turned to look at the paintings with proprietary pride.

Dale gave his elbow a light squeeze. "You did the right thing," she whispered. "Your father's just lost the presidency of the business he worked his entire life to build. There isn't very much left that's meaningful to him. Those paintings are about it. But you don't need me to tell you that. You understood that."

"I did," he confirmed. "Yes, I did."

CHAPTER 49

Steven sipped a cup of coffee as he finished the *Wall Street Journal*. The maid was clearing the sideboard in front of him. She moved cautiously in order not to disturb him. The occasional rustle of her starched uniform and the tick of silver hitting china were the only sounds in the room. "May I bring you anything else, Mr. Fraizer?" she asked.

"No, thank you." If he wasn't mistaken, he thought, the sound of his answer to the maid still ringing strongly in his ears, his voice was beginning to sound more like his father's every day. He folded the paper and put it down on the dining room table as he pushed his chair away. There was a smile of contentment on his face as he straightened his jacket and picked up his briefcase from the table in the entry hall.

"The phone for you, sir," said the butler, cutting him off in the hall at the point where the library door opened from the passage. "Mr. Phillips."

Steven walked briskly into the library and picked up the receiver.

"Are you sitting down?" Herb asked. Steven felt the color drain from his face. "What is it?" he asked. His voice had the chill of fear; it sounded light and breakable.

Herb didn't waste time on any formalities. "Fraizer's stock has a buyer who's reached the five percent mark," he told him. "They've just filed a 13G with the S.E.C. Someone's making a run to take over controlling interest of the company."

"Who the hell is it?" Steven asked. He knew that the choice of a 13G meant the buyer had no immediate intention of trying to take over his company, and yet his words had a nervous edge to them.

"I figured you'd know," Herb said, sounding surprised. "The corporation's called Broome Street."

"Doesn't mean a thing to me," Steven replied. As he searched his mind the name reminded him of something he should have known but didn't. "Who are the owners?" he asked, hoping to clarify things.

"I don't know," Herb told him, "but I put in a request for the information." He waited for a few seconds to give Steven time to gather his thoughts. "Listen, Steven," he said kindly, "I don't know what's going on over there but I have to tell you as a friend that if things keep churning at Fraizer's the way they have been for the past month you're going to have an S.E.C. investigation added to your load of troubles. I don't want to tell you how to handle things, but I do think you should keep that in mind."

"But, Herb," Steven began to protest.

His friend cut him off quickly. "I don't want to hear it, Steven," Herb told him. "What I don't hear I don't know. And what I don't know I can't tell under oath. Keep your mouth shut unless you're sitting with your attorney. And now I am talking to you as your underwriter."

"Thanks, Herb," Steven said as he replaced the receiver. He sat down heavily behind Kenneth's desk. "Thanks for fucking up my morning." He put his head down in his hands, closed his eyes, and tried to think. Then he slowly stood and walked out of the library.

He went into the living room and approached the Matisse. He took it carefully from the wall, and wrapped it in a quilt. He pulled the Cézanne from the wall next. It seemed heavier than it should have, as if an unseen hand, his father's or his grandfather's or even someone further back, was holding it away from him. He became impatient with himself. Get hold of your imagination, he said as he felt the anger rising in him. It seemed to be seeping slowly at first, creeping into every wrinkle and recess of his brain. And then it began to rush, like the brush fire of one wild cell carrying a cancer throughout his body, turning everything well and healthy in him into something sick and repulsive.

He knew it was because they'd grown on him since they'd been hanging in his home. He resented them for that. It really was as if they'd brought a sense of family with them. He'd found himself feeling more complete every time he'd been in the room with them. He hated them for that. He knew that it was silly, and yet it seemed to have happened. It was a feeling of sentimentality he couldn't afford, he told himself, if he expected to survive.

He carried them to the curb, where the driver waited with the car. As he reached for them, Steven became distracted, and in his nervousness he let go of them too soon. For an instant as he watched them begin to fall he felt the sort of thudding drop inside himself that he would have expected if he were losing something precious to himself. He caught them and steadied them into the trunk. They're paintings, he told himself. Like any other paintings. You've had thousands of them pass through your hands every year. These have just come full circle. They helped your grandfather to survive, and now they'll do the same for you.

He counted the blocks as they drove through the press of Manhattan's traffic. He touched the speaker button and gave directions to the driver. Then he settled back and tried to relax during the short drive that lay ahead of him.

CHAPTER 50

Steven drummed his fingers impatiently on the burled wood trim of the limousine door. He sat as if he were ready to spring out of the car at any provocation. He was angry. Worse than that, he was frightened. As he sat there in the teeming faceless traffic, he realized the enormity of what he had done. He'd had the ending pictured differently.

For the first time in his life the thought of suicide seemed palatable, or at least the thought of crawling away, never to be seen again. Immediately he rebelled against it and decided to come out swinging instead. As long as he came out the winner there was no need to even think of that.

He ticked off the list of his European brokers again. He'd have to wait until morning to start calling and buying back the Fraizer's stock he'd sold. By then he should have a check in hand from the painting he was about to sell that would cover the transactions. Herb had been right. The less he knew the better, and keeping him clear of these new transactions was one way to insure his ignorance.

"We're here, Mr. Fraizer." Steven stepped onto the sidewalk and made his way quickly to the Wildenstein Gallery's front door. He walked in impatiently, intent on conducting his business as expeditiously as possible. He brought an aura of unrest in with him, in contrast to the gallery's other patrons who stood thoughtfully and judiciously studying every work in the exhibition that was mounted on the first floor.

The downstairs receptionist could see that he was short on time and temper. He'd called ahead, and so he was immediately escorted to Daniel Wildenstein's private office. He looked at his watch as he went through the door. He wanted to consummate this deal as rapidly as possible and get to the house.

"Good to see you, Steven," said Wildenstein, rising to greet him as he entered. He looked curious. It wasn't unheard-of for the head of an auction house to sell through a private gallery, but it was certainly irregular. From the way that Steven had described them to him over the phone he was handing over paintings that would have meant a small fortune in commissions to Fraizer's had they gone on the block. Experience had imparted a healthy skepticism to Daniel Wildenstein, but he was more than willing to look and, if everything appeared to be as represented, to buy.

"How's your father?" he asked as Steven carefully

placed the blanket-covered canvases on the couch that spanned one side of the room.

Instead of answering, Steven started to remove the wrappings from the pair of paintings. A nagging doubt started in the back of Wildenstein's mind. There wasn't any way to know why he was selling on the private market instead of waiting until one of his regularly scheduled auctions. At least not so long as he refused to talk about it there wasn't. So maybe it's none of my business, he thought. Then his inquisitive side reminded him that he hadn't survived for decades in the arena of multi-million-dollar art sales by minding his own business, and that this morning might not be the best time to change his style.

"Thanks for seeing me on such short notice, Daniel," said Steven. Daniel indicated two easels that had been set up in the center of the room, and encouraged Steven to finish unwrapping the paintings and put them on display.

"The price for the pair is seven million," Steven said, once he had arranged them.

"Possibly," replied Wildenstein. He moved in for a closer look.

Side by side the pair presented a breathtaking tableau. Each represented the best period of a master's work. Together they were the sort of duet that major collectors strive unsuccessfully for a lifetime to acquire. Wildenstein examined each one closely. He was quiet for what seemed like an eternity. Backing off, he measured them from the perspective of distance. "Remarkable," he said at last. "Truly remarkable."

"Seven million," Steven repeated to him. He felt a sense of pride seeing Wildenstein so taken by the pair.

"Would you consider seven hundred?" the wiry dealer asked in a tone of perfect seriousness.

"For such a 'remarkable' pair?" Steven laughed, assuming that Wildenstein was joking.

"For such a remarkably well-forged pair," Wildenstein replied. "In fact," he added, "two of the best fakes I've ever seen. Tell me who put you up to this?" he asked after a moment's pause. "At first I thought you were trying to put something over on me," he chuckled. "I was ready to tell you to try a dealer who doesn't have an eye instead of trying to dump your fakes in here. But then it occurred to me that it had to be a joke." He continued to smile as he removed the paintings from their easels and stacked them like cordwood on the corner of his desk. "Come on," he pried. "Tell me which of my fellow dealers has this sense of humor." He settled the canvases safely, though without a great deal of care, and looked back to Steven for an answer. Then he moved quickly across the few steps that were between them and placed a steadying arm under the younger man's elbow. Steven Fraizer had turned an alarming shade of white. Wildenstein suddenly realized that he hadn't been in on the joke. He guided him to a chair and poured him a shot from the decanter of brandy that stood on his sideboard. "Take this," he said solicitously. "It looks like you need it."

Steven sat as still as death. His eyes had the empty look of a catatonic's. His hands lay like moribund creatures in his lap. Wildenstein became increasingly alarmed. "Drink it," he repeated. Steven looked up at him, hearing him for the first time. His eyes were glazed, out of touch with his surroundings.

"No," he told Wildenstein in a voice that sounded mechanical and far away. "No. I've got to leave." Without one further word he gathered the two paintings under his arms and walked out of the office.

The rush of winter air in the street outside brought him to his senses. A single thought obsessed his mind. Forged. The paintings were forged. He'd sold his Fraizer's stock to buy a pair of forged paintings that weren't worth the canvas they were painted on. He'd never doubted he could slowly buy back his controlling interest as cash flow allowed. And now—there was this nightmare. He barely held himself in check as he directed the driver to take him to the House of Fraizer.

He could have kicked himself for buying the paintings. He didn't really understand why he'd done it. He only knew he was at his most vulnerable when it came to his father's requests. It had been that way for as long as he could remember. He couldn't recall a moment—infant, child, or man—when he hadn't loved his father immeasurably. How many years he had tried to become like his father he couldn't now count. Nor was it totally clear in his mind on what day he realized he couldn't insinuate himself into his father's flesh and bones, or even into his position of respect, until Kenneth had ceased existing. For one flash of a moment he hated his father for leaving him in that untenable position.

He opened the door of the car and leaped from the back seat. He stormed through the lobby with the pair of paintings in his arms. He rode the elevator up to the third floor without so much as a glance at the other employees who were sharing it with him. He walked past Barbara's desk without a word. By the time he burst into his father's office perspiration was beaded on his forehead and his face was flushed with the heat of the blood that was pounding through his veins. The sight of his father seated across from Dale, the table between them massed with photographs and copy about the London gallery opening, was enough to send him to new heights of fury.

He walked across the room and stopped a step or two from where they were sitting. He leaned the canvases against the side of the couch. He slowly bent down and picked up the first of them. He lifted it until it was as high as the level of his head. It covered his face, completely masking his emotions. Then with frightening force he sent a fist right through it, shattering the crossbars that kept the canvas stretched out tight and ripping the fabric into a jagged gaping hole. He threw it onto the floor like refuse, then looked up defiantly and into his father's face.

Kenneth looked at the ragged canvas as if it were a tattered twin to his hopes and dreams. Then he looked at his only son, his eyes gaping, wounded, as adrift as the eyes of a man who is trapped in a nightmare. Dale reached across the table and grasped his hand to give him her support.

Steven returned his gaze, at first audaciously. A sort of stillness surrounded them, a total absence of awareness of anyone or anything else in the room, the kind of deadlock into which a pair of duelists fall before one dares to fire the first shot. But as he watched his father he began to understand his terrible mistake. "My God," he said to Kenneth as he watched his father's face fall into a living mask of tragedy, "you weren't in on it, were you?"

Kenneth didn't speak. He slowly shook his head as if to clear away the confusing jumble of his thoughts.

"They're fakes," Steven told him, holding up the one undamaged canvas. Wildenstein told me." His father cut him off.

"You took them to Wildenstein?" he asked Steven. Kenneth's face no longer showed shock, just resignation. He accepted it like someone who's expected bad news for some time and has finally seen it arrive. He almost looked relieved to have the worst out. It didn't make the wounds go away, but at least now that they were exposed they could be ministered to. He stood and walked over to face his son. "How could you sell them?" he asked. His voice was low, the things he was saying were too unthinkable to share with the world. "You knew that they were the things I treasured most in the world. You could have done anything else to me and I would have found a way to overlook it. But this—to take my only real memories of my father—to sell your own roots. I'm afraid I just don't understand it," he said, shaking his head in astonishment.

Steven hesitated for a moment, but when he answered all the anger and frustration that had built up in him over the years were disgorged in a torrent. He might as well tell it all. The game was up anyway. "I needed the money. And I guess it just seemed like a fair exchange to me," he said. "Your memories in trade for my survival. It almost makes up for everything you stripped me of over the years. My self-respect. My independence. You gave me the best schools, the best clothes and friends, even picked out the best wife for me. But you took my mind and soul and made them over to your liking. Not once did you ever let me make any decisions on my own. Not once did you give me a chance to feel like a man. And so everything you gave me added up to nothing. Nothing . . . do you hear me?" he asked, his voice rising until it echoed off the beams and bookcases. "It's always been Kenneth's way or no way around here. You never really loved me," he spit out. "If you had, you would have respected me."

"Steven," Kenneth interrupted him. "There was a world of resources and possibilities for you here at Fraizer's if only you had been able to make them work for you."

Steven looked at him, through him. "There would have been if you'd respected me. If you'd been willing to give me some authority. If I'd ever been able to believe that someday—not right away, but someday—you'd actually let me hold the reins and control this business. But you weren't going to do that, were you? I realized that years ago.

"At first I took out my anger by working harder, by driving myself for long hours here at the house, by searching for new ways to impress you. But later, when it became clear to me that nothing would change you, I looked for a way to hurt you as much as you were hurting me. It was difficult to come up with something that would make you feel that kind of anguish," Steven went on. "Nothing matters to you besides the House of Fraizer."

Kenneth's eyes looked pained. He walked a few steps away from his son, sadly nodding his head no.

"I discovered my weapon late one night when I was looking at the catalogue for an upcoming sale," Steven told him. "For the first time I really read our 'Conditions of Sale.' Do you remember what they say?" he asked rhetorically. "'Notwithstanding any other terms if within twenty-one days after the sale, the buyer of any lot returns the same to Fraizer's in the same condition as at the time of sale and satisfies Fraizer's the lot is a deliberate forgery, then the sale of the lot will be rescinded and the purchase price refunded.'" He paused for a moment to let the import of his words sink in.

"I began to consider whether it was really possible, whether I could really bring myself to have a work of art forged and then to slip it into one of your auctions.

"I spent months picking out the right painting," he went on, "then more time tracking down someone to do a perfect forgery. While I waited for it to be completed I made plans for the switch. It all had to be timed to the minute. Of course no one noticed what I was doing. They never did notice me around here.

"That first one, the Delacroix, when it was brought up on center stage I thought I'd throw up from fear. And yet when the hammer came down I felt a new kind of high. It was euphoria I'd never experienced before, and its source was simple. For the first time in my life I held the reins. I was the only one who knew the truth. It gave me power.

"A month passed before it was returned. I was flying when you called me into your office to tell me the story, flying without wings. You showed me the forged painting, and then you announced without any further conversation that you had decided to pay the buyer back from Fraizer's funds to avoid alerting the insurance company and creating unfavorable publicity. You didn't turn to me for advice. I had thought you would, but you didn't.

"At first I felt a twinge of remorse when you told me. There was no need for you to spend that kind of money; that was what insurance companies were for. But I could see, even as I argued against it, that you weren't listening. You were determined to absorb the brunt of the forgery yourself.

"I left your office in the most intense state of frustration I've ever known. For the first time in my life I had thought I was in control, and I wanted to prolong it. But you spoiled all of that. Without even knowing it, without even trying, you regained the power I thought I had. You took all meaning out of it.

"I vowed that I wouldn't ever do it again. I realized I hadn't really wanted to hurt you, I'd only wanted you to listen to me. But I couldn't stop." For the first time Steven began to look remorseful. "The pattern grew faster and more frequent. Whenever you hurt me, I attacked you in my own way.

"The only problem was, I didn't really need the money that I made—even at underground auctions the originals brought in a lot. It just kept piling up at Crédit Suisse. Then I came up with the master stroke. An idea of what I could spend the money on.

The answer was stock," he said, smiling wisely, "stock in the House of Fraizer. All I had to do was steal enough to force you to go public. And I did, didn't I? It took the thefts and my trust fund but between them, I was able to get majority interest. And for six short months I've been the one who's controlled you."

"I feel sorry, Steven," Kenneth told him as he walked over to his desk. "For both of us," he said.

Steven turned on his heel and walked out of the room without another word. Kenneth sat at his desk looking like a beaten man. His eyes, when he looked up to Dale, were sad. He swiveled his chair to face the window. He was in time to see Steven striding away from the House of Fraizer. He quickly turned away again.

"You know, you gave me a terrible fright," Dale told him with concern in her voice. "The look on your face when Steven put his fist through that painting was terrible. I thought you were going to have a heart attack on the spot."

"I felt like he'd taken a knife to me," Kenneth said. "He couldn't have hurt me more if he'd murdered me."

"It's my fault. They were fakes. I arranged for them."

"I knew that," Kenneth acknowledged. "The minute I looked carefully at them I realized I couldn't send them out for authentication."

"And you didn't say anything?"

"I trusted you. I knew those paintings were there for a reason. I knew you'd managed to figure out what's been happening here the last year. And now," he said softly, looking into her eyes and motioning for her to sit down with him, "now I wish you'd let me in on it too."

It took about twenty minutes for her to relate the story, twenty minutes during which she could see

Kenneth gradually shrink into a shadow of his usual self. "Kenneth," she sighed as she finished, "if I'd had any idea when I agreed to look into these forgeries that it would turn out to be such a horrible mess, I wouldn't have done it. Do you think it can ever be right between you and Steven again?"

Kenneth thought for a moment. Then in a shaky but clear voice he spoke. "I remember Oscar Wilde's line," he told her. "'Children begin by loving their parents. As they grow older they judge them. Sometimes they forgive.'"

CHAPTER 51

Dale looked at her watch. Six-thirty. Ivan's plane must have arrived already. She wanted him there. She could picture him at Kennedy, waiting for his luggage to swing around on the conveyor belt, towering a good head above most of the other men there. It made her feel tender inside, then her brain intruded, shutting off the feeling as quickly as it had occurred. She'd felt dejected since Steven had torn out of the office. The volume of Kenneth's troubles weighed on her, an unexpected load. Maybe the sight of Ivan would help; she hoped so.

He opened the door quickly and eagerly. The lines of fatigue that travel always brings were traced into his face, but his expression was alive. His smile faded when he saw her face. "It's already happened?" he asked her.

"About half an hour ago," she confirmed. "Steven

showed up here in a fury. He'd just been to Daniel Wildenstein's and tried to sell the fakes."

"I take it it wasn't pleasant," Ivan said.

"It was horrible," Dale murmured. "I hope I never live to see another human being's face look the way Kenneth's did today." She was on the verge of tears, and he had an immediate urge to reach out to her. To hold her and comfort her in a way her father never had. It made him angry every time he thought about what that man had done to her. He hoped that he would have a chance to make it up to her during the years to come.

"So, my friend in Europe did his job well?" Ivan asked. "The paintings passed for the real thing?"

"Kenneth saw they were fakes, but he didn't say anything. So they passed until Wildenstein saw them. Which was exactly what I was counting on."

"Don't you think it's about time you let me in on all the details of how this little scheme of yours worked? You didn't really tell me much in London."

"I've been waiting for you to arrive so I could," she assured him. "I was hoping you'd be here before the blowup. Kenneth could have used you this afternoon."

"Steven admitted doing the forgeries?" Ivan asked her. Dale nodded slowly, numbly in the affirmative.

"Did you tell Kenneth how you'd decided it was Steven?" Ivan probed.

"I told him the whole series of things," Dale confirmed. "All the little things that began adding up. No one of them was strong enough to give him away. But together—well, it was too much circumstantial evidence to ignore.

"The first thing that caught my attention was the list of charges at the Dorchester when we were there for the London art auction. When I picked up the bills that night, there was a list of phone calls that had been made from Steven's room. He'd requested that they be kept separate but the hotel slipped up. I couldn't tell much from looking at them, they were just numbers and prefixes. The manager gave me a little help. He was able to pick out Geneva, Madrid, Hong Kong, and Chicago. I dialed some of the others myself. They were stock brokerages. Stock brokerages scattered all over the world."

"That's what you told me at breakfast. But what did that mean to you?" he asked her.

"Not much at the time, I admit. Only that something out of the ordinary was going on. Add that to the fact that Steven had the other qualifications of the thief—that he had access to every part of the house and knowledge of art—and I thought it might mean something. The only thing he didn't seem to have as far as I could see was motive. Stealing from Fraizer's was stealing from himself. It was all going to be his someday."

"If he was patient," Ivan reminded her.

"Right. And he wasn't. I found that out when I got back to New York. There was a copy of the new security systems proposal with the cover letter that had been submitted by Manhattan Security waiting on my desk. When Mr. Crown told me it had been turned down by Mr. Fraizer, I assumed that meant Kenneth Fraizer. It didn't. It was Steven." Ivan was giving her his full attention, filling in all the pieces he hadn't heard about in London. "It was Deborah who tied it all together. I knew she'd been having an affair; I'd never been able to get her to tell me who he was. Well, she did after London, with a vengeance. It had been Steven all the time, and he made the mistake of telling her good-bye."

"A woman scorned."

"Don't get mad, get even. That was Deborah's motto. When Kenneth was forced into resigning by the stockholders, she came marching into my office and let me know that it hadn't happened because they wanted Kenneth out. It had happened because they wanted Steven in. And why shouldn't they? 'They' were Steven. Fraizer's stock had been purchased by a series of D.B.A.s under a corporation controlled by Steven."

"Easy to say. Not so easy to prove."

"Not so tough considering he'd used Deborah's apartment as a mailing address for receipt of the certificates."

"I've always known you could never trust a woman not to open your mail," Ivan joked.

Dale glared at him, then went on.

"He'd set up an account in a Zurich bank. A code could trigger the bankers to clear stock trades and pay for them in his absence. The code was presented by the brokers making the trades."

"And so he managed to accumulate a majority of the stock," Ivan summarized.

"Right. When the original underwriting went through the Fraizer family retained fifty-one percent of the stock in the House of Fraizer. Twenty-six stayed in Kenneth's name, the other twenty-five went to Steven. The Zurich stock purchases gave him another four percent and a controlling interest, enough to let him swing a vote in his favor whenever it became necessary. The percentage was small but critical."

Ivan gave a low whistle. "Kenneth should have given Steven more credit all along," he said.

"That's for sure. It was a sophisticated, complicated set of maneuvers. It took the raw skills of a genius to forge the art and the diamonds, to sell the originals, hide the money, and in the process put Kenneth into a cash bind tight enough to make him take the company public. But for a few small errors, he would have gotten away with the whole thing."

"But for Dale Kenton," Ivan corrected her.

"I was just lucky," she told him. "If he had directed all that energy and thought in a positive direction he could be running his own auction house now."

"I must be obtuse. I still don't totally understand what part the faked paintings played in all of this."

For the first time Dale smiled. "I was certain that it would have taken all of his available cash to make the secret stock buys. But he couldn't tell his father that his trust fund money was gone, leaving him short when the paintings came in. The only way Steven could afford to buy those paintings for his father was to sell some of his stock, enough to reduce his majority percentage. As long as it was floating out in the public market he felt vulnerable—but not too vulnerable. He'd already gotten the presidency, and as long as he exercised some restraint he could keep it. And gradually, as he earned money from it, he would be able to accumulate stock to replace what he had sold."

"It's true. That shouldn't have been a problem."

"It wouldn't have been if he'd had enough time. Thanks to your paintings he didn't."

Ivan looked confused.

She smiled at him mysteriously, then slowly started to guide him through it. "I used the money he paid for the fakes to buy all the stock he had sold. I formed a corporation called Broome Street to do it—I thought that would mean something to Kenneth. It was the street where he and his father had their first store. It just seemed like poetic justice. As soon as Broome Street reached the five percent mark it had to be reported to the S.E.C. That's when Steven realized something was wrong. He knew he had to get controlling interest back fast—he had to buy more stock or face the possibility that he'd be asked to resign by a majority of the stockholders. Just the way his father had been. Once he saw that we owned Broome Street he knew we'd team up with Kenneth to do it."

"You're amazing," he said with affection. He put his arms around her and happily swung her off the floor.

"Ouch," Dale protested, but his excitement was contagious and as he swung her around him she broke out into a gusty laugh. "Ivan, you're mad," she giggled. He loved her even more when those deep-set blue eyes were free of worry. It had touched him to see how quickly her smile could disappear when the happiness of people close to her was threatened.

"Quite a scheme," he congratulated her. "A real beauty." He had to admit that he felt a certain satisfaction when he thought of Steven casting around wondering where he'd go next and what he'd do with the career that had ground so abruptly to a halt. Loyalty was strong in Ivan's nature, and he couldn't stand the idea of Kenneth being betrayed.

"I don't know," Dale replied. She looked as downcast as she had when she arrived. "I don't know if Kenneth will ever really recover from what happened today."

"He'll feel better once we give him the stock certificates," Ivan said encouragingly.

"Part of him will, I suppose," she answered. "But I think there's another part of him that will never heal." She looked at Ivan, waiting to see if he could understand that.

"You're right," he answered. His tone became serious. He looked at her as if he never wanted her eyes to waver from his. "There is a part of you that's never whole again once you lose someone you really love." He took her hand in his with a grip that was strong and firm, but to her surprise she could feel his hand begin to shake as he spoke to her again. "That's why you have to come back to London with me. Why you have to marry me. Neither of us will be whole if you don't. You know that. Admit it to me. And to yourself."

She quickly withdrew her hands from his and as

rapidly broke eye contact and looked away. "Ivan," she pleaded. Her voice was filled with pain. "I can't. I've told you . . ."

"You told me you couldn't because you had to prove yourself," he interrupted. "Well, that's not the case any more. Not after today. You've proven yourself beyond anything that was ever expected of you."

"It's more than that, Ivan. You know it is."

"Dale," he said. His hand gently cupped her chin and moved her face around until she was looking at him once again. "I won't leave you. Never. But you have to realize that no one can leave you totally alone any more. Your satisfaction, your self-confidence, they're inside you now. You don't have to lean on someone else for them any more. You bring them to yourself. Succeeding has done that for you. Succeeding on your own, with no help from anyone else. You can trust now—you can afford to. Because no one can go off and leave you without a foundation. You've built your own. Take this," he said, pulling a small black box out of his pocket and thrusting it into her hand.

She opened it cautiously. A diamond winked out at her, small but brilliant. "It's the one you found the first day you were here," he told her tenderly. "The one that started all of this. It's come full circle now, back to you. I couldn't think of any other stone that would mean more to you, no matter how large it might be. So I had this one mounted for you."

"When did you do it?" she asked in wonder.

"Weeks ago," he admitted, sounding slightly embarrassed. "I never had any doubt that you would succeed."

She suddenly burst into tears. Ivan was alarmed until he realized that they were tears of joy. He nestled her in his arms, stroking her hair, her forehead, and wondering how long it would take for the full impact of what he had told her to sink in. Holding her close to him, he spoke the words that he had held until the very last. "I love you, darling," he whispered to her. "I want to be with you always. I want to marry you. I don't want us ever to be apart." She listened to him, but she didn't say a thing. "Dale, did you hear what I said?" he asked her.

She pulled back from him a little and looked into his trusting eyes. They helped her to make her way through the confusion of her thoughts, to fashion an answer for him.

She felt the strength of his arms around her, folding her into him with all the soft, warm comfort of a lamb's-wool blanket. It was the most natural feeling in the world. She reveled in it. It made her want to crawl closer, to be part of him, to stay there until the day when they were too old and too tired to hold on to each other any more. She vowed to make up for all she had lost in the needlessly solitary years. "Do you think that I'll ever be able to make you as happy as you've made me?" she asked him.

His smile was enough. He didn't have to say anything more. "We should find Kenneth, don't you think?" he asked her.

"I don't know, Ivan," she answered. The thought of Kenneth's pain threw a sudden pall over her own happiness. "I know he's going to be happy when we give him the stock. I'm just not sure that now is the right time."

"He won't have stopped grieving over Steven by tomorrow," Ivan chided her. "He may still be suffering from it years from now. But we've made our decision," he said, taking her by the softly molded muscle of her upper arm. It felt deliciously giving to him. "If you're coming to London with me he'll need to make plans around it. It's not fair to him to hold back and not let him know," he reminded her. "You're not going to be that easy to replace. Ask me," he laughed. "I tried. He'll need all the time he can get to look for someone else. Do you have the envelope with the stock certificates?" he encouraged her when she didn't make a move. "Believe me, Dale," he told her when she still continued to hesitate, "giving him the stock certificates now, letting him have something to be glad about today, is the right thing to do."

She squeezed him once again before she stepped away from him. Even though she was giving in and doing what he had suggested, he could see the uncertainty in her eyes.

"I wanted to do it over dinner, Ivan," she told him. "With champagne and toasts and caviar. I wanted it to be such a special night for Kenneth."

"Well," Ivan told her, "I don't have champagne chilling in my office. But I do happen to have a bottle of very good Scotch in my desk. Will you settle for that?" Dale looked at him in surprise. "It's been tough sitting around and waiting for you to make up your mind," he explained to her hurriedly. "You have no idea how hard that can be on a man."

"In that case, I don't suppose you have three glasses, do you?" she asked him.

"Just wait right here," he instructed her as he started for her office door. "There's no end to the extraordinary things that I have hidden away, as you are now in a perfect position to find out."

Kenneth sat in the empty salesroom. His eyes scanned it. He'd been drawn there in the late hours of the afternoon, as if by some stupendous magnet of the soul. He'd thought there was some reason for it, some part of him that knew he'd start feeling better if he was at the scene of some of his greatest triumphs, but that hadn't happened.

Instead he found it desolate. It was as if the more active a room has been, the less purpose it seems to have when that animation has gone. It was like sitting in one of the art world's great ghost towns. All the people that were its lifeblood had been sucked out of it—all the family at least. The tote board was set on zero. It didn't have a function when it wasn't clicking. Chairs were pushed back against the walls. They looked so temporary without bodies in them. There were naked walls where artwork should be hanging, and dividing panels placed willy-nilly around the room in no set pattern. Velvet ropes were draped through stanchions, but there were no spectators to hold back.

He realized as he looked at it that excitement, like any other emotion, can't really be missed until it's been present somewhere. But then, if it goes, the place seems emptier with the absence of sound than another kind of room might have been. It was depressing as hell. Worse than a wake. At least a wake has food and liquor and one or two well-meaning and cheerful drunks. Kenneth watched himself give in to self-pity, and he hated himself for it.

His eyes settled on the deserted stage. He remembered now, in these quiet minutes, that he'd never seen Steven at the podium. He'd always hugged the back of the room during an auction, pacing from one spot to another, attaching himself like a limpet to the part of the room that promised the most action. He'd always thought it was because Steven preferred it that way, but maybe he'd been wrong.

He turned to the front left side of the room where Katherine used to sit. Katherine. There wasn't a day that went by without his thinking of her. How he missed her easy manner and the way they had once talked. She had been a special light in his life then, one that had been snuffed out too soon.

"I'd like to propose a toast. To the Chairman of the Board of Fraizer's, and to its President."

He turned, startled, back toward the podium. Dale

stood there, one hand lifted, a glass held high. He had felt so solitary it was like seeing a ghost.

"And to a good and dear friend," Ivan added in a voice thick with emotion. His hand was raised in an identical gesture. The overhead light that hung from the high ceiling caught a facet of his glass and sent its glimmer back across the rows to Kenneth's eyes. He was too surprised to reply, and too unhappy to fake a smile.

Ivan climbed carefully down the steps at the side of the stage and began to come down the aisle toward the row where Kenneth sat. In one hand he held a half-empty bottle of Scotch. He carried an extra glass, identical to his own, by hooking one long finger into it and pressing it next to the bottle. In his free hand he had an envelope, long, white and unadorned except for the name Kenneth Fraizer, which was written across the front in Dale's practiced script.

"Here," he said, standing over Kenneth. "You know how much Dale and I love and respect you. We think that this belongs to you. Always has, always will." He put the envelope into Kenneth's outstretched hand.

He turned it over several times before he began to open it. Then he painstakingly slit the top with a finger. He started to take out the contents, then thought better of it and spoke instead.

"The two of you are like family to me," he told them. "I think you know that." The force of his sentiment almost made it impossible to go on.

"Will you open the envelope, please," Ivan ordered him. He tried to make his voice sound gruff, but the fondness he felt for Kenneth showed through like skin behind a fabric that's started wearing away in places.

Kenneth finished the tear with deliberate circumspection, lingering over the envelope and extracting the papers inside in slow motion. His eyes began to glisten as he looked at them and saw that they were stock certificates for Fraizer's that had been conveyed to him from the Broome Street Corporation. He struggled to hold back the tears as he looked up at his two friends, Ivan who had been such an integral part of his background, and Dale, once Katherine's friend and now his as well. His eyes joined with his friends. Not a word passed between them. There wasn't any need.

Ivan turned a chair around to face the one in which Kenneth sat. He held it for Dale, seating her with courtly grace that would have seemed out of proportion to the moment and their surroundings if it hadn't been accomplished so artlessly. Then he threw his own long leg over the seat of another and straddled it, facing Kenneth as he leaned against its back.

"Have another," he said, lifting the bottle and holding it, partially tipped, over Kenneth's glass as he waited for an answer. Kenneth nodded, watched his glass fill until the amber liquid stood at least an inch and a half high, then tossed it off with the speed of someone who is trying to forget.

"I think that some of these should be yours," he said to Dale as he ruffled the stiff edges of the stock certificates with newly steadied fingers. "You've worked too hard to save Fraizer's not to own a part of it. And I'm going to need you here even more now that Steven is gone. I never thought it would make me feel good to be giving away part of my company," he said, looking into her eyes, "but your case seems to be the exception."

Dale returned his gaze, and hesitated. For all the excitement she had felt whirling around her office with Ivan an hour before, she understood that this was the true moment of decision. Once she turned down the stock in Fraizer's, she would have set off upon a path from which there was no turning back.

A familiar set of feelings flooded through her. The security that she had anticipated would come once she had earned the ability to take care of herself, independent of her father or any other man. The pride that she had felt as she grew in her work and in her skills. Even the thirst for success and acquisition that had surprised her with its intensity as she held the five-million-dollar check that Steven had handed her in payment for the forged paintings. It had symbolized more than money to her. It had been the means for Broome Street to buy the stock in Fraizer's and, in the process, to barter for power as well.

For the first time she began to appreciate how difficult giving it all up would prove to be. She turned to Ivan, who was watching her and waiting for her words. Looking into his eyes, where belief in her brimmed as precariously as the water in a too-full glass, she knew it would be even harder to disappoint him. The pain of indecision had shown on her face as she realized that as substantial as her gains within the company were, there was no real success without him. She could never have imagined how meaningless it would all seem once she got it.

"There's something that I need to tell you, Kenneth," she said seriously. And for the first time in her life she understood the meaning of the word love. Her fervent wish was that Kenneth would be able to find it, too.

Kenneth's eyes misted as Dale told him she was moving to London so that she and Ivan could be married.

"I can't tell you how happy I am for you both," he told them. "If you get married here I'll give the wedding dinner. Congratulations, Ivan. You've got yourself one hell of a girl."

Dale took Kenneth in her arms. "I've got an idea about how you might replace me," she said.

"Another idea? I'm not sure my heart can stand any more of your ideas right now." He laughed for the first time that day.

"Ned has closed his firm here," she went on. "Miriam is still the finest expert in her field in New York. I think you should call her. The two of you were tied together for too many years. She needed a breather. She got it. Now the two of you need each other. You really do, Kenneth. You know that."

"You never give up, do you?" Kenneth cried, holding up his hands to stop her. They all laughed.

"She's right. You can't run Fraizer's, and head the paintings department at the same time. Not to mention taking care of the details for the London branch that will need your attention," Ivan said. "Dale and I are good. We all know that"—a twinkle came into his eyes—"but we'll need your input, Kenneth. You can't cover the whole board."

"It seems I'm outvoted," he conceded. "The truth of the matter is I do miss Miriam, her and her cigarettes. I'll try to work it out with her."

"Join us for dinner, Kenneth?" Ivan asked.

"No thanks, Ivan. You two go on ahead. I've got a lot to think about. And to do."

Ivan took Dale's hand as they walked along Park Avenue. "It's been quite a day, hasn't it?"

"I'm just sorry it had to be Steven. He could have had it all if his energies had been put to use in a productive way. I even think he and Katherine could have worked it out. He was too preoccupied with his scheme to meet her halfway. He was so detached and unemotional that she turned to Kenneth. My guess is that she loved Kenneth all along, but if things had been more normal with Steven, those feelings for Kenneth would never have reached the surface."

"Just how do you know all these things?" Ivan asked. Dale gave him a small smile. "A woman can tell.

"At least she finally stood up to her mother," Dale went on. "Let her know in no uncertain terms that it was time for her to stop meddling. One bad marriage and a miscarriage was all it took."

"I hope Betty understands now that it wasn't you who was to blame for every step her daughter took off the path she'd so carefully laid out for her."

"Oh, I don't think she'll ever stop blaming me. It hardly bothers me any more," Dale lied.

"What's Katherine going to do? Has she made any plans?"

"She's contacted the Sorbonne to see if they'll give her the grant back. She'd like to go to Paris and put all of this behind her. I'm sure when she finds out Steven was in back of it all it will be even harder on her."

They walked along in silence for several blocks. Dale was content just holding Ivan's hand. For the first time in years she had a feeling of inner peace. Ivan was a safe harbor in a terrible storm, one that had lasted too many years. She looked up at him, her face glowing with the happiness she felt. "Sweetheart, I think it's all such a waste. Kenneth and Katherine. They love each other. We know that. Each of them is feeling so guilty over Steven that they'll never make a move toward each other, not now."

"It's unfortunate that they can't get together," Ivan agreed. "But it will take a miracle to unravel that mess."

Ivan saw Dale's face light up. He knew that expression all too well.

CHAPTER 52

Dale crossed Third Avenue and continued along Sixty-seventh. She was a short half block from Steven's new office, and she still wasn't sure whether he would see her, or what she would say to him if he did. Pray for divine guidance, she thought as she opened the door into the small foyer.

It looked upper-crust, though not as imposing as Fraizer's. A neatly dressed young woman sat behind the information desk, stacks of catalogues arranged in front of her. Dale had a flash of déjà vu as she asked for Steven Fraizer—it was so nearly the way they had met, the way it had all started.

At first glance he looked the same—the impeccable dark suit, the navy and red rep tie. But as he came closer his eyes, touched with sadness that hadn't been there three months ago and surrounded by a web of fine lines that no amount of sleep could erase, gave him away. "Just happened to be in the neighborhood?" he inquired, smiling.

"Not really. I'm leaving New York next week. I wanted to see you before I left."

He didn't show any hint of curiosity, but then he'd always been able to hide his feelings well, she remembered. "Let me show you the place," he suggested as he led her down the corridor that opened off the entrance. "I hear you and Ivan got married last month. You'll give him my congratulations, won't you?"

"I'll do it when he calls tonight. He's in London now," she explained, seeing the question in his eyes, "settling the last details for the opening of the New Bond Street branch."

"That's a tough way to start out, separated like that."

"The only ones who are pleased about it are the stockholders of AT&T," Dale laughed. "We call each other at least twice a day."

"This is the salesroom," Steven told her, walking her through the first door on their right. She was able to take it all in with a glance. It wasn't a third the size of Fraizer's. "What do you think?" he asked, stepping on to the stage and sliding behind the podium.

"It's as if you were born to it," Dale told him. She couldn't keep the sadness out of her voice. He sensed it immediately and stepped back down beside her.

"How's he going to do once you and Ivan are gone?" he asked suddenly, surprising Dale with the concern that came through in his tone.

"Your father will have Miriam to help."

"Dale," Steven answered, taking her hands in his, "I think you know what I meant. It's not the house I'm worried about. He can run that in his sleep."

"Oh, Steven," she said unhappily. "I feel so sorry for both of you. There could have been another way."

He opened one of the folding chairs that leaned against the wall for her, and one for himself as well. Then he sat down, facing her. "I can see that now," he admitted. "Twenty-twenty hindsight. But then . . . then I so much wanted to be a man in my own right." He looked down at his hands, the guilt he had lived with for the past months coming to the surface. He took a handkerchief from his pocket and wiped his face, but it didn't erase the memories.

"Do you still want to?" Dale asked, hoping the moment was right. He looked at her, not comprehending. "If you're sincere," she continued, "there is something you can do. About Katherine."

He looked perplexed. "Katherine and I have talked it all over," he told her. "She'll never condone what I did. I don't blame her. But she's given me every kind of support since I started this," he said, sweeping the salesroom with a large gesture. "Emotional support. And straight answers, too. I think she's the best friend I've got," he said, smiling wistfully. "Ironic, isn't it?"

Dale nodded her agreement. "So you really do care about her?" she asked. "Then you should want her to be happy."

"I do," he agreed. "I'm hoping as much as she is that the offer from the Sorbonne can be resurrected."

"That won't make her happy," Dale told him impatiently. "That's just her way of running away."

"Running away? Don't be ridiculous. From what?" Steven asked.

"From you, Steven. But more than that, from Kenneth. Steven, you must know that Katherine and your father feel a strong attraction for each other. Neither one of them will call the other, even though both of them are suffering. Your father feels responsible for what you did. He thinks he caused it, and he thinks you still love Katherine and that he'll hurt you all over again if he calls her."

"And Katherine?" Steven asked.

"She feels guilty about loving your father, about the failure of your marriage. You're the only one who can release her."

"My father's lost to me. She's the only one who cares about me. If I give her up, I won't have anything left."

Dale looked around the room that Steven had struggled so hard to earn. She could see that even now he had begun to stamp his personality on it. "That's where you're wrong," she told him with great warmth and understanding in her voice. "If you let her go, they'll both come back to you."

"I don't know if I can do it. I don't know if I can face my father."

"I think you can," she reassured him. "He'll be in Arnold Swerdlow's office at Chase Manhattan at ten tomorrow if you want to take the chance."

The indecision in his face stayed with her as she walked back out along the corridor. But there wasn't anything else she could have said. Now she could only hope.

CHAPTER 53

Kenneth took Dale's arm as they walked in Central Park. He realized as he did that it would probably be the last time that they would walk to an appointment like that, easy and relaxed in each other's company. She would be leaving within the week, and, though it would only be a partial loss since she and Ivan would be working with him in London, he knew that he would sorely miss them.

It seemed like the final blow after a difficult period. The three months of summer that had just passed had been blistering. All around the city people had bantered about frying eggs on the city sidewalks, then had fled with all possible speed to the Hamptons or Cape Cod or almost any other place that held the promise of a cool, clear breeze.

There hadn't been any respite for him. The losses from the ranks at Fraizer's had left him overseeing every little detail within the house. Luckily Michael Edwards had been able to pick up some of the burden once he'd been cleared of suspicion. He'd almost thrown it all over and gone on a vacation, but it would have been his first in fifteen years, and at the last minute as reservations were being confirmed and bags packed, he'd gotten edgy and canceled all the plans. Then just when he decided he couldn't stand it any more, a day like this came along all bronze and gold and alive with the scent of leaves growing crisp in the dry cold air of the city and he knew that Manhattan was about to pull him back to her breast like a mother reuniting with her punished child.

They cut through the park on one of the trails that led southward. The asphalt, swept clean by the last evening's breezes, had become an almost pristine path of mottled black, littered only by the dappled shadows of the branches that hung overhead, playing in the morning sunlight.

Dale took deep breaths as she walked, enjoying the sensation of crispness that burned like brandy in her throat. She returned the smiles of passersby who looked surprisingly relaxed and tanned. The entire population seemed to be feeling the electricity of the fall season that was about to burst forth.

Her stride faltered as they drew abreast of the Tavern on the Green. Kenneth had given their wedding dinner there. Sitting in the big, glass-walled room with shadowy shapes of stirring trees watching them from outside the windows, he'd wished them all happiness. But as he'd done it, Dale could tell that he was hiding a personal disappointment that had been made more obvious by their joy in each other.

She hesitated, afraid to broach the subject that had been nagging at her for so long. There was no good putting it off any more. Once she was in London it would be too late to tell him heart to heart and face to face. It was now or never.

"You know I think of the wedding dinner you gave us every time I pass here," she told him, squeezing his arm with an affectionate reminder of their closeness. "That's one night I'll never forget as long as I live."

He glanced at her in profile, looking so young and hopeful and beautiful by his side, bathed in the morning light. He felt good about life at that moment. He was struck by the sense of renewal that the joining of two lives into one strong link can bring.

"The only thing missing for me was Katherine," Dale said cautiously. "I wished she could have been with me. I was her maid of honor. She should have been mine."

Kenneth's steps faltered. He barely resisted the urge to turn and walk away from the conversation that seemed to be developing. He had wished that Katherine could be there to see it, too. She would have rounded out their little circle so completely. He missed her, too, and he suspected that Dale understood that. He fought back the desire to ask Dale where he might find her, as he had fought it back so many times before.

"Don't you ever wonder where she is?" Dale asked. It was as if she had read his mind.

He felt suddenly old. His mind filled with dark, forbidden thoughts. It was as if he would have to die to live again. And as he thought about it, he admitted the reason to himself for the first time. He needed to kill the old Kenneth, the father, the caretaker of his son. He knew what his sin was, his most serious sin. He had violated Steven by coveting his wife. He had cheated him since the moment Katherine moved in. He had loved her.

"I do wonder where she is," he admitted. "But I have no right to meddle. It's her affair and Steven's now. And since he's not speaking to me, I can't just intrude on their lives."

"Kenneth," she said. She stopped then, stark still in the center of the path, paying no heed to the fact that people had to walk around them. She just looked into his eyes and wondered how to explain it to him. She knew there should be a certain natural order to things. That parents should die before their children. That children should care for their parents, as they themselves had been cared for. That each generation leads to another in a rhythmic, predictable way. But Kenneth and Katherine were different. In their case the sequence was broken. They were a reach across the generations that was out of the norm, and for them the complete and balanced circle of life threatened to turn inward on itself and crumble because its line had been disturbed. They simply weren't like the rest of the world. It was an accident of fate, and she had to convince him not to feel guilty about it. He had too many other things to punish himself for already. He had buried Steven alive. He was the root of his son's behavior. He hadn't allowed him any dignity. That was his real transgression, and it was time that he admitted it to himself and then gave himself the gift of forgiveness for his mistakes.

"She's in love with you, you know," she told him.

He tried to look away, but her voice was relentless. Kenneth felt his insides recoil in horror. He didn't want to hear it, not even if it were true. Katherine wouldn't, couldn't feel right with him so long as she ran the risk of hurting Steven with their relationship, and he loved her too much to put her in the position of trying and failing. Only his son had the power now, with everything that had happened between them, to free her from that sense of loyalty.

"She's in love with Steven," he protested. He sounded like a man who was trying to convince himself.

Dale nodded her head slowly in disagreement.

"Why do you think she ran away from you after the night you made love to her, Kenneth?" she prodded him. "Why do you think she came running over to stay with me? Fear, that's why. Fear that she wouldn't be able to handle it. She overreacted for a reason. She finally realized she loved you, too. Realized it with the first real kiss you gave her. The desire to have you was so strong she had to run away from it."

"She told you that?" Kenneth asked.

"Not in so many words. But close enough."

Dale waited for a reaction, but he stayed silent, uncompromising. "It's time for you to call her now," she told him. "To have an honest talk with each other. She really does love you."

"She has to work it out with Steven," Kenneth told her wearily. "If she doesn't, I would never forgive myself. I've done so much to hurt him already. I can't take her from him, too." A shadow of despair passed over Kenneth's face as he thought of it. Steven would never release Katherine, not so long as he suspected she would be going to Kenneth. Impossible, Kenneth thought, the way Steven hated him now.

"He doesn't love her," Dale whispered. "He married her because he thought it would please you. He stayed with her for the same reason."

"Just like everything else he did," Kenneth said. There was a sound of defeat in his voice. He moved heavily, slowly, to a bench at the side of the path and lowered his body onto it with the movement of an old man. "Always to please me. I'm responsible for what Steven's become." Kenneth tried to summon up a sense of anger toward his son for the things that he'd done and found he couldn't. He'd made so many mistakes with Steven that, no matter how wrong his son's actions had been, he was, in some small sense at least, the cause of them. He couldn't ever forget that. It would follow him like a curse as long as he breathed and thought and remembered. As he thought about it he held his head in his hands.

"What Steven is today," Kenneth said quietly, "is what I made him into. Anna wasn't there. I brought him up, taught him about life, gave him his sense of morality and ethics. I see his face when he was six. So innocent. He was a clean slate waiting for me to write. Everything he knows, everything he does, is a product of me—either of my actions, or, worse yet, of my neglect. How could it have gone so wrong?" he asked her. He kept his head hidden in his hands and began kneading it like an aching muscle that couldn't be soothed, but that might be forgotten if he could exert enough pressure elsewhere.

"You never let him go," Dale agreed. "Everyone has to make independent decisions eventually. Children go away to college. Grow up. Get married. Are on their own. Except Steven. He was protected all his life. And when he chose to break out, he did it in the wrong way."

Kenneth thought back on it. She was right. Steven had walked a long road with him, but he had never been allowed to take a step on his own.

"Perhaps if Anna had been here," he said, "things might have been different." His voice sounded dead, his expression was leaden. "I can see that I must have done something terribly wrong. Maybe it was too hard, the way I tried to bring him up. And yet," he said, reaching up and running his fingers through his hair in a distracted gesture, "preserving the family, preserving the business, seemed so important to me. I was always pushing him in the wrong direction," he said regretfully. "Even his marriage. I thought in my heart it was the right thing for him, for the family. I've been proved wrong, miserably wrong, there, too."

"Kenneth," Dale said, grasping his hands in her

own, "can't you see that the mistake you made before was in not letting go? Not letting go of the business, of authority, of anything when it came to Steven. And now you're doing that again. Only this time you refuse to let go of what's happened in the past. You're carrying it around your neck like an albatross. Not letting go was a mistake before. It's a mistake again. If you don't believe me, ask Katherine. She'll tell you."

"I can't do it," he said with finality. "Steven loves Katherine. He's just afraid to admit it, because he thinks that once he does I'll take her away from him. The way I've taken everything else, including his dignity. Stop," he said, as she began to protest. "We have to hurry," he said, ending the conversation by standing. "We have an appointment to get to.

"You know I'd gladly pay double the amount of those forgeries if I could find a way to deny I've lost my son," he told her as they started down the path. "To deny that I've lost him forever." At the thought of Steven he felt a searing pain of such magnitude he wondered whether he was going to be able to survive it. He tried to let the sights and sounds around him wash the sudden thought of his son away. The pain of it had been unexpected, like the sudden painful jab of a mugger's knife coming at you from behind. He didn't want to linger with it, to walk with the ghosts of the past on such a glorious day, and so he turned his attention to preparing for the appointment he was going to instead.

It must have been two years since he'd seen Arnold Swerdlow, but he still remembered how to flatter him. He regretted now not having kept up with the bank trustee. This was the sort of call he would have sent Steven out on before; he'd had to remind himself before he started out exactly how Chase Manhattan's method of bidding out estates functioned.

There'd been a lot that he'd remembered since Steven had gone. It took the necessity of doing them to remind him of how menial some of the tasks that went into running the house were, and how much he'd hated them before he'd shunted them off to his son. Well . . . Steven had probably been doing a few things he wasn't used to as well. There were hours, even days sometimes, when Kenneth managed to block the whole thing out of his mind, only to be reminded of the existence of Steven's infant auction house when he picked up the Arts and Leisure section of the Sunday *New York Times*. Invariably they managed to run his son's advertisements exactly next to his own, which never failed to jolt him, and occasionally even set a little tinge of competition coursing through his veins.

Steven Fraizer sat in Arnold Swerdlow's waiting room. His eyes quickly darted to the entrance door each time he heard a sound in the corridor. He felt nervous waiting like that, knowing that at any second his father would be coming through the door. He'd been looking forward to this meeting ever since Dale had come to see him, and yet he had been dreading it too. He was ashamed of what he had done, and probably always would be. It had cost him a lot of sleep in the last few months, and the night before had been no exception.

He sat there quietly, his fingers making a small pyramid in front of him as he thought. He was still there, remembering, as Dale and his father came through the door.

By the time Kenneth entered Arnold Swerdlow's office, his face was flushed with color. He was flooded with a sense of déjà vu when he looked into the room and saw Janice, Swerdlow's secretary, sitting in her accustomed spot. She was a familiar marker on a much-traveled road, a landmark that never seemed to change. She smiled at them and motioned to some chairs across the room.

"Running late, as usual," Kenneth said good-naturedly.

"Some things never change," she said. "Niagara won't ever stop falling. He won't ever learn to interrupt someone who's in the middle of their sales pitch. Still take your coffee black?" she asked him as she reached for the tea tray that rested on the shelf behind her.

"Some things never change," Kenneth reminded her. He took the cup that she extended to him, and then turned to walk to the seating area in the corner.

He'd expected to find everything at Chase Manhattan basically unaltered. Like most large institutions, Chase's systems, and most of their upper-level personnel, were as immovable as the great pyramid. What he hadn't anticipated, however, was that he would find Steven sitting on the small couch in the corner. He stopped dead in his tracks for an instant, and then acknowledged him with a nod. He could feel his gut begin to shake as he continued across the room.

"You knew he'd be here, didn't you?" he accused Dale as they walked toward the couch. She simply pretended she hadn't heard him.

He took the seat beside him. For the first time in his life he wished that he used cream and sugar. He could have played at stirring with the spoon, he could have used it as an excuse to be preoccupied while he tried to come up with something to say.

Dale sat very quietly, and as the silence grew she stood up and began to survey the paintings that were hanging on the other side of the office, leaving the two of them alone.

Nothing seemed appropriate. They were trapped in an awkward silence, like actors who have forgotten their lines. They looked away from each other, wary and wordless, each trying to find something to say that would express the seriousness of what had happened between them without bringing the distress that was attached to it back to set them apart all over again.

Kenneth strained to find the words, and as he did he could see Anna with her simple practical wisdom telling him to use the insignificant events of every day as a base, and to let the more momentous words grow out of them.

"I hear you're doing quite well," he said, angling his body on the cushions until he was looking at his son.

"Not badly," Steven replied in a strained voice, "but it's a struggle."

As he looked at him, Kenneth believed him. His face, once so clear and fresh looking, had added lines and wrinkles. The half-circles that lay under his eyes had turned the stale color of ashes. His eyes had lost a lot of the fight that had smoldered in them in the few short months that he'd been gone.

Steven fretted under his father's scrutiny. He rose from the couch and began pacing the room. "How much longer do you think it will be?" he asked Janice when he reached her desk.

"Your guess is as good as mine," she told him without looking up.

He stood in front of her, then almost visibly straightened, as if he'd reached within himself and pulled some puppet wire that was attached to the bottom of his spine.

He returned to the spot right where his father was sitting on the short couch.

"I've been going for some help, Dad," he told him as he resumed the spot next to him. He leaned toward him and grew close, as if their coming together would be added evidence of his sincerity. His eyes held the utter fatigue of a man who's been so close to the brink of a breakdown it seemed to him that it was the rest of the world which was unbalanced, and who, once having realized the problem was his own, was emptied out by the enormity of his mistake. "I left you and I started having nightmares, horrible nightmares. I hope some day you can forgive me. You'll never know how sorry I am."

Kenneth's heart stopped as he listened to him. He was so carefully focused on him that he heard his voice crack with emotion. In the past he had loved Steven the way you would a child. As he looked at him now and listened to him, he would now be able to love him another way, with pride and respect.

"Steven," he told him, trying not to choke on the emotion that he'd been holding inside for so long, "this has given me more pain than you can imagine. I drove you to it. I never let you grow up," he said, berating himself. "If I had, this wouldn't have happened. I started out by thinking I could make things easier for you than they'd been for me. I ended up by isolating you from all the sense of hardship and of struggle that you needed to go through to become a man. It was so stupid," he said. "I've spent so many hours going over it in my mind and wishing that I could start over."

Steven's hand moved slowly over to his father's knee. He squeezed Kenneth's leg reassuringly to let him know that it was going to be all right. Though he didn't actually smile, an expression of relief came over Kenneth's face. They had only uttered a few sentences, and yet they had explained all that was important between them, and somehow within themselves each had found his own sort of peace. They were silent for a time, and then Kenneth, looking straight ahead of him, told his son, "I wish there had been some other way for you to learn to make your own decisions, without opening your own business," he explained sorrowfully. "I wish that I had given you one. Maybe you could come back now," Kenneth said suddenly, hopefully. "It would be different, you know. I promise you that."

Steven hesitated. He looked at his father with renewed love. Then he slowly shook his head in the negative.

"I can't do that, Dad," he told Kenneth. "Not now." Then for the first time that day Steven smiled. "Who knows," he told his father, "maybe someday we can merge. Of course I wouldn't even consider it," he joked, "until I've gotten to be bigger than you."

Kenneth smiled back, then he took the risk and asked the question that was troubling him most. "How's Katherine?" he inquired. "Have you two gotten back together again?"

When Steven answered, his face was untroubled and the words flowed easily. "We've talked a lot, Dad," he told Kenneth. "We both realize we never should have gotten married. We were both too young. We didn't know the difference between a loving friendship and real love. We've come to terms with it, and with each other.

"Are you worried about her, Dad?" he asked compassionately.

"Of course I worry about her," Kenneth said. "But loyalty and honor are important virtues to Katherine. I don't expect she'll ever call." It was as close as he had ever come to admitting the true nature of his relationship with her to his son. It was nebulous as a galaxy, but they both understood with perfect clarity what he was saying. They sat side by side, each lost in his own thoughts. The ensuing silence was broken by Janice, who came over to them and announced, "Mr. Swerdlow said that he could see you now, Mr. Fraizer." She began to become flustered as she looked from one to the other. "I'm sorry," she apologized, "I'm not sure which Mr. Fraizer he meant. I'll be just a minute."

As she hurried away in a flurry of clicking heels and efficient gestures, Steven stood up and looked down, long and hard, at his father. His eyes penetrated the facade to the strong and caring man beneath. There was a hardness about him, the outer reflection of ethics and principles. But underneath there was a glow of loving concern that softened the steely exterior.

He intercepted Janice as she came back through the door. "May I have a pen and a piece of paper, please?" he asked her. She handed them to him, and he quickly scrawled a few lines, folded it, and handed it to Kenneth without another word. Then he followed Janice into Swerdlow's office.

Kenneth waited a few seconds before he opened it. When he did he saw that what Steven had written there was short and to the point. "Katherine Fraizer, Westbury Hotel, 535-2000."

Kenneth didn't bother to say anything to Janice. He got up, walked out of Swerdlow's office, and out of the Chase Manhattan Bank. He left the estate of Mr. James Stanley in the hands of Mr. Steven Fraizer.

EPILOGUE

It had been an archetypal English day. Legions of tall black London taxis had passed down fashionable New Bond Street and Fraizer's front door in an uninterrupted stream since the early hours of the morning. Occasionally an inquiring passerby peered through its open front doors and was politely turned away until the late hours of the afternoon.

Dale missed seeing most of it. She was locked away within the inner recesses of the house, directing the finishing touches that would make the difference between good and great. It was almost six before she finished and relaxed enough to run back to their flat and change into the gown of violet Charmeuse that she had ordered for this special night. As she stood now, surveying the pre-auction reception that was milling and eddying in the room in front of her like the perpetual motion of the waves that lick the seashore, she was a singular column of shimmering violet, interrupted only by a small but lovely old mined-diamond pin that Ivan had given her. She had placed it where the plunge of her throat could be seen to stop under the high neck of her dress, and the curve of her breast to begin. Her eyes were filled with good humor, nervousness, and excitement. They'd taken on the smoky purple tones of amethysts, though they surpassed them in intensity.

The party was in full swing. Women dressed in crushed satin and velvet evening gowns glittered beneath collections of jewels that must have taken centuries for their families to amass. The men, though handsomely attired in tuxedos, seemed to blend into an uninterrupted brushstroke of black that served as a splendid backdrop for the flash and sparkle of their women. Photographers, both inside the foyer and on the sidewalk, were having a field day. Their cameras clicked like tap dancers during a grand finale.

Dale scanned the room. She was satisfied with what she saw. Would-be bidders were browsing now among the Reynoldses and Gainsboroughs, Turners and Constables that ringed the room. It had been Ivan's idea to open Fraizer's London branch with a sale of English masters, and there were so many on display it looked as if he had invaded every great house and castle between Dover and Windsor, and made off with everything of value that had been locked up inside their stone walls.

Long strips of molding had been mounted in wooden stripes at different levels on the walls. They held the larger canvases, which were propped up in them against the plaster, their bases securely tucked into the three-inch recess of the molding. Underneath, the smaller canvases hung in a single orderly row that circled the entire room.

The moldings stopped before they reached the front left corner. The podium was placed there. It was an imposing structure of carved wood that stood at least fifteen feet high. They'd been lucky enough to find it as it was stripped from an Anglican church that was about to be refurbished. Now it was newly polished and secured where it would guarantee that the auctioneer would be seen by bidders in every corner of the room. Microphones had been placed in front of it in preparation for the sale, and a small video camera had been hung overhead, its blinking red light indicating that it was taping all that took place below.

Long tables covered in baize that matched the entrance halls stretched out on either side of the podium. They were covered with caviar that was scooped onto beds of crushed and liquid ice like small mountains of coal, and triangles of Scotch salmon that had been laid out in a sea of flesh pink that stretched for ten or twelve feet. Behind the tables a phalanx of bartenders opened champagne so rapidly they sounded like a troop of Boy Scouts battling with popguns.

Newly hired department heads and assistants were at their posts throughout the room, watching clients pick up catalogues and search for information. They made an appearance to provide answers when perplexed looks were seen, and remained unobtrusive when they weren't. Dale's gaze swept the room one more time and confirmed that everything was going well.

Her eyes sought out Ivan, who was talking to a handsome English couple in the center of the room. He looked debonair in his tuxedo, though his pants had a slightly rumpled look that was definitely out of character. A secret Mona Lisa smile began to glow on her face as she remembered how they'd gotten that way, the kind of smile that had the couples on either side of her looking at her inquisitively, although she was too preoccupied to notice them. She wondered what the proper Englishman that Ivan was addressing would say if he knew as well. Before she had a chance to relive the moment herself, Ivan was coming toward her from across the room.

He put an arm around her with a gesture that

showed love and pride. She felt as if they were alone there, instead of in a crowd of hundreds.

"Who were you talking to?" she asked him curiously.

"Lorraine and Ramond Stair," he told her. "I think they're interested in the Turner."

"I don't blame them," Dale interrupted him. "I wouldn't mind having it myself."

"It's going to take us a few seasons before we'll be able to have a Turner hanging on our wall," he told her lightheartedly.

"Well, the Stairs seem like a nice couple," Dale said. She looked them over appraisingly. "I guess it will be all right if they take care of it for us for a year or two."

"They may not have the chance," Ivan told her. "Dave Barnes over in the other corner there has taken quite a fancy to it as well. I imagine he pictures it hanging at Amelia's."

"It looks as if we've got a winner here," she told him, a thread of pent-up excitement running through her voice like a sparkling silver strand. "Though I must admit I'll be happier once this first sale is over."

"You worry too much," Ivan told her. He squeezed her gently around the waist. She reached around and took one of his hands.

"And I wish that Kenneth and Katherine could be here," she added as the lights began to dim and the spectators started to take their seats.

As the hammer came down on the first Constable she began to relax. It was going to be all right, she realized. The bidding was already fast and furious, more so than she would have expected early on in the evening. The people who were sitting there seemed to have been brought by the champagne and caviar to a fever pitch of acquisitive madness. The girls on the phones were as busy as the auctioneer. The atmosphere in the room was electric.

The singsong of the auctioneer was getting faster. Like a wheel that's turning quickly, the motion merely served to make the sound seem more even and uninterrupted. Soon she found that she was losing track of the breaks that came between the auctioning of various pieces, and was being lulled, instead, into a relaxed and soothing dreaminess.

It carried her back into the early part of the evening, when Ivan had come on her like a thief as she dressed, and, snaking up on her in the bedroom from behind, had captured her and thrown her down on the bed as if he'd been a student of rape and ravishment for a lifetime. His fevered sexual assault had quickly given way to careful tenderness. As she'd risen rhythmically underneath him she had felt as if their love was a swelling, growing, living thing that would continue on and would create something shared to survive them. As he had held her, cupping her breasts in his hands and stroking the swelling roundness of her hips, she had wanted it to last forever.

She was remembering how quickly he had needed to pull his pants on again, retrieving them from the crumpled heap where they had fallen, in order to get to the house on time to greet the first arriving guests, when he joggled her shoulder to get her attention. That wonderful small smile had spread across her face again, and he had looked at her strangely, wondering if he would ever learn to understand how women think, before he'd spoken to her. "Over ten million gross," he told her, surprised himself by the extent of their success.

"Who got the Turner?" she asked him slowly, as if she had just been awakened from a dream.

"It went to a phone bid," he said.

"Maybe it was Ned Whytson," she teased. "Maybe he was just afraid to show his face around here."

"I'll take his money," Ivan told her absentmindedly. His attention had shifted to one of the runners who was heading across the room in their direction. When she reached them she held out a note to him. "The man on the phone said to hand this message to you," she said and left.

Ivan opened the folded paper and read it quickly. "If that isn't just like him," he said as he refolded it and slipped it into his pocket. Dale waited for him to explain but rapidly lost patience. "Who?" she asked him.

Ivan withdrew the paper from his pocket. He did it slowly, drawing out the moment. Then he handed it to her as if the words that she was about to find would explain it all. As she read it she began to struggle to hold back the tears.

"I never got a chance to give the two of you a wedding gift," it started. "I hope you like the Turner as well as I do. Katherine, Betty, and Ronald join me in my wishes for a long and happy life. Love, Kenneth."

Dale reached for Ivan's hand and held it as she smiled up into his face. "It will be the beginning of our own collection for the House of Fraizer."

Their arms wrapped around each other, and without another word being spoken, they knew that they would skip the post-auction dinner party and instead go home together to see how the Turner looked by firelight, and to marvel at the way in which the full and rich tradition that Kenneth Fraizer had so valued was about to be passed on to another generation.

Sex...Glamour...Money...

PRETENSIONS by Sally Rinard
Set in the glittery world of high fashion and high society, where money is a weapon and sex the means of exchange, this dazzling tale combines the erotic, exotic, and the cutthroat world of business.
"A glitzy contemporary novel that's a delight to read."
—*Publishers Weekly*
_____ 90301-4 $4.50 U.S.   _____ 90302-2 $5.50 Can.

LISA LOGAN by Marie Joseph
Ambition and pride take Lisa Logan from poverty to the heights of success in haute couture. Money, power, fame, she finally has it all—except the man she wanted most.
_____ 90218-2 $3.95 U.S.

DECISIONS by Freda Bright
Dasha Croy rockets to the top in a brilliant law career, but will her marriage be the price? Can love and security compete with the seduction of power?
_____ 90169-0 $3.95 U.S.   _____ 90171-2 $4.50 Can.

HER ONLY SIN by Benjamin Stein
Susan-Marie had the beauty, brains, and sexuality to achieve her dream of heading the biggest studio in Hollywood, but her ambitions could cost her her love and even her life. "A power-packed, star-studded page turner."
—*Los Angeles Herald-Examiner*
_____ 90636-6 $4.50 U.S.   _____ 90637-4 $5.50 Can.

IMAGES by Cara Saylor Polk
"A hip, inside, behind-the-scenes page turner about a woman's climb to prime-time in big-time television news."
—Dan Rather
_____ 90456-8 $4.50 U.S.   _____ 90458-4 $5.50 Can.

ST. MARTIN'S PRESS—MAIL SALES
175 Fifth Avenue, New York, NY 10010

Please send me the book(s) I have checked above. I am enclosing a check or money order (not cash) for $_____ plus 75¢ per order to cover postage and handling (New York residents add applicable sales tax).

Name _____

Address _____

City _____ State _____ Zip Code _____

Allow at least 4 to 6 weeks for delivery

Fascinating Fiction from St. Martin's Press

JOURNEYS by Judith Summers

The powerful story of two sisters, bound by blood and tradition, but separated by an ocean, by the most tumultuous decades of the century, and by the forbidden journeys of their hearts—in the grand storytelling tradition of Cynthia Freeman.

_____ 90535-1 $3.95 U.S.

FAMILY MONEY by Doris Shannon

Poor Cousin Elizabeth, cheated out of her share of the family fortune, betrayed by her cousin's wife, turns that betrayal into her key to her sweet dreams of having everything...especially sweet revenge.

_____ 90463-0 $3.95 U.S.   _____ 90464-9 $4.95 Can.

ORIENTAL HOTEL by Janet Tanner

Rich, lovely Elise Sanderson has everything: a reasonably happy marriage, a young son...but when World War II strands her in Cairo her world is turned upside down by Gerald Brittain—and a passion neither of them can resist.

_____ 90480-0 $4.50 U.S.

ST. MARTIN'S PRESS—MAIL SALES
175 Fifth Avenue, New York, NY 10010

Please send me the book(s) I have checked above. I am enclosing a check or money order (not cash) for $_____ plus 75¢ per order to cover postage and handling (New York residents add applicable sales tax).

Name _____

Address _____

City _____ State _____ Zip Code _____

Allow at least 4 to 6 weeks for delivery